THE SHOCKING LORD STANDON

LOUISE ALLEN

Louise Allen loves immersing herself in history. She finds landscapes and places evoke the past powerfully. Venice, Burgundy and the Greek islands are favourite destinations. Louise lives on the Norfolk coast and spends her spare time gardening, researching family history or travelling in search of inspiration. Visit her at louiseallenregency.co.uk, @LouiseRegency and janeaustenslondon.com

THOSE *Scandalous* RAVENHURSTS

VOLUME 2

THOSE
Scandalous
RAVENHURSTS
COLLECTION

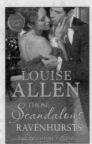

February 2016   May 2016

THOSE
Scandalous
RAVENHURSTS
VOLUME 2

LOUISE
ALLEN

First Published in Great Britain 2016
By Mills & Boon, an imprint of HarperCollins*Publishers*
1 London Bridge Street, London, SE1 9GF

THOSE SCANDALOUS RAVENHURSTS VOLUME TWO
© 2016 Harlequin Books S.A.

The Shocking Lord Stanton © 2008 Louise Allen
The Disgraceful Mr Ravenhurst © 2009 Louise Allen

ISBN: 978-0-263-92221-9

09-0516

Printed and bound
by CPI Group (UK) Ltd, Croydon, CRO 4YY

Author Note:

Gareth Morant, Earl of Standon, is upright, eligible—and a bachelor who views the chancy business of falling in love with alarm.

Marriage just isn't for him, and certainly not marriage to his wild childhood friend Maude. But Maude is going to be in deep trouble if she doesn't marry the highly respectable Earl, so what is a gentleman to do but create a scandal?

It isn't easy to become a rake overnight, as Gareth and I discovered, but finding a naked governess in a brothel certainly helped and, with the enthusiastic support of his cousins Eva and Sebastian Ravenhurst (*The Dangerous Mr Ryder*) and Bel and Ashe Reynard (*The Outrageous Lady Felsham*), Gareth succeeds in shocking society.

But by then Gareth has dug himself into a moral, emotional and social hole, and he has to climb out of it, greatly hindered by his own treacherous heart, Maude's appalling acting and the surprising allure of the chaste Miss Gifford, who just wants to get back to teaching the piano and the Italian tongue. Or so she says.

I do hope you enjoy the progress of this reluctant rake as he discovers that falling in love is perhaps the most shocking experience of all.

My exploration of the life and loves of THOSE SCANDAL-OUS RAVENHURSTS takes me to France next, where bluestocking spinster Elinor is assisting her scholarly mama amid ecclesiastical ruins, quite unprepared for the eruption into her orderly life of *The Disgraceful Mr Ravenhurst*, her black sheep of a cousin Theo. He's the last thing she needs—unfortunately she soon discovers he's the one thing she wants.

Chapter One

London—late February 1816

'My lords, your honours, gentlemen! Your attention, please! At midnight, upon the stroke of the hour, Madame Synthia's School of Venus presents our famed Parade of Beauty. Ladies of rich and varied experience! Exotic creatures of every hue! Country-fresh innocents willing and eager to learn their business at the hands of dashing London beaux! Posture girls of amazing flexibility and ingenuity for your delectation! In half an hour, my lords and gentlemen—take your places early and do not be disappointed!'

The ex-town crier employed at considerable expense by Madame Synthia—formerly known as Cynthia Wilkins of Camden Town—shouted himself to a stop and left the platform at the end of the Grand Assembly Lounge. Footmen began to set chairs around the stage and keen patrons jostled to fill the front row, despite there being half an hour to go before the start of the performance.

'Morant, come on.' Gareth Morant, Earl of Standon,

winced as Lord Fellingham nudged him sharply in the ribs. 'Those posture girls are all the go, but you need to be close up to get a proper eyeful.' Fellingham licked his rather full lips. 'They hold up a mirror and there are candles…'

'I doubt they have any feature that any other woman you have had congress with was lacking, Fell.' Gareth set down his almost-full champagne flute and regarded the scrimmage around the stage with bored distaste. 'This place is a vulgar dive, I cannot imagine what we are doing here.'

'You're off your oats, old fellow, in need of a tonic, in my opinion,' Fellingham retorted. 'You're no fun these days, and that's the truth of it. Look at you— you've sat by the fire, toying with one glass the entire time Rotherham's been upstairs with those Chinese twins, and never a word out of you but grunts.'

'Indian twins.' Gareth got to his feet and stretched. 'They are Indian. I'm off to White's, see if I can drum up a decent hand of cards.'

'We can't go without Rotherham,' his friend protested, one eye on the rapidly filling seats before the stage. 'And besides, I want to see this show. I've heard all about it, that's why I wanted to come—remember? Let's go and get old Rothers and watch it and then we'll all go to White's. He must be finished by now, surely. What do you say? Don't be a killjoy.'

'Very well.' Gareth picked up his glass with a suppressed sigh, tossed back the contents and stood up. 'Do you know which room he's in?'

'The Mirrored Chamber. Damn good room that, mirrors all over it, even the ceiling.' Fellingham made for the stairs, pushing his way against the tide of men intent on reaching the stage.

'So I collect. The name gives a slight hint.' Damn it, Fell was right, his temper was short, nothing appealed any more. He wanted—no, *needed*—something, but he had no idea what, although it most definitely was not to be found in this temple to commercial sexual gratification. And the *respectable* novelty being pressed upon him—marriage—held no charms whatsoever either.

His friend snorted, good humoured despite Gareth's tone. 'Jaded, that's what you are, you sarcastic devil. What you need is a good woman. No, make that a thoroughly bad one!' Roaring with laughter at his own feeble wit, Fellingham struck off down a dimly lit corridor. 'Down here somewhere, if I recall.'

'Give me my clothes back!' Jessica Gifford made a wild grab at the bundle of drab garments before the maid tossed them out of the door and slammed it. Outside, the key turned.

'Now then, don't give me trouble or I'll have to get Madame Synthia up here, and you won't like that, believe me.' The maid grinned and went over to the wardrobe with a sway of her hips that indicated that the skimpiness of her gown was more than just an accident in the wash.

'This is all a terrible mistake.' Jessica stood there shivering, stark naked and too bemused and angry to be properly afraid. But at the back of her mind there was a growing awareness that she should be. She should be very frightened indeed, she realised, for it seemed that all the far-fetched tales she had heard about innocent

country girls being snatched off the street by evil pro-
curers were nothing less than the truth. But she wasn't
some innocent young milkmaid, she was a grown-up,
independent, educated woman—this should not be happening to her!

'There has been some error.' She tried a reasonable
tone, keeping her breathing light in an attempt to control
it. 'I am a governess, here to take up a new position.'

'You'll take up one of those all right.' The maid
laughed. 'Lots and lots of new positions. You *are* a
virgin, aren't you?' The glance she sent Jessica's shivering, goose-bump-covered body was scornful.

'Of course I am! I said there was some mistake. I
asked the woman who greeted me as I got off the coach
if she was Lady Hartington's housekeeper and she said
yes and took me to a carriage and the next thing I know,
I am here.'

'Yes, well, Lady H. won't be wanting your services
for her precious brats after tonight, especially as Lord
H. himself is here and is likely to bid high for you. He'll
be getting you to show him the use of the globes, I'll be
bound. Or perhaps he'll be slow at his Latin and'll need
a good birching. Put these on.' She tossed a handful of
flimsy scraps of fabric on to the bed.

'This *is* a brothel?' *As well to have it clear*, the logical,
sensible part of Jessica's brain told her, while the rest of
it screamed in silent panic.

'Lord love you, of course it is. Best vaulting house
in town. Wonder if we ought to do something about
your hair.' The maid peered at her. 'Nah. I'll just unpin
it, give you that *ready to be tumbled* look. They like that.'

'There has been a mistake,' Jessica repeated, adopting

the tone of clear reason she found effective with some of her more dense pupils. 'I am a governess, I am in the wrong place. If I am kept captive here, that is kidnapping and when I complain to the magistrates someone is going to be in very serious trouble with the law.'

'How're you going to do that, then?' The maid advanced on her with a hairbrush and began to pluck out hairpins. 'You'll stay here until you're properly broken in, then there's nowhere else for you to go because no one respectable will want you. If you want to chat to a magistrate or two, I'm sure there's some here tonight. Very sympathetic they'll be—want to make you feel right at home, I'll be bound.'

Cold fingers of fear slithered down Jessica's spine. She had been earning her own living for three years and she knew just how perilous was the position of an unprotected young woman with the slightest hint of scandal attaching to her name. She knew, all too well, the consequences of that one step off the slippery path of respectability.

If she got out of here and complained, most likely she would be ignored. If she were believed, then she was as good as ruined, whatever happened.

'How can you help them do this to another woman?' She put her hand on the other girl's arm imploringly. In this situation she was not too proud to plead. She would be on her knees begging in a minute. Whatever it took to end this nightmare. 'Don't you want to be out of here yourself?'

The maid stared at her as though she was mad. 'Leave here? I'd be crazy to,' she said shortly. 'Warm room, good food, lots of company, gentlemen giving me good tips. All I have to do is lie on my back on a clean comfy bed and do what comes natural. Leave here and go back to what? A filthy slum in Wapping, that's what. And there you do it up against the wall for a handful of coppers and a black eye.' She peered in the mirror and pinched her own cheeks, bringing some colour into her pert, sharp-featured face.

'Look, you silly cow,' she said suddenly, with what Jessica realised was an attempt at kindness, 'it ain't so bad after the first time. Why make it difficult for yourself? If you make a scene, Madame will just send up some of the doormen to break you in, and you won't like that, believe me.'

Jessica sank down on the end of the huge bed, oblivious to the cold slippery satin under her bare behind. The choices appeared to be to be deflowered by a group of bully boys, to be sold to some debauched gentleman or to throw herself out of the window. Only that was barred with iron.

Life had been hard, these past three years, but she had her modest savings, a respectable profession, her self-respect and she was dependent on no one. Under no circumstances was she going to give that up. Her mind seemed to move beyond terror into a desperate resolve.

The maid was gathering up her fallen hairpins. Jessica put her foot carefully on one of them. 'All right,' she said, having no trouble letting her voice shake. 'What happens now?'

'There, that's better! See how much easier it is if you stop being so foolish about it? What's your name?'

'Jessica.'

'Well, Jessy, I'm Moll. We get's you into your

costume—that won't take long, there ain't much of it— then at midnight the show starts. You're the only virgin on the bill, so the bidding'll be brisk. You'll get a nice rich gentleman who'll tip you well after, I'll be bound, seeing you're the real thing.'

'What's the time now?' Jessica reached for the scraps of muslin the maid held out.

'Twenty to the hour.'

'Well, if there isn't any other option… Isn't there a costume that's a nicer colour?' she asked, feigning petulance. 'I don't like lilac. It looks so insipid with blonde hair.'

Moll did not appear to find the sudden change of tone suspicious. 'I think there's a green one, that'll be pretty with your eyes.' She opened the wardrobe doors again.

The maid's shriek was cut off by Jessica bundling her bodily into the clothes press. One piece of muslin was around her wrists, the other gagging her mouth before she could recover her wits. Jessica pulled down more pieces from the hooks, tying the struggling girl's ankles.

'If you make a noise in the next half-hour, I'll hit you on the head,' she warned, hoping she sounded convincingly fierce. 'If you are quiet, nothing will happen. Understand?'

Wide blue eyes stared at her over the gag, then Molly nodded energetically. Jessica shut the wardrobe door, wedged a chair under the handle, retrieved the hairpin and set about picking the door lock.

In sensation novels, the sort governesses are supposed never to read and in fact devour by the shelf full, the beleaguered yet valiant heroine can pick a dungeon lock in seconds as she escapes from the wicked duke's evil clutches. Her hands shaking, cold sweat standing out all over her, Jessica could only conclude that either wicked dukes employed inferior locksmiths to brothel keepers or the authors of the Minerva Press were sadly misinformed.

After five minutes she stood up in an attempt to relieve her cramped knees. 'Open, you beastly thing,' she said, almost weeping with frustration, and fetched the lock a thump with her clenched fist. With a click it did just that.

Jessica was out into the corridor before she could think. Opposite her a shadowy figure moved. She gave a yelp of fear and realised that it was her own reflection in a full-length mirror. And she was stark naked.

Behind her the door swung to, the catch snicked closed. She could not go back, that was where they would come for her. *Clothes.* That was the priority. Like this she had no hope, and she was finding it very hard to think clearly. One of these rooms, surely, must contain something she could wear.

She opened the first door that she came to and peered round the edge. Inside was a big bed and on it a welter of naked flesh. Gasping, Jessica made out six legs, two pairs of buttocks, a glimpse of hairy chest... How many people? Doing what? She shut the door, flattening herself instinctively into the recess. The participants in the orgy had appeared totally preoccupied, but even so, she did not think she had the courage to sneak in and steal clothing while *that* was going on.

It was ridiculous to feel even more alarmed and fearful than she was already—how much worse could her predicament possibly get?—but that glimpse into carnal matters beyond her comprehension had shocked her out of any delusion that this was a nightmare. There, for real, was what she risked becoming if she could not escape.

Jessica drew in a deep breath and forced herself to plan. To assume the worst was a self-fulfilling prophecy. Her fate was sealed if she panicked. Steadier, she surveyed the corridor in which she found herself. Opposite was the door she had just escaped through, behind her the room with the orgy in progress. On either side were two more doors and then, in both directions, the passage turned. More cautious now, she applied an ear to each door in turn and from each came the sounds of gasps and sighs, and, from one, the crack of a whip.

Which way to go? Her sense of direction had quite deserted her in the hectic few minutes when she had been bundled out of the carriage and up the stairs. Then, as she hesitated, her arms wrapped around her chilly ribs, the decision was made for her by the sound of a door opening and loud voices from out of sight to her right. Without hesitation Jessica fled around the other corner.

It might have been better, she realised in the second she thudded into a solid wall of male muscle, if she had been looking where she was going and not wildly back over her shoulder.

Her nose was buried in a shirt front, the crisp upper edge of a tailored waistcoat stuck into her chin and her shivering body was pressed against warm superfine and knitted silk. The immovable object stood quite still as the voices behind her grew louder.

Jessica tilted back her head and found she was squinting up past a chin that was already shadowed by an evening beard into amused grey eyes. One dark eyebrow rose. 'Help,' she whispered, her voice fled along with her hope. 'Please help me.'

'This is the room,' a slurred voice from behind the man announced. 'Come on, Morant, in we go.'

'By all means,' a voice as amused as the eyes answered, turning Jessica around and putting one firm hand on her shoulder. 'In we all go.'

Her quivering flesh seemed to steady at the warm touch and the thought came to her that at least, if she was about to be ravished, about to lose her virginity, at least he was not the slavering monster of her imagination; not the gross, sweating horror she had been trying not to think about.

The room was brightly lit, glittering with candles reflected over and over from mirrors all around. It was like being inside a chandelier. Jessica, her eyes hunting frantically around the chamber for some escape, saw three figures entwined on the bed, closed her eyes and stumbled.

The hand on her shoulder tightened, holding her up. 'Come on,' the deep voice said softly in her ear. 'Pay attention, I can't do this all by myself.' He still blocked the door, she realised, as the two golden-skinned women on the bed sat up, a pair of pagan idols, and turned identical faces to watch them. Silken black hair flowed down their backs and, between them, his face mercifully hidden by the thighs of one girl and his loins by those of another, was the prone form of a naked man. A fallen Greek statue.

The man holding her reached out his other hand and lifted an exotic brocade robe off a chair beside the door. 'Put this on.'

With a gasp of relief Jessica struggled into its heavy

silken folds as a plaintive voice said, 'Move, would you, Morant!' She found herself gently turned to one side as the big man stepped into the room and his companion barged in behind him, closing the door.

Jessica pulled the deep collar up to hide the lower half of her face. With clothing came some semblance of inner calm; it was incredible how the very fact of being naked clouded the wits. She found she could look around her and see the whole room, not tiny details of it magnified as though in a nightmare. The two women on the bed became clearly twin mortals; the room was not a crystal palace of light, but simply a tawdry chamber lined with smoke-smudged mirrors; and the naked god sitting up on the rumpled sheets was just a blond young man with an incipient pot belly and a flushed face.

'Hello, Fell, Morant,' he managed before slumping back on to the pillows. 'Brought your own, have you?'

'What?' The man at the back—Fell?—pushed past and stared. 'Where did you get this little ladybird, Morant? We didn't have her with us when we started out, did we?' He reached towards Jessica.

'Hands off,' the big man said easily, pushing his friend towards the bed. 'You go and help Rotherham get his money's worth: he doesn't seem to be up to it, all by himself.'

The two black-haired girls held out their arms in welcome and Fell stumbled forwards, collapsing on to the bed with a hoot of laughter amidst his friend's vehement protests.

The big man reached out and scooped up a pile of clothing from the chair, then propelled Jessica out into the passageway again. 'Get dressed.' He dropped the things at her feet. A tall silk hat rolled away, teetered on its brim for a moment, then fell over.

'These are men's clothes.' Jessica clutched the silk robe even tighter around her.

'Exactly. Do you think you are going to walk out of here dressed like that?' He gestured at the robe. Jessica had a vivid mental picture of her hair, her bare feet, the naked skin under the lush brocade.

'You are taking me with you, then?'

'Oh, yes.' She could not see properly, but she knew he was smiling—it was in his voice. 'I am certainly taking you.' Something inside her, something very complicated indeed, was making it hard to think. He would take her out of here, yes, but his words meant more than that—or did they? She shook her head: *deal with the immediate problem, Jessica.*

'You are right, this is a good idea.' She picked up the pantaloons and hauled them on under cover of the robe, rummaged and found the neckcloth and used it to tie round the waist to hold them up. 'Turn round.' The passageway was barely lit, she could make out the shape of him, the flash of white teeth as he grinned, the shape of a closely barbered head.

'I've seen all there is to see already, sweetheart.'

'Well, I don't want you seeing it again,' she retorted and to her amazement he turned a shoulder with a grunt of amusement, leant against the panelling and began to whistle softly while she shucked off the robe, dragged the shirt over her head and pulled on the greatcoat. It came down to her feet. Her bare pink toes peeked out. 'Shoes?' she said.

'And hair.' He turned back and looked at her. 'Heaven help us. Here.' His hands on her hair were ruthless. With one hand he gathered up the whole unruly mass, twisted it into a knot and then into the tall hat, which he jammed on her head. It came down to her nose.

He was heeling off his own evening slippers. Balancing on one foot, he dragged off the black silk socks, then repeated the gesture with the other foot before putting the shoes back on. 'Try these. At least your feet won't seem to be bare. If they notice my bare calves, they'll think I was too fuddled to get dressed properly.'

This was insanity, yet now, with this man she could not even see properly, she felt safe. She had no idea how he could rescue her, but somehow she knew that he would. She was going to survive this. But the illusion of safety was just that, an illusion, and she must not forget it.

Feeling like an exceptionally well-dressed scarecrow Jessica stood in front of the looming dark bulk of her rescuer. 'We will never get out of here with all these people still awake.'

He pulled a watch out of his waistcoat pocket and held it up close to his eyes in the gloom. 'Oh, yes, we will, it is two minutes to midnight. Come on.'

What midnight had to do with it Jessica could not imagine, although images of coaches and pumpkins floated into her mind. She obediently padded along in his wake, one hand holding the hat so she could squint under the brim, the other clutching the coat around her.

They reached the head of a broad staircase, not the narrow one she had been so unceremoniously bundled up, struggling and scratching, only an hour before. The heat and the noise rising from the room below were overwhelming. Jessica took a firm hold of the man's coat tails.

'Don't do that,' he said mildly, 'My valet will complain. Here, beside me.' She forced her clenched fist to relax and, stumbling in her trailing greatcoat, went to stand on his left side. She tried to look up, see him now the light was better, but the hat brim defeated her.

'You are drunk,' her rescuer ordered, his deep voice calm and definite. 'You can do that?'

'Yes.' Actually she wanted to scream, have the vapours and faint dead away. Do all the things, in fact, that the well-bred women lucky enough to be in a position to think themselves her superiors would do if they found themselves captives in a brothel. But she owed it to herself, and to this calm capable man, to have courage, even if she was going to have to pay for her rescue by losing her virtue in his bed. She could not imagine any man would remove a naked woman from a brothel and not expect the logical reciprocal gesture. After all, why else would he be here, if not for a woman? That was what he had meant when he had said he would take her.

'Slump against me, then, and, whatever happens, don't panic.' One arm came round her shoulders and clamped her to his side. *He smells nice*, Jessica thought irrelevantly. Spicy citrus and clean linen and leather. 'And whatever happens, hang on to that hat.'

They began to stagger down the stairs, the man keeping up a slurred, grumbling commentary that taught Jessica, in two terrifying minutes, more cant and bad language than she had ever heard in her life.

The noise swelled, overwhelming her; the stink of hot oil, candle wax, alcohol, sweat and excited masculinity enveloped her, driving away the comforting smell of the man beside her. Then their feet hit the level floor of the entranceway and she drew in a deep, sobbing breath. They were down. The door was right in front of them.

'Off already, gentlemen?' It was the false-genteel accents of the woman who had picked her up at the inn, the woman whose face she had glimpsed, hard and merciless, as the bullies had swept her up the stairs into the nightmare of captivity. Madame Synthia.

'Unfort…unfortunately, Madame, Lord Rotherham ish…is overcome. We will have to return another night—see your famed midnight ex'bition.'

Jessica pressed herself against the tall, gently swaying figure as the madam took her rescuer's other arm and tried to urge him into the room. 'He'll be all right, my lord, one of the girls will look after him. Or I'll get the lads to keep an eye on him. Here, Geordie…'

'Hat,' he hissed, sweeping her up and over his shoulder. Jessica made a grab and held it on. 'Too late, Madame, you don't want him throwing up on your nice marble floor.' Then the doors were open and with an exaggerated stagger they were out. Out into the blissful cold of the night, out into the quiet of a side street with only a hackney cab driving past.

'Cab!' The carriage reined in. Jessica tried to catch a glimpse of the man's face in the light from the windows of the brothel, but he bundled her into the musty interior before she could focus.

'Well.' The door slammed shut and he settled down opposite her in the darkness. 'Here we are, then.'

Chapter Two

The dark shape opposite her did not become any clearer, however hard she stared. Dots began to swim in front of her eyes and Jessica gave up. Seeing him clearly was not going to make any difference—she was in those large, capable hands whether she liked it or not.

Count your blessings, she always said to pupils who whined or complained, knowing as she did it just how infuriatingly smug it sounded. But it was the sort of thing expected from teachers. Now she tried to apply her own good advice.

Blessing One: I am not naked, I have clothes on—but they belong to some man who is currently disporting himself in a house of ill repute. Blessing Two: I am not in a brothel about to be ravished by goodness knows who—but I am in the power of a complete stranger who probably has my ravishment high on his agenda. Blessing Three… She appeared to have run out of blessings.

Know your enemy. Another useful dictum. Especially when you did not know how much of an enemy he was.

'My name is Jessica Gifford.' She ignored the impulse

to give a false name. Life was complicated enough without that. 'Miss,' she added with scrupulous care.

'And mine is Gareth Morant.' The deep voice was curiously calming. She had noticed that in the corridor in the brothel, but then, at that point, anyone who had not drooled or sworn at her would have been comforting. Now that her panic had subsided into cold fear she expected to be rather more discriminating—but he still made her feel safe. *Safe-ish*, she corrected scrupulously.

'Mister?'

'Lord.' She could hear he was smiling. 'Earl of Standon.'

'Thank you for rescuing me, my lord.' There was no call to be impolite, even if you were quaking in your silk-stockinged feet. *His* silk stockings. That felt almost more indecent than wearing that other man's pantaloons.

An earl. An aristocrat. Oh Lord, she really had jumped from the frying pan into the fire. A nice, respectable baronet might be concerned with rectitude and reputation. A plain gentleman might be law abiding and bound by the conventions of church and received morality.

But everyone knew about the aristocracy. They did what they liked and to hell with anyone else's opinions or values. So long as they paid their gambling debts they disregarded with impunity every standard held dear by lesser mortals. They gambled, they spent with wild extravagance, their sexual morals were a scandal, they duelled and they did not give a fig for the opinion of anyone else outside their own charmed and privileged circle. *Look at Papa,* she thought with an inward sigh. *And look at Mama—which is rather more to the point under the circumstances.*

'So, what am I going to do with you, Miss Gifford?' Lord Standon enquired. The thread of amusement was still there in the deep voice—he knew exactly what he was going to do with her, she supposed.

'Take me to a respectable inn?' she suggested hopefully.

'You have your luggage safely somewhere, then?'

'No. They took it all.'

'But you have some money?'

'No.' Obviously she did not have any money, he must know that perfectly well.

'Some respectable acquaintance in London to whom I could deliver you?'

'No,' she repeated through gritted teeth. He was finding this amusing, the beast.

'Then I think you are coming home with me.'

Where you will expect me to show my suitable gratitude for this rescue, she thought with a sinking heart. The trouble was, it was not sinking quite as much as it ought, given that she was a respectable virgin completely in the power of a rakish aristocrat. There was something about his size that made it very hard not to feel safe with him, and something about the amused kindness in his voice that made her want to talk to him. *And something about the sheer masculine splendour of him that makes me want to put my hands on him. All over him...*

'Are you frightened?' he asked suddenly.

'Yes.' It was the honest truth. Frightened of him, frightened for the future, terrified of her own, purely female, responses to him.

'Sensible of you.' He did not appear insulted by her response. She supposed she should have tried a little feminine fluttering: *I feel so safe with you, my lord...*'In fact you are an admirably sensible female, are you not, Miss Gifford? Strange how one can tell that in a mere twenty minutes' acquaintance.'

'Not sensible enough to avoid being tricked by a brothel keeper,' Jessica said bitterly. She was not flattered to be told she was sensible. She knew she was, it was her chief virtue and stock in trade and, try as she might, she could not sound anything else.

'Well, you will not be caught a second time. If my solution is not to your liking, what would *you* like me to do with you?'

Have your wicked way with me? she thought wildly, then caught herself up with a effort. She was exhausted, frightened and completely out of her depth, but that was no excuse for hysteria.

'Would you lend me some money, my lord? Then I can go to a respectable inn tonight and seek employment from an agency in the morning. I am a governess.'

'Go to an inn dressed like that? I am afraid all the shops are shut and I do not carry ladies' clothing on my person.'

'Oh. No, of course you do not.' He must think her completely buffle-headed.

'However, I do have some available.' He let the sentence hang. 'At my house.'

'You mean your wife will lend me something?' she enquired sweetly. How she knew it Jessica could not say, but this man was quite definitely not married. The clothing in question was doubtless the silks and laces of some past or present mistress.

'I am not married.' She had the impression that she had slightly unsettled him. 'If I were married, I would not be patronising establishments such as the one we have just left.'

'You have no need to explain yourself to me, my lord.' And having a wife at home made no difference to whether a lord kept a mistress or frequented the muslin company.

'No,' he agreed with the calm that appeared to be natural to him. 'I was explaining it to myself. A tawdry place—there is little excuse for its existence.'

'Other than that gentlemen patronise it.' She thought sadly of Moll, grateful to be employed in a brothel because there she had regular food and nobody blacked her eyes. She hoped someone had found her by now and released her from the clothes press.

The hackney cab drew up with a lurch. 'My town house,' Lord Standon said, getting up and opening the door. He held out his hands to help her down and Jessica paused in the doorway, seeing him for the first time in the light of the torchères either side of the wide black front door.

He was big. She already knew that. His hair was dark and she could not make out the exact colour, but what held her was the power of his face. No one would ever call Gareth Morant handsome, but no one would ever be able to call him less than impressive. Someone—she could not imagine who, unless it was a blacksmith with a hammer—had managed to break a large nose that had not been particularly distinguished to start with. His jaw was strong and determined, in contrast to the peaceable tone he seemed to habitually employ. His eyes, which she already knew were grey, were shadowed below dark brows and his mouth, which she could see all too clearly, was wide, sensual with a lurking smile.

He was waiting with patience for her to move and to alight from the hackney. Jessica thought frantically. Had she any option other than to enter this man's house? No, she had not. 'Thank you, my lord,' she said as placidly as she knew how, and allowed him to take her hand as she jumped down to the pavement.

Doubtless she should embrace death rather than dishonour, but that seemed both unpleasant and disproportionate under the circumstances. *Like mother, like daughter.* The thought flickered through her brain and was instantly banished. Mama…Mama had been *different.* And beside any other considerations, Miss Jessica Gifford believed strongly that one honoured one's obligations. Up to now that had sometimes been onerous, but never quite so frightening to contemplate.

She stood and waited while he paid the driver, her stockinged feet cold and damp on the flags, her ridiculous hat pulled down over her face, then allowed him to take her arm and guide her towards the shallow steps. Despite the hour a butler materialised as Lord Standon closed the door behind him.

'Ah, Jordan. Is Mrs Childe still up?'

'No, my lord, she retired an hour ago, as have all the maids. Would you wish me to rouse one of them?' His very lack of interest in the bizarrely clad figure shivering beside his master revealed the superiority of an upper servant, but Jessica would have been grateful for a look of surprise—she was beginning to feel invisible.

'No, there is no need to disturb them. This young lady has had an unpleasant experience and requires a bedchamber, some supper and some suitable clothing. A fire in the room, please, Jordan.'

'Yes, my lord. Would the young lady care to come into the library to eat while her room is prepared? There is a fire there as usual.'

'Yes, that would be best.' The earl turned and regarded Jessica, who stared back from under the brim of her hat. Her feet were beginning to grow numb on the cold marble. 'Clothes first, though. Come along, Miss Gifford, we should find something in the Chinese bedchamber.'

He led the way to the sweep of stone stairs rising from the chequerboard marble. Jessica grabbed her trailing coat and struggled up after him, clutching the elegant wrought-iron handrail with her free hand. The position gave her an unrivalled opportunity to study long well-shaped legs, narrow hips and broad athletic shoulders. Having run into him at speed, she did not make the mistake of imagining that Lord Standon's figure owed anything to his tailor, who must give thanks daily for a customer who did so much credit to his creations.

On the other hand, she thought critically as she reached the landing and he turned to make sure she was following, he definitely was not a handsome man. The good light showed that her impression outside on the pavement had been correct. At least, she corrected herself, as she plodded along in his wake, trying to lift her tired feet up out of the thick carpet, he was not a *classically* handsome man. Neither Lord Byron's romantically tumbled locks, nor Mr Brummell's much-vaunted beauty need fear competition from the Earl of Standon. On the other hand, he was unmistakably a very virile, masculine creature and she knew perfectly well that his size was provoking a thoroughly unwise desire to cast herself upon his broad chest and beg to be looked after.

Jessica reminded herself that she was not a woman who could afford to succumb to romantic notions, but one who lived by her intelligence and common sense, and that what she was striving for in life was respectable, dull, safe security. Men played no part in that ambition and aristocrats who frequented brothels, however kind they seemed, and however much one wanted to wrap one's arms around as much of them as possible, were the shortest way to the primrose path that led inexorably downwards to shame and degradation. *Look at Mama.*

Well, possibly shame and degradation were rather strong words for it in Mama's case, but it had certainly led to her being cut off without a penny, shunned by her family and living the sort of life that Jessica had sworn, at the age of fourteen, that she would never, ever, risk. Mama had thought the world well lost for love; then, when that love itself had gone, she had lived on her wits, her beauty and her charm.

As far as Jessica was concerned, falling in love ranked somewhat below wagering one's entire substance on a lottery ticket as a sensible way of carrying on for a woman.

Sensation novels promised true love would find you if you only waited long enough and the Old Testament was littered with prophets being sustained entirely by faith and passing ravens, but a good education and hard work seemed more positive routes to security, food on the table and a roof over her head to Jessica than prayer and patience.

Lord Standon stopped and Jessica walked into the back of him. 'Sorry. It is this hat.'

'I believe you might safely remove it now, Miss Gifford.' He opened the door and she stepped inside, pulling off the tall-crowned hat as she did so. There was no point in being a ninny about this. She must do what she had to do to get her life back on course. This was an interlude, then she could get back to being Miss Gifford, superior governess—pianoforte, harp, water-colours and the Italian tongue included.

They had entered what was presumably the Chinese bedchamber. Jessica stood inside the door while his lordship touched a taper to the candelabra standing around the room, trying not to be overawed by the fine painted wallpaper, the golden silk hangings or the rich carpet. It was, when all was said and done, merely a room for sleeping in. She swallowed, hoping that whatever happened before the sleep was not going to occur here under the jewelled eyes of dragons. Common sense and resignation were not proving as fortifying to the spirits as she might have hoped.

'There should be night things at least.' He pulled out drawers and turned over fabrics. 'Yes. Help yourself.' A carved panel opened at a touch and revealed hanging rails. 'And there are robes in there as well, and slippers. Will you be able to find your way down again? Jordan will show you where the library is.'

So, it was not going to happen here and now in this room. Jessica placed the tall hat on a chest and nodded, managing her breathing somehow. 'Thank you, my lord. I will not be long.' He smiled and went out, closing the door behind him. Jessica went to look down into the open drawer at the fine lawn and rich Brussels lace, the satin ribbons and the shimmer of silk. It seemed she was going to lose her virtue whilst lavishly dressed—if that were any consolation.

Gareth stood frowning down at the meal his butler was setting out on the side table in the library. 'Jordan, Miss Gifford was kidnapped by bullies from a brothel as she arrived on the stage this evening.'

'Tsk. Shocking. One hears about such things, of course. How fortunate you were able to assist her.' The man shook his head at the wickedness of the world and adjusted the position of the cruet slightly. 'Miss Gifford will doubtless be hungry, my lord. Snatched meals at post inns are not sustaining fare and I presume she has had nothing since. I will bring a slice of fruit pie in addition to the sweetmeats.' He regarded the table, apparently satisfied with its arrangement. 'Will Miss Gifford be staying with us long, my lord?'

'Until I have settled her future, Jordan.' There was a tap and the door opened. 'Ah, that is better.' Gareth regarded the slim figure in the open doorway and found himself fighting back a grin. Top to toe in Julia's luxurious lingerie, Miss Gifford still managed to look like a governess. Her hair was braided down her back, her feet were neatly together and her hands clasped at her waist. She had managed to find the plainest of the robes and, from the lack of frills showing under it, one of the simplest of the nightgowns.

The memory of her naked, her hair in glorious disarray around white shoulders, those small, high, rounded breasts pressed against his shirt front, filled him

with a pleasurable glow that none of the exotic pleasures promised at Madame Synthia's had evoked.
Something must have shown in his eyes, for her chin
came up a fraction and those wide green eyes narrowed
into suspicious slits. However naïve Miss Jessica
Gifford had been in stepping into a brothel-keeper's
carriage, she was not lacking in either courage or per-
ception.

'Come and sit down by the fire and eat, you must be
hungry.' He pulled out a chair for her and waited while she
came and seated herself, managing it neatly and without
glancing down at the chair as he pushed it in. *Used to
dinner parties*. Gareth added the fact to his slim mental
dossier on Miss Gifford. Obviously a superior governess,
and one with much to lose from this night's events.

'Thank you, my lord.' She waited, hands folded in her
lap while Jordan pulled out a chair for him. 'I confess
I am a trifle peckish.'

'Tea, Miss Gifford? Or lemonade, perhaps?' Gareth
saw her glance from the waiting butler to the opened bottle
of white Chablis standing in an ice bucket by his side.

'Wine, if you please.' There was a touch of defiance
about the choice. *Dutch courage*, he thought, wondering just why she was still so tense. There would be a
period of uncertainty while she recovered from the
shock, no doubt, but she would feel better in the
morning. Mrs Childe would find her ready-made clothes
and she could visit some agencies. He had no doubt she
would soon find a suitable appointment; in the
meantime he would have to find her somewhere to stay.
Maude would help.

She was eating elegantly, he noticed, yet with a
single-minded approach that was making inroads into

the cold meats before her. Her lack of the vapours appealed to him and he plied her with food until she sat back with a sigh of repletion. 'Thank you, my lord. I cannot remember when I last ate anything beside the merest snack.'

'You have travelled far to London?' Gareth picked up his wine and stood to pull back her chair. 'Shall we sit by the fire?'

She gave him a long, searching look from under lashes that seemed ridiculously lavish for such a neat, self-contained creature. 'Yes, thank you,' she said at last, picking up her own half-empty glass and moving to the chair he indicated.

'I have come down from Leicestershire,' she explained. In the big, masculine, winged chair she looked more fragile than he had thought before. Despite her poise, she also seemed vulnerable in a way that was different from her panic in the brothel. Her eyes were wide and watchful on him and she seemed braced for something. 'My last position ended when my pupil went to stay with her grandmother in Bath. I have…had…a position with Lady Hartington to teach languages to her two older daughters. I understand that Lord Hartington was at that place tonight.'

'Yes. In any case, you are better off not employed in that household, Miss Gifford. Lady Hartington is a bitter woman and her husband has a poor reputation.'

Jessica shrugged, a slight, unconsciously graceful gesture. 'It is my job to fit in and make the best of what I find. Few households can be said to be ideal.'

'No doubt you are right. Finish your wine now, it is time for us to retire.' He got to his feet and reached for a candle to give her.

There was no mistaking the tension that shot through her at his innocuous words. She stood up, lifted her chin and said with just the merest tremor in her voice, 'Of course my lord. I am quite…ready.'

Ready for what? Then he realised what the tightly clasped hands and the pulse beating visibly at her throat meant. She thought he had brought her home to—*Damn it, does she take me for some libertine?* Gareth leashed his temper with an effort. 'So, you think you have jumped out of the frying pan into the fire, do you, Jessica?'

Her eyes widened at his use of her name, the pupils expanded so their green light became almost black. 'You had gone to that place for a purpose and thanks to me you were not able to accomplish it.' She stood quite still, although he could see the edge of the nightgown moving. She was trembling and suddenly that made him furious.

'Are you a virgin?' he asked, his voice harsh.

She went white. 'Yes. I am.'

'And you think I am in the habit of ravishing virginal young ladies?'

'I am not a lady, I am a governess.' Her lips tightened for a moment. 'From my observations, the aristocracy regards governesses in much the same light as chambermaids.'

'As fair game?' Obviously being an aristocrat weighed heavily against him.

'Yes.' She gave a little huffing breath as though to recover herself after running. 'And I owe you for rescuing me—I pay my debts.'

'Indeed?' Gareth set the candlestick down with a snap, suddenly too angry to analyse why. 'Would it be

worth my while, I wonder? Virgins are no doubt interesting, but then there is the lack of experience…'

'I learn quickly my lord.'

'Do you, Jessica?' He closed the distance between them
and cupped his hands around her shoulders. Under his big
palms her bones felt fragile. 'Let us see just how quickly',
and he bent his head and kissed her full on the mouth.

Chapter Three

Jessica had just enough warning to drag a breath down into her lungs and then her world changed. One moment she had no idea what a man's mouth felt like, what a male body crushed against hers would feel like or how her own body would react to such contact—and the next everything became a sensual blur filled with this man's heat and scent and taste and the pressure of his lips devouring hers.

She was up on tiptoe, held hard to him, his big body forcing hers to curve and mould into his. His mouth moved on hers with purpose that confused her until she realised that he wanted her to open to him. With a little gasp she did so and his tongue filled her, hot and moist and indecently exciting. She could taste the wine they had been drinking and something else that must be simply him. He was possessing her mouth with what she hazily realised was an echo of a far more complete possession and she melted, boneless, shameless, against him.

When Gareth Morant lifted his mouth from hers and set her square on her feet again she had lost the power of speech, of movement and, utterly, the will to resist him. Jessica gripped the powerful forearms as his hands steadied her. She tried not to pant.

'Miss Gifford.' Unfortunately he did not appear to have been reduced to the same state. His breathing was perfectly even, his face calm, his colour normal. 'Miss Gifford, you are a delightful young lady and a pleasure to kiss, but I hope you will believe me when I tell you that I have not the slightest intention of taking you to my bed. I went to that place this evening at the behest of my friends, not to seek a woman, and you may rest assured that even if I had that intention, I am capable of suppressing my animal instincts for one night.'

'Oh.'

'And I am not in the habit of ravishing virgins, nor of extracting a price from someone whose plight should have prompted any gentleman to rescue her.' He paused and the corner of his mouth twitched. 'Or even any aristocrat.'

'Oh.' Jessica struggled to get her brain out of the morass of warm porridge into which it appeared to have fallen and to say something coherent. 'Then I must say that was the most embarrassing mistake I have ever made,' she admitted with painful honesty.

'Kissing me?' His eyebrows shot up. Obviously his lordship was not used to having his caresses dismissed as embarrassing. He was probably offended that, having reduced her to a quivering puddle, she was not begging for more.

'No. I had no choice about that, had I?' Jessica glared at him. 'I mean, assuming that you would expect—you know.'

'Well, I do not.' He picked up the candlestick again

and handed it to her. 'I will ring for Jordan to show you to your room.'

'Why *did* you kiss me, my lord?' She had not meant to say it, she had meant to say *Thank you* in a calm and dignified manner, but the question just escaped.

'Because you made me cross.' He stood watching her and she made herself stand up to the scrutiny without fidgeting until the corner of his mouth quirked into a ghost of a smile. 'And because I wanted to.' He reached for the bell pull. 'You may sleep in peace, Miss Gifford, my curiosity has been satisfied.'

Well, that was a flattening piece of reassurance to be sure! Jessica produced a perfectly correct curtsy and stalked out in the butler's wake. So his lordship's curiosity had been satisfied, had it? And what if it had not been? Would he have persisted? Obviously he was used to far more sophisticated kissing than she could provide.

'Your room, Miss Gifford.'

Her agitation melted away on a sigh. Warm firelight flickered on rose-coloured walls. A bed heaped with white linens sat comfortably in the far corner. Steam curled upwards from the ewer standing on the washstand and the curtains were closed tight against the damp London night and all the dangers it held. This was not some rake's love nest. Lord Standon was treating her as a guest and she had cast aspersions on his motives.

'Oh dear.'

She had realised she had spoken aloud. Jordan turned. 'Miss Gifford? Is something wrong?'

'I have just realised that perhaps I expressed my gratitude to Lord Standon insufficiently just now.'

What might have been a fleeting smile passed over

the impassive countenance. 'It is easy, if I might make an observation, miss, to misinterpret things, especially when one is tired and in some distress.'

'Yes. Thank you, Jordan.' The man bowed and left her. Jessica took off the heavy apricot satin robe, pulled the cream silk nightgown over her head and went to pour water into the basin. Her feet were filthy, but her whole being felt contaminated from those desperate hours in the brothel and she stood for long minutes lathering the sweet-scented soap over every inch of her body before she began to feel clean again.

Fresh and dry at last Jessica slipped back into the nightgown, luxuriating in its soft fabric and luxurious detail. Sinful behaviour obviously had its rewards, she decided, climbing between the warm sheets and snuggling down, wishing now that she had chosen one of the more elaborately trimmed garments—she would never have the opportunity to indulge in such opulence again.

It had been an eventful day. She had been inside a brothel, she was sleeping in silk—and she had been kissed by a man. Jessica blew out the remaining candle and lay watching the pattern of firelight on the walls. She should be making plans, but…. As her agitation slowly ebbed away and she relaxed into the warmth and safety of the bedchamber, the sensual memory of that kiss flooded back. She had resigned herself to never being kissed— the path she had set herself precluded any relationship with men beyond that of employee and employer.

Now she knew what it felt like to be held so tightly, and yet want to be held tighter yet. She knew what a man tasted like, how his skin smelt, how her own body yearned to betray every standard and scruple just to experience that glory again. And that was just a kiss. What would it be like to be made love to by Lord Standon? Perhaps, if she willed herself to sleep, she would dream about him.

The rattle of curtain rings woke Jessica from a deep sleep undisturbed by the nightmares of Madam Synthia's or the bliss of Lord Standon's arms.

'Good morning, Miss Gifford.' Jessica sat up and found a neatly clad maid setting a tray down beside her bed. 'I am Mary, miss, and I'm to look after you while you are here. Mr Jordan told us about what had happened—what a dreadful thing, miss!—and Mrs Childe will be going out in a minute to buy you some day clothes. Here's your chocolate, miss, and his lordship says, would you care to join him for breakfast? In your dressing gown's quite all right, miss.' She ran out of breath at last and stood beaming.

'Thank you, Mary.' Jessica took a reviving mouthful of chocolate. *Oh, the luxury!* It seemed to stroke down inside her like warm velvet, soothing and invigorating, both at the same time. 'How will Mrs Childe know what size clothes to get for me?'

'His lordship lined us all up and said Polly was just the right size, miss.' Mary bustled about. 'I'll fetch your hot water, shall I?'

Oh Lord! So he had told them Polly was the right size, had he? Just in case the rest of the household had no idea that their master had had the opportunity to scrutinise her in intimate detail. Jessica had become very familiar with the inner world of households, their miniature social hierarchies, their taboos and their rules. The servants would not be kind about a governess gone astray; she and her kind were usually regarded as being neither gentry nor servants and as a result were an outcast class between the two. Not that Mary appeared hostile.

The maid bustled back with the water and drew the screen round the washstand. 'Here you are, miss, I've brought a fresh nightgown as well.'

Gareth pushed back his chair as the door opened on to the breakfast parlour and Jessica walked in. He saw with relief that she did not appear much affected by her adventures the night before—neither the kidnap nor his insane kiss. He was still kicking himself about that, and he had suffered long sleepless hours reviewing just how unwise it had been to yield to temptation. He was not sure whether it was the ache in his groin or in his conscience that had most disturbed his slumber, but they had both proved damnably uncomfortable.

'Miss Gifford. I trust you slept well?'

'Very well, thank you, my lord. That was a most comfortable room, I could not have been better cared for.' She hesitated, one hand lying with unconscious elegance on the back of a dining chair. 'I leapt to an unforgivable conclusion last night, my lord, and I apologise for it.'

Coals of fire heaped on his tender scruples. 'And I apologise for what followed. I suggest we both forget about it, Miss Gifford. Now, would you like to take a seat and I will fetch you some breakfast from the buffet?'

She inclined her head and Gareth felt a flicker of admiration for her poise. 'Very well, thank you. But I will not forget your kindness. And please, do not let your own meal get cold, I will help myself.'

He sat, watching with a carefully suppressed smile of appreciation as she walked past him to the back of the room where the chafing dishes had been laid out on the sideboard under their silver domes. This morning rich silk ruffles flounced from under the heavy hem of the apricot robe and her hair had been brushed until it shone and then caught up with skilful simplicity. There was far less of the prim governess on show this morning. Julia always said Mary was the most accomplished of the maids.

'Mrs Childe has gone shopping on your behalf,' he began, reaching for the mustard pot.

'So I understand.' There was a muted clang as she turned back a lid and began to fill her plate. 'I understand you could accurately identify Polly as being just my size.' *Ah.* Mary might be skilful as a lady's maid, but she was obviously somewhat lacking in tact. 'Goodness, black pudding, what a treat.' There was another clang. Gareth began to amuse himself following Jessica's progress along the buffet by sound alone. 'Who else is coming to breakfast, my lord?'

'Just us.' He bit into the rare sirloin.

'Indeed? How lavish it is.'

He suspected he was on the receiving end of a very governessy look, to do with extravagance and possibly gluttony. Gareth grinned at his rapidly diminishing steak and contemplated what response would be most calculated to tease her.

'I do not believe in stinting—' He broke off at the sound of raised voices in the hall. Or at least, of one, very familiar, female voice raised in argument and Jordan's even tones attempting to head her off. Impossible, the man should know that by now.

'—his lordship is up!' The door swung open. 'You see, he was in here all the time. Good morning, Gareth darling.'

'Maude.' Gareth got to his feet and submitted to being pecked on the cheek by the black-haired whirlwind who swept in, thrusting her vast muff into Jordan's hands. 'What on earth do you keep in a muff that size? A small pony? And what are you doing here at this hour of the day and without a chaperon?'

'They are all the crack this size. And as for chaperons—piffle.' She sat down next to him, tugged off her bonnet and reached for a cup. 'Is that coffee?'

'Yes.' Resigned to the invasion, he sat down again and passed the pot. 'And it is not piffle. Do you want to end up marrying me?'

'Lord, no!' She laughed at him, glossy black curls bouncing, the morning chill colouring her cheeks and lending sparkle to her blue eyes. She really was the most lovely creature and he was strongly tempted to box her ears. 'That's why I am here, this marriage thing is getting serious. Papa has Pronounced. Say what I will, he is fixed upon our union. You are the only man for me, in his opinion—as well as being well bred, healthy, in your right mind and rich, you are also, he tells me, a pillar of rectitude and just what a flibbertigibbet like me requires in a husband.'

'I don't want to marry you,' Gareth said flatly. 'None of this is news, Maude. You don't want to marry me either. Our parents came up with this idiot agreement, it isn't legally binding.'

'I know that! But most of society believes we are betrothed. Gareth, how am I ever going to find a man to marry if they are all afraid of you?'

'What do you want me to do about it?' Gareth poured them both more coffee. 'I have never confirmed the rumours, I have never given your father any indication that I might do as he wishes.'

'He will not listen. And neither do all the gorgeous men out there who are avoiding me like the plague!' Maude set her elbow on the table, put her pointed chin on the palm of her hand and gazed at him earnestly. 'There is only one thing to do Gareth, you are going to have to embark on a life of sin and debauchery.'

The gasp behind him had Maude swinging round on her seat, her eyes searching the less well-lit end of the room. 'Gareth! You fraud—you've already started.'

The eruption into the room of one of the loveliest young women she had ever seen froze Jessica in front of the buffet. Even in the flat light of a winter morning the intruder seemed to gleam like a highly finished piece of jewellery. Her hair was a glossy mass of black ringlets, her clothes had the dull sheen of silk and merino, her eyes glinted like Ceylon sapphires and her teeth as she laughed at Lord Standon were white and perfect.

Jessica stood quite still, her plate clasped in both hands while this lovely creature, quivering with barely suppressed energy, swept on. Despite her lack of a chaperon, she did not need Lord Standon's words to realise that this was a lady and not, despite her scandalous presence in an unmarried man's breakfast parlour, one of the muslin company. Maude, whoever she was, was quite obviously well bred, wealthy and supremely self-confident.

'…you are going to have to embark on a life of sin and debauchery.'

Jessica gasped, all too aware of the picture she must present. There was no way out of the room unseen.

Maude swung round, her face lighting up into a picture of delighted mischief at the sight of Jessica. 'Gareth! You fraud—you've already started.'

'I—' Jessica put down her plate and walked towards the door. 'Excuse me, you will wish to be alone, Lord Standon.'

'Miss Gifford.' He stood up. 'Please, sit down and have your breakfast. Lady Maude is just going.' He held out a chair for her on the opposite side of the table and waited. Jessica sat while he retrieved her plate, placed it in front of her and poured her coffee. There did not appear to be any choice.

'Thank you, my lord. But—'

'My pleasure. Maude, go home.'

'Certainly not, this is far too interesting.' Lady Maude settled herself squarely to the table and reached for the bread and butter. 'Introduce us properly, Gareth.' She beamed at Jessica. 'That's Julia's robe, I was with her when she bought it. Are you a friend of hers? I was rather hoping that you were an exotic bird of paradise and that Gareth was about to launch himself into a life of scandalous dissipation and save us both. But I can see you are a lady. Which is a disappointment, I must admit.'

Jessica blinked in the face of this torrent and plucked out one name. 'Who is Julia?'

'Lady Blundell, Gareth's sister. Would you pass the honey? Thank you so much.'

So she had completely misjudged him. He had lent her his sister's clothes, not his mistress's, he had no intention of ravishing her—and now she was embarrassing him by being here when this extraordinary young woman descended upon him.

Jessica shot Lord Standon a cautious sideways glance. He had pushed his plate to one side and had buried his face in his hands, which she supposed was a reasonable reaction from anyone attempting to deal with Lady Maude. She looked back at the other woman. Maude gazed back, her lovely face a picture of cheerful curiosity. Jessica succumbed to it, unable to think of a single fabrication that might cover her presence there.

'My name is Jessica Gifford. I am a governess and yesterday I was abducted off the stage by a brothel keeper. Lord Standon rescued me and his housekeeper is buying me clothes so I can go to an employment agency today and secure another position.'

'Goodness. How beautifully concise and organised you are. I shall see if I can match you. I am Maude Templeton, my papa is the Earl of Pangbourne and my entire ambition at the moment is not to end up married to Gareth.'

'Why?' Jessica enquired bluntly. 'His lordship appears eminently eligible to me.' This was greeted by a faint moan from the head of the table. Lady Maude rolled her eyes.

'Gareth, stop it. Miss Gifford is obviously a woman of sense and her breakfast is getting cold. We can all agree that you are completely eligible, utterly gorgeous and I am demented not to want to marry you. Likewise I am lovely, desirable, incredibly well bred and amazingly well dowered. You must be all about in the head not to want me. Let us all finish our breakfast and then we can decide what to do about it.'

'I know exactly what I am going to do.' Lord Standon

lowered his hands and regarded both of them with disfavour. 'I am going to ring for Jordan, who will put you in your carriage and send you home, Maude. Miss Gifford is going to finish her breakfast and then, when Mrs Childe returns with her new clothes, I will send her in the barouche to interview as many employment agencies as she sees fit to visit. You, meanwhile, will stand ready to provide whatever references Miss Gifford requires to cover the period of unemployment she is currently experiencing. In fact, come to think of it, she can stay with you until she finds a new position.'

'Lord Standon, I could not possibly impose upon La—'

'Of course you can. What fun. Do call me Maude, we are going to be great friends, I can see.' Maude smiled at her, then turned a gimlet stare back on Lord Standon. 'Gareth, what about me? I am truly desperate and if you don't—'

The door opened, Jordan positively slid through the gap and closed it behind him, his back to the panels. 'My lord,' he murmured, his voice hushed, 'Lord Pangbourne is here, demanding an interview.'

'Papa?' Maude stood up with a faint shriek.

'Yes, my lady.'

'Shh!' Lord Standon set down his coffee cup. 'Tell him I am not at home Jordan.'

'I attempted so to do, my lord. The earl says he will wait in the hall. He has resisted all my efforts to establish him comfortably in your study—he appears suspicious that you will attempt to evade him.'

'Damn right,' his lordship said grimly.

'Jordan!' The masculine voice from the hall had all

three of them at the table regarding the door warily. The handle rattled. 'Is Standon in there?'

'Just coming, my lord,' the butler called back, then lurched forward as the door partly opened behind him.

'Maude,' Lord Standon hissed, 'get under the table and take your bonnet with you.' As she slid out of view he was on his feet, pulling Jessica to hers.

'What—?'

'I'll make this up to you. Promise.' His fingers were in her hair, dragging out pins, sending her curls tumbling around her shoulders, then he yanked open the satin sash, pushed the robe back off her shoulders and fell back in his chair, Jessica tumbling into his lap. 'Kiss me.'

The door burst open. Her mouth captured by Gareth Morant's, her body held hard against his, all Jessica could do was to fight to keep her senses. The pressure on her mouth eased a little. 'Help me, I can't do this all by myself,' he whispered. The echo of his words to her in the brothel. Jessica stopped struggling. This was how she could repay him.

She snaked her arms around his neck, opened her mouth under his and arched her back. The robe slithered free and the warm air caressed the swell of her breasts revealed by the silken gown. Deep in his throat he made a soft sound, a growl. Something inside Jessica turned to liquid fire. Was this only playacting?

An infuriated voice thundered, 'Damn it, Jordan, get out of my way.' There was silence, broken only by the thunder of her heartbeat. Then, 'Morant, you libertine! What the devil do you think you are doing?'

Chapter Four

Lord Standon shifted Jessica in his arms so that her face was hidden in his shoulder. She clung, quivering with mingled excitement and embarrassment.

'I am attempting to eat my breakfast in my own dining room,' he replied coldly. 'You will forgive me if I do not get up. I believe Jordan did attempt to intimate that I was not receiving.'

'You've been avoiding me, Sir! And neglecting poor Maude—and now I see why.'

'Maude is hardly moping without my presence, Templeton.' Jessica gave a little wriggle as she felt the satin of her nightgown sliding over his knees. Lord Standon closed his hand more firmly over her hip and pressed her to him.

'You are betrothed to Maude, damn it,' the older man snapped. Jessica could imagine him, red faced with bristling eyebrows.

'Forgive me, but we are not betrothed, whatever you and my honoured father cooked up between you. And neither of us wish to be. With respect, sir, you cannot force me to make a declaration to Maude.'

'I can stop her marrying anyone else. What do you say to that, eh?' Jessica, her senses filled with the smell and feel of the man who held her, struggled to focus on what was happening on the far side of the table. Lord Pangbourne appeared to be pacing.

'I would say that I find it hard to believe that you would be such an unfeeling father.'

'Bah! I'll talk to you again, Morant, when you haven't got most of your mind on your doxy. I give you good day!'

The door slammed. Lord Standon exhaled, his breath feathering hot all down her neck. 'You can come out now, Maude.' Jessica wriggled, sitting upright, but he still held her on his lap, apparently forgetting that they were merely playacting. The sensation of a man's legs pressed so close to her derrière was breathtaking. Jessica felt the shift of thigh muscles and sat very still.

Maude popped out from under the table, pushing back her tumbled curls. 'You see? He is quite impossible.' She brushed down her skirt and stood regarding them. 'Gareth, are you still supposed to be cuddling Jessica?'

'What? Lord, I beg your pardon, Jessica, you felt so right there I quite—' He broke off, shaking his head as though surprised at his own words and opened his arms. Jessica slid off his lap and returned to her own place, her cheeks glowing.

'My lord…' She pulled her robe into some sort of order and pushed her hair back over her shoulders. This was a madhouse and she needed to extricate herself from it and go and interview employment agencies before she became any more embroiled.

'Gareth. I think we have gone beyond the use of titles, do you not?'

Gareth. It suited him, a solid, warm name. But she could hardly imagine herself using it, except in her head.

'You see, don't you, Gareth?' Maude continued. 'Papa finds you in the torrid embraces of a scarlet woman, and *still* persists in saying we should marry. What on earth do you have to do to make him realise we are not suited?'

'Perhaps Lord Standon could marry someone else?' Jessica suggested. She suppressed the turmoil the last few minutes had thrown her into and tried to apply some logic to the situation. Someone had to. 'It seems the commonsense solution.'

'So it is, if there was anyone I wished to marry.' Gareth grimaced, pouring more coffee. 'I'd sooner marry Maude than some female I don't like.'

'Then why?' Jessica persisted, determined to make sense of it all. Her food was lukewarm. She pushed the plate to one side and started on the bread and butter and honey. 'Why is Lord Pangbourne so insistent and why, when you obviously both like each other very much, don't you do what he wants?'

Maude and Gareth exchanged looks, then he shrugged and gestured for her to start. 'Once upon a time,' she began, her voice taking on the singsong tone of the storyteller with a much-told tale, 'Gareth's uncle fell in love with my aunt. Our families' lands march together and it was true love and a marvellous romance. He was the son of the duke, she was a great beauty. Everyone was thrilled, but on the eve of the wedding they were killed in a carriage accident. Both families were plunged into deepest mourning and our fathers vowed that when we grew up—I had just been born— we would marry and recreate the legendary love match.'

Jessica's thoughts—that this was a piece of sentimental nonsense—must have shown, despite her careful lack of comment, for Gareth grinned. 'It was not such a foolish piece of romance as you might assume. As we grew up it became obvious that because of her poor mother's continuous ill health Maude was going to remain an only child—and there we were, presenting the perfect alliance to unite two great estates.'

'Our fathers exchanged letters formally agreeing to the betrothal,' Maude picked up the story. 'And here we are.'

'But you are not legally bound?'

'No, this is not the Middle Ages, thank goodness, but Papa controls my money until I am thirty or I marry with his consent. And he has made sure everyone believes us to be betrothed.'

'Then why don't you do as he asks?' Jessica persisted. 'You can hardly object to Lord Standon, surely?'

'Thank you Jessica,' he said gravely.

'I meant,' she said repressively, kicking herself under the table for thinking aloud, 'you are apparently highly eligible and you like each other.'

'They made the mistake of bringing us up like brother and sister—we simply can't think of each other except as that. And I know perfectly well that somewhere, out there, is the man I am going to fall in love with,' Maude said flatly. 'And I do not want to be married to someone else when we meet. Doomed love and broken hearts may be all very well in novels, but I have no intention of subjecting myself to such discomfort.' She attacked an apple with a pearl-handled knife and a fierce expression. 'But I will never get to know any men to fall in love with because no one will do more than make polite conversation because they are all scared of Gareth.'

'He is rather formidable,' Jessica agreed, eyeing his lordship's brooding figure at the head of the table.

'Thank you,' he said again, politely. 'We are agreed that I am eligible and formidable and that Maude cannot be sacrificed upon the altar of matrimony other than to a man she truly loves. You will also have observed that her father is a thick-skinned old termagant who won't take *no* for an answer. You are a young lady whose common sense is her stock in trade—what do you suggest?'

Jessica pondered the problem, her abstracted gaze fixed on the rather attractive whorl of Gareth's left ear where the crisp brown curl of his hair set the defined shape into sharp relief. She knew exactly what the skin there smelled like.

'Um… You could pretend to become betrothed to someone else. Lord Pangbourne would admit defeat then, surely? But that means you need to find a complacent lady who would not mind such a charade, and you risk finding yourself permanently attached if she proves unscrupulous. Or you could do what Lady Maude suggested and embark upon a course of debauchery so public that even Lord Pangbourne will be forced to admit that he cannot marry his daughter to you. After all, he has just surprised you apparently making love amidst the marmalade.'

Maude suppressed an unladylike snort. Jessica contemplated another slice of bread and honey, decided that she was eating merely to keep her mind distracted from Gareth's proximity and sucked the tips of her sticky fingers. Then she realised his gaze was resting on her lips and promptly snatched up her napkin. 'The latter course would be safer—the debauchery, I mean, not the marmalade.' Maude gave way to giggles. 'I imagine that you could hire a professional without risk of finding yourself sued for breach of promise.'

She closed her eyes for a moment, imagining Gareth back in that brothel interviewing candidates for a charade of debauchery. Only, once having paid for them, she assumed it would require a saint not to avail himself of the services thus acquired, so playacting would not be required. *He is a man*, she reminded herself briskly. *That is what men do. And in any case, what is it to me?*

'Excellent. We have a plan.' Maude tossed her napkin on to the table and stood up, ignoring Lord Standon's grimace and shaken head. 'You see, Gareth, Jessica agrees with me.' She smiled across the table. 'Now, I will drive home and then send my carriage back to collect you and take you round the agencies. As soon as that is done you can come and stay with me until you are settled.'

'But Lord Pangbourne has seen me.'

'He saw a wanton female with her hair down, half-dressed in a improper nightgown and from the back. He will not recognise you, Jessica, take my word for it.' Gareth walked across and opened the door. 'Maude's offer of the carriage is a sensible one.'

Gareth strolled through the doors of White's, nodded absently at the porter who relieved him of his outer garments, and climbed the stairs to the library. He needed some peace and quiet to think about Maude's predicament. For himself, although it was tiresome,

Lord Pangbourne's ambitions were merely a nuisance. He could, and would, marry where he chose. One of these days. When he got round to it.

But Maude was a considerable heiress and, if her father truly intended to, he could keep her financially dependent on him until she was thirty. She could choose herself a husband, he supposed, always provided she could find someone prepared to ignore the persistent rumour that she was already betrothed to him, or who was prepared to take a dowerless wife, but that was assuming a case of love at first sight and a determined lover at that.

He could put an advertisement in the paper, denying the rumours, but that would create a scandal—the presumption would be that there was some reason discreditable to her, which was why he did not want to marry Maude. He could carry on denying it whenever it was mentioned—but no one believed him when he did. By common consent, he would be insane to refuse to marry a lovely, high-born, wealthy young woman who would bring the Pangbourne acres to join his own. And everyone knew that Gareth Morant was no fool. He was simply, the gossips concluded, in no hurry to assume the ties of matrimony.

Meanwhile poor Maude was effectively out of bounds to any gentleman who might otherwise court her, unless he took the first step and married.

Gareth picked up a copy of *The Times* and found a secluded corner to read it in. Ten minutes later it was still folded on his knee and he was passing in review each of the young ladies currently on the Marriage Mart and dismissing all of them. There was a new Season about to start in a week or two; that would bring the new crop fluttering on to the scene.

Gareth steepled his fingers and contemplated marriage to a seventeen- or eighteen-year-old. It was not appealing. He liked intelligence, maturity, wit, sophistication…

'Morant, thought I might find you here.'

Hell and damnation and… 'Templeton.' Gareth tossed his newspaper on to a side table and got to his feet. He might feel like strangling Maude's father, but good manners forced him to show respect for the older man.

'Gave me a shock this morning! Ha!' Lord Pangbourne cast himself into the wing chair opposite Gareth and glared around to make sure they were alone. 'Young devil.'

'If I had expected you, my lord—' Gareth began.

'You'd have kept your new doxy upstairs, I'll be bound.'

'And what makes you think she's a new one?' Despite his irritation, Gareth was intrigued.

'No sign of her before. Discreet, that's good. I was a bit out of sorts.'

It was, Gareth realised, an apology of a kind. The best he was likely to receive. He snatched at the sign of reasonableness. 'You know, my lord, that neither Maude nor I wish to marry each other; we have told you time and again.'

'You'll grow out of that nonsense.'

'Sir, I am seven and twenty. Maude is only four years younger. She'll be on the shelf if she has to wait much longer.'

'She's on *your* shelf, that's the thing.' The older man looked smug. 'Snuff?'

'No, thank you.' Gareth scarcely glanced at the proffered box. 'And if I do not marry her?'

'You will, I have every confidence in your good sense. You are perfect for her and she'll bring the Pangbourne estates with her when I go. Mind you, I'm not going to put up with these vapours of hers much longer. One more Season I'll stand for and then she can go back to the country and wait for you there.'

Frustrated, Gareth tipped back his head and stared up at the chaste plasterwork of the ceiling. Maude would go mad in the country, and no suitor was going to find her stuck in rural solitude. If that was what the old devil intended then he, Gareth, was probably going to have to make the sacrifice and marry someone else.

'Is there anything,' he said between gritted teeth, 'that would convince you that I am not suited for your daughter?'

'Nothing.' Lord Pangbourne beamed at him, his hands folded neatly over his considerable stomach. 'I watched you with some anxiety in your salad years, I have to admit. Never can tell which way you young bucks will go—and I wouldn't have given her to you if you'd been some rakehell, not fair on the girl to have to live with scandal and dissipation.' He grimaced. 'Diseases and all that. But look at you now. Perfect.'

Gareth felt far from flattered. 'This morning you called me a libertine,' he pointed out. 'I was exhibiting behaviour that might well be characterised as both scandalous and dissipated,' he added hopefully.

'Mere irritation of nerves on my part—that daughter of mine is enough to try the patience of saint. Keeps telling me that her own true love is out there somewhere and she can't find him with you in the way. True love, my eye! Balderdash! As for your little ladybird—don't expect you to be a monk, my boy, just be a bit discriminating and don't upset Maude while you're about it.'

Lord Pangbourne hauled himself to his feet and nodded abruptly. 'I'll be off. See to it now, Morant—make her a declaration and all will be right and tight.'

Gareth watched the broad shoulders vanishing behind the book stacks with a sense of being caught in a trap. His thoughts churned. *Damn the old... Scandal and dissipation...*Coherent phrases spoken in a clear, dispassionate voice penetrated his anger. *Embark upon a course of debauchery so public that even Lord Pangbourne will be forced to admit that he cannot marry his daughter to you.* That was what the eminently sensible Miss Gifford had counselled.

It had been Maude's idea first, but, fond of her though he was, Gareth was used to Maude's schemes—most of them hare-brained, to put it mildly. Miss Jessica Gifford with her wide green eyes, her clear gaze, her common sense, her sweet, high breasts and innocently generous mouth—*Stop that, damn it!*—her calm governess manner, now she would not suggest something hare-brained.

A business arrangement, that was what was needed. He needed to create a scandal with no repercussions once it was all over, so that Templeton accepted he was too unreliable for his Maude.

Gareth steepled his fingers and tapped the tips absently against his lips. London was filled with highly skilled courtesans with a flair for the dramatic and a love of money. Finding one to misbehave with would be simple. And distasteful. He tried to sort out why. He had taken mistresses in the past, but that had been a straightforward relationship. Something made him recoil from involving a stranger in his business and Maude's feelings.

His errant memory conjured up a cool voice observing that a lady could hardly object to Lord Standon, a pair of warm, innocent lips against his and a slight figure shivering at his side in Rotherham's clothes, terrified yet gamely playing her role. Playing a role…

'Morant, there you are! I've been looking for you everywhere—what have you done with my clothes, you—'

Gareth got to his feet as his friend marched into his sanctuary, his chubby face set in a scowl. 'Rotherham, if you want to pluck a crow with me, you'll have to do it some other time. I'll get my man to pack them up and send them round this afternoon. I'm busy now.' He added something under his breath as he passed Lord Rotherham, giving him an absentminded slap on the shoulder as he went.

The younger man stood staring after him. 'I say, Morant, did you just say you were off to create a scandal?' He received no response. 'Damn funny way to carry on,' he grumbled, picking up Gareth's discarded newspaper and dropping into his chair. 'Damn funny.'

An hour after breakfast, her hair braided into severity, and clad in one of the sombre and respectable gowns and pelisses Mrs Childe had purchased, Jessica began her round of the agencies. She knew them all by experience or reputation, although her previous employment had been as much as a result of answering personal advertisements as through their efforts. She did not expect much trouble in finding something suitable. Her accomplishments were superior, her references excellent and Lady Maude Templeton's address could only, she was certain, add a certain *cachet*.

By four in the afternoon Jessica was hungry, thirsty and dispirited. No one, it seemed, was seeking superior governesses just now. The Climpson Agency could offer her a family of lively small boys—Jessica knew enough to interpret that as *thoroughly out of control*. Another bureau suggested a family in Northumberland who were seeking an *adaptable* governess for a daughter who, as the owner Mrs Lambert explained, was 'Just a little, er…eccentric.' Yes, she confirmed, there was rather a high turnover of governesses for that post.

And, as always, there were any number of middle-class families who were looking for governesses who would also act as general companions. Jessica had heard about those sort of positions; they translated as general dogsbody to the lady of the house.

'It will be the start of the Season soon,' Mr Climpson explained, running an inky finger down his ledgers and shaking his head. 'People have made arrangements already so they can concentrate upon social matters. There are sure to be more opportunities once the summer is upon us; many people make changes then for some reason.'

'I had hoped to find something suitable more quickly than that.' Jessica looked down at the dark blue wool of her skirts. Every stitch she wore was borrowed, she had not a penny piece of her own until she could write to her bank in Leicester. And then she would have to dig into her precious savings, her only and last resource. How on earth was she going to cope otherwise—unless she took one of those posts that no one else wanted?

'Your references and experience are excellent,' Mr Climpson added, obviously intending to be encouraging. She knew they were, and knew without arrogance that they were the result of her own hard work and careful selection of posts. To take anything less would diminish her status, but it did not appear she had much choice.

How long could she possibly impose upon Lady Maude? A week perhaps? 'I will call back in a few days.' She stood up with a bright smile—it would not do to appear desperate. And there were always the newspapers to scan. Lord Pangbourne's household would be sure to be well supplied with those.

The coachman was waiting patiently outside the agency. 'That will be all for today, thank you.' Jessica smiled as the footman flipped down the steps for her and held the door. 'Please can you take me to Lady Maude's house now.' The carriage was such a luxury with its lap rug and heated bricks—it would not do to become used to such things. Jessica sat up straight and gave herself a mental talking to. She was lucky to be here, she knew it. If it had not been for Gareth, she would be living a nightmare of degradation and shame. She had begun from very little when Mama had died—now she had experience and references. Soon she would find employment and, in the meantime, at least she had a safe and comfortable refuge for a few days.

The carriage drew up and she peered out of the window on to the gloomy early evening scene. This must be the Pangbourne's residence. A door opened and a tall liveried footman ran down the steps and opened the carriage door. She half-rose, expecting him to offer her his hand to descend.

'Miss Gifford? I have a note from Lady Maude.'

Jessica unfolded it, confused, tipping the note to read it in the light from the open door. Maude's handwriting was as bold as her personality, the words slashing across the expensive cream paper.

Dear Jessica, Things have got Much Worse—but Gareth has a plan, if only you will help us. Please will you go back to his house? Papa must not see you. Imploring your understanding, your good friend, Maude.

She looked up at the impassive footman. 'Please tell Lady Maude I will do what she requests. Will you ask the driver to return to Lord Standon's residence, please?'

He closed the door and the carriage rumbled off into the light drizzle. Jessica felt her shoulders sagging again, and this time found it an effort to straighten them. Now what was going to become of her?

Chapter Five

'When did you last eat?' Gareth demanded, his hands fisted on his hips as he looked at her.

It was not what Jessica was expecting and she stared blankly at him while she made herself think. Jordan removed her bonnet and pelisse from her unresisting hands. 'Breakfast?' she hazarded.

'I thought so, you look ready to drop. Jordan! Food for Miss Gifford, in the library as soon as possible.'

'At once, my lord.'

'I thought you were the sensible one in all this—what were you thinking of, to starve yourself?' Gareth was positively scolding as he guided her into the book-lined room and sat her firmly down in one of the big wing chairs in front of the fire.

'There were so many agencies to get round,' Jessica protested, stretching out her feet to the hearth and letting her tired back rest against the soft old leather. It was seductively easy to allow him to take charge and organise her. It gave her an entirely false sense that all would be well and she knew she could not succumb to that: she was in charge of her own destiny and no one could help her but herself.

'This is not a race—you know I will find you somewhere to stay for as long as you need.' Gareth dropped into the chair opposite and crossed his legs, the silver tassels on his Hessian boots swinging. A pair of those boots would keep her for months. It was a timely reminder of just how far apart their worlds were.

'It seems the residence you suggested for me is not so suitable after all.' Jessica held out the note. Gareth took it, scanned it and grimaced. 'And I am afraid I was unable to find anything in the way of employment today. I will have to look at the newspapers and try the agencies again in a day or two.'

'Nothing suitable? Please, Jessica, don't let it worry you.' He read the note again. 'Maude has such a taste for the dramatic it is a pity a career on the stage is so ineligible.' Gareth screwed it up and tossed it on to the fire. 'It is true that if you agree to our plan it will be impossible for you to stay with her, but did you think we were going to cast you out?'

'I am having trouble thinking clearly at all,' she confessed. 'I am so disorientated, so much out of my depth. I fear I must ask you for a loan of money until I can get funds from my bank in Leicester.'

'You have funds?' He was regarding her steadily, his face thoughtful. It was like being interviewed for a post.

'My savings.' *My precious savings.*

'Well, you will not want to dip into those.' She found herself nodding agreement and forced herself to sit still. It was dangerous to agree with anything he said. 'Jessica, I have to say I am selfishly glad that you have not secured employment yet. I have a proposition for you. Maude may be dramatic, but she is right, things have deteriorated.'

'Yes?'

He smiled at her wary tone, and she wondered why she had not thought him handsome before. *And Maude does not want him? She must be about in her head...*

'You are right to sound so cool, my sensible Miss Gifford. Ah, here is something for you to eat. We will talk when you are a little revived.'

It took considerable self-control to sit quietly and eat the savoury omelette, the soft white roll and butter and the dish of lemon posset that the footman set out on the little table before her. Jessica sipped the glass of red wine Gareth poured and schooled her tongue and her patience.

When she had finished she waited while he lifted the table to the side and then folded her hands in her lap with as much composure as she could muster. 'You say you have a proposition for me, my lord?'

'Gareth.' He waited until she repeated his name. 'You made an eminently sensible suggestion at breakfast, Jessica.'

'That you should appear to follow a path of dissipation with a mistress and scandalise Lord Pangbourne so that he will consider you unsuitable for Lady Maude?'

'Indeed. He called upon me at my club this morning and made it very clear that he means what he says—but he also betrayed the fact that openly scandalous behaviour would not be tolerated. I think it is the only solution if I am to free Maude from this situation.'

'And yourself?' she asked, curious about his own

position. He must be of an age where he was looking to marry, set up his nursery, ensure the succession to the title.

'I have no desire to marry yet and, when I do, I foresee no problem. In this case it is, as so often, the woman who is weakest.'

Jessica nodded, surprised at his understanding. It seemed Gareth Morant could comprehend the difficulties of women more generally than just those applying to his friend Maude.

'Then in what way can I assist you?' The only possibility she could think of was that Lady Maude might require a companion to support her in this masquerade if Lord Pangbourne became even more difficult. It might even help to have another virtuous female voice echoing Maude's assumed shock and outrage.

'I would like you to be my mistress.'

The empty wine glass fell from her fingers and rolled away on the Oriental rug unregarded until it clinked against the table leg.

'*What?* Outrageous! What do you take me for?' Jessica sprang to her feet and took three strides away from the fireside before she swung round to face him, more words of righteous indignation trembling on her lips. And then it hit her—the memory of his mouth over hers, the heat and the smell and the feel of him. The long, hard body—

Furious and horrified at herself, Jessica shut her mouth with a snap as Gareth got slowly to his feet. 'A masquerade, Jessica. I am asking you to *pretend* to be my mistress.' His voice was steady, but there was a trace of colour across his cheekbones. 'I would not insult you by proposing anything else.'

'I… You… No, you would not. You made that clear last night. I beg your pardon; I seem to be more tired and less rational than I thought.' Jessica walked back to her chair and sat, her legs suddenly stiff and awkward. She knew why she had reacted with such vehemence: Mama, of course. But mostly it was because of her own guilty desires. Self-knowledge, an admirable trait she had always thought, did nothing to improve her mood.

'You must be tired.' Gareth sat again too, making the silver boot tassels swing as he crossed his long legs. Jessica found herself staring at them and dragged her eyes up to meet his somewhat rueful gaze. 'It is the shock of yesterday's experiences; you should not underestimate the effect such trauma has on the body and mind. And then you have spent the day without proper refreshment or rest. Not very sensible of you, Miss Gifford.'

'Then let us be sensible at all costs,' she retorted, taking a grip on her emotions. 'What, exactly, are you proposing, my…Gareth?'

He steepled his fingers and bent his head to touch the tips to his mouth as if collecting his thoughts, then he raised his head and looked at her steadily. *How changeable his eyes are. From the light grey of a cloudy sky to hard steel from moment to moment.*

'I believe the course of shocking Lord Pangbourne is the only way to reach a speedy resolution of this problem. But I am reluctant to involve a professional—actress or Cyprian—in our personal affairs. One places too much trust in their discretion and too much power in their hands should they choose to make mischief later: I cannot risk that with Maude. Nor, I find, can I contemplate some vulgar piece of play-acting.'

Gareth paused, marshalling his thoughts. 'I believe this wants more than simply my apparent misbehaviour with one of the *demi-monde*. A man of Pangbourne's generation considers that almost routine. The scenario I believe would be most effective is a flagrant dalliance with a lady on the thin edge between scandal and respectability. To have the maximum impact my liaison must be conducted under the noses of the *ton*, not merely observed at the theatre or in the park.'

'But who, then, do you want me to be?'

'A wicked widow.' Gareth smiled suddenly, and she found her own lips curving in response. She caught herself and pressed them tight together. 'A lady returned from abroad where her husband died. A lady on the fringes of respectability, yet with an entrée into London society as she searches for her next protector. And I am going to fall head over heels in my blatant pursuit of her favours.'

'I can see that that would, indeed, cause talk and scandalise Lord Pangbourne, especially if you insultingly ignored Lady Maude in the process,' Jessica agreed. 'But firstly you will need to secure an entrée for this impostor and secondly—look at me! Do I look like a glamorous and dangerous adventuress?'

As she spoke she gestured at the overmantel mirror that reflected the upper parts of their bodies as they sat before the fire. Her blonde hair was still neatly in its governess's braids and bands, its colour pretty, but, in its tight confinement, quite ordinary. Her gown was high at the neck, shrouding her figure that, while brisk walks and healthy eating might have kept neat, was by no means the voluptuous form she assumed such a siren as Gareth was describing would possess. And her deportment was that of a respectable professional woman—contained, controlled, immaculate, designed to be the very opposite of obvious.

'Not at the moment, I must agree.' That smile again, turning a well-looking man into one of dangerous appeal. 'You look charming and eminently respectable. But you forget, I know exactly what you look like without that drab gown and those neat braids.' He ignored her inarticulate sound of protest and her reddening cheeks and added, 'And you *could* look spectacular, Jessica. No, do not shake your head at me—it will take two things, the transformation of your wardrobe and your coiffure and for you to think like an adventuress, a woman on the edge, a dangerous, predatory, beautiful huntress.'

Despite everything Jessica's sense of humour got the better of her. She laughed at him, 'You think the church mouse can turn into the hunting cat, Gareth?'

'No, I think the fireside tabby can arch her back and flex her claws and become a tigress.'

She shook her head, unconvinced. There was no need to panic over his scandalous scheme—it would fall at the first hurdle, her inability to be the woman he was describing. She would humour him a little.

'And who are you going to prevail upon to let this dangerous female loose in a respectable setting?'

'My cousin Bel, who has recently remarried. She and Maude are both deeply involved in a charity to secure employment for soldiers returning from the wars. One of Maude's schemes to raise money for this cause is to hold a subscription ball, but as she is an unmarried

girl the hostess issuing the invitations will be Bel, now
Lady Dereham. Everyone who is anyone will be there,
for they plan to make it one of the grand opening events
of the Season—and that will include Lord Pangbourne.'

'And how, exactly, am I going to prevail upon the respectable Lady Dereham to invite me?'

'She would do it as a favour to me, but for the public
explanation of the acquaintance we depend upon
another cousin of mine, Bel's brother, Lord Sebastian
Ravenhurst. He is married to Eva, the Grand Duchess
of Maubourg.'

'But I read about that in the newspapers—it was a
most romantic affair by all accounts!' The dashing Lord
Sebastian had snatched the Grand Duchess from the
claws of French agents and had smuggled her across
France to arrive in Brussels on the day of the Battle of
Waterloo. The Grand Duchess had been reunited with
her son in London and returned to Maubourg with the
young Grand Duke and the man she had fallen in love
with on their perilous journey.

'It was, and there was considerably more romance to
it than you would guess, even reading between the lines.
However, for now I think we can agree that your late
husband was employed in some manner by the Duchy. As
an economic adviser perhaps? I will ask Eva's advice.'

'She is in England?' A few days ago Jessica had been
attempting to instil the basics of Italian conversation and
Mozart sonatas into the daughter of a baronet. Since
then she had been kidnapped, flung herself naked into
the arms of a man, escaped from a brothel and been
kissed for the first time. Now, it appeared, she was to
be thrust into proximity with minor royalty.

'She and Sebastian divide their time between his estates here—where she is Lady Sebastian Ravenhurst, a private citizen—and Maubourg where she is the Grand Duchess and Sebastian seems to have taken over as Minister for Agriculture, although I am not sure I entirely believe that. Fréderic, her son, is at school at Eton. Eva has decided she would like to do the London Season for a change, so they arrived last week and the Duke of Allington, Sebastian's brother, has loaned them the town house.'

And now dukes, Jessica thought faintly, then pulled herself together. She was never going to be the sultry temptress Gareth was deluded enough to imagine, but at least she could continue to apply common sense to this madcap scheme.

'And where am I going to live whilst I am scandalising London?'

'In Bel's house in Half Moon Street, which is currently empty while she decides whether to sell it, keep it or lease it out. You will appear to have purchased it.'

'Or perhaps the Grand Duchess has done so in recognition of my late husband's contribution to the Duchy?' She had meant to be faintly sarcastic, but Gareth nodded.

'Good idea.'

Jessica sat and regarded him, trying to convince herself she was not dreaming. Although whether this was a dream or a nightmare was debatable. 'I arrive, transformed by some miracle into a *femme fatale*. We conduct a very public, flagrant liaison, Lady Maude goes into a shocked decline, Lord Pangbourne cuts your acquaintance—and then what?'

'We keep it up for the Season.' *Three months of flirting—or worse—with Gareth? Oh, my God...* 'And then you vanish off to Maubourg, seduced by one of Eva's court, perhaps, and I am left a sadder and wiser man. One who is, most obviously, unworthy of Templeton's ewe lamb.'

'And I return to seeking work as a governess, with no doubt some good explanation of what I have been doing for three months?'

Gareth dropped his hands and clasped them together, his eyes on her, searching, it seemed, for some insight into her thoughts. Jessica felt they should be more than obvious.

'Do you enjoy being a governess? No, let me rephrase that—do you have a dedication to education?' She shrugged. 'Why then do you seek employment in that way?'

'Because I wish to eat! And I find I am a good teacher.'

'You have no relatives?' he asked, frowning at her snappish tone.

'Yes—an aunt, cousins.' Jessica began to see the drift of his questions and produced her usual prevarication—it was not so very far from the truth in some ways. 'You wonder why I do not live with them? I do not chose to be beholden to anyone and dwindle into an unpaid companion, dependent on family charity for my very existence. I wish to be independent and to provide for my old age. I have no aptitude as a milliner or a dressmaker. There is very little money or security as a paid companion. But I do have skills that I can teach and I have chosen my employers with great care to enhance my references and my reputation.'

Gareth nodded as though she was confirming his own thoughts. 'So your long-term aim is for financial security and respectable independence?'

'Exactly.' It seemed she was getting through to him at last. 'And I can think of few things more damaging to that ambition than flaunting myself in London society as your mistress!'

'Certainly if you wish for further employment, I can quite see that.' He appeared unconscious of Jessica's frowning regard. 'Would I be accurate if I said that you would hope to reach the point one day where you could afford a small house in a charming village or market town with adequate funds to employ a small staff and perhaps own a gig? To be in the position where you had no need to work, but might, if you wished, take the occasional pupil for individual tuition in an instrument or a language?'

'You have painted a picture of my exact ambition.' The image of roses round the door, a cheerful maidservant bringing in a tea tray, an earnest child happily learning the piano, flickered before Jessica's gaze. 'And to achieve the half of that I need to work. Work hard for years,' she added.

'I am offering you work.' Gareth stood up and walked round the chair to lean his folded arms on its padded back while he watched her. 'I am asking you to take on an onerous acting job for three months and then I will give you the house and an annuity that will allow you to do just as you please.'

'But—'

'You think I am offering too high a price? I can assure you—'

'I think you are offering a very fair price for such an outrageous request,' she retorted robustly. 'Gareth—look at me. Do I look like a seductress? Do I seem to you to have any wiles, any aptitude for casting out lures? I have never flirted in my life, not even mildly. How do you expect me to learn?'

'I will teach you,' he said and the smile he sent her was pure, wicked, promise. 'I will teach you so well, Miss Gifford, that half the men in London will be at your feet and every lady in society will wish to scratch your eyes out.'

'No...I could not.' She had to be strong. It was impossible, she could never do this.

Gareth walked round and picked up her hand as it clasped the arm of her chair. His fingers were warm and his thumb brushed gently against the soft mound of flesh at the base of her thumb.

'What colour are the roses round the door in your dream house?' he asked her, his eyes intent and dark on her face.

'Red,' she murmured. And was lost.

Chapter Six

'How do you intend teaching me these arts of fascination?' Jessica rescued her hand from Gareth's grip and tried to make her voice as businesslike and brisk as possible. He sank back in his chair, recognising her capitulation and, she could only hope, not seeing the churning mix of terror and anticipation behind her question.

'It will be easier for you once you have your new hairstyle and your new clothes, I imagine. I will send a note around to my cousin Bel and ask her to call tomorrow and take you under her wing.'

'Will she agree?' Jessica wondered. 'It is a scandalous deception. She might well disapprove.' He had not answered her question, she noted. One faculty life as a governess taught you was to recognise evasion when you saw it. Lord Standon might not be a naughty eight-year-old with a toad in his pocket, but in her opinion all males of whatever age were that boy under the skin.

'Bel? I suspect not. She was first married to Lord Felsham, who was generally accounted to be the most boring man in the *ton*. When she was barely out of mourning she encountered Ashe Reynard, Viscount Dereham, who was just back from Waterloo. By all accounts it was a lively courtship. I have no idea of the details, but our highly respectable bluestocking of a cousin Miss Elinor Ravenhurst, who is a great friend of Bel's, blushes whenever she mentions Reynard.'

'It would be a relief if she does help us, because I do not feel we should involve Lady Maude in this.' Jessica waited, trying her best stare to see if Gareth was going to answer her question about her lessons in flirtation.

'I agree. Tell me, Jessica, why are you regarding me as though I have not finished my Latin exercises?'

'I am waiting for an answer to my question about how you intend to teach me—and I fear you may be evading one.'

'Very well. This is not something I have attempted before, believe me, but I will try. May I be frank?'

'Ye…s,' she responded, suspicious. His lordship was studying her closely. She felt uncomfortable meeting his gaze, but it was equally unnerving trying to find something innocuous to look at. Her immediate field of view seemed very full of large, disturbing, male. She settled upon his neckcloth and attempted to regard it tranquilly.

'You are a very contained person, are you not?' Startled, she nodded, the neckcloth and its intricate folds forgotten. 'You sit very still, you occupy your own space and do not intrude into that of other people. You communicate with your voice and with the force of your argument, not with touch, or teasing or cajoling.'

'Yes. That is appropriate to my role in life.' That stillness and self-control had been hard-won, but necessary.

'But not to your new one. You are to become a

creature of the senses—all five of them. You want to touch silks and skin. You want to taste champagne and kisses. Your eyes will long for luxury, your ears for flattery, you will want to move within clouds of scent from lavish flowers and from exotic perfume. You will talk with your hands, with your eyes, with your laughter. Instinct will appear to dominate over thought.'

'Appear?' She felt breathless, her mind reeling from thoughts of silk, skin, kisses, perfume.

'Underneath you will be thinking very hard indeed, because you will be acting, and the woman you are portraying will be thinking hard too. She is not a heedless flirt, she is a determined adventuress.' He leaned forward, his forearms on his knees. 'Unless we can release the inner hedonist in you.'

'I am not sure I have one,' Jessica confessed. Hedonism required money, time and self-indulgence. The first two she could not afford, the third she dare not permit. Until now.

'In that case we will take one sense at a time and work on it. Which shall we start with? Not taste, for you have just had your supper, and not smell, because this fire seems intent on smoking. I shall have to think about hearing a little. Sight—or touch, Jessica?'

'You choose.' She threw the question back as fast as if this were a ball game and the ball red hot.

'Oh, no. You must also learn to be demanding and capricious. You will always be the one to choose, whatever the question.'

Sight sounded safest. It was probably the one he expected her to say. 'Touch,' she decided, her eyes meeting his defiantly.

* * *

He had been sure she would decide upon sight, an apparently safe sense, although he was having ideas about that. Inwardly Gareth gave Miss Gifford points for courage.

'Close your eyes.' She stiffened immediately, her fingers curling tight around the arms of the chair. 'Do you not trust me, Jessica? We are not going to get very far with this if you do not.'

Clear green eyes looked into his. For long seconds he watched her thinking. 'Yes,' she decided finally, her mouth quirking into a rueful smile. 'Although quite what I trust you to do I am not certain.' The long lashes that contrasted so piquantly with her tightly bound hair lowered, feathering her cheeks and she waited, blind, outwardly tranquil. Except for her death grip on the leather arms.

'Stroke the arms of the chair,' Gareth said, keeping his voice low. A frown line appeared between her brows, then she nodded and relaxed her fingers. 'Tell me what you feel.'

'It is smooth, warm from where my hands have been.' She felt further down. 'Cool here. It feels strong. Somehow I can tell it is thick.' He waited while she explored further. 'It is smoother here, where hands have rubbed; I can feel the grain lower down.'

Gareth felt in his pocket and pulled out the clean linen handkerchief his valet had placed there that morning. On the table beside him was a sample of heavy silk Maude had forgotten last time she had sat in this room. He leaned over and dropped both pieces of fabric into Jessica's lap. 'And these?'

She scooped them up in her cupped hands and rubbed with thumb and forefinger, then bent her head to bury her face in them. 'That is cheating,' Gareth said mildly and she raised her head and smiled in the direction of his voice.

'Very well.' She dropped the silk into her lap and concentrated on touching the linen. 'Expensive, very fine Irish linen. I imagine one could see through it. But a strong, masculine feel.' Her fingers found the whitework monogram in the corner and rubbed gently. 'Excellent work.'

'And the other?' He found he could not take his eyes off her face.

'The silk? Beautiful. A dress weight, expensive again. I imagine it is coloured, although I have no idea why.' She ran it through her fingers and sighed. 'It is alive.'

'Which would you prefer to wear?' Gareth asked. Jessica frowned. She was thinking too much still, not feeling. 'Next to your skin?' he added outrageously, intent on shocking an instinctive reaction out of her.

Jessica gave a little gasp at his effrontery, but answered, as he had hoped, without reflection. 'The silk. Utterly impractical, but like bathing in warm oil. See how it slides and slithers.' Eyes still closed, she held it out to him and he took it, warm from her hands, and let it slip through his fingers. It was no longer possible, for some reason, to sit still. Gareth got to his feet, standing in front of the chair so close their toes nearly touched.

'Will you stand up, Jessica?'

Obedient, she did as he asked. 'You are standing very near.' It was a matter-of-fact observation but he could sense the reserve behind it.

'How can you tell?'

'Your voice. And I can feel your—' She swallowed, making the chaste muslin fichu veiling her throat move. 'Your heat.'

Heat? Gareth felt suddenly as though he was burning up, the colour in his cheeks as high as that on Jessica's. He dragged air down into his lungs and kept his voice steady. 'Touch me.' It might have been steady—he could do nothing about the huskiness.

'What!' Her eyes flew open and she took a half-step back until the edge of the chair hit the back of her knees.

'Jessica, I am not asking you to make love to me…'

'Good!' She looked deliciously flustered.

'But the new you is going to touch men all the time,' Gareth explained, in haste before one of Miss Gifford's clenched hands found his ear. 'It will be part of your charm, one of your weapons. The slightest, fleeting touches. A caress with your fingertips on a sleeve, a flick to remove an imaginary piece of lint from a lapel, a handshake held just a fraction too long. You must be completely relaxed touching a man.'

'I see.' She narrowed her eyes at him, still suspicious. 'I think.'

'You think too much Jessica, just feel.'

'Hmm.' She put her head on one side, reminding him irresistibly of an inquisitive robin who has just spotted a worm. 'Like this?' She reached up and brushed her fingertips across his lapel, her movement wafting a faint scent of Castile soap and warm woman to his nostrils.

'Yes. Just like that. Now, find some other ways.'

There was a glint of mischief in her eyes now and she caught her lower lip in her teeth for a moment. The heat flooded Gareth again, this time sharply focused in his groin. If his reaction to an inexpert touch from Miss Gifford, dressed like a governess, was this, what effect was she going to have in her new guise?

'I need to find excuses to touch, and they should be so brief that the man concerned will not know if they are an accident, an impulse—or a message. An invitation, even.' She nodded to herself, then, smiling, raised her hand and brought it up to pat her fichu into order, managing as she did so to brush the back of her fingers against his. The tingle reached right up his arm. 'Like that?'

'Perfect, Jessica.'

'But I need to hold your eyes as I do it, I think, to make you even more unsure of my intentions. You must not know whether I meant to touch you or not.' The limpid green gaze held nothing but the faintest question and then she was smiling again, a polite social smile.

'Excellent,' Gareth managed, wondering what the hell was wrong with him. True, he had spent a decidedly fraught twenty-four hours, but that was no excuse for feeling like a randy eighteen-year-old simply because he was toe to toe with a buttoned-up governess.

'Oh!' She was peering up at him now. 'My lord, I do believe there is a money spider in your hair.' Jessica stood on tiptoe, reached and flicked lightly at the side of his head, her fingers just skimming his temple before they ruffled into his hair. This time the tingle went straight down to the base of his spine with predictable results. 'There.' She held up slender fingers for him to see the tiny red dot that was swinging from them. 'What luck for me.'

There was a faint ink mark on her forefinger. It would

need work with a pumice stone—seductresses did not have ink blots. Jessica blew softly and the red dot landed on his lapel and vanished into his neck cloth. *This one does...* 'You gave it back.'

'We can share it—I expect we are going to need all the luck we can get to pull this off.'

'You have not changed your mind?'

The half-hidden seductress vanished to be replaced with the governess, her expression severe. 'I said I would do it—I do not go back on my word.'

'No.' Gareth studied her straight back, raised chin, determined expression. 'I can see that.'

'My lord. Her Ser...' There was a muffled exchange from the hall. 'I beg your pardon, Lady Sebastian Ravenhurst and Lady Dereham are here. I explained that you were at breakfast, my lord, but—'

'Show them in, Jordan, bring more cups.' Resigned to yet another turbulent breakfast Gareth pushed back his chair and got to his feet as his cousin Bel and her sister-in-law Eva, Grand Duchess of Maubourg, swept into the room in a flurry of flounces. At the other end of the table Jessica stood too, schooling her knees not to knock together. These two elegant, assured, sophisticated matrons would take one look at her and laugh Gareth's plan to scorn.

'Gareth, we came at once, Maude said things have reached a crisis.'

'Thank you, Bel.'

So that would be his cousin, Lady Dereham. A tall brunette, she kissed him on the cheek, and stood aside to make room for an equally tall, rather more statuesque brunette whose deportment could have been used as a model of perfection. The Grand Duchess.

'Gareth, you poor man. Lord Pangbourne appears to have become quite irrational, even allowing for Maude's tendency for the dramatic.' Her English accent was perfect, her gaze direct. 'Your message was cryptic, but we will do our very best to help.'

'Then allow me to introduce Miss Gifford, who has agreed to play the critical role in this scheme.' Both ladies turned and Jessica sank down into her best court curtsy. She knew how to do it in theory, but she had never had to do it in practice. It was murder on the thigh muscles, she discovered, rising with relief as the Grand Duchess stepped forward and caught her hand in her own kid-encased one.

'Your Serene Highness…'

'Lady Sebastian, please. Except for court appearances, I do not use my title outside the Duchy. Miss Gifford…' she looked at her, a smile lighting up her face, '…you poor thing—what theatricals have Maude and Gareth prevailed upon you to join?'

'Good morning Miss Gifford.' Lady Dereham came to shake hands, then sank down on a dining chair and peeled off her gloves. 'Yes, we insist upon knowing all the details at once.' She lifted the silver pot before her. 'I fear we will need sustaining with considerably more coffee.'

'Templeton has become fixed in his intention to carry out the exceedingly mawkish scheme he cooked up with my esteemed parent and marry off Maude and myself.'

'Not so mawkish if you consider the land holdings,' Lady Dereham observed, stirring sugar into her cup.

'Templeton's no fool—he is dangling an estate almost the size of your own before you.'

'Quite. How can I refuse? That is the problem. He has decided I am perfect for Maude—but it is obvious that even he would draw the line at marrying her off to a libertine. Or, at least, to one who created a public scandal. He has a strange way of showing it, but he is fond of Maude and would not want her to be hurt by her husband's public infidelities.'

'His private ones would, no doubt, be of no account,' Lady Sebastian remarked wryly. A flicker of memory came back to Jessica—Lady Sebastian's first husband, the Grand Duke, had been a notorious rake, leaving a trail of highly visible liaisons across Europe.

'Exactly. I, therefore, must become not just a rake, but a very public philanderer.' Gareth reapplied himself to his sirloin, then looked up to find three pairs of eyes fixed upon him, sighed and put down his knife and fork. 'Our intention is that Jessica, who is the widow of a gentleman who performed some service for the Duchy…' he raised an eyebrow at Lady Sebastian, who nodded '…has returned to London to re-establish her life. Bel has leased her the Half Moon Street house as a favour to Eva and will introduce her to society at Maude's charity ball. Jessica, it will soon become apparent, is an adventuress at whose feet any number of gentlemen are about to prostrate themselves.'

Jessica could almost feel the effort it took the two ladies not to turn and look at her in disbelief. 'I,' Gareth concluded, 'will make a complete cake of myself over her, conduct a flaming *affaire* in the full glare of the Season and Templeton will cast me off.'

'I see,' Lady Dereham said with what Jessica regarded as almost supernatural calm. Suddenly she could see the family relationship between them—Lady Belinda was exhibiting the same calm as she had seen in Gareth in the brothel. A sort of watchful stillness. 'And our role—other than providing an *entrée* for Miss Gifford—is to be what exactly?'

'I am very much afraid that Lord Standon expects you to transform me into a dashing adventuress,' Jessica said, bracing herself for the polite laughter that must surely follow. 'A glamorous siren,' she added, heaping on the improbabilities.

Both ladies did turn at that, fine dark eyes under arched brows and amused grey ones regarded her. Neither woman laughed. They must feel it was past a joke to achieve such a task.

'Oh, yes,' Lady Dereham said. 'Hair first, don't you agree, Eva? And then see what suggests itself once we know what colour we are working with?'

'Monsieur Antoine.' Lady Sebastian nodded. 'Gareth, would you be so good as to ring for Jordan, I must send a note immediately.'

'You think it is not impossible?' Jessica shook her head. Not only did she have to appear stylish enough to be seen with leaders of the *ton* such as these, but in addition she must seem alluring and dangerous.

'I think Gareth is showing remarkable insight,' his cousin said with a mocking smile in his direction. 'Lord Fellingham was saying to me just the other day that Gareth seemed jaded; one can only be relieved that he is not so bored that he missed this opportunity.'

'Fellingham is an ass,' Gareth retorted, pushing his

plate away and reaching for the toast. 'Bored? I have estates to run, a speech to write for the House, that damned orphans' charity Maude nagged me into chairing…'

'You enjoy it, you know you do. If you did not, why did you invite them all down to Hetherington in the summer and teach the boys to play cricket?'

Gareth grimaced. 'Smashed half the glass in the succession houses, young hellions.'

'So did you when you and Sebastian were boys,' Lady Dereham retorted. 'You don't fool me, Gareth Morant—you are working hard for those orphans, and you enjoy it. But being busy does not preclude becoming jaded; this will do you a power of good.'

'We are doing this to rescue Maude from an impossible situation, not me from the *ennui* of my duties. Ah, Jordan, Lady Sebastian wishes to have a message delivered.' The butler bowed his way out with instructions to deliver the hairdresser on Lady Sebastian's doorstep in an hour equipped with sufficient tools of his trade to create a transformation. *What if he is not free?* Jessica wondered, then smiled at her naïvety. Not free for a Grand Duchess, the sister-in-law of a duke?

Jessica sat, eating her breakfast in the unobtrusively quiet manner life as a paid dependent in numerous households had taught her, and watched with the focus she would have applied to learning a new instrument.

She watched the unselfconscious grace and command of the two women, she listened to the freedom with which they conversed and the lightness with which they teased Gareth. And she allowed her eyes to feast on their clothes, on carriage dresses in the very latest stare, crafted from fabrics of quiet luxury, trimmed with exquisite detail. She looked longingly at the smart gloves, tossed carelessly to one side, the thickness of the grosgrain bonnet ribbons, the pretty clasps on the reticules. How could she even learn to treat such luxury with nonchalance, let alone seduce men to her side while she did it?

'What name will you be using?' Lady Dereham asked, cutting across her increasingly alarming thoughts.

'Name?' On top of everything else she had to lose her identity as well, it seemed. Her mind went blank.

'Francesca Carleton,' Gareth said. Three women looked at him in enquiry. He shrugged. 'It just came to me.'

'Well…' Lady Sebastian got to her feet, gathering up her possessions '…in that case it is time for Mrs Carleton to come with us.' She paused on the threshold, waiting while Gareth came round the table to open the door for her. 'Be prepared for a surprise, Gareth.' As she looked at Jessica her eyes twinkled in a smile of pure naughtiness. 'We are going to have so much fun.'

Chapter Seven

Jessica sat in the closed carriage and tried not to look anxious under the combined scrutiny of the ladies opposite.

'How on earth did you become entangled in this madcap scheme?' Lady Dereham enquired, in much the same tone as she might have used to enquire whether Jessica had enjoyed a concert.

'Lord Standon rescued me from a brothel.' Lady Sebastian opened her mouth, then closed it again without speaking. It seemed there was something that would shake their *sang froid* after all. 'I am a governess.'

'I rather thought you might be.' Lady Dereham nodded.

'I was kidnapped when I arrived on the stage and taken to the brothel.' She shivered—repeating the story did not make it any less horrible. 'Gareth—Lord Standon—rescued me. Before anything too awful happened,' she added hastily. She did not feel up to explaining that she had careered down the corridor stark naked, observed two orgies and had escaped slung over Gareth's shoulder while wearing Lord Fellingham's pantaloons.

'What was Gareth doing in such a place?' Lady Sebastian enquired, interested. 'No, do not tell me, I can imagine.'

'Nothing, actually.' Jessica felt bound to defend him. 'He was accompanying Lord Fellingham and Lord Rotherham, but he was rather cross and bored by it, I think.'

'But how did you go from your rescue—for which we must be profoundly grateful—to this?' Lady Dereham was looking understandably puzzled. You did not know Gareth before, did you?'

'Like all the men of your family, Bel dear, Gareth is nothing if not ingenious.' Lady Sebastian's smile was one of pleasurable reminiscence. Jessica remembered the circumstances of the Grand Duchess's unconventional romance. 'I presume Miss Gifford is unknown in London, is presently unemployed and, being a young lady of intelligence and integrity, is a much safer partner in this deception than one of her frailer sisters.'

Jessica nodded. 'You are quite right, Lady Sebastian. Gareth, er…Lord—'

'Call him Gareth,' Lady Dereham interjected. 'And I am Bel and this is Eva. We are all going to become very good friends before this is out, I should imagine.'

Jessica cast a dubious glance at the Grand Duchess, who smiled her wicked smile again. 'Eva,' she confirmed. 'Now, you were saying, Jessica?'

'Gareth is concerned that Lady Maude is not implicated in this, in case it goes wrong, and he was also anxious not to involve anyone who might be less than discreet.'

'And what is to become of you when this is all over?'

Bel enquired. 'I imagine that reverting to being a governess again—unless in the Scottish Highlands—might be somewhat dangerous.'

'I receive a cottage and a pension.' Jessica braced herself for some critical comment about such largesse, but none came.

'Very reasonable,' was all Bel said. 'You will enjoy that better than being at the beck and call of some demanding employer and their obnoxious brats, I dare say.'

'Not all brats are obnoxious,' Eva remarked. 'My son, naturally, is an angel.' Somehow, if he took after his mother, Jessica doubted it. 'As will yours be, I am sure,' she added with a sly sideways and downwards glance at Lady Dereham's waistline.

'Eva! How did you know?' Bel laid one hand protectively over her flat stomach.

'When I saw Reynard last night he was looking stunned—I recognise the symptoms of a man coming to terms with incipient fatherhood—and you are looking a trifle pale.' Eva smiled, 'However, I suspect mine will be born first.'

'You, too? Eva, how wonderful!' The two embraced while Jessica sat in tactful silence through a confusing exchange about what Freddie would make of it, how insufferably smug Jack was, dates and something about sea air that made Bel blush.

'Jessica, I am sorry.' Eva turned to her, her cheeks flushed, her expression apologetic. 'We are neglecting you.'

'Not at all. May I offer my congratulations to you both?'

'Thank you. Oh, look, we're here. Borrow this and

use the veil.' Eva whipped off her bonnet and placed it on Jessica's head.

The door was opened, the steps let down and Jessica found herself in a wide hallway, confronting a man whom she supposed from his clothing must be the butler. With his brawny frame and broken nose he appeared to have been recruited from the prize-fighting ring. Perhaps the Grand Duchess employed him as a bodyguard as well.

'Grimstone, is his lordship at home?'

'No, my lady. I understand Lord Sebastian is at his club.'

'Excellent. This is Miss Gifford, Grimstone. You have not set eyes on her, nor have you ever heard of her.'

The butler gazed at a point somewhere over Jessica's head without a flicker of expression. 'Monsieur Antoine is in your dressing room, my lady.'

Jessica regarded the room and its occupants with some trepidation. A large dressing table draped in net supported a wide mirror and an elaborate silver-mounted vanity set. Next to it was a wash stand with ewer and basin and, standing waiting before it, was a slender, intense-looking man in a black suit, a languid-looking youth and a woman she guessed was Lady Sebastian's dresser.

She tried not to stare about her at the array of gowns draped over chairs or hanging from the blue brocade screen in the corner. Hat boxes teetered in a pile and gloves spilled out of their packaging. Bel was not so reticent.

'Eva, you must have bought out every shop in town!' She picked up a gauze scarf and ran it through her fingers.

The Grand Duchess laughed, shedding her furs and

gloves into the hands of her silent dresser. 'Thank you, Veronique. But of course I have been shopping—I haven't been to Paris yet this year. One must dress, my dear! Ah, Monsieur Antoine.'

'Your Serene Highness.' Eva did not correct him and from the elaborate flourish of his bow Jessica guessed he would have been mortified if he been unable to extract every drop of enjoyment from his contact with royalty. 'In what way may I serve you?'

'This lady, who as you see has naturally a most modest and elegant style…' *Elegant?* '…has, for reasons which I cannot reveal, to appear in society in quite another guise. Naturally, this matter requires the utmost discretion. I trust I may rely upon you?'

'A matter of state!' Eva did not disabuse the coiffeur of this useful notion. 'Our lips are sealed, your Serene Highness. May I enquire in what way *madame* should be transformed?'

'Into a lady of some…experience. A lady who will be invited to the very best parties, naturally, but one who will be *popular* with the gentlemen, shall we say?'

'I comprehend entirely, ma'am. Dashing, a little dangerous, perhaps? A lady of powerful attraction.'

'Precisely,' Bel said, perching on a stool and untying her bonnet. 'Dangerous.'

The hairdresser advanced upon Jessica with finicking small steps, his head on first one side, then the other. She tried to look experienced, dashing and dangerous and knew she was failing comprehensively to look anything but a governess out of her depth. It was an effort of will not to shift from one foot to the other under the intensity of his stare.

'If *madame* will kindly shed her pelisse and bonnet and sit here.' He gestured to a stool set before the dressing table. The dresser darted forward, removing the items and taking Jessica's gloves. Feeling as though she was going to the dentist, Jessica sat.

'Remove the pins!' The acolyte darted forward and began to deconstruct the tight, careful coiffure pin by pin, then combed out the braids. Her hair, blonde, waving and long enough to reach to her elbows, fell about her shoulders. 'Hmm.' Monsieur Antoine picked up a strand, rubbed it between his fingers, peered closely at it, then dropped it dismissively. 'A natural, most English blonde.' That did not appear to be a recommendation. Jessica seemed to recall hearing somewhere that blondes were out of fashion.

'It is a very pretty colour,' Bel said supportively.

'But not dangerous,' Monsieur Antoine pointed out incontrovertibly, beginning to prowl again. 'Not dashing.' He came close and stared into Jessica's eyes as she blinked back. 'Gold, that is what is needed, with just a hint of red.'

'Won't that be a touch brassy?' Anxious, Jessica frowned into the mirror at her pale skin and long— but blonde—lashes. What would she look like with brassy hair?

'Brassy? *Brassy?* Madame, remember, I am an *artiste*! We speak here of guineas, of glow, of subtle excitement. Of *élan*, panache!' He scowled, perhaps daunted by the reality in front of him, then made a recover. 'And curls. This demands curls. The scissors, *Albert.*'

'You are not going to cut it?' Jessica grabbed handfuls defensively.

'But of course; as it is it is impossible—the hair of a governess.' He stood poised, the scissors in hand, having delivered what was apparently the ultimate insult. 'I assume *madame* has come from the Continent...'

'I have?'

'She has,' Eva confirmed. 'The very latest French style, if you please, *monsieur*. It will grow again,' she pointed out to Jessica.

'Oh, very well.' Jessica released her grip and clasped her hands in her lap. Curls and gold it was. In for a penny, in for a...guinea. At least it should soon be over.

Two hours of snipping, washing, soaking in strange substances, more washing, combing, the application of a thick red paste, rinsing, drying and curling later, Jessica stared dumbfounded into the mirror again.

A mass of shiny guinea-gold curls framed her face in an outrageously flattering manner. The curls were short enough to cluster naturally, except at the back where they were half-teased down into flirty ringlets on her shoulder and half-pinned up to give some mass to the coiffure. The wide-eyed woman looking back must be her—after all, the eyes were green, although they looked darker and more intense than she remembered, the mouth was the same, although now it was parted in a gasp of surprise and the plain blue gown was certainly the one she had arrived in.

'Oh,' said Jessica. 'That is me?'

'It most certainly is,' Eva said with satisfaction. 'A most excellent result, *Monsieur* Antoine, exactly what I had hoped for. You will call upon *madame* daily once she is established and you will maintain this look, with appropriate variations depending on her social diary.'

The hairdresser and his assistant bowed themselves out, leaving two satisfied ladies and one stunned one behind them.

'Now,' said Bel with resolution. 'Now we shop.'

'After luncheon,' Eva said firmly, walking Jessica to the door. 'When we have made lists.'

'But who is going to pay for all this?' Jessica protested, waving a hand in a gesture that encompassed the pile of parcels and hat boxes that surrounded the three of them and the even larger list of items that would arrive from the workshops of the *modistes* and milliners they had spent the afternoon visiting. It might well be vulgar to mention money, but someone had to—Bel and Eva appeared oblivious to the amount that was slipping through their prettily gloved fingers.

'Gareth is,' Bel said. 'Now don't frown, Jessica— sorry, *Francesca*. We really must become used to calling you that or we will make slips later. He can well afford it and, if this is to be done, it must be done properly or no one will believe it. And these things are not so very extravagant, just suitable to your supposed background. Here we are, your new home.'

Jessica peered out and her wavering spirits rose at the sight of the neat narrow house with its black brick and shining door knocker and the pair of clipped bay trees by the green front door. Her own house, even if it were only for a few weeks. Somewhere that was all hers, not a plain room in someone else's house where she was regarded as barely above a servant and entered a reception room on sufferance. However difficult this task she had accepted was going to be, at least there would be a safe haven to retreat to at the end of each day.

'I have left it fully furnished,' Bel was saying as they climbed the steps and the door swung open. 'And I will leave Mr and Mrs Hedges and the rest of the staff to look after you. Good afternoon, Hedges, this is Mrs Carleton. I hope you received my note this morning and everything is ready for her?'

'Yes, my lady.' This butler was cut from a very different cloth than Lady Sebastian's ex-pugilist, but his expression as he regarded the incongruous figure before him with the dashing hairstyle and the governess's clothes was a masterpiece of tact. 'Mrs Carleton, ma'am. Mrs Hedges has prepared your room.'

'Thank you, Hedges.' Jessica had long since learned not to show that she was intimidated by superior butlers, but now she hesitated. If this really was her house now… She glanced at Bel, who gave a slight nod of encouragement. 'Could you bring tea to the drawing room, please?'

'At once, ma'am.' He moved to throw open a door and Jessica smiled, inclined her head and swept through it. *Goodness*, she thought faintly, *that worked*.

'I have left all my staff in place here except for my dresser, and that is going to be an important position under the circumstances.' Bel sank into a chair and put her feet up on a beadwork footstool. 'Ooh, why is shopping so tiring?' She did not wait for an answer, her brow clearing as an idea seemed to strike her. 'I wonder if Lady Catchpole's dresser has found a new employer.'

'Lady Catchpole?' Eva frowned. 'I do not know her.'

'She was Rosa Delagarde, one of the leading lights of the stage for the past three years, but she caught herself a baron and they married last week. Now, knowing George Catchpole, he might have married an actress, but he is going to want a command performance as a lady from her in future. I would not be at all surprised if he will insist on a starched-up dresser of the highest respectability.' She got up and went to the French writing desk at the side of the room and drew out some paper. 'I will write at once. *La Delagarde* was always turned out in the most dashing style—just what we need.'

'But would she be discreet?' Jessica wondered.

'There was never any gossip about the Catchpole romance before the announcement, and that would have made her dresser some good money if it had been leaked to the scandal sheets.' Bel folded the note, stuck on a wafer and addressed it as Hedges brought in the tea tray. 'Hedges, please see this is delivered as soon as possible.'

They sipped tea in companionable silence for a while. Jessica had no idea what was passing through the minds of her two companions, but her own thoughts were a muddle of impressions, worries and, lurking under everything else, excitement.

I am taking tea with a countess and a Grand Duchess, I have been shopping in the most exclusive shops in London and I am about to embark upon a Season of scandal with a man who has a completely reprehensible effect on my pulse rate.

'Can you dance?' Bel asked, cutting across Jessica's ruminations on just how Gareth Morant made her feel and how shocking it was that he should have such an effect.

'Yes. In theory,' she added with scrupulous honesty.

'I have taught all the country dances and so forth, but I have never waltzed, nor have I danced a cotillion.'

'A dancing master, then?' Eva reached for her reticule and extracted her note tablets. 'Another list is called for, I can see.'

At least, Jessica consoled herself as she surrendered to having her life, her appearance and her wardrobe organised, she would be able to spend this evening in peace and quiet reflection.

The door opened and Hedges coughed. The ladies turned to regard him. 'Lord Standon has sent to say that he hopes it will be acceptable if he joins you for dinner tonight, Mrs Carleton.'

Jessica realised with a start that he was speaking to her. 'Where?'

'Here, ma'am. He has sent Mrs Hedges instructions for a detailed menu.'

'Has he, indeed?' Jessica meant to sound sarcastic, but the butler merely inclined his head.

'Yes, ma'am. Mrs Hedges has sent the footman out with a shopping list now.'

No one appeared to think that she might refuse this suggestion. Or was it an order?

'And how many people is his lordship intending that I entertain to dinner this evening?'

'I understood from the note that it was to be a private occasion, ma'am.' Hedges bowed himself out.

'He is impossible!'

'Hedges? But I always found him—'

'Gareth. Impossible. What on earth are the staff to conclude from him inviting himself here for a dinner *à deux*? That we are lovers?' Bel and Eva both smiled and

Jessica felt the colour rising up her cheeks. 'Whatever he wants people to think for the purposes of this masquerade, I have no intention—'

'Of course not,' Bel soothed. 'I will have a quiet word with Hedges. He and Mrs Hedges already understand that you are helping Gareth with a tricky family problem.'

'Thank you.' Jessica brought her agitation under control with an effort. If she was going to make a public spectacle of herself with Gareth Morant, it might seem out of proportion to worry about what the servants thought, but she had to live with them for several weeks and the prospect of reading contempt or condemnation in their eyes was not easy to bear.

'What are you going to wear?' Eva put down her tea cup and looked thoughtful. 'What a pity so many of your gowns will take several days and we only have the ones we bought ready made.'

'Well, obviously I will dress for dinner, but would Gareth expect me to make a special effort?'

'I imagine that Gareth is intending to teach you the arts of dinner-table flirtation,' Bel observed.

'And remember,' Eva interjected, 'Francesca Carleton *always* makes an effort. She would not be seen outside her bedchamber less than exquisitely gowned and coiffed and with a subtle use of maquillage. Or in it, come to that,' she added, 'if she has a companion.'

That is not *going to arise,* Jessica reassured herself. *The only man I will appear to encourage is Gareth and he will not want to enter my bedchamber in any case.* After all, he had kissed her only to satisfy his curiosity and he had already seen her, stark naked and covered in goose bumps. There was no erotic mystery there. Thank goodness.

'From now on you will never appear except in character, although you will not be ready to burst upon society until Maude's ball in three weeks' time. Meanwhile, you must practise with us, with Gareth and with your new dresser until your image and your story is perfected.' Eva's smile held sympathy as well as kindness. 'I do not expect you have ever been encouraged to be thoroughly selfish, have you?'

'I have not had that luxury,' Jessica confessed. 'I have been earning my own living in a way that does not allow for mistakes or self-indulgence. Common sense, practicality and self-control are my talents.'

'But Miss Jessica Gifford, superior governess, is an act too, is she not?' Eva turned her dark, intelligent eyes on Jessica. 'It is an act you have worked on and perfected, but it is not you. What were you before you made that decision, chose that path, I wonder? If you could subdue your real self to become her, you can free something of you to become Francesca.'

Bel, nibbling on a macaroon with a faraway look on her face, was not listening. 'The pale green silk,' she pronounced. 'It needs taking in, but with a sash it will be perfect for this evening.'

'Yes, thank you.' Jessica turned, eager for the distraction from Eva's disconcerting theory. Was there really something in her of the wanton, daring creature she needed to portray?

Mama...Wide green eyes peeping provocatively over the edge of a fan, the soft teasing voice that could charm birds out of trees, the careless shrug of her shoulders when Jessica, aged thirteen, had worried about the rent being in arrears yet again.

'Oh, I'll go and smile at Mr Gilroy, darling,' she would say. 'He'll give us another week.'

Jessica had vowed she would never be in a position where keeping the roof over her head relied on her ability to smile at a man until she turned him into a fool. But then, Jessica had never had one-tenth of her mother's natural charm, so she had believed. Or had Miss Miranda Trevor, banker's daughter, learned those arts out of sheer necessity when she had run away with Captain the Honourable James Gifford and found herself living the life of a gambler's wife?

'Shall we help you change before we go?' Bel offered and the disturbing thoughts vanished, obscured by the immediate worry of what Gareth Morant, Lord Standon, was going to make of her first steps in the shoes of Mrs Francesca Carleton.

Chapter Eight

Gareth mounted the steps to Jessica's new front door with an anticipation that surprised him. He already knew that he enjoyed her company but the necessity for this masquerade was a tiresome interruption to his life and he should be resenting it. He paused, his hand on the knocker, examining his feelings.

He was not resentful, he was not even vaguely irritated. He was stimulated and he rather thought he was going to be amused. Was Rotherham right? Had he become bored and jaded with the round of careless pleasures and unavoidable duties?

The door opened and he let go of the cast metal with a thud.

'Good evening, my lord.' Hedges regarded him benevolently. Gareth decided that the staff must approve of their new, temporary, mistress. 'Mrs Hedges has followed your instructions for dinner to the letter, my lord.'

'Excellent.' Gareth shed his heavy coat and handed the footman his hat, cane and gloves. He did not know whether Jessica would have the gowns to enable her to dress for dinner yet, but he had done the occasion justice with silk knee breeches, striped stockings and his newest swallowtail coat.

'Lord Standon, madam.' Hedges threw open the drawing-room door and Gareth walked through.

'My lord.' A slender lady in pale almond green silk rose from the fireside and dropped a slight curtsy. 'A most inclement evening, is it not? I do hope you did not become chilled.'

Gareth returned the courtesy with a bow, unable to repress the smile that curved his mouth. It was Jessica, but not the Jessica who had left his house that morning, wide-eyed and in the more than capable grasp of his cousin and Sebastian's new wife.

'Mrs Carleton. It is indeed very raw out, but I took the precaution of wearing a heavy coat.'

The door closed softly behind him as he walked to the fireside. 'Please, do sit.' She extended a hand as though to show him which chair to take, pale fingers emerging from the tight ecru lace sleeves, and the tips just brushed his knuckles.

So, she had remembered one lesson from the night before. Gareth said nothing, but caught and held her gaze for a long moment as they both sat. The colour rose, charmingly, under her skin, then she laughed. 'Oh dear, I am afraid I simply cannot control my blushes.'

'They are charming,' he said, meaning it. Her hair was astonishing, the soft curls opening up her face and taking at least two years from her appearance. The severity and the attempt to look older had been deliberate, he was sure; now Jessica was the most intriguing mixture of sophistication and innocence.

'What is it?' she asked, her eyes narrowing at him. All of a sudden she was the governess again and he reminded himself that she was neither the innocent nor the sophisticate. Jessica was a respectable, intelligent woman who was making her own place in the world and had been managing that very well until the rotten under-belly of polite society had ensnared her.

'I was admiring your hair,' he said, with partial honesty. 'It is delightful—exactly the look I think we should aim at, yet it is still you.'

'I am not certain about the colour.' Gareth found himself watching the play of expression on her face: the frown as she worried about the colour, the look of rueful acceptance that it was suitable for their masquerade and then the amusement at her own doubts banishing the seri-ousness from her eyes. 'I know it is exactly right for our purposes. I will get used to it and it will wash out in time.'

'I like the style. You will keep that, will you not? Af-terwards?' He wondered if there was any length left in it—the back was elegantly pinned up provoking an in-convenient fantasy of unpinning it.

'Perhaps.' She was silent while he wondered whether a comment on the gown she was wearing might push her from frankness into reticence. She was wearing a fine lace fichu around her shoulders. Was the subtle glimpse of flesh through the lace deliberate or modesty? He decided to keep silent on the subject, although he was admiring the effect of softly draped silk on a form he was only too aware was sweetly rounded and warm.

The memory of the sensual shock as she had hurtled into his arms in the brothel came to him with almost painful intensity and he crossed his legs, trying not to think about the lovely elegance of the line from shoulder to the swell of her hip. He was quite certain that Jessica had not the slightest idea of how beautiful her body was.

And why should she? She is inexperienced and respectable, he reminded himself sternly. He was here for one reason only, and that was to equip her for the role she was to play. And it *was* a role, not reality.

'Did you enjoy your shopping expedition?'

'Very much. Your cousins are so kind. But it is not real,' she added, echoing his thought. 'I cannot believe that it is me, sitting in all those fashionable shops, being waited upon, making decisions, choosing between ribbons for my slippers as though I have a dozen pairs already and can toss them aside the moment they show wear.'

Gareth thought of telling her that she must keep all the clothes and accessories they bought for the deception, then caught himself in time. Jessica had accepted payment for what she was doing because she was a professional woman and knew she was worth her hire. But he guessed she might have a very different reaction to accepting fine clothes and fripperies—they were too close to the presents a true courtesan would expect.

She was restful to be with, sitting there with her clasped hands, her eyes resting on him as though she was studying him, which he supposed she was. Miss Gifford was not a woman who went headlong into something unprepared. That mixture of restraint and sense, combined with the image of the girl who, stark naked and terrified, had picked a lock and set about rescuing herself from a situation where most would have been in a dead faint of horror, piqued more than his amused interest—it stirred something inside him.

'I assume that this evening's meal is so that we can explore the sense of taste?' she asked, cutting across his uncomfortable self-examination. He did not feel Jessica Gifford was so restful after all.

'Yes. The sense and sensuality of food and how you can use it for flirtation and seduction.' Her eyebrows rose. 'Are you hungry?'

'Very,' Jessica admitted. 'Have you any idea how tiring spending large amounts of money is?' Her smile seemed to glow and she gave a little wriggle of pleasure, as though someone had run a finger down her spine.

Gareth took a deep breath. He was enjoying this too much; that had to cease. It was not what he was here for, they had work to do.

'Well, being hungry before meals in public must stop at once,' he said severely. 'Food must become a luxury, a game, a tool in your armoury of seduction. Before any meal taken when men are present, you must consume something solid and sustaining at home first.'

'Dinner is served, madam.' Hedges stood holding the door while Jessica closed her lips on what he suspected was about to be a withering comment on the foolishness of fashionable life.

She stood instead and placed the tips of her fingers on his proffered forearm, glancing up at him from under her lashes as she did so.

'Very nice,' he murmured, escorting her through the door and into the dining room. Their chairs had been placed as he had requested, with hers at the head of the table and his on her right. On the white cloth there were only the place settings, a flower arrangement, a candelabra and two dishes, one before each place.

'I wanted to concentrate on one thing at a time,' he explained, holding her chair for her. Jessica sat, regarding the almost empty table dubiously.

'Oysters?'

'Do you dislike them?' He sat beside her. 'If you have no objection to dining alone with me, I will pour the wine and we can ring when we require the second course.'

'Yes. Thank you, Hedges, that will be all for the moment.' The butler closed the door behind him. 'That is a relief; I do not feel comfortable having this sort of lesson before an audience.' She lifted her fork, then put it down again. 'I've never eaten raw oysters, I have only had them in beefsteak-and-oyster pie.'

'Oysters are regarded as a highly erotic food. Look at them.' He wondered if she would understand the symbolism and watched as she studied the six open shells set out on an extravagant bed of crushed ice.

'Erotic?' Jessica murmured, lifting one shell delicately and advancing it closer so she could stare down into the fleshy folds moving gently in their briny liquid, cradled within the opalescent shell. He knew the exact moment she caught his meaning from the blush that coloured her cheeks. 'Well, really! Do men think of nothing but sex?'

Gareth had been watching her over the rim of his wine glass as he took a sip of the white burgundy. At her question he choked, half-laughing, and put the glass down. 'I'm afraid we do think about it quite a lot,' he admitted apologetically.

Jessica knew she was blushing. She put the oyster back on the plate and lifted her own glass, hoping for a little Dutch courage. 'You mean that in dining rooms all over the country people are sitting down to oysters and the men are looking at them and thinking they look like... And then *eating* them?'

Now what have I said to amuse him? she wondered as Gareth gave another gasp of laughter.

'Yes.' He did not appear capable of elaborating.

'I see.' She eyed the offending shellfish. 'How exactly does one eat a raw oyster?'

'You squeeze on a little lemon juice, then raise the shell to your lips and tip it in.' Garth suited the action to his words, chewed a couple of times and then swallowed. 'Sublime. In *very* polite company one eats it with your knife and fork, but that need not concern us.'

'Hmm.' Jessica knew she was sounding prim, although something inside her was wanting to giggle, partly because the whole idea of food as erotic seemed nonsensical and partly because she was beginning to feel as though she was in a dream, or had had far too much to drink, or both. Not that she had ever had more than one glass of wine at once in her life, but she supposed this light-headed, bubbly sensation was how intoxication felt.

She picked up her oyster, regarded it severely and tipped it to her lips. Cool, salty, fleshy and sensuous, it was like nothing she had ever tasted, and certainly not like the rather rubbery constituents of a pie. Jessica bit, swallowed, thought about it and smiled. 'It is fabulous!'

'Then let me give you another.' Gareth squeezed lemon, then lifted one from his plate and advanced it to her lips. Jessica sat back, a little shocked. 'Oh quite, absolutely scandalous behaviour, and you do not do this at polite dinner parties, not until we have reached the stage of really setting the *ton* to talking. But we might be seen sharing our oysters in a box at the theatre.'

Jessica opened her lips and Gareth touched the shell to them. 'Keep your eyes on me,' he murmured as, instinctively, her lids drooped. His eyes, as she lifted hers to them, were dark and something hot burned at the back of them. 'Just so, we are exchanging unspoken words, messages that cannot be said out loud in company. And everyone else will know that is what we are doing.'

This time she let the flesh slide into her mouth and the memory of his tongue, tangling with hers, as hot as this was cold, filled her. 'What is it?' He was instantly alert to her mood. 'What are you thinking about?'

Too startled by her own reaction to prevaricate, Jessica answered honestly, 'You kissing me', and was rewarded by the knowledge that she had both surprised and disconcerted him.

The heat in his eyes flared and she knew he was remembering too, but his voice was dry as he said, 'Those are exactly the thoughts you should be conjuring up— they will add verisimilitude to your acting.'

'Excellent.' If he thought he was going to disconcert her, he had another think coming. And in any case, she was more than capable of disconcerting herself, without his help. 'My turn.'

This time, as she held out the shell and the oyster slid between Gareth's lips she ran the tip of her tongue over her own and he almost choked. 'You are worryingly good at this,' he said when he was recovered and they laughed and ate the remaining oysters chastely from their own plates.

Jessica rang the little bell by her plate and the next course, 'A pea fowl, larded, removed with a ginger soufflé and asparagus, madam', was brought in.

The guinea fowl led to a much less disconcerting discussion about taste and texture and a good-natured dispute about the amount of port in the sauce, which Jessica lost as she had never knowingly tasted port before. She thought she had scored points by batting her eyelashes prettily and imploring Gareth to carve, because he was certain to be *so* good at it.

The ginger soufflé melted on the tongue, leaving an unexpected heat behind it. By this time she found she was paying as much attention to taste and texture, heat and cold, spice and sweetness as she had to the feel of the items Gareth had had her touch the night before.

'That just leaves the asparagus,' he remarked innocently.

Jessica eyed the thick green shafts, glistening with melted butter and the giggle finally escaped. She had eaten asparagus often enough in the past, daintily with knife and fork, casually with her fingers, the butter running down her chin; now, fuelled by the atmosphere of sensual indulgence and the experience with the oysters, she had no doubt at all what asparagus was supposed to be symbolising.

'No,' she gasped, not worrying that the end of her nose must be turning pink as she laughed or that this was not behaviour expected of either the governess, or of the lady who wore a fashionable silken gown. 'This is too funny to take seriously.'

Silence. She had overstepped the mark with the man who was, when it came right down to it, her employer.

He was paying her to take this seriously and she was giggling. What was the matter with her? Miss Jessica Gifford *never* giggled.

Eva and Bel had wanted her—expected her—to wear the gown without a fichu, to let her hair down, to rouge her lips and blacken her lashes. But her instincts had told her that the first time that Gareth saw her in public he had to see someone who would shock him in truth. His reaction must convince a jaded, cynical audience.

So she had found a fichu, pinned up her ringlets, left her face scrubbed and innocent—and laughed at the game he was trying to teach her. And now he was looking at her, his face shuttered. Those grey eyes were wet-flint dark and the mobile mouth still. Jessica held her breath, wishing she could not remember what his lips had felt like against hers, wishing she had no memory of the scent and the heat of him.

His mouth moved She saw the tip of one white, sharp, canine catch at the corner of his underlip, and then Gareth smiled at her, a slow, lazy smile that caught her breath in her throat and had the stumbling words of apology tangling into silence on her tongue. *Oh, my God*, she thought, shocking herself, *he is gorgeous.*

All he said, mildly, was, 'Sex often is very funny.'

'Oh.' Jessica, charmed out of her embarrassment, regarded him, curious. 'I thought it a subject men had little sense of humour about. That…place was so cold, so joyless. Would you ever hear laughter there? Joyous laughter?'

'Perhaps not.' Gareth picked up his wine glass, twirling it gently between thumb and fingers. 'But there are more aspects to the relations between men and women than that—and, yes, men, despite our fragile sense of self-worth, do enjoy being with a woman with a sense of humour and wit.'

'I shall remember that,' Jessica said primly, wondering whether Gareth was being ironic about the fragile sense of self-worth or whether even large, calm aristocrats had their insecurities.

'Tell me about your family.' He changed the subject abruptly as she rang the bell.

'I was about to leave you to your port and nuts.'

'You have an absorbing novel, or perhaps some stitchery to occupy yourself?' Gareth leaned back in his chair to allow the footman access to his plate.

'Neither, I confess.'

'Then stay and keep me company,' he suggested as the man placed the decanter at his side and the dish of nuts before him.

'Is that not rather…unusual behaviour for a lady?'

'Rather dashing—but then…' Gareth waited until the door closed behind the footman '…you are rather a dashing lady, are you not, Mrs Carleton?'

'So I understand. May I try some port?'

Gareth poured a little into her empty wine glass, then cracked a walnut and placed the meat on her side plate. Jessica sipped, wrinkling her nose. 'Very heavy.' He took a swallow of his, watching her over the edge of his glass. Strangely it did not make her feel uncomfortable; it was as though she had spent many an evening companionably in his company. She put her elbows on the table, nibbling the nut, her port forgotten. 'What should I be doing tomorrow?'

'What do you want to do? More shopping?'

'No!' Jessica rolled her eyes. 'I have shopped until I can shop no more—at least for a day or two. I shall wait until everything is delivered, then Lady Dereham and Lady Sebastian will come and we will go through it all and see what further accessories I need. I cannot imagine anything can be missing, but they insist there will be all kinds of things we have forgotten.'

'If you have no engagements, there are two things we need to see to.'

'Really?' Jessica frowned and absently sipped her port. The rich taste was beginning to grow on her.

'Perfume and jewellery,' Gareth said and it seemed to her he was watching her for her reaction.

'Jewellery?' she enquired coolly. There were only two sorts of women a man bought jewellery for—his wife and his mistress.

'I rather thought you might take it like that. How would it be if I promise to take it all back at the end, every last pearl? If I promise to leave you with not so much as an amber bead?'

'That, my lord, would be acceptable.' At least, it would be socially acceptable. Jessica found her heart was beating erratically with a mixture of disappointment and the thought of wearing such jewellery, if only for a short time. The picture of Gareth showering gems upon her was shamefully pleasurable—and yet she had never so much as coveted a diamond in her life. Mama's pearl set was in the bank along with her savings, Papa's signet ring and her coral-and-silver christening rattle.

Governesses did not wear any jewellery beyond, perhaps, a chaste cross. Had a few hours with this man seduced her from her acceptance of her true station in life to such a extent that she had fallen prey to the shallowness of fashionable life?

The feeling that had give risen to the giggle was stirring again and a little voice was murmuring in her ear to stop being such a prig. She was going to earn her holiday from reality; if that meant revelling in a little shallowness, then she, Miss Jessica Gifford, was going to do so with gusto.

Chapter Nine

'May I have diamonds?' Jessica asked, hoping Gareth would realise she was joking. In for a penny, in for a thousand pounds, the reckless little voice urged her, while common sense told her that aquamarines, pearls and garnets would be the sensible thing for him to buy.

'Of course. Of the finest water, naturally, although, with *your* eyes, emeralds should be your stone. But only a limited number of pieces.' Without thinking she raised her eyebrows in enquiry, surprised at his sudden lack of liberality. 'To be in keeping with your cover story. The late Mr Carleton would have earned good money from his royal service, but not so much that he could shower his wife with jewels. And perhaps you have already sold a few pieces to finance your London adventure.'

'Oh, I see.' She tried another sip of port, beginning to enjoy the warm slide of the wine down her throat. 'I am, perhaps, just a little bit desperate to find a new protector?'

'Not desperate yet, but certainly a trifle concerned. This London adventure is a big gamble for you.'

'And yet I am retaining the good will of the Grand

Duchess?' Jessica took the fresh walnut that Gareth cracked for her, frowning over the intricacies of her new character. She seemed as convoluted as the whorls of the nut.

'Eva is a continental—London society will expect her court to be a touch more…relaxed. And I am sure she will let it be known that the family owed your late husband a debt of gratitude for some service. Given the intrigues of *her* late husband, the exact nature of the service is naturally something we do not speak about. It would explain a little indulgence on her part.'

'May I ask a personal question?' What was making her so bold? Perhaps the port, perhaps the intimacy of sitting like this with a man with the curtains drawn tight against the cold, damp night and the candlelight flickering. Or perhaps it was just this man

'You may, although I cannot promise I will answer.' He smiled at her, a look heavy-lidded and amused. 'In return I will ask you again about your family.'

'Very well.' She did not have to tell him everything, after all. 'If you met this Mrs Carleton in real life, would you pursue her, attempt to become her protector?'

Would he answer? 'I don't know,' Gareth replied, his expression becoming speculative. 'I haven't met her yet.'

Very clever, my lord, Jessica thought, determined not to let him escape with word play. 'But in principle?'

'In principle, possibly.'

'Even if you were not trying to shock Lord Pangbourne?'

'Possibly.' He watched her face. 'Now have I shocked you?'

'No.' Jessica shrugged, hiding the fact that, yes, she

was a little shocked. Which was foolish. Did she think this man was different from all the rest in some way? 'It is the way of the world. Or at least, of so-called polite society.'

'And not-so-polite society, I can assure you. Enough of my moral deficiencies—where do you come from, Miss Jessica Gifford?'

She had thought about this moment and what she could safely reply. 'My father was a military man. And a gamester. He and my mother eloped and both families cut them off. He was killed in an argument over cards when I was twelve.' She paused, wondering how much more she might tell him.

'Twelve? Were you the only child?' She nodded. 'How did your mother support you?'

Tell him the truth, the shocking truth I only realised when I was sixteen? Tell him that I was raised and sent to a good school in Bath on the proceeds of Mama's great charm and thanks to the liberality of her protectors? No.

'Mama had many good friends. I was well educated and able to take all those expensive additional lessons that have equipped me for life as a superior governess. I can play the harp as well as the pianoforte, speak three languages, paint in watercolour. Mama died of a fever when I was in my final year at school in Bath.'

The protector of the moment had disappeared before his paramour was even laid in her coffin. She fought back the memories of those days when she could not allow herself to give way to her grief, days while she sold every piece of jewellery, every pretty trinket, every length of lace, buried her mother decently and bought herself the good, but sombre, wardrobe befitting her new role in life.

'And those good friends could not support you?' Gareth asked, the concern in his voice almost upsetting her careful control.

'One—a vicar—did offer to take me into his home, but I do not care to be beholden.' *And certainly not to a pious hypocrite who preached virtue to his flock while visiting Mama every Saturday night!* And there was always the fear that those men might expect her to carry on in her mother's footsteps.

Mama had done the shocking, the unthinkable thing and had sacrificed her virtue and her reputation to give her daughter a future. Jessica could only guess at what that had meant for a woman who had loved her husband, with all his faults, and who had been brought up in the strictest respectability.

'You do what you have to do, darling,' she had said once when Jessica had protested that the Honourable Mr Farrington was anything but honourable. The reality of what Mama had been to those men had never been spoken between them, the fiction that Mama was merely keeping them company was always maintained, even when Jessica dabbed arnica on bruised wrists or listened to her mother's stifled sobs late at night.

You do what you have to do. And now she was all but standing in her mother's shoes, only she was doing it to gain her own independence, once and for all, and to repay a debt to a man who had rescued her from degradation and shame.

'I see.' Gareth poured himself more wine and sat back, loose-limbed, relaxed, in the high-backed chair. 'I must confess to even more admiration for you than I was already feeling. Your independent career and high standards are to be applauded.'

'Thank you.' Jessica felt embarrassed. She knew, without false modesty, that she deserved the praise and yet it was strange to have someone recognise what she had achieved, what it had cost in sheer hard work and determination. 'Now, tell me about tomorrow.'

He smiled, obviously recognising that she was trying to turn the subject. 'I will go and buy your jewels and you and Maude can go and have your scent designed.'

'Designed?' Jessica stared at him.

'But of course. When you pass by, men will inhale, entranced, and know it is you, and only you.'

'Poppycock!' Jessica retorted roundly. 'You are teasing me.'

'Not at all.' Gareth regarded her for some moments, then stood up. 'Will you come here, Jessica?' Wary, she stood and walked towards him. 'Give me your hands.'

Biting her lip, she placed her palms in his outstretched hands. His fingers meshed with hers then lifted, carrying her inner wrists up to his face. His breath feathered the fragile, exposed skin and her own breath caught in her throat.

'You have your own, unique, fragrance. I can smell it now, warm and female and Jessica.' His voice was husky, the words, spoken so close to the sensitised flesh, was like the brush of feathers across her pulse. 'But it is subtle, a scent only a lover will know and recognise.' *And you*, she thought, unsteady on her feet. *You will know the scent of me again.* 'We need to give you a scent the hunting male can find and then seek out.'

'That is a disconcerting thought,' she murmured.

Gareth's eyes lifted, met hers across their conjoined hands, and she thought she glimpsed the hunter there, in front of her, dangerous, more of an animal than a man. She drew their hands towards her, pulling down until his knuckles were level with her mouth, then inclining her head until she could inhale the heat from the back of his hands.

'Warmth and man and Gareth,' she murmured. His very stillness told her she had startled him, even without the sudden hammering of his pulse against her wrist. She kept her eyes on the clean lines of his tendons, the blue veins under the skin, the healing graze on one big knuckle. A man's hands engulfing hers, and yet, at this moment, who was the stronger? She rather thought it was she.

'You learn your lessons well, Miss Gifford,' Gareth said after a moment, and she admired the control in his voice. 'You are going to become a very dangerous huntress.'

'Count upon it, my lord,' she promised, releasing his fingers and turning on her heel to walk to the door. As she opened it she turned to see him still standing there watching her, a smile of reluctant admiration on his lips.

How I dared, Jessica thought, distracted, as Maude's carriage drew up in front of a small bow-fronted shop entrance. *Todmorton's* it read in spindly gilt lettering above the door. *Craftsmen Perfumers*. At a gesture from Maude she pulled down her veil and stood to follow her out of the carriage.

It had been keeping her awake all night, tossing and turning. How she had dared turn the tables on Gareth like that, behave like a woman of the *demi-monde*, how it had felt to hold him in her thrall for those long, shimmering moments while his blood raced in his veins and his skin heated in her clasp.

It was power and it was dangerous power and he was not the man to practise it on. There were *no* men it was safe to practise such wiles upon and certainly not the one with whom she had to act out this masquerade. She did not need to seduce, only to give the impression of seduction. But it was all becoming too real.

'What did you say, Jessica?' Maude turned from her contemplation of a display of giant bath sponges in the shop window. 'Did you say *frightening*?'

'Er, yes. Frightening being out like this, in disguise,' she extemporised as the footman opened the shop door for her and they entered into fragrant gloom.

'Not to worry, no one will know you veiled, and afterwards, no one could make any connection with you wearing that frightful stuff gown,' Maude reassured her, blissfully unconscious of the fact that such dreadful gowns were Jessica's everyday uniform. 'Mr Todmorton, good morning. Yes, I am in the best of health, thank you. Now, this is the friend of mine for whom we require a scent. Something unique, something *tantalising*, yet discreet. Can you help us?'

'Lady Maude, an honour to assist a friend of yours. Clarence, a chair for her ladyship and show her our new range of triple-milled soaps while she waits.' The man who bustled forwards, stirring the air into a swirling rainbow of scents as his long apron swished across the floor, was of an indeterminate age. His bald pate gleamed, his white hands were clasped across his rotund belly and his smile was wide and ingenuous.

'Madam, please, come into my workshop.'

* * *

Jessica felt awkward, sitting disguised by her heavy veil in front of the neat, professional figure of the perfumer in his workroom. She looked round, curious at its ordered rows of labelled drawers from floor to ceiling, its racks of bottles and phials and its clean, bare surfaces. She had expected to smell a riot of perfumes like the fragrant shop outside, then realised he must need to work with nothing to distract his sensitive nostrils.

'Would you mind removing your glove, madam?' With the coolly impersonal tone it was like going to the doctor. Jessica stripped off her right glove. 'And holding out your hand, palm upwards?'

It was like the encounter with Gareth last night, and yet utterly unlike. This man made no attempt to touch her, merely leaning forward until his nose was above her bared wrist and inhaling. He might, she thought with an inward chuckle, be a cook smelling the soup to adjust the chervil.

'Hmm.' Mr Todmorton sat back, nodded sharply and reached for a notebook. 'You wish for a scent for evening and for day, madam?'

'Yes.' She supposed she did, although a daring dab of lavender water, or essence of violets on her handkerchief was the sum total of Jessica's experience with perfume.

'And the impression you wish to create?'

She stared at him, failing to understand, then realised he could not see her expression for her veil. 'I am sorry, I do not quite comprehend.'

Again, she might have been with a medical man, she embarrassed to discuss some feminine problem, he entirely at his professional ease.

'Do you wish to be seductive and subtle or flamboyant? Do you wish to be unique and memorable, or merely sweetly feminine?'

'Subtle,' Jessica said hastily. 'But seductive, memorable. Definitively unique.'

He nodded, apparently unsurprised by her requests, which seemed to her contradictory. 'Now, which family? That is our first question. Florals as a main group are insufficiently memorable, and besides, will not last well on your type of skin. The woody, leather and *fougère* groups are too heavy and perhaps too masculine.' He jotted another note and frowned. 'Chypre or amber?' It was apparently a rhetorical question, as he shook his head in thought. 'Chypre. Mystery, warmth, natural depth. Floral undertones rather than moss, perhaps? Yes, I see it clearly now. I will prepare something in a *parfum*, an *eau de toilette* and a very light dilution for scenting linen.'

Jessica, who had been expecting to be offered samples to sniff and choose between, found herself being escorted to the workroom door, a decision made without the slightest involvement on her part. It was a relief, she decided, buttoning her glove again; how she would have recognised a suitable scent she had no idea, although it would have been amusing to have sniffed her way along the array of intriguing bottles.

Maude was perched on a stool in front of the counter, a predictably large stack of packages in front of her. The assistant was folding white paper crisply around what appeared to be the final box, although Maude's gaze was roving the shadowed interior with all the concentration of a huntress in search of prey.

The assistant knotted string and reached for the sealing wax as she saw Jessica. 'Well? Mr Todmorton, have you found just the thing?'

'I will *create* just the thing,' he corrected in gentle reproof. 'If you and madam return in three days, Lady Maude, I will have the first bottles ready.'

'Oh, look at these lovely little things!' Maude jumped down and went to rummage in a basin of miniature, fine-grained sponges.

'From Corfu, my lady.' The assistant knew his trade, Jessica thought, amused. 'Young girls dive for them; each is selected with great care to be perfect for cleansing the face…'

'We must have some, see how fine they are. Catch!' Maude tossed one to Jessica across the width of the little shop. A featherlight ball, it wavered in the air and she reached for it just as the door opened.

The sponge bounced off the broad chest of the gentleman who entered and he reached up and caught it one handed.

'Gar—' No, it was not Gareth, it was quite another man altogether, Jessica realised, puzzled why she had made the mistake. This man was as tall and as broad, but he was far darker, both in hair and eyes, but also in skin tone as though some Mediterranean blood flowed in his veins. She was spending too much time with Gareth, that was the trouble. Thinking about him too much led to seeing him everywhere.

Frowning over why that should be such a very bad thing, it took Jessica a moment to recall the people around her, then she saw Maude's face. There was a faint rose flush on her cheekbones, her lovely lips were parted as though she had just gasped and her eyes were wide. The gentleman, apparently impervious to this vision of loveliness, turned the sponge over in his fingers for a moment, then handed it to Jessica, his eyes sliding over her veiled face with polite indifference.

'Thank you, sir.'

'Not at all.' He inclined his head, unsmiling, giving her an opportunity to observe a nose that would have done credit to a Grecian statue, dark brown eyes and severe, well-formed lips.

There was nothing further to be said. Jessica stepped forward and placed the sponge on the counter. Maude was still standing to one side clutching an over-spilling double handful of tiny globes. 'Here, let me.' She removed them and dropped them back into the basin, her back firmly to the gentleman. 'How many do you want?'

Maude blinked at her, a frown of irritation between her arched brows. *'Move,'* she hissed.

'What?' Jessica hissed back. She could almost feel the three men staring at them. 'More, did you say?' she added in a clear voice. 'Shall we take six?' She stepped to one side before Maude could physically shove her aside as she appeared about to do, and began to select another five sponges, delving amongst them to find the ones of the finest grain. 'Please,' she half turned and spoke to the assistant, 'do serve the gentleman, we may be some time.'

'Thank you.' Again, that polite, chilly, inclination of the head. Beside her Jessica heard Maude moan faintly. *What on earth is the matter with her?*

'The order for the Unicorn, Mr Hurst?'

Unicorn?

'Indeed. And two dozen of those small sponges, if you please—send them round later. I will take the main order, *madame* awaits it.'

'Certainly.' The assistant retrieved a package from under the counter and handed it over with reverent care. 'If you will just keep it this way up, Mr Hurst.'

'Thank you. Good day.' He nodded to Mr Todmorton and the assistant and raised his hand to the brim of his hat as he passed the ladies.

The door closed behind him, the bell jangling into silence. Jessica frowned at Maude, who appeared to have been struck dumb. 'Maude, we need to pay.'

'What? Oh, put it all on my account, Mr Todmorton. *Who* was that gentleman?'

'Mr Hurst, Lady Maude. He owns a number of theatres, including the Unicorn.'

Jessica scooped up their shopping and took Maude firmly by the elbow before she could make any more outrageous enquiries about a strange man. 'Thank you, Mr Todmorton, I look forward to my new scent. Good day.'

It seemed she had not lost her touch with recalcitrant pupils. Maude was outside on the pavement before she could protest, her mouth open indignantly.

'Jessica! I wanted to find out more.'

'You cannot interrogate shopkeepers about gentlemen, Maude, it just is not done.' She broke off as the footman jumped down from the carriage and hurried to take the parcel. 'Thank you. We will walk a little. Hyde Park is that way, is it not?'

'Yes, ma'am, just along there, left into Piccadilly and a short walk and you'll be there.'

'How am I going to find out about him if I do not ask?' Maude said with crushing reasonableness.

'But why should you want to?' Jessica snuggled her gloved hands into her wide sleeves and wished she had a large muff like Maude's. The day was chill and a touch misty, but they could hardly have this conversation in the carriage for the servants to overhear.

'Why?' Maude sounded incredulous. 'Did you not think him the most attractive man you have ever seen?'

'He was very good looking, if you like icebergs,' Jessica agreed. 'But I would hardly call him the *most* attractive man I have seen. Although when he first walked in, I thought for a moment he was Gareth.'

'Gareth is a very well-looking man, but nothing to compare with Mr Hurst,' Maude pronounced reverently. 'But the name is an odd coincidence, do you not think?'

'What do you mean?' Jessica side-stepped to avoid a snapping pug being led along by a liveried footman with his nose in the air.

'Well, Gareth is a Ravenhurst—at least, his mother is. He and Eva's husband and Bel, and goodness knows how many others—I lose count, some of them are abroad—are grandchildren of the Duke of Allington. Hurst—Ravenhurst. Perhaps he is a connection.'

'Hurst is a very common name, especially in the North, I believe,' Jessica said repressively, rather spoiling the aloof effect by adding, 'That cock won't fight, Maude—you are not going to be able to get to know him on account of him being some sort of distant relative of your Ravenhurst friends. And besides, your papa is not going to want you speaking to a theatre owner, however well off.'

'His clothes were very superior, were they not?' Maude sighed, walking straight past a shop window containing an array of bonnets labelled *Fresh in from Paris* without a sideways glance.

'I did not notice.' Jessica studied as much of the lovely, determined face as she could while it was screened by a wide-brimmed bonnet. Maude looked uncommonly focused. 'Maude, I am not going through this masquerade in order to free you from Gareth just for you to commit some indiscretion with a tradesman!'

Her companion stopped dead and glared at her. 'Mr Hurst is not a tradesman.'

'Well, he certainly does not have vouchers for Almack's,' Jessica retorted. 'You have glimpsed him for five minutes—you know nothing about him! Maude, what are you planning?'

'I don't know.' Jessica sighed with relief: that sounded genuine. 'I shall have to think about it. I refuse to give up. Did you see the way he looked at me?'

'Maude, he looked at both of us as though we were part of the furniture,' Jessica said repressively. 'And you were throwing sponges about and then moaning—he probably thought you were slightly about in the head and I was your keeper.'

'Oh.' Momentarily cast down, Maude began to walk on and Jessica hid another sigh of relief which rapidly turned to one of exasperation as Maude gave a little skip. 'I must look through the newspapers and see what is on at the Unicorn. He cannot be made to think of me unless I am very much in his way, now can he?'

Gareth is going to have to sort this out, Jessica decided. It was beyond her. She would write and ask if he would take breakfast with her, then she could be sure of a private word before any of her enthusiastic supporters descended upon her for the day.

Chapter Ten

Gareth lay naked on his back on the bed, looking up
into the shadows as the firelight sent them dancing over
the ceiling and cornices. It was past one in the morning,
but he felt too indolent to get between the sheets, too
awake to snuff out the candles and sleep. He turned his
head, restless, and saw the light catch the gemstones in
the open boxes he had left on the bedside stand.

He had enjoyed choosing jewellery for Jessica,
wished that he could see it at once displayed against her
white neck, on her slender wrists. He smiled at the
thought of her pleasure when she tried each item on for
the first time. The smile broadened as he remembered
the chill in her eyes when he had first mentioned buying
her jewellery and the mischief as a purely feminine
desire both to tease him and to wear such baubles
overcame her.

It was amusing having Jessica to talk to, he mused,
like having an unconventional friend—if one could be
friends with a woman. Maude was like a younger sister,
a beloved, charming, worrying responsibility. Miss

Gifford was his responsibility, too, but in quite a different way. For a start, his feelings for her were not brotherly. He was not quite sure what they were—those of an employer? A guardian? No, neither of those fitted. He would have to settle for friend.

He dragged himself up against the pillows, reached for the boxes and picked out the pieces, one by one. A pair of emerald drop earrings, edged with diamonds. Good stones, but not over-large. Tasteful and appropriate. He dropped them and lifted a thin necklace of diamonds, supple and snakelike as it flowed over his hands. Matching ear bobs. A pearl set. Aquamarines for day wear, two silver gilt wrist clasps and a gold chain.

Yes, a suitable collection of respectable jewellery for a widow with good taste, hinting that she would appreciate something better. And he did have something better.

It had been ridiculous to buy it, Gareth told himself as he reached out for the red morocco case and thumbed the catch. The lid fell back and he blinked at the fire reflected from the diamonds, the almost fierce green glow of the emeralds. It was a full parure: necklace and armlets, rings and earrings, a tiara—the sort of jewellery a nobleman bought for his wife, not what a lady such as the fictitious Mrs Carleton could ever hope to wear.

But he had seen it, seen Jessica's eyes in the shimmer of the stones, and the compulsion had gripped him and he had bought the set. Madness. He could always resell them. They were of the best quality, an investment.

Gareth set the case down and lifted the finest piece from its setting. A great diamond-cut emerald designed to be a brooch or to sit in the front of the tiara or to fasten to the necklace. It lay in his palm, the colour of Jessica's eyes when she was angry.

A glint of gold caught his eye and he looked down the length of his naked body. It was scattered with gems where he had discarded each piece. The earrings lay on his flat belly, twinkling indecently amidst the central arrow of dark hair. The diamond necklace snaked over his thigh, an unsettling contrast with hard, masculine muscle. A gold chain slithered down his chest as he shifted and he started as it caressed his left nipple.

His fist clenched over the great gemstone as he stared down, uncomprehending, at the blatant evidence of his own arousal. *Bloody hell*. What had brought *that* on? He was as rampant as a stallion and he had not even been thinking about sex. Surely to God he was not aroused by handling jewellery? That was a perversion he had never heard of before and had no wish to contemplate now.

There was a pain in his palm, as sharp as the insistent nagging in his groin. He opened his hand and glared at the emerald as though it could answer his puzzle.

'Oh, no.' The words were a whisper. The stone did not speak, but his imagination did, taking the image of the parure, decking his memory of Jessica's white, naked body with it. Only it was no memory, this was impurest fantasy, for the Jessica he could see now was not a desperate, cold fugitive. She was warm, smiling, turning to him, holding out her hands…

'*No!*' Gareth swept the sparkling ornaments to one side and rolled off the bed, pacing across the room as though to shake off an incubus that had descended upon him in his sleep. How could he? It was dishonourable, disgraceful—and downright painful.

Up until two minutes ago he would have sworn an oath on everything he held most dear that his intentions towards Jessica Gifford were chivalrous and good. He would protect her through this masquerade and then, from a distance, ensure her well being in modest comfort and security for the rest of her life. Yes, he had kissed her, but in anger—and he had not enjoyed it. Much. And she had understood about that. He hoped.

Gareth made an abrupt turn and paced back again, swearing as his naked left instep made painful contract with an earring. He enjoyed flirting with her a little as he tutored her in the arts of seduction. Of *pretended* seduction, he corrected himself. But mild flirtation was almost second nature to him—and she gave no sign of being either alarmed or confused by it. No, rather she appeared amused by the entire exercise.

It was simply that he was unused to being so close to a woman, yet not sexually involved with her, that was all. And certainly not a woman he had seen naked. He winced as his right foot made contact with the other earring and he bent to scoop them up and toss them into their case.

He hadn't had a woman for a while, that must be it. His restless pacing brought him up in front of the tilted cheval glass and he stared critically at his reflected image, glaring at his offending penis. It had, thank Heavens, subsided somewhat. How long was it since he had made love? Too damn long. The treacherous member stirred hopefully and he snarled at it as though it were an uncontrollable wild animal, not part of his own body.

Common decency insisted that he stop thinking about Jessica like that. All it would take was a little self-control. And that, of course, he had in abundance. Of course.

* * *

Jessica was sitting eating a particularly succulent slice of ham when Gareth finally arrived at Half Moon Street for his breakfast. She had risen early, having succumbed to the first clear, sharp morning for days and taken a brisk walk around Green Park with a footman trailing with reasonably well disguised resentment at her heels.

Now she was eating with an appetite, contemplating her surprising new life with some pleasure. The shock of her adventure had subsided, she was amused and stimulated by her lessons in flirtation. Maude was proving a true friend, if a worrying one. Her nerve-racking imposture had not yet begun and Jessica realised she felt as though she were on holiday.

'Good morning,' she said, observing that Gareth flinched at the brightness of her greeting. In fact, now she looked more closely, he appeared to have spent a night of either severe insomnia or indulgent dissipation. Or possibly both. 'Would you like to sit down and I will fetch you some breakfast?' He appeared to drag his gaze to her face with an effort. 'You seem a little tired.'

'Yes. Yes, I am. Tired.' His eyes roamed over the buffet, then back to the table. 'I will have coffee, thank you. Nothing more.'

She lifted the silver pot and poured, adding a dash of milk and no sugar, just as he liked it. 'Would you like some toast?'

'No. Thank you.' Gareth took the cup and sat opposite her. 'There is no call for you to wait upon me.'

It was not said with a smile. Jessica felt the sick knot of embarrassment tighten in her stomach and knew she was colouring up. She had presumed upon her position, one of the unforgivable sins for a governess. She was treating this breakfast table as though she was truly mistress of the household and not an amateur actress incompetently learning to play a part. And she had summoned Gareth to come to breakfast without a second thought. There were doubtless all kinds of ways in which she had offended and now Gareth—Lord Standon—was displeased.

'I beg your pardon, my lord.' She folded her hands in her lap, dropped her eyes to her plate and wondered how soon she might slip from the room.

'What the devil?' He grounded his cup with enough force to crack porcelain. Jessica winced. Causing him to shatter Bel's Spode morning service would simply be the last straw. 'What are you apologising for? I'm the one behaving like a bear with a sore head.'

'I was presuming too much upon my position, my lord. I should not have asked you—'

'Your *position*? Your position is the mistress of this house and as a lady—and the only one in residence—I would hope you would feel free to take charge of any meal in it and order the servants as you see fit. And what is this *my lord* nonsense?'

'I thought you were offended by my presumption. And asking you to call was indiscreet.' He smiled and the knot unravelled itself and she unclasped her hands. It was all right. And in any case, she had to get used to being liberated from the restricted position she had disciplined herself to accept in the past. She had a personality, opinions—and she could give herself permission to exercise both

'It was a touch unconventional, perhaps, but I came in through the mews and the back garden.'

'You are not usually so…tense,' she ventured. 'Or at least, not in my short acquaintance with you.'

'I am usually too lazy to be tense, is that what you mean?' His smile was wry. 'Indolent, perhaps? Normally I see little merit in losing one's temper or becoming fraught over problems. A little thought, a little calm planning and most things resolve themselves. At the risk of labouring the point, Jessica, I am angry with myself because I have miscalculated over something, not with you.'

'And that cost you a night's sleep?' she asked sympathetically, nudging the plate of toast and the butter in his direction and controlling the quirk of her lips as he reached out and took them. She risked pushing the ham across as well, then topped up both their coffee cups.

'It did. That and a…friend of mine who has a mind of his own and appears set upon directing mine along quite the wrong paths.' Gareth cut into the ham and bit into his toast with a fierceness that made her glad she was not the object of his displeasure.

'A close friend?'

'Very. A lifelong one, you might say. We are attached.' He shifted in his chair and silence fell. Jessica tactfully busied herself with buttering toast and mentally reviewing how she was going to tell him about Maude's sudden fascination with the completely ineligible Mr Hurst.

'Why are you still dressing like that?' Gareth demanded, making her jump. 'Have your new clothes not arrived?'

They had, a collection beyond her wildest dreams, gowns for every occasion. Bel and Eva might have assured her they were entirely appropriate for her apparent station in life and were not at all extravagant in comparison with others she would see, but to her they were simply luxury made manifest.

'Yes. They are all in my room.'

'Then why do you continue to dress like a governess? And your hair—you are doing your very best to turn a dashing crop into a prim nothing. You dress like a governess; no wonder you feel you should behave like one.'

'I *am* one, and I am not ashamed of it. No, please listen.' He closed his mouth again as she held up a hand. 'The masquerade has not yet begun. When it does, you will meet Mrs Carleton, for the first time, in public. You cannot risk showing you are familiar with her—I must be as much of a shock to you as possible.'

She had thought it all through as she had twisted her elegant new ringlets into stiff braids, and she knew she was right. And she also knew that she wanted to flaunt herself for him alone in her new satins and laces and watch his face, see the hot, wicked darkness come in to his eyes again as it had when he had kissed her. And that was dangerous madness, even if all it meant was that she needed approval and reassurance.

'Very well.' He sipped his coffee, then added, 'I will send round the jewellery.'

'Oh, thank you. My scent is being made up; I enjoyed that very much, although I did not have much to do— Mr Todmorton simply inhaled the air about two inches above my wrist and pronounced!'

'You mean to say you did not ransack his shop?' His mood seemed improved now, perhaps he was simply one of those men who needed several cups of coffee in the morning. Jessica nudged the jam across and rang for more toast.

'I did not. Maude did. Um…'

'Um?'

'While we were there, a gentleman came in.'

'You were veiled?'

'Oh, yes, there is no risk he could recognise me again. No, it is Maude. I am sure I should not tell you this, but I fear I have absolutely no influence with her and—'

'Who is it?' Gareth said with resignation. 'I would not worry. She will flirt, but then she is not going to come to any harm with most of the men she will meet this Season.'

'I doubt she will meet this one at Almack's,' Jessica worried. 'His name is Hurst and he owns theatres, the Unicorn included.'

Gareth cast up his eyes. 'Oh, Lord. She has always been fascinated by the theatre. Not that she can act for a groat. Whenever we are at house parties and someone suggests a theatrical entertainment, Maude has to be persuaded to be the prompter or look after the costumes.

'All of us Ravenhurst cousins seem to have an ability as actors—purely amateur, with the exception of Sebastian, Eva's husband, who was a government agent and had as many faces as Edmund Kean—and Maude says she is jealous of our skill. It is just the glamour of the theatre, that is all. It will wear off.'

'I do not think it will be so easy. She was struck dumb just at the sight of him. I suppose he is probably the most handsome man I have ever seen.' Gareth's eyebrows rose. 'If one finds icicles attractive.'

'In that case she will get frostbite.' Her worry must

have shown for he smiled, the old, lazy smile that should have reassured her and instead made butterflies dash madly about in her chest. 'Don't tell me—we are going to be making up a party to whatever is showing at the Unicorn at the moment?'

'I fear so.'

'Well, Maude will have to concentrate all her dubious thespian abilities on extracting herself from our so-called engagement before she can focus on persuading Lord Pangbourne that he wants a theatrical manager for a son-in-law.'

'True. I am refining too much upon it, no doubt. Gareth…' She found herself suddenly, ridiculously shy. He sat, politely waiting for her to speak. 'My final two lessons—sight and sound? How are those to be achieved?'

'Sight we will do today, this afternoon. I intend de-spatching you with Bel and Eva and Maude for a nice drive in the park. London is still a little thin of company, but there will be enough for you to work upon. When you return I shall expect a report detailing which ladies you consider to be rivals, which you should cultivate and which may be safely ignored. But, more importantly, I want you to be Mrs Carleton inside your head. I want you to look—really look—at all the men you see. Sum up each one with a view to seduction. Fix them in your mind. What might be their weaknesses, what attracts you to them, how will you approach them, how you would set out to seduce each one and how dangerous each is.'

'Gareth!' She stared, shocked. 'In cold blood, just like that? You want me to look at men and…'

'Assess them. Yes. You did a good job summing up Mr Hurst, the handsome icicle, did you not?' He drained his cup and stood up. 'Thank you for breakfast, Miss Gifford. Enjoy your drive.'

Jessica sat staring blankly at the Dutch still life hanging on the wall opposite. There had been a sardonic note in Gareth's voice, a set to his mouth that somehow told her that he did not exactly relish setting her that task. On the other hand, thinking about it, it was certainly good tactics to familiarise herself with the prominent players on the stage she was to inhabit for the next few weeks.

The ladies arrived in Bel's barouche with the top down, all well wrapped up and with hot bricks at their feet and lap rugs over their knees. Maude handed an enormous muff to Jessica as she climbed in. 'This is for you, I saw you didn't have one. They are all the crack.'

'Thank you!' Jessica struggled to control the fur muff that was about the size of a medium dog, although mercifully lighter. 'What a lovely day.'

'It is ideal for the task Gareth has set us,' Eva shifted in her seat, allowing Jessica an even better view of her pelisse with its fur epaulettes, collar and cuffs. Another Paris fashion, she guessed. 'Everyone who is anyone will be out in Hyde Park with the sun shining like this.'

Reluctantly, for she was enjoying the crisp air and the sun on her face, Jessica settled her veil securely and they set off. 'If necessary, I shall introduce you, rather vaguely, as Miss Smith,' Bel explained. 'Just bow slightly. People will assume you are a companion, or a visiting relative.'

'A poor relation,' Jessica murmured, smoothing a hand over the skirts of her plain brown pelisse.

'Precisely. We do not want anyone putting two and

two together and making five when I launch Mrs Carleton into society,' Eva said with a crisp decision that made her sound, for the first time, like the Grand Duchess she was.

The carriage swung through the gates into Hyde Park, the driver reining back to steady his team as he insinuated it into the mass of carriages and riding horses that thronged the wide tan-covered drive. 'Very thin,' Bel observed, sounding disappointed. 'We shall have to do the best we may.'

Jessica was glad her veil hid her unsophisticated amazement at what her companions obviously thought was a quiet day in the Park. Bel was already waving and bowing to acquaintances.

'We need to concentrate on the men,' Maude reminded her *sotto voce* as a landau containing an elderly lady drew up alongside.

'Three nephews,' Bel murmured back. 'Lady St Margaret, how do you do!'

Carriage after carriage stopped, oblivious to the traffic jam they were creating around the Dereham carriage. It was rapidly becoming obvious that Bel was a leading light in London society and that Eva was a star, the ladies simpering and looking conscious as they carefully addressed her as *Lady Sebastian*, the exciting words *your Serene Highness* trembling on their lips.

'You are going to be lionised,' Bel commented after they had disposed of a particularly effusive matron.

'All the better for our purposes,' Eva replied with a sigh. 'But such a bore. Ah, now that's better, here are some men at last.'

Three uniformed officers on raking cavalry mounts

reined in beside their carriage, doffing their hats. Maude smiled, causing a noticeable effect. 'Lady Sebastian, may I introduce Major Aulbarre, Captain Lord Heathcote, Captain the Honourable Charles Grahame?' Bel deferred to Eva. 'Gentlemen, I believe you know Lady Maude? Oh, yes, and Miss Smith.'

Amused, Jessica graded the depths of bows. All three managed suitably deep inclinations for Eva, despite their high pommels. For Maude they all imbued their greetings with implications of admiration, and, in the case of the Major, deep homage. Jessica received two nods and a thin smile from Captain Grahame.

As they rode off, having expressed their eager anticipation of the first ball of the Season, four pairs of feminine eyes studied their retreating figures, then turned back. 'Captain Grahame is a very good-looking gentleman,' Jessica ventured, feeling it was an inadequate assessment.

'Too much so for his own swollen head,' Bel declared. 'And not enough money. Lord Heathcote is the man to concentrate on from that little group.'

'I thought him haughty,' Jessica demurred.

'Indeed he is, and well connected, rich and highly competitive. What we want is someone to create a stir when Gareth makes his move to secure your favours.'

'Surely we do not want to provoke a duel?' Jessica was horrified. 'Someone could get hurt!'

'But it wouldn't be Gareth,' Maude assured her. 'I am sure he is an *amazing* shot.'

'We do not want things to go that far.' Bel had gone a little pale. 'I have endured the suspense of one duel, I am not going to put up with another.'

'A duel? What happened?' Maude was, predictably, agog. 'Who was fighting over you? Was it Ashe?'

'Yes, and I am not going to tell you who the other man was, so it is no good asking, Maude. They both deloped, thank goodness, but I swear it put ten years on me, waiting for the result.'

'But—' Maude broke off and directed a wide smile to their left. 'Lord Bourton, good day! Grandfather was a West Indies merchant, father made a baron, but the son has a shocking reputation for the ladies,' she summarised in a murmur into Jessica's ear.

Again, Jessica was ignored, but this time she made herself disregard that and study the man driving the high-perch phaeton. His dress was slightly extreme to her, admittedly still untutored, eye. His horses were flashy and his air of self-consequence considerable. Having said all that, he was certainly a strikingly good-looking young man, if one ignored a definite weakness about the chin.

'Pretty,' she observed two minutes later as he drove off, attempting to get his fidgety team under better control. 'And spoiled. He won't like it if he does not get what he wants.'

Half an hour later she had resorted to jotting notes, unable to hold so many names and faces in her head. Goodness knows, it would cause a scandal if her notebook ever fell into anyone else's hands—her observations were nothing short of libellous.

Her head was spinning, but she appreciated Gareth's idea in setting her this task. She had never done more than glance indifferently at a gentleman; staring at one was quite out of the question. And she had certainly never assessed them in the light of seduction. Now she felt she could cast a bold eye over any man she met in the course of her masquerade.

Even the man riding towards them now.

'Well,' Jessica observed with heartfelt appreciation, 'now that is what I call a truly handsome man.'

'So do I,' Eva said, a smile twisting the corner of her mouth. 'But he is out of bounds for your games—I am married to this one.'

Chapter Eleven

'Oh my goodness! That is Lord Sebastian?' Jessica subsided in blushing confusion as the man brought his raking chestnut sidling up to the barouche. 'I do apologise!'

Eva smiled wickedly. 'There is no need to apologise, my thoughts on first seeing him were considerably more explicit.'

Lord Sebastian Ryder looked fit, lean, and, in some indefinable way, dangerous. His grey eyes were fixed on his wife's face and Jessica took a shaky breath. What would it feel like to have a man look at her like that? Eva reached out her hand and he bent and caught it, pressing a kiss on the inside of her wrist before releasing her.

'My love. Maude. Bel, my wicked sister, what are you up to? I sense mischief.' Bel shot him a reproving glance and inclined her head reproachfully towards Jessica. Jessica did not make the mistake for one moment of thinking he had not noticed her already. 'And Miss Jones, I assume?'

'Miss Smith, my lord,' Jessica answered, suppressing a laugh. She liked Eva's husband, she decided.

'Indeed you are,' he agreed gravely. 'And what course is this barque full of beauty bound upon?'

'We are collecting men for Jessica to study,' Maude explained, provoking a grin from his lordship and a mortified gasp from Jessica.

'Heaven help the entire male sex if you three are hunting,' he observed with every appearance of sincerity. 'Here comes another poor victim for you to add to your tally. Good day, Morant.'

'Gareth!' *Oh Lord, I spoke aloud.* Jessica was aware of Maude's rapid, intelligent glance that appeared to penetrate her veil before flickering away as Gareth came to a stop next to Lord Sebastian.

'Ryder.' There was respect, even affection there between the two cousins, she noticed, struggling to keep her attention on observation and to still the ridiculous flutterings inside that Gareth's unexpected arrival had provoked. What was the matter with her? He was hardly going to test her on her observations here and now.

Think, look, she reproved herself as though she were a slow student failing to grasp the principles of sketching. *Are they alike?*

She could tell that Lord Sebastian was Bel's brother—there was a similarity in colouring and in the way they smiled, the turn of their heads. There was nothing of Gareth that immediately spoke of a relationship, yet when you saw all three together she could sense the kinship.

How wonderful to have that easy familiarity, that tie, she thought wistfully.

Gareth turned from making bantering remarks about his cousin's new horse and fixed his gaze on Jessica's veiled figure. 'Are you having a successful drive, Miss Brown?'

'Smith,' Sebastian corrected helpfully.

'Not really,' Maude interjected. 'Jessica thinks that you two are the only handsome men she has seen all afternoon.'

'Maude! I said no such thing.' Jessica struggled to keep both the schoolmistress and the flustered innocent out of her voice. 'There were Lord Bourton and Captain Grahame, and any number of pleasant gentlemen.' There, that was said with a light-hearted, sophisticated air. 'And I made no observation whatsoever about Lord Standon,' she added, ruining things.

Lord Sebastian grinned at her, but mercifully made no comment, Eva choked back a laugh and Gareth gazed at her, disconcertingly expressionless. Surely his feelings were not hurt? 'Never say I instructed you to flirt with married men, Miss Smith.'

Jessica had got her breath back, although why she had been feeling slightly winded in the first place she could not say. 'Certainly you did not, my lord,' she retorted. 'And I was not flirting with Lord Sebastian— my remarks about his person were made while he was well out of earshot.'

Sebastian gave a shout of laughter, making a nervous chestnut hack being ridden past them shy away and several dowagers turn their heads to see what was occurring. 'Miss Smith, I am flattered. Morant, I have a suspicion you have been bested.'

'I am certainly constantly being surprised,' Gareth countered. 'And find myself quite off balance. I had no idea that the bombazine bodices of our educationalists hid spirits of such independence.'

'Jessica does not wear bombazine,' Maude protested indignantly, making them all laugh.

'We should all be wearing overcoats,' Bel said with a shiver. 'I think it is time to be turning back; the day has turned quite raw.'

Gareth gave instructions to the coachman and the group turned towards the gate, joining a log-jam of other vehicles whose occupants had obviously become as chilled as Bel's party.

'This is such a miserable time of the year,' Jessica observed. 'The nights draw in so early and the air is so damp and chill most of the time. I find it hard to keep up my spirits, especially if I am teaching children who do not have any natural liveliness.'

'Oh, but I think it is one of the best times.' Maude was adamant in her contradiction. 'The start of the Season. There is something magical about going out in the cold and the dark and then into a house lit up with hundreds of candles and warmth and noise.'

'Did you have no chance of a come-out?' Eva asked.

'No.' Jessica shook her head. More questions; well meant, kindly, but full of pitfalls. 'My mother died. We were already not well off. I had my living to earn.'

Gareth glanced down, wishing he could see Jessica's expression beneath the heavy veil. She was not comfortable with being questioned about her past, he had noticed it when he had asked. It was not something to her own discredit, he was sure. Perhaps simply the memory of hard times and past slights.

His grey hack sidled and snorted, not liking being kept to a slow walk in this crowd of horses and vehicles. Normally he would have touched his hat and ridden on, out of consideration for his mount, if nothing else, but now he soothed it with his voice and stayed where he was. Sebastian would stay too; concern for his newly pregnant wife showed in his every glance in her direction.

Love and marriage changed a man, Gareth mused, blanking out the conversation in the barouche now the talk had turned to hats and Jessica had relaxed. He would never have dreamed he would see Ryder dancing attendance on a carriage full of ladies. He was a man more at home bluffing his way through the courts of Europe on secret government business or sliding like a pike through the murky waters of some back slum. At least, Gareth corrected himself, not unless one of the ladies was a spy or there were stolen diamonds secreted in the upholstery.

Or take Sebastian's brother-in-law, Ashe Reynard, Viscount Dereham. He had returned from Waterloo, a hardened military man and a devil-may-care rake by all accounts. He had encountered Bel—under circumstances that made them both grin reminiscently, but which they steadfastly refused to discuss—and the next thing anyone knew, he was leg-shackled, faithful and a pillar of society.

It was enough to make a man nervous. Neither of them had been intending to fall in love, let alone get married. That, apparently, was not enough to protect you. Gareth grimaced, guiding the grey through an opening gap and managing to hold it for long enough for Bel's coachman to get past and clear of the gate. Why was he even brooding on the subject now? He had his careful scheme in place to save him from having to marry Maude and he was under no particular pressure to get married at all—there were male Morant cousins a-plenty if he managed to fall off his hunter and break his neck. It was all this talk of flirtation and Jessica's worries about Maude's unfortunate *tendre* for the un-suitable Mr Hurst, that was all.

He turned in the saddle and raised a hand in farewell before trotting off down Park Lane with a view to a lei-surely bath before that evening's promised card game at the club. There wouldn't be many free evenings for idleness in male company once the Season opened with Eva's ball and he was plunged into his false flirtation with the lethal Mrs Carleton.

The sound of hooves right behind him had him turning his head. 'Ryder?'

'Bel says to tell you that she is making up a party to the opera tonight and do you want to come? Miss *Smith* will be there, I gather; she said something about the fifth sense if that means anything to you.'

'Opera.' Not his favourite form of entertainment—he enjoyed the music, but not the fuss and feathers that went with it. On the other hand, it would be an excel-lent opportunity to talk to Jessica about the place of sound in seduction.

'All right, I'll come.'

'Our box is well placed,' Ryder offered as consola-tion as he turned his black gelding to make his way back through the traffic. 'Bring your earplugs.'

Jessica had never been to the opera; it was not some-thing that a governess would have the slightest excuse to accompany her charges to and she certainly could not afford to go on her own account.

'What do you think?' Eva stood in front of the long glass in her dressing room and regarded her reflection critically. 'Madame Hortense assures me it is in the very latest French mode.'

A white silk slip dress plunged from beneath a miniscule blue satin bodice which was cut so low and ended so high under the breast line that it barely contained the Grand Duchess's bosom. From the short sleeves of the bodice gauze under-sleeves billowed out to be caught in at the wrist by the pleated gauntlet cuffs of white kid evening gloves. Her dresser settled an immensely long silk stole, embroidered white on white, about her shoulders, remarking critically as she did so, 'You won't fit in that much longer, not with the young gentleman growing at the rate he is.'

'I think it is lovely,' Jessica assured her. No one, looking at Eva's slim but curvaceous figure, would guess she was expecting. 'The hat, er…headdress is certainly original.'

'I was not sure about it.' The round cap topped with small white plumes perched on top of Eva's head like some sort of exotic crown.

'It makes you look very regal,' Bel contributed, peering over Eva's shoulder at her own reflection in a confection of silk, tulle and bird-of-paradise feathers with some complacency. She had collected Jessica and driven her to Eva's so all three could go with Lord Sebastian as escort. Lord Dereham, Bel's husband, was still out of town.

Jessica guessed Eva knew she was being teased, for she merely looked down her nose and refused to be drawn.

'Will it not seem very odd that I am veiled?' Jessica asked. She had assumed that the simple dark blue silk gown she owned would be suitable and that a veil might not look out of place. Now, seeing the splendour of the other two in their opera dress, she had doubts.

'I shall say you are my companion and in mourning,' Eva said.

'And attending the opera?' Jessica was dubious.

'By my command,' Eva said imperiously. 'Any eccentricity is excused foreign royalty, I have discovered. Even when I insist that here I am simply Lady Sebastian, no one pays it any account. Very tiresome.'

There was a discreet tap at the door. 'Lord Sebastian's compliments, ma'am, but are you going to be all night? Not that he has any objection to missing the first three acts, he says.' Grimstone remained outside, so whether he was keeping his face as straight as his voice could only be imagined.

'We are coming now.' Jessica followed behind, clutching Eva's fan and the reticule that Eva's dresser thrust into her hands at the last moment.

Lord Sebastian helped Bel and Eva into the carriage, then turned to Jessica as she waited on the doorstep. 'You look very well this evening, Miss Smith, but I suggest you lower your veil now.' He followed her in and sat down carefully beside her, taking care not to crush the folds of her skirt. 'I confess to some curiosity at seeing Miss Smith shed her disguise and emerge as Mrs Carleton.'

'I am not so much curious as very apprehensive,' Jessica admitted. 'The suspense is beginning to prey on my nerves and I would welcome the thing starting.'

'Only ten more days,' Eva assured her, 'and then the Season begins with my ball.'

Gareth was waiting for them at the box. Jessica, jostled by the chattering throng and the focus of many an enquiring stare, despite her position by Eva's side, let out a sigh of pure relief at the sight of him.

He stood and she went to him instinctively, laying one hand on his forearm and whispering, 'I am so glad to see you!'

He seemed to understand without further explanation, for he turned her slightly and showed her a chair in the deeper shadow where the edge of the curtain was caught back. 'Sit there,' he suggested. 'You can put back your veil, no one outside the box will be able to see you.'

It was not until he patted her hand that she realised she was still touching him—*clinging more like*, she chided herself. Her palm lay on the warm black cloth that covered the supple muscle beneath and she snatched it away. She made a business of lifting her veil over the careful top knot that she had created to be as unlike her new hairstyle as possible while the glow in her cheeks subsided.

Sebastian sat at the furthest side from her with Eva next to him and then Bel. Gareth moved his seat away from Bel and into the shadows with Jessica. 'We can whisper,' he said, leaning sideways in the straight gilt chair until his shoulder just brushed hers.

'I have never been to the opera before,' she confided. 'What will they be performing?'

'Mozart, the *Marriage of Figaro.*'

'Oh, how interesting. I have played some of the music on the piano, but it is not the same.'

'How does music make you feel?' Gareth had no need to make such an innocuous question a secret, but he kept his voice low. It felt as though the two of them were hiding in this sheltered corner. Jessica shivered, surprised at herself for enjoying the *frisson* the thought brought with it.

'Feel?' She frowned at him. 'If it is challenging, then it is interesting to master. Familiar tunes are soothing.'

She could not see the expression in his eyes, but she could tell from the enquiring tilt of his head to one side that he was puzzled. 'And that is all the emotion music evokes? No passion, romance, nostalgia, *joie de vivre*, sadness?'

'Church music has the power to evoke reverent feelings.'

He made a noise somewhere between a snort and a laugh. 'Reverent feelings is not what we are about here, Jessica. Listen to the music, hear the emotion. You are not a governess any longer, bound to get up a piece exactly so as to be able to teach it. Open your mind and your heart to it. Never mind the plot, just *feel* and then tell me about it. Remember, you are to become a creature of emotion.'

Intrigued by the intensity of his directions, Jessica murmured, 'I will try.' She understood Italian and knew the story, so following the progress of the opera would not be hard and she could concentrate on the music. The orchestra tuning up, the swelling noise of the audience taking their places, filled her with an anticipation that was almost nervous. Or perhaps it was Gareth's closeness, the heat of his body reaching hers through the thin silk only inches from his shoulder.

'Can you see all right?'

She nodded, craning to see the empty stage, the flickering lights, the blur of faces in the distant boxes on the other side of the auditorium. There was applause as the conductor walked out, raised his baton and the overture began.

By the time Figaro strode on to the stage, Susanna dancing at his heels and trying on her new hat, Jessica was lost in the enchantment of the scene. The chattering from the stalls, the laughter from one of the boxes where a group of young bucks were entertaining their *chères amies*, failed to break the spell.

She listened, amused, as Figaro, convinced that the count had immoral intentions towards his fiancée, begins to plot. 'If you want to dance, my dear little count, I'll play the tune for you on my guitar…' she sang softly under her breath.

'You can translate?' Gareth asked, his breath whispering in her ear.

'Yes. Figaro is going to teach his master a lesson. Hush, here comes Marcellina.'

They laughed together over Cerubino's love-lorn sighings. 'I talk of love when waking, I talk of love when dreaming…' Jessica sang, her voice reaching only Gareth's ears. He leant closer, slid his arm along the back of her chair to lean in towards her. 'He's so sweet,' she whispered. 'So silly and young and romantic.'

'You will have to deal with equally silly young men soon,' Gareth teased as the characters came and went on the stage, entangling themselves deeper and deeper in their misunderstandings.

'But you will deal with them for me?' Jessica turned to look at him, anxious.

'Oh, yes. The young sprigs and the old roués and the dangerous rakes.' His eyes were amused, yet intent. Surely the flames that flickered in them were simply a trick of the light? 'I will protect you, Jessica, never fear.'

'Thank you,' she whispered.

'You are mine, after all,' he added, turning a little to look at the stage, leaving her confused and oddly breathless…*Mine* in the little drama they were going to enact, or *mine* in the sense of his responsibility now? Or something else entirely?

She forced her concentration back to the stage where the village girls were singing the praises of their undeserving count and Figaro was teasing Cerubino with scary stories of what he could expect in the army. Whether it was the composer's skill or Gareth's instruction to let herself feel, but Jessica realised all her emotions seemed to be on the surface.

She quaked for poor Cerubino, yearned with him for his hopeless calf-love. She felt Susanna's anger at the count's amorous intriguing and cheered on Figaro's plans for his master's come-uppance. But most of all her heart was aching for the countess's unhappiness.

Beside her she was aware, constantly, of Gareth's closeness, of him sharing the experience with her. From time to time they half-turned to one another, exchanging a smile.

Then she realised the point the opera had reached.

'Who—?' Gareth began to whisper.

'Hush!' Without thinking she raised her hand and touched her fingertips to his mouth. 'It is *"Dove sono"*. So beautiful…' The countess, alone, her heart breaking, began to sing as Gareth's breath warmed her flesh.

'*Dove sono*…where are the beautiful moments of sweetness and of pleasure, what happened to the promises of that lying tongue?'

Chapter Twelve

The aching loveliness of it silenced even the young bucks in their box. The voice floated high and pure and sad through the crowded space and Gareth turned to watch Jessica's face.

Her eyes were closed, her lips curved in pleasure at the exquisite sound, but her eyelashes were tipped with tears, glinting in the light like tiny diamonds. The countess sang the last, heartbreaking, line and stood for a moment, then left the stage. Gareth, without being able to understand a word of it, found himself caught in Jessica's emotion, bending closer as she gave a little sigh.

Her eyes fluttered open as the count and Antonio began the next scene, but it was clear she was still in that last aria and so, caught in the shimmer of her eyes, was he. Her hand, still raised from where she had silenced him with that featherlight touch to his lips, brushed his cheek as she lowered it.

They were so close he would hardly have to bend his head to kiss her. He wanted to, wanted to comfort her, as though she, not the countess, had been betrayed. For a long moment they were still, locked in the music.

'That is so sad,' she murmured. 'She loves him, forgives him, yet she knows he will betray her again and again. Her only hope is that, by remaining loyal to him, his ungrateful heart may change.'

'He will not change,' Gareth said. 'She is doomed to be betrayed.' He drew his handkerchief from his pocket and passed it to her. 'Your lashes are wet.' For a moment he thought of pulling her against his shoulder to hold her while she recovered from the emotion, then he controlled the impulse.

'Oh!' Jessica took the linen and dabbed at her eyes. 'I had no idea how it would affect me. When I read it, I thought her foolish to persist in loving him, but hearing it, you can understand that she will love him until death, despite everything.' She sat with the fabric crumpled in her hands, then handed it back. 'Thank you.'

Gareth reached for the handkerchief, his hand closing over hers. It was small and warm and vulnerable within his grasp and he simply held on, letting their joined hands rest on the arm of her chair. He felt her fingers curl against his palm, then relax as her attention was caught again by the unfolding story and her hand remained linked with his.

Jessica came to herself with a start as the curtain fell for the interval. She was pressed close to Gareth, her hand locked in his, her head almost resting on his shoulder. With a little gasp she sat up. Her veil, falling to her shoulders, snagged on his lapels and she freed her hand before the others, who were beginning to stand up, could see. Whatever had come over her?

'We will go and visit the Hetheringtons' box opposite,' Eva announced. 'She is beckoning and it will be safer than having goodness knows who coming in here.'

'Jessica and I will stay.' Gareth stood to set back the chairs. 'Could you have them bring us refreshments? I do not think it wise for her to be mixing too much.'

'But—' Alone with him, with all those emotions still surging around inside her? Jessica felt as light-headed and foolish as Cerubino, and about as reliable.

'You are probably right.' Eva nodded. 'I'm sorry, Jessica, I should have thought. But you will not be bored with Gareth's company.'

Boredom was the least of her concerns. Jessica assured her friends that she would be perfectly fine and resumed her seat.

'How do you feel?' Gareth spun a chair round at right angles to her secluded niche and straddled it.

'Flustered,' she confessed, too shaken at her own feelings to conceal them. 'The emotion of that music simply carried me away. Was it Mozart's genius, or was it hearing it performed so well?' *Or was it you?*

'Both.' Gareth ran a hand through his hair, wreaking havoc with his elegant style, and Jessica realised that he too had been affected, although he was not going to admit it as readily as she. 'And you had given yourself permission to simply experience it—not as a task to learn about, not as a piece to study.'

'Do you think the countess is a fool?' she asked abruptly, realising as she asked it that the question had been lurking there at the back of her mind. 'To love such a rogue, even though she can see him so clearly for what he is?'

'No.' Gareth frowned. 'No, I do not. I do not understand her, but I do not think she can help herself. A year ago, perhaps I would have dismissed her as weak. Now—' He broke off, the frown still creasing between his brows.

'What has changed for you?' More comfortable now the focus was off her and her feelings, Jessica twisted round in her chair so she could look at his face more easily.

'Seeing Reynard and Sebastian fall in love.' The frown vanished as he spoke of his friends. 'You haven't met Reynard—Lord Dereham—yet. But when you do you will see, he and Bel are like Sebastian and Eva: utterly devoted, totally as one.

'They are two of the bravest men I know,' he continued, frowning. 'And two of the most self-reliant. A soldier and a secret agent. And yet now they have given themselves something to fear, something that would bring them to their knees—the thought of losing the women they have fallen in love with. You only have to watch them when they look at their wives.'

'As you say—it is love,' Jessica pointed out, secretly amused by his bafflement.

'Yes, but they did not seek it. They were not looking to get married—and yet they were struck down with it like a fever.'

Jessica laughed. 'There is no need to make a normal human emotion sound like a dangerous disease!'

'It might as well be—it attacks as remorselessly and without warning,' he retorted grimly. 'Look at them now. Both Bel and Eva are expecting. Reynard and Sebastian are more afraid than they have ever been in their lives— at best their wives are going to have to endure childbirth, at worst, they may lose them. What were they thinking of?'

'They are in love; wanting to have children together is perfectly normal for people in love.' Jessica shook her head at him. 'It is perfectly normal for married people who are not in love, come to that.'

'Getting married should be a rational process,' Gareth grumbled, defeated by her logic, but refusing to leave the subject. He got to his feet to unlatch the door at the sound of a knock, took a tray from the waiter and locked it again. 'Then people go falling in love in a positively irrational manner.'

'I have not met Lord Dereham, as you say.' Jessica took the glass of champagne he handed her and sipped thoughtfully. 'But Bel seems very happy, and Eva and Lord Sebastian obviously are, so love cannot be so bad, can it?'

'It is unpredictable. They are well suited, I will admit. But what if the person you fall in love with is utterly unsuitable? Or married? Or does not love you in return?'

'Then you have to learn to live with it somehow, I suppose—or in the case of an unsuitable love, throw convention to one side and marry them anyway.' She shrugged, smiling. 'I don't know, I have never fallen in love. But don't worry, it may never happen to you.'

'Falling in love or suffering a broken heart?' Gareth grinned back at her. Apparently he had shaken off his gloom at the prospect of an erratic god of love firing off random arrows at blameless noblemen.

'Either, I suppose.' She tried to imagine Gareth with his bachelor world, indulgently organised to suit his every whim, turned upside down by the eruption of love into his life. He was no pampered sybarite, she knew he had a well-developed sense of duty and worked hard for his estates, his charities and dependents, she had seen him and heard Maude talk of it.

But Lord Standon had no one's will to consider but his own and marriage, let alone love, would change all that. It would probably do him good, she told herself robustly, trying not to feel a twinge of envy for the unknown but fortunate young lady concerned. 'You are going to have to act it soon when Mrs Carleton comes into your life.'

'What you will be seeing then, my dear, will be an exhibition of unbridled lust and desire.' Gareth produced a comical leer.

Jessica failed to suppress an unladylike snort of laughter, but she still wanted to probe this scandalous relationship she was supposed to be participating in. 'So, you do not intend to be feigning love?'

'The Mrs Carletons of this world are not the sort of women the Earl of Standon would marry.' He said it so matter of factly that Jessica was taken aback. It almost felt as though she—and Mama—and not the fictional adventuress had been snubbed.

'Indeed? Then let us hope, for your sake, that the next time you come across such a lady in reality, Eros is looking in the opposite direction,' she retorted tartly, annoyed with herself for caring. 'Making statements like that could be tempting fate.'

And letting her concentration slip so that she half-believed this was real life and not fantasy was even more dangerous. Gareth was an attractive man and one as far beyond her reach as a royal duke. Finding herself enjoying his company, feeling a *frisson* when he came close enough for his breath to caress her skin was madness. She, Jessica Gifford, was a spinster governess. She now had the opportunity to become a lady of modest independent means and that was the height of her ambition. Anything else was for three-o'clock-in-the-morning dreams or the hazy aftermath of an orgy of novel reading.

Gareth topped up her glass, apparently unmoved by her warnings. 'I shall learn by my friends' downfall and simply not permit myself to become attracted in the first place.'

'I see,' Jessica said, her face straight despite this ludicrous masculine logic. *As if it were as simple as that!* 'So, are my lessons in the senses complete now?'

'The theory is, certainly. It all boils down to feeling, emotions, sensuality. Now you will have to practise. I will look forward to seeing your progress when I return.'

'You are going away?' Jessica wondered at her own feeling of alarm. It was ridiculous. She had Bel and Eva to support her, Maude's frivolous encouragement, a respectable house to lodge in and her own wits to rely upon. But the feeling of calm strength that had reached her from him in the brothel and had led her to trust him was weakening to her own self-reliance.

'Not for long, and only into the country to my estate on business. I will be back just before Bel's ball.'

Jessica gave herself a mental shake. She had never depended upon a man before—certainly not dear Papa—why was she weakening now? Gareth feared falling in love; she should fear this kind of feminine weakness.

You should be ashamed of yourself, Jessica Gifford, she scolded inwardly. *All it takes is a pair of broad shoulders and steady grey eyes and look at you! You are employed by this man to carry out a task. An unconventional one to be sure, but a task. If he had left me to instil deportment and the French tongue into a pair of schoolroom chits, I would do it without needing more than his initial instructions. This is no different. I do not need protection, I do not need support. I most certainly do not need further tuition!*

She had lectured herself into a state of resolute independence when he stood to answer another tap at the door. The orchestra was filing back in and beginning to retune their instruments, the interval was almost over.

'Whatever have you two been arguing about?' Bel asked, amusement rippling through her voice.

'Nothing.' Gareth looked puzzled. 'Nothing whatsoever.'

Bel looked at Jessica. 'Well, if I were one of Jessica's pupils, I would be feeling highly apprehensive at the moment. I remember that look from my governess all too well—it's the one that accompanies the lecture on frivolity and slacking.'

'I am neither frivolous nor slack,' Gareth responded amiably. 'Jessica is naturally of a more sober disposition than you are, cousin.'

'I was mentally lecturing myself,' Jessica interposed as Bel seemed ready to settle down and tease Gareth. 'I am allowing myself to enjoy this life of leisure and pleasure far too much.'

'No fear it will last,' Lord Sebastian observed with a sly smile at his wife as he held the chair for her. 'Eva and Bel will drag you from ball to party, from reception to masque, from dress shop to milliner, all in the name of doing your social duty.'

'Or, in my case, in the cause of this masquerade I will be enacting.'

'I am so looking forward to it,' Eva said with a pleasurable shiver. 'I do so enjoy a masquerade.'

The days before the ball slipped by with terrifying speed. Word of the charity extravaganza spread like wildfire throughout the smart set who were pouring into London for the start of the Season and invitations were eagerly anticipated, angled for and, in some cases, blatantly solicited.

'Could you believe your ears?' Maude was saying with horrified amusement to Eva as the pair of them were shown into the Half Moon Street drawing room a week before the event. 'Good morning Jessica darling.' She pounced, hugged, her cold cheek tingling against Jessica's warm one for a moment, then tossed her floss-trimmed bonnet onto the sofa. 'That odious shabby-genteel Mrs Harrington—'

'Harrington-Smythe, Maude, *please*,' Eva corrected with a wicked smile.

'Harrington-Smythe, then, as though that makes her manners any better.' Maude stripped off her gloves and went to perch on the fender to warm her hands. 'She positively bounced up to me in the Exeter Exchange—'

'If you will patronise such a middle-class emporium,' Eva interrupted, 'what do you expect?'

'Dagger-cheap silk stockings, that what I expect,' Maude countered. 'We don't all have your limitless dress allowance, Eva. Anyway, up she comes, bold as brass and says, "My dear Lady Maude, I am so looking forward to your wonderful ball!" Gush, gush, smarm.

"But I can't imagine what has happened to our invitations. I said to the girls…' Maude opened her eyes wide in cruel parody, '"Mark my words, girls, they'll have gone astray in the post, for Lady Maude will be wanting all her friends to support her efforts for those brave soldiers.' And then she said with a silly simper, "Even if they are just rough common men." I nearly boxed her ears.'

'What did you say?' Eva hooked a toe under a footstool and put her feet up with a grateful sigh.

'I said that it was not my ball because, after all, I was just an unmarried girl and naturally couldn't be hostess at such an event—you would have been *amazed* at how demure I sounded, Jessica—but I knew Lady Sebastian and the Grand Duchess had drawn up the most exclusive guest list so I had every confidence that all my most *particular* friends would be invited.'

'Cat,' Eva remarked appreciatively.

'It isn't that I mind her husband being a coal merchant or her frightful taste in puce satin gowns, and I'll take anyone's money for my rough, common soldiers. It is just that she toad-eats so,' Maude complained. 'Her poor daughters would be perfectly acceptable if only she didn't dress them in pink silk on every possible occasion and frizz their hair.'

'I'll invite them to a masquerade,' Eva promised. 'But never mind them, how are you, Jessica? Are you quite prepared for your grand opening scene?'

She exhaled a long breath and smiled ruefully. 'I think so.' Listening to Maude's airy talk of who was in and who was out made her realise just how ignorant she was of this whole gilded, privileged world—and how easy it would be to blunder over the simplest thing, let alone her pretence of being a dangerously seductive adventuress.

'Don't worry,' Eva reassured her, her sharp eyes apparently spotting more apprehension than Jessica thought she was showing. 'You must remember that you have been out of the country for years—if you do something you realise is odd, just say *Oh, that's how we do it in Maubourg*. And you will look the part—that is nine-tenths of the battle.'

That was true, Jessica thought, grateful for the reassurance. Even though she was keeping to her modest gowns and her severe hairstyle for the moment, the knowledge that the silks and the lawns and the cashmeres were hanging in her wardrobe, and the glimpses of her guinea-gold hair, made her feel a different woman already.

She was practising her seductive arts too, not certain whether she was glad or sorry that Gareth was not there to see her improvement. Without him she felt fidgety and supposed it was the lack of his guidance she was missing. Yet at the same time the strange tension she felt when he was near was gone and she found her concentration was much better. Altogether it was very odd, and she had a sneaking suspicion that the memory of that kiss was responsible for her conflicting feelings about Gareth Morant.

She had secured the services of Lady Catchpole's ex-dresser and Mirabelle spent much effort demonstrating the uses of the fan in flirtation. Jessica spent an hour a day perfecting each trick—the slow unfurling to draw the eye, the seemingly thoughtless use of the closed fan to draw down the line of one's neck or across the bosom of one's dress. Then there were the messages that could be sent—resting the fan on one's heart, peeping over it half-open, running fingers across the ribs, slapping it into the palm—they were all to be learned.

'You have just told me that I am ugly, that you want to talk to me and I am breaking your heart,' Mirabelle had observed critically only that morning. 'What did you intend to say, Mrs Carleton, ma'am?'

'That you were making me jealous looking at other women, and that I could not be with you as I was being watched,' Jessica confessed, sending them both off into peals of laughter. 'More practice,' she said ruefully. 'Show me again.'

After much thought they had decide to tell the dresser the false story of Jessica's identity and to enlist her help in fitting her new mistress for the task of finding a protector in London society as though that were Jessica's true purpose. It was too risky to let her know the truth, however discreet she had been in Lady Catchpole's employ, and the effort of keeping up the pretence in the house did help fix in Jessica's mind who she was now supposed to be.

Dancing lessons had progressed well, Bel's daily lectures on everything from orders of precedence to who was sleeping with whom and the latest *on-dits* about the royal family were dutifully absorbed and Jessica took every opportunity, heavily veiled, to drive out with one of her three new friends, observing the rich and the famous and the merely pretentious as they flaunted their finery through the fashionable promenades and the shops.

She even had the opportunity of practising her new skills and wiles on real men, for Bel and Eva volunteered their husbands for intimate dinner parties in the Half Moon Street house.

'It is a pleasure to meet you, especially here.' Lord Dereham, bowing over her hand, had a wicked smile that sent appreciative shivers all down Jessica's spine, despite the presence of his wife, smiling, equally wickedly, in the background. 'This house has many very happy memories for me. But it is you we must concentrate upon, is it not, Mrs Carleton? I have been brought up to date with this scheme you are all hatching to rescue poor Maude from Gareth's clutches and I understand that Sebastian and I are under orders from our wives to flirt outrageously with you.'

Jessica had blushed rosily, despite her very best efforts to look sophisticated and unconcerned by the attentions of two of the best-looking, most sophisticated and certainly the most teasing males she had ever come across. It was difficult at first to respond to their allusive jokes, their elegant compliments, dropped carelessly into the conversation, the half-serious repartee that had her laughing and blushing. But then she grew in confidence, applied her intelligence to the situation and found she could turn the tables on them with increasing confidence.

'Ah, if I had a heart to lose, ma'am,' Ashe Reynard, Lord Dereham, said in apparent seriousness, gazing deeply into her eyes while she gazed limpidly back. 'But, alas…'

'You had many of them to squander last night, my lord,' Jessica retaliated pertly. 'I saw you lose hand after hand of them at the piquet table. How could I trust you to look after mine any better?'

He chuckled at that, confiding later to his wife—

who promptly reported it back the next day to Jessica—
that no unattached man was going to be safe and he had
grave doubts about some of the married ones at that.

So her confident words to Eva were almost the truth.
She would look the part, she could act the part—but
could she convince the world that she had it in her power
to make Gareth Morant, Earl of Standon, fall head over
heels in love with her?

There were only days before she would find out.

Chapter Thirteen

Once more her nostrils were full of overwhelming smells and her ears with the braying of excited voices. For a brief, panicky, moment Jessica shut her eyes, trying to blank out the memory of that descent of the brothel staircase into the heat and stir of a room full of lascivious men.

'Mrs Carleton, ma'am? Are you all right?' *What is his name?* Jessica struggled to recall. It was only an hour after Eva and Bel had taken their places at the head of the receiving line and it was already obvious that their charity ball was going to be a complete crush. Which might signal its overwhelming success, but meant equally that Jessica's head was spinning.

'Quite well, Mr Hamilton, thank you. It was just the noise. I have been living quite retired, you understand.' She summoned up a brave smile and was rewarded as he patted her lightly on the arm with his white gloved hand.

No, these sensations were different—it was the well-bred laughter of ladies, the noise of the *ton* all trying to make themselves heard above the hubbub without actually shrieking, the scent of flowers and expensive scent. There was no coarse laughter here, no stink of male sweat and cheap perfume and cigarillo smoke.

She, Miss Jessica Gifford, governess, was at the opening ball of the Season of 1816 and was enjoying the giddying knowledge that she was the focus of considerable male attention. She could not believe it, after so short a time, but her dance card was almost half-full, three gentlemen were at her side, vying to entertain her with their witticisms and compliments, and a fourth had hastened off to fetch her a glass of champagne.

'I cannot believe you ever succeeded in living retired, Mrs Carleton,' the youngest of her attendants said with an attempt at a knowing smile. As he was all of nineteen, this was not entirely successful. 'Wherever you are, the gentlemen will beat a path to your door.' He leaned closer and whispered, 'Your bedchamber door.'

'Lord Chevering, that is a very naughty suggestion,' she pouted, rapping him lightly on the forearm with her fan. He blushed and smirked. *This is ridiculously easy, they are such idiots!* 'You forget, I was under the protection of her Serene Highness.'

She glanced towards Eva as she spoke. The Grand Duchess was in laughing conversation with an ambassador, someone who had been pointed out to Jessica as a High Court judge and two leading politicians. With her uncanny knack of seeing all that was going on Eva caught the glance and smiled, a small, wicked sign of encouragement.

'And you will be delighting us with your presence for the entire Season, ma'am?' That was the third gentleman, Sir Oscar Remington, who appeared more delighted with his view down the front of Jessica's alarmingly low-cut gown than with her personality.

'I expect so—I have been made *so* welcome.' She unfurled her fan and shot him a slanting look over the top of it. The fan also had the advantage of covering up her bosom, at least temporarily.

'It is a pleasure to welcome such a lovely new face into our midst.' Sir Oscar moved a little closer, managing to crowd out Mr Sayle, who had returned with her champagne. 'And one belonging to a lady of, shall we say, experience? Not yet another of the naïve young ladies who are flocking here for their first Season.'

'Experience, Sir Oscar? Oh, thank you, Mr Sayle.' She took the glass from the flustered gentleman with a smile that made him blush and sipped. 'I have no experience of London society, I fear. Why, I was the merest child when Mr Carleton married me and whisked me off abroad in the late Grand Duke's service.'

'Of life, dear lady, of life.' Sir Oscar was definitely getting too close and she had not been expecting such a full-frontal approach quite this early in her debut.

'Oh, yes. Life.' She sighed soulfully, half-turning so she could gaze into Mr Sayle's eyes as she drank deeply from her glass. 'Life is so full of…opportunity, is it not?'

'I should say so,' he agreed enthusiastically, his voice changing to a more discouraging tone. 'Oh. Hello, Grahame.' One of the riders Jessica recognised from her first carriage expedition to the park appeared, clicked his heels and executed a bow, which gave her ample opportunity to admire his dress regimentals.

'Won't you introduce me to the new star in our firmament, Sayle?' Jessica bit the inside of her lip, uncertain whether to laugh or sneer. She was looking very well, she knew that without false modesty. The combined efforts of her supporters had sent her out looking as attractive as she had ever felt herself to be. But the ballroom was full of much lovelier ladies than she. The reason that she was surrounded by men was that she was giving out signals that she might flirt, might be indiscreet, might even, if the incentive was right, be *available*.

'Mrs Carleton, may I present Captain Grahame.'

'Captain.' Jessica dipped a slight curtsy, leaning forward, just a little, to give the captain a glimpse of those features so much admired by Sir Oscar. How she was managing all this without a blush of shame she had no idea. It was as though she had donned Francsca Carleton and her dubious morals along with her silken gown.

'Madam! Your devoted servant.' He even had a thin moustache, which he brushed up with the back of his finger as he spoke. It was either a nervous mannerism or an attempt to look dashingly military. 'Might I have the honour of a dance—or more than one?'

'You'll be lucky,' Lord Chevering blundered in, earning himself a glare from the captain for his gaucheness. 'Mrs Carleton won't give us an aye or a nay, no matter how we plead.'

'Now you are being naughty again, my lord,' she chided, tapping his cheek with her fan and provoking a delighted laugh and a crimson blush. *Really, after a classroom of inattentive small boys, this is almost too simple!* 'You know a lady must be careful with the dances she gives—think of my reputation, gentlemen. I am not certain I will be dancing at all this evening.'

The thought of what Mrs Carleton's reputation might

be produced a glazed expression in four pairs of male eyes and a glare from a starched-up dowager sweeping past close enough to catch, if not the words, at least the atmosphere of innuendo.

Jessica repressed a sigh. This was all very well, but a whole evening of it, even with dancing, was going to prove tiresome. She chided herself; it might be ridiculous, flirting with a group of over-amorous gentlemen, but at least she was being very well paid for it and had the prospect of a good supper and a snug house to go back to. It could have been the draughty house in the wilds of Northumberland with the 'eccentric' daughter, or the chaos of a home full of ill-disciplined boys to contend with.

And even though she had to put up with—no, encourage—their dubious attentions, there was no danger they could go any further than that. Lord Sebastian and Lord Dereham were there, unobtrusively watching over her. And soon Gareth would be here and the masquerade could begin in earnest.

But where is Gareth?

Jessica shifted a little so she could watch the part of the room just beyond the receiving line. Maude was there, her father Lord Pangbourne at her side, jovially making conversation with the new arrivals about the work his daughter and her friends were doing for the wounded soldiers. He was a good-hearted man, she acknowledged, even if he had such a blind spot about Maude and Gareth.

The orchestra in the ballroom through the wide arch had stopped playing light airs and were tuning up for the dancing and there was still no sign of Gareth. Maude was behaving with poise and decorum, dutifully standing at her papa's side and laughing at all his sallies. If she was on the look-out for Mr Hurst, to whom she had insisted the committee send an invitation, one could not tell.

'Ride with you?' She pulled herself together and focused on what the Captain was saying. If she was not careful, she was going to blunder through sheer inattention. 'How kind, but I am afraid I do not have a riding habit in my wardrobe.' She plied the fan again, delighted at how versatile it was proving to be. 'But I hope I might see you in the park while I am driving out. I am certain you must look so dashing on your charger.'

He laughed at her flattery, assuring her that he had left his charger behind in barracks. 'No, I will be exercising my hunters, ma'am…'

His overconfident voice faded in her ears as some sense sent all her attention towards the door. *He is here.*

There was a stir around the receiving line, Maude stiffened and Lord Pangbourne beamed as Lord Standon turned from a laughing exchange with his cousin and strolled towards father and daughter.

Oh, but he looks wonderful. Maude, Bel and Eva seemed to dismiss Gareth as merely a *well-looking man*, and to be sure he was no match for Sebastian and Ashe in pattern-book good looks. But as she watched him stroll across to Maude, smiling at acquaintances as he crossed the parquet floor, she thought him their equal in masculine presence and in virile elegance with his broad shoulders and slim waist and long easy stride.

That deceptively lazy smile hid a decisiveness she had seen in action, the humour a seriousness and sense of honour and obligation that both she and Maude could be grateful for, and the broken nose and rugged chin lent character that, in her opinion, matched Lord Sebastian's saturnine looks and Lord Dereham's blond glamour.

Then she saw the laughter lines crinkle round those clear grey eyes as he greeted Maude and something twisted inside her. She had not seen him since he had left for his estates over a week before. It was agreed that it would seem most natural if they did nothing to rehearse this supposedly first encounter and the realisation of how much she had missed him hit Jessica with a force that almost overset her. *What is the matter with me?*

Then, *I desire him*, she thought, aghast. She fought for poise, attempting to rationalise her feelings, but they would not be ordered or controlled. *At least it will help my acting*, she thought wildly as some part of her managed to chatter on inanely to the circle of men around her. She watched out of the corner of her eye as Lord Pangbourne beamed upon Gareth's head, bent over Maude's dance card.

Gareth sketched a gesture to one side of the room and Jessica guessed he was saying he would escort Maude in to supper later. Her father must be delighted with this show of attentiveness; he was probably choosing the hymns for the wedding service even as he stood there, poor man.

Gareth, laughing at something Maude had just said, shifted position and began to scan the room casually as though looking out for acquaintances. The group around her shifted, blocked her view, moved again. Jessica knew the moment he saw her, felt the grey eyes lock with hers, saw the laughter ebb out of his face.

They could all act, the Ravenhurst cousins, he had

told her. But were any of them good enough to force the blood from their own cheeks? Gareth had gone white.

Maude said something to him, her hand on his arm, but he walked away from her as though she had been an importunate street hawker, straight across the room to where Jessica stood in her circle of bucks and beaux, as direct as if they had been alone in the room and the crowded reception hall clear space.

Startled looks followed him, ladies drew their skirts back, affronted by him brushing past them without ceremony. A man began, 'Ah, Morant, I need to talk—', but was ignored. They had wanted to cause a stir—it seemed they were about to brew a scandal.

Maude was overacting to a ridiculous degree, Gareth thought, bowing low over her hand with an exaggerated courtesy that had Lord Pangbourne beaming with pleasure.

She gazed at him wide-eyed with an expression of simpering adoration on her face that almost had him laughing aloud. 'Maude, my dear. You look ravishing tonight.' And so she did, the minx, no doubt in the expectation that her unsuitable theatre fellow was going to put in an appearance. She was doomed to disappointment. Gareth had done some investigating and Hurst was not given to attending *ton* parties. Work appeared to be his world and he had made no attempt to break into society, despite wealth and looks that would doubtless have won him an *entrée* of sorts.

'Now, how many dances are you going to allow me?' he teased. 'Or have they all gone, snapped up by other lucky fellows?'

'As many as you like,' Pangbourne put in. 'No need to stand on propriety, Morant, everyone knows the way the land lies, eh?'

'Three, then?' He took the proffered card and filled in a country dance, a waltz and the supper dance, making a production of it, drawing the attention of the gaggle of matrons and chaperons who were covertly watching them. The gossip mills would be working overtime; within minutes word would spread that the long-awaited betrothal was on the verge of being announced.

Someone else was watching him, he could feel it. Not a hostile gaze, but one of an intensity that brought the hair up on his closely barbered nape and sent a *frisson* of anticipation down his spine. *Jessica.*

'So, we are agreed on supper?' he asked, turning slowly to sweep the room with an apparently casual glance.

He couldn't see her. Frowning, he searched again and then a knot of men by one of the large flower arrangements shifted, parting to reveal a single woman in their midst. She was looking at him.

In the part of his brain that was reminding him how to act as a sophisticated gentleman, Gareth knew his jaw had dropped. He shut it, but no amount of inculcated poise and manners was going to stop him staring. *Jessica? It has to be, but...*

He was moving without conscious volition, vaguely aware of Maude's voice, sharp, behind him, 'Gareth!' and of Pangbourne spluttering.

She isn't beautiful, something said inside his head. *But she's enchanting. I want her.* This was not supposed to be happening, he thought in the kind of daze he had not experienced since he was in his teens. He chose the ladies who received his admiration, he wasn't dragged into something by the parts of his anatomy that were even now overriding his brain with painful intensity. This was a carefully staged simulacrum of instant attraction, it was not supposed to be a genuine *coup de foudre. Not for a prim governess with a talent for common sense...*

Not beautiful. He clung to that thought, vaguely aware that his sleeve was brushing too close to someone. She was looking directly at him, although her lips, warm, rose pink, were moving, talking. Her face, framed by the artfully tumbled curls, was pale and her eyes as clear and transparent as spring water. Everything about the simple sheath of almond silk that turned her figure into a graceful column said cunning artifice, glamour, and yet the woman he saw radiated a kind of clarity and honesty that stopped the breath in his throat.

Not beautiful. 'Damn it—' Someone was irritated with him, he realised vaguely, striding towards his goal. He didn't care. All he cared about was managing to drag air down into his lungs so that he could articulate when he got to her.

'Madam.' *Thank God. I can speak, and it is Jessica and she looks perfect—and if this pack of bucks, bloods and coxcombs has so much as laid a finger on her...*

'Sir.' She dropped a curtsy nicely calculated to indicate that she had no idea of his rank and to show off an expanse of milk-white bosom.

Gareth choked back an order to get into the retiring room that minute and make herself decent. 'We have not been introduced, ma'am. Grahame, if you would be so good?'

'Of course.' Captain Grahame, too wise to show his

chagrin, did so with apparent good grace. 'Mrs Carleton, may I present the Earl of Standon? Standon, Mrs Carleton has returned from Maubourg with Grand Duchess Eva. Her husband was in service with the Duke.'

'The late Grand Duke and my late husband,' Jessica clarified, carefully making her widowed status quite clear. 'My lord, you are related to Lord Sebastian, I think?'

She was wearing the pearl set. Gareth had a sudden memory of the necklace slithering down his own naked body and an image of how it would look if he unfastened it now and let it slide over those milky curves, down into the shadowed valley of her low-cut bodice. 'Indeed. We are cousins, ma'am.'

It was a miracle he was making any sense, he thought. He had expected to have to guide a nervous Jessica through this first momentous meeting, yet she seemed the calm one, if he discounted how wide her pupils were, and the fluttering of the pulse in the angle of her throat.

Why had he not expected this? He had assured her over and over again that she would be perfectly convincing in her role as seductive adventuress, and he had not been lying to her. But faced with the sceptical, upright, prim governess, he had somehow not been able to imagine the full impact of the woman in reality.

'You will dance with me,' Gareth said curtly.

Jessica's eyes widened at the tone, then she tapped him on the arm with her fan in mock reproof.

'So hasty, my lord! I was just telling these gentlemen that I may not dance at all this evening.'

'You will dance with me, ma'am,' he said evenly, stepping closer and lifting the wrist from which the tiny gilded dance card and pencil dangled.

'You are very forceful, sir.' Jessica smiled, cat-like, apparently basking smugly in this masculine attention. Only Gareth, he was certain, saw the question in her eyes, the nervousness at his tone. 'One each, then, gentlemen. Lord Chevering asked first…'

'You misunderstand, Mrs Carleton.' Gareth untied the gold cord card and took the dance card between forefinger and thumb of each hand. 'You will dance with *me*.' The thin card ripped as he tore it across and then again, the pieces showering to the floor.

'Dammit, Standon!' Captain Grahame took a step forward, his face darkening. 'The lady—'

'The lady has no objection. Has she?' Gareth asked softly, staring deep into Jessica's eyes. For a moment the clear green clouded with panic, then her gaze sharpened, focused and she smiled that pussycat smile again.

'My lord!' The fan swirled open and she looked over the top of the cream-and-gold lacquer with something like devilment. 'I yield to your command. Gentlemen, I confess I find myself swept off my feet—perhaps another evening when you find yourselves more…persuasive?'

She laid her hand on Gareth's proffered forearm and, with a dimpling smile to either side, allowed herself to be led towards the ballroom. Gareth concentrated on relaxing, sauntering, trying not to look like a man expecting to have a challenge hurled at his back at any moment.

None came. The room seemed hushed. Eyes were following them, he knew without looking. He had his scandal.

Chapter Fourteen

'What do you think you are doing?' Jessica demanded in a hissing whisper. 'I thought there was supposed to be a gradual onset of your infatuation over several meetings, not you acting like the Grand Turk in the middle of the reception room! La, my lord!' she remarked more loudly as they passed a group of goggling matrons at the entrance to the ballroom. 'I swear you have quite undone my resolution not to dance.

'And I never thought I would hear myself say *La!* either,' she added bitterly, *sotto voce*.

What *was* he doing? A very good question. He could hardly respond with the truth, that he was in the grip of an attack of mind-numbing lust, or she would probably flee the room screaming.

'I saw the opportunity to create an effective scandal immediately,' Gareth improvised. 'Why shilly-shally about?'

'Why, indeed?' He could almost hear Jessica's teeth gritting as they came to a halt on the dance floor. 'I do wish you could have warned me, though. My heart was in my mouth—I thought you were about to provoke a challenge just then.'

So did I. Gareth took his place at her side at the head of the set as other couples followed them on to the floor. He tried to ignore the sensation of curious eyes burning into his back and looked down instead to meet Jessica's sideways glace. To an onlooker she would appear to be looking up at him flirtatiously, but he could see the governess-look in her eyes. For some reason it did nothing to diminish this heat that was surging through his veins, pooling in his belly.

The music struck up and they linked hands across their bodies and began to lead the set down the room. In the manoeuvre Jessica's knuckles accidentally brushed the front of his thin silk evening breeches, with predictable results. Gareth fought to think of cold horse troughs and Parliamentary reports.

They reached the end, separated, turned to face each other in concert with the other dozen or so couples and Gareth made himself focus on the steps and on strategy, although he rather feared he was beyond that. Beyond tactics even, he told himself with wry humour. He had probably reached the stage where improvisation was all that was going to save the day.

It was their turn to step forward and promenade again. 'Do remember we have only just met,' Jessica murmured, smiling with every appearance of enjoyment and pressing rather too close for propriety as they turned.

Yes, there was that. He was feeling so overset by that lightning strike of desire that he was in danger of forgetting the overall plan. What was the most convincing thing for him to do next? Retire into some secluded, but visible, corner and flirt, seemed the answer.

The dance was interminable. Jessica applied her mind to her recent dancing lessons and turned and skipped, dipped and linked hands, reciting the steps in her head as though she were conjugating irregular verbs.

People were still staring; she could feel the touch of their eyes like the press of fingertips on her skin. And Gareth—had he any sense of the wave of desire that had swept through her when she had seen him? It was difficult to think of that, and the dance and the person she was supposed to be, all at once.

'Thank Heavens that is over,' she murmured with heartfelt relief as he led her to a *chaise* in a curtained alcove.

'Champagne.' Gareth clicked his fingers at a passing waiter and snagged a full bottle and two glasses from the tray. 'Here, drink this.'

'On an empty stomach?'

'Pretend.' He sat down beside her and she was overwhelmingly aware of the size of him, so close and hot on the fragile piece of furniture. 'I have taken your lure, the hook is in my mouth, now you have to reel me in.'

'You make it sound as though you are a hapless victim of my toils—and that is what you are supposed to be, is it not?' Jessica took an incautious sip of the wine and choked. 'But you did not seem very hapless back there, Gareth, believe me. And none of those gentlemen thought it either. Some of them were very capable of putting their weaker brethren in their place, I saw them do it earlier—but they hardly dared twitch when you snatched me from under their noses.'

Gareth tossed back his champagne and refilled his glass, his eyes roaming the room, as though alert for any raiding party intent on regaining his prize. It seemed to her that he was controlling his breathing.

'In fact,' Jessica persisted, 'you felt very domineering and masterful and positively scary.'

That brought his attention back to her with a jolt. 'I am sorry!'

'No, please do not apologise,' she said earnestly, fixing her eyes on his face. 'Actually it was most…stimulating.' The flush stained her cheeks as her own words registered and she opened her fan, making rather a business of it, and waved it in the hope of a cooling draught. 'I must be getting into the part rather too much.'

There was a silence, one that crackled with unspoken questions and, on Jessica's side at least, rather too much horrified self-awareness for comfort. Gareth was holding her gaze and she watched, fascinated, as the stormy grey eyes darkened and his lids drooped into a sensual stare that had the goose bumps prickling wildly up and down her spine.

Then he smiled and she let her breath go with an audible gasp. 'I hadn't realised what a dangerous game this acting is,' he said lightly. 'Do you think when Kean is playing Macbeth, he goes home at night with the urge upon him to murder kings?'

Jessica felt the blood ebb and flow in her cheeks. Did he mean that he realised she wanted, in truth, to be his lover or that he wanted to be hers? Or both? Or neither? What to say? How to ask?

Words, for once, failed her. She was saved by an amused voice remarking, 'You *have* set the cat amongst the pigeons, Gareth.' It was Bel, eyes twinkling with mischief. 'Eva has sent me over to ask what the devil you are playing at—her words—and on the way I was accosted by Lord Pangbourne demanding to know what I thought was the best thing to do in the face of your apparent brainstorm.'

'Oh, Lord.' Gareth looked conscience-stricken. 'Maude.'

'You did snub her quite outrageously,' Jessica put in. She felt guilty, too—from the moment she had set eyes on Gareth, nothing and nobody had mattered. But what he had done was a very different matter than the gradual erosion of his supposed engagement to Lady Maude— he had swept the whole thing away with one stroke and very publicly at that.

'Actually, Maude is perfectly fine,' Bel reassured them. 'She is doing the rounds, stirring the pot and assuring everyone—in the strictest confidence, naturally, which means it will be all over town by tomorrow—that she always knew you were a rake and a libertine at heart, but could never convince her father of it. Her tale is that she had been browbeaten into acceptance of your forthcoming proposal, but now that you have exposed your true nature for all to see, she is deeply relieved.'

'That is a mercy. Thank goodness Maude is so uninhibited.' Jessica sank back against the hard bolster cushion. 'Our mission has been accomplished, it seems.'

'Yes, but you cannot stop yet,' Bel pointed out. 'It would be obvious that it was a ploy if you suddenly vanish and Gareth returns to being his usual well-behaved self.'

'Couldn't I vanish and he could brood for a few weeks in dark despair like a Byronic hero?' Jessica suggested.

'No, he could not,' Gareth interjected, getting to his feet with an energy that sent those wretched goose bumps going again. 'He would feel a complete idiot. He, since you two insist on discussing me in the third person, is going to carry on his rakish way with Mrs Carleton for a good while yet, believe me.'

'Heavens.' Bel blinked at her cousin. 'You look just like Sebastian when roused.'

Gareth gave a snort of laughter, rather spoiling his domineering stance. 'Is that a compliment?'

'Oh, yes,' Jessica assured him. 'Ladies will tell you that such masculine forcefulness is most attractive.'

The look he gave her was sceptical, as though he suspected her of teasing him, but there was a heat lurking behind it that made her swallow hard. 'That damned fellow Byron, I suppose.' He shot a wary look over Bel's shoulder. 'We are attracting attention again.'

'I am sure we are. I shall go now, radiating distress at having my diplomatic mission spurned and tell Eva within earshot of, I think, Lady Greyshott, that I very much fear her protégée is in the process of seducing our cousin from the paths of righteousness.'

'Will she have to appear to cast me off?' Jessica worried.

'No, she will shrug and drawl something like, *Nonsense, it is only masculine urges, quite natural, dear Gareth is such a rake*—causing Lady Greyshott to have the most enjoyable fit of the vapours—and everyone will laugh sycophantically at her outspoken foreign ways.'

'Off you go, then,' Gareth urged her, 'and we will take to the floor again, radiating defiance.'

'I must confess to feeling decidedly shaky,' Jessica admitted, wondering whether it was the situation or the fact that she was achingly aware of Gareth's body so close to hers. She found her eyes were fixed on the play of long muscles under the thin silk breeches and wrenched them away.

He filled her wine glass and passed it to her. 'More champagne,' he ordered. 'We will dance the next waltz and then, I think, we will leave.'

'Leave?' It came out as a squeak. 'Together?'

'Definitely more champagne.' He laughed at her. 'Don't look so appalled, Jessica—people will wonder what I am suggesting to you.'

'I doubt they will be wondering! I am sure their imaginations can supply an answer perfectly well,' she countered. 'Leave for where?' A couple passed their alcove, glancing in. She hastily adjusted her expression and raised her glass in a teasing toast, clinking it against the rim of his and holding his eyes until the inquisitive pair were gone. They were visible to virtually the entire room, she reminded herself, hoping that her face reflected sophisticated dalliance and not any of the other, real, emotions she was experiencing.

'I wish them well of their lurid fantasies,' Gareth said, raising a hand to brush an errant curl back from her cheek. The touch made her shiver and she turned her head fractionally, following the caressing fingers. 'In fact, I will take you home to Half Moon Street. And your chaste bed,' he added.

Was that an ironical twist to his lips as he said that,

she wondered, or a wry one? The thought of her own chaste bed held no appeal whatsoever, she realised, shocking herself profoundly. Gareth's no doubt thoroughly unchaste one, on the other hand…

'Shall we?' He stood, holding out his hand.

Oh, yes, please…Jessica forced a smile, put down her glass and placed her fingers in his as she got to her feet. Was he wondering why she was no doubt as pink as a peony? She hoped her scandalous thoughts were not written plain on her face for him to see, or that, if they were, he simply thought that she was overacting her part.

It was a waltz—it would have to be, she thought with a kind of resignation. The dance that would keep her in his arms throughout, the dance that would hold them face to face while she struggled to act the wanton and yet not let him see the truth of her desires in her eyes. It seemed, unless in her inexperience she was very much mistaken, that this situation had aroused Gareth to the state where he had no need to act his part. *But is it me, or is it simply male competition, the hunting urge, the need to best the other powerful males? And if it is me—surely not?—what then?*

'Why so solemn?' he murmured, taking her in his arms as they reached the floor. It seemed that the other couples left a space around them, despite the crush. Rejection—or was it that prurient curiosity demanded more room to watch?

'I am worrying about my steps,' she confided with earnest dissimulation.

'No need.' Gareth gathered her closer, his hand at her waist making her draw herself up, breathe in sharply, as surely as the strictest corset. No wonder unmarried girls needed permission before waltzing! 'I have you, just follow my lead.'

They swept into the dance and she was lost from the first note, the first step. Gareth was close—too close for propriety—he was strong, he was dominant and once again she found herself yielding to that in the most disconcerting manner.

They moved as one—in truth, she had little option. If she had fought against his direction, she knew he would simply have lifted her off her feet and carried her on with him, her skirts swirling round his long legs, her breasts crushed to his chest. As they almost were now, Jessica realised, thankful that at least this close stance meant she could not see his face.

Dizzyingly seduced by the music, the gliding sway of the dance, of Gareth's body hot and strong and close, Jessica could not have said coherently where she was in the room, or even if she was on her head or her heels. But Gareth, it seemed, was fully in control of things. As the last notes died away she came to herself and realised they were at the reception-room end of the ballroom and, as she glanced around, close to Eva and Lord Sebastian, who were standing talking to a group by the door.

'Make your farewells.' Gareth released her, then, taking her elbow, guided her towards the Grand Duchess. Heads turned. Jessica caught a glimpse of Maude, colour flying in her cheeks, standing just behind. Their eyes met and one of Maude's lids dropped in an unmistakable wink. She was enjoying herself.

'Your Serene Highness.' Jessica curtsied and Eva turned, one eyebrow raised in haughty amusement.

'My dear Mrs Carleton, you are enlivening our staid English ballroom, are you not?'

'Ma'am?' Jessica achieved a look that she thought combined injured innocence with knowing roguishness. 'I do hope not, although I confess to finding it all very new and strange. Might I be excused, ma'am?'

'A headache?' Eva enquired, tongue almost visibly in cheek.

'Yes, ma'am. Lord Standon has most kindly offered to escort me home.'

'I am sure he will look after you,' Eva said blandly. 'Will you call tomorrow afternoon?' It was a command.

'Yes, ma'am, thank you.' Another curtsy and they were walking away, out of the ballroom.

Gareth's carriage was a haven of blessed quiet and privacy after the staring eyes and whispered speculation. Jessica lay back against the squabs and sighed with relief. 'Oh, my goodness, how are we going to keep this up for weeks?'

'One appearance at a time,' Gareth said, folding himself down on to the seat opposite her. 'There is no need to put you under such pressure next time—a drive in the park is probably the logical progression.'

'And am I supposed to be under your protection by then?' she enquired, grimacing slightly at the euphemism.

'There is nothing to prevent you appearing to look around for a better offer.' Gareth sounded calm about the prospect.

'Indeed? So you can call someone out in defence of your property?'

'Is that how you see yourself?'

'It is how the world is being asked to see Mrs Carleton.'

'And you dislike that?'

'I most certainly dislike the sensation for myself, even though it is pretence.'

'And what exactly is it that you dislike, Jessica? The exchange of money for sexual favours I understand you would recoil from. But do you dislike also the idea of male possession?' There was something less calm about him now, although she could see as little of his face as she could that first evening, escaping from the brothel.

'Possession? Yes, that I do not find easy to accept. I have been independent for too long, my lord, to see it as anything but a form of servitude. Should I ever find myself in a relationship with a man, I would need equality of thought and action.'

'You are in a relationship now, with me,' he pointed out, his tone reasonable. Once again she was visited with the impression that he was controlling his breathing.

'You are my employer, Gareth. I expect to follow your direction, so far as I feel morally able to do so.' It was a shock to realise that she too was having to steady her diaphragm so that she could speak steadily. He was not touching her, yet it felt as though his scent and his presence enveloped her.

'Ah. The governess is back in control again, I see, not the actress who was swept up in her part.'

'I was not the only one swept up,' she retorted, unable to deny what he had said.

'True. But I do not have an inner governess.' He said it lightly, as a joke, but she could not hear from his voice that he was smiling. 'We are back already.' He leaned forward to look out of the window. 'All in darkness except the fanlight. Have your staff deserted you?'

'I told them to go to bed and leave a shielded lamp in the hall. I do not expect to need to call my dresser for this gown and I do not see why they should lose their sleep.'

The groom was opening the door and pulling out the steps. To her surprise Gareth jumped down before her, holding out his hand to help her alight. 'I'll walk back, Griffin,' he called up to the driver.

'Very good, my lord.'

Jessica stood on the pavement, her hand in Gareth's, watching the retreating vehicle. 'I have my key in here somewhere,' she said, freeing herself and delving in her reticule.

'May I come in for a moment, to discuss our plans for the next few days?'

It was most improper, but then who was there to censor her—except herself? And he was her employer, after all, and she had to be clear in her mind just how things were to proceed now.

'Certainly.' Jessica handed over the key and allowed herself to be shepherded over her own threshold into the dimly lit hall. 'I will just turn the lamp up.' She moved to do so, caught her heel on the trailing edge of her mantle and stumbled against Gareth.

His arms went round her, supporting her. And then he was no longer holding her up, he was crushing her against his chest and his mouth, hot and hungry and utterly irresistible, was on hers. And to her shock and delight, she was kissing him back.

Chapter Fifteen

~~~
&∞&
~~~

The feel of him, the scent of him, the need for him, were all familiar things, it seemed. Her body knew what she wanted without her conscious awareness. Her arms were around Gareth's neck, her fingers sought out the point where his hair was clipped close into his neck, knowing by instinct that their pressure—*just there*— would make him gasp against her lips. Her own lips parted easily under his and the thrust of his tongue into her mouth was not shocking, only deeply arousing.

Wanton, she touched her tongue to the invader, teasing, inciting, gasping as the heat spread down, down her breasts, peaking her nipples, down to her belly, down the insides of her thighs. She ached and she knew that only his body, his hands, would stop the torment and yet she wanted him to increase it, push her further.

The world spun somewhere beyond the darkness of her closed lids, dizzying her, but she was held tight, pressed back until his body moulded against the length of her and her shoulders were hard to the wall. Jessica threw her hands wide, groping for stability, for something to lace her fingers into and hold on to against the sensation that was sweeping her up.

The handful of hard, prickly stems made her cry out, jerking her back to reality as effectively as a thrown bucket of cold water. 'What? What's wrong?' In the half-light, his eyes black, his mouth swollen, Gareth looked primeval, ready to fight whatever had attacked her.

'Holly,' Jessica gasped, shaking her hand free of the arrangement she had set in the vase only that morning. 'Oh. Gareth.' She was still crushed against the wall, his chest rising and falling with the hard breaths he was controlling. 'Gareth—we shouldn't…'

'No. We shouldn't,' he agreed, his voice husky. He didn't move.

'I don't know what—'

'It's called desire,' he said flatly, his hands tightening on her waist.

'Gareth—I'm a virgin.' She was panting, aware of every inch of him against her, aware of the heat and hardness pressed to her stomach. Somehow, with a desperate effort of will, she stopped herself rubbing against him.

'Yes. It is all right, Jessica. I won't—'

'But I wish… Oh!' She buried her face in his shoulder. She wanted him desperately, knew she must not lie with him, yet the will was simply not there to push him away, walk away.

'I wish too,' he murmured against her hair, his grip suddenly gentle. 'So much.'

The gentleness almost undid her. Jessica felt tears prickling the back of her eyes as she reached up and encircled his shoulders with her arms again, nuzzling into his neck.

'Hell,' he muttered under his breath and scooped her

up in his arms, shouldered the door open and carried her through into the dark of the drawing room.

'Gareth!'

'Shh,' he soothed, setting her down on the *chaise*. 'I want to kiss you, Jessica, that is all, just kisses, I swear.'

Just kisses. There was no *just* about it. How could something like kissing be so complex, so rich? It seemed like a simple thing, an exchange of touch, but Gareth made it an intricate bartering of breath and of heat, of taste and of touch. Somehow he had shed his coat, her own fingers were tangled in the once-immaculate folds of his neckcloth, searching for the skin beneath. And then he released her mouth.

'Ah...' Jessica sank back against the cushions, trembling. He had stopped as he had promised, he would leave her now. But how was she to move again when her body was limp and yet tense all at once, when the aching demand for more—anything, something—racked her?

Then his lips found the warm, sensitive skin beneath her ear and he began to kiss and lick down the column of her neck as she arched her head away to give him access, then up to catch the lobe between his teeth, biting gently until she sobbed his name and he murmured reassurance in words she could not catch, words that both soothed and inflamed her.

The torment of his mouth trailed down, over the curve of her breasts, down until his tongue could flicker around the point where the peaks dipped into the dark, perfumed valley between them. His hands were moving and Jessica was suddenly aware that the bodice of her gown was open, that only the fine lawn of her chemise was veiling her nipples, thrust up to meet his questing mouth by the boning of her corset.

'Gareth!' She did not know whether it was a protest or a plea, but as his lips fastened on the tip it became a mindless whimper of pleasure. The strange tension racking her intensified, deepened, became more complex as his tongue laved first one aching nub and then the other. *Only kisses*, she told herself in the part of her rational mind that was still struggling against sensation and instinct. *Only kisses.*

Then he nipped her right nipple between his teeth, so gently as she arched up beneath his weight. His tongue flickered, stroked the imprisoned, aching flesh and everything came undone, unravelled, as though something had both imploded and exploded inside her all at once. There was light, there was darkness, there was Gareth's voice a long way off and then there was nothing but a long, delicious fall into utter limpness.

'Jessica?' She lay in his arms in total abandon, her eyes shut. In the shaft of light from the hall he could see her lips were parted, sweetly curved. Colour stained her cheeks and her breast, her heart beat against his palm like a wild thing. 'My God.' Gareth stared at her, awed and a little shaken. How could he have guessed that she would be so sensual, so responsive? He had touched her nowhere but her breasts. His palms curved protectively under their weight, cupping them as she moaned.

'Hush, sweet.' He bent and kissed her, then stood on legs that were strangely unsteady and went to get the lamp from the hall. She blinked in the light as he brought it in, the picture of sweet wanton disarray on the sensuously curving *chaise*. He knelt beside her and gently re-arranged her bodice lest she be embarrassed when she came to herself.

'Gareth? What happened? What was that?' She sat up, pushing her tumbled hair back from her face and reached out a hand to touch his cheek as though to reassure herself that this was not a dream. Or, he thought with a sudden twinge of conscience, to confirm that it was all too real.

'It was a climax.' She blinked at him. 'An orgasm.'

Her blush showed that she understood what he was saying, even as she shook her head in puzzlement. 'But—we didn't make love.'

'No.' Gareth sat back on his heels, fighting the instinct to get up and go, flee before this became any more complicated, get somewhere alone where he could think. But if course he could not. This was Jessica; she was completely inexperienced and she was his responsibility. 'That was most unusual. You are a sensual woman, Jessica. A very sensual and responsive woman.' He let the back of his hand trail up her forearm and she shivered. Gareth pushed on, determined to make things clear. 'Normally that would not happen until we had become considerably more intimate.'

'And you promised we would not.' She frowned, causing a little line to appear between her brows. He half-lifted his hand to smooth it away, then stopped himself. 'I'm sorry.'

'*Sorry?* Jessica, it is deeply flattering to a man that a woman would respond so when he caresses her.'

'Really?' She sat up more, interested, her embarrassment giving way before her habitual instinct to learn.

When he nodded, she smiled and something knotted tight inside him, reminding him that he was deeply aroused and completely unsatisfied. Something must have shown in his face, for the frown reappeared. 'What about you?'

Gareth did not pretend to misunderstand her. 'It will pass, you do not need to concern yourself.'

'You won't go to that horrid brothel?' she worried.

'No, I promise not to.' He got to his feet and went to the mirror, taking the lamp to set on the mantelshelf while he retied his neck cloth.

In the glass he could see her swing her legs down from the *chaise* and twitch her bodice properly closed. 'Gareth—this isn't going to happen after every time we appear together, is it?'

'Certainly not!' He jabbed himself painfully in his Adam's apple with his tie pin and swore under his breath. 'We both got rather carried away with the atmosphere and the playacting.' *Only it wasn't playacting, that's the damnable thing. I want her, I want her in my arms and in my bed and it would not take much to have her there.* He looked up and met her eyes in the reflection. *And she'd hate me for it afterwards. I cannot, must not ruin her.*

'Yes, that must be it,' Jessica agreed. 'Does reacting like that mean I am naturally wanton?'

'No,' Gareth said firmly, racking his brains for an analogy that would stop a virtuous, chaste lady worrying about such things. 'It just means that you have an innate talent—like good pitch for music, or a true sense of colour.'

She shot him a somewhat quizzical glance, but did not question him further, simply stating, 'It is going to feel very awkward when I meet you again.'

'No more so than if we had both become rather tipsy and had shared indiscreet confidences,' he said easily, getting into his coat again. Without his valet's assistance it was not a speedy business and provided a welcome distraction from Jessica's unsettling observations. 'I will come and collect you to go driving at half past ten tomorrow, if that is convenient.'

'Yes, whatever you think is best.' She stood too, smoothing down her skirts with an unconsciously graceful gesture that had him hardening all over again. 'I have been summoned to Eva's presence in the afternoon, if you recall.'

'She will probably give us marks out of ten for our performance at the ball,' he joked, one hand on the door knob. 'Can you bolt the door after me?'

'Yes, I can reach.' She joined him in the doorway, too close for comfort, her subtle scent rising from her heated body, almost overwhelming to his sensitised nerves. 'Good night, Gareth.' The brush of her fingers on his cheek burned and he turned abruptly, wrenched the door open and stepped out into the blessed cold dampness of the night.

Jessica sat primly in the drawing room, her gloved hands folded in her lap, her saucy bonnet on the *chaise* beside her. She had made herself come and sit on the offending article of furniture while she waited for Gareth, unsure whether it was a form of penance or a piece of outrageous self-indulgence to place herself where last night's earth-shattering improprieties had occurred.

She could not be said by even the most charitable observer to be in the best of looks, she decided, glancing up at her own reflection in the overmantel mirror. One could not drink champagne at one's first, very stressful ball, then indulge in outrageously immodest behaviour with a gentleman and in consequence spend the night tossing and turning, wrestling with conscience and desire, and expect to escape without dark shadows under one's eyes and a wan complexion.

There was no doubt that Gareth would have slept perfectly well. He was, after all, a sophisticated man of the world. Jessica had worried a little about his feelings. She, at least, had experienced that exquisite, shattering, release; he had not. He had promised not to visit the brothel, and she knew, although she had no right to have asked it of him, that he would take that as a promise to visit none of them. Would the chill night air have had a calming effect on his passions? She had heard that immersion in cold water had that effect on a man. But of course, one could not ask.

Unable to sit still any longer, she jumped to her feet and began to pace. She had realised, as the clock had struck four that morning, that there was no doubting that she desired Lord Standon—it was not simply the heated delusions brought on by their playacting. In fact, she was probably suffering from some sort of infatuation for him. This was a shameful thing for a well-conducted, rational, professional female of her age to be admitting to, but one might as well be honest with oneself.

The chief thing was not to let him guess. Despite his reassuring words, he would naturally have the impression by now that she was a wanton who was not fit to undertake the education, moral or academic, of young ladies. If she were to disabuse him of that—and for some reason it was particularly important that Gareth

Morant thought well of her—she must be a model of rectitude from now on.

Which was going to be a problem, considering that she was dressed in a clinging garment that could, at best, be described as dashing, and was supposed to be spending the next hour appearing to flirt heavily with him in public.

Gareth himself was, of course, an experienced man and would not be thinking anything of what had passed—other than to hope, she supposed, that she was not foolishly besotted with him.

He was very prompt. Jessica snatched up her bonnet as the knocker sounded and went to stand before the mirror to fix it.

'Lord Standon, madam,' Hedges intoned from the doorway.

Her theory had been that it would be less embarrassing to make eye contact in the mirror. It certainly solved the question of the correct etiquette. How *did* one greet a gentleman in whose arms you had shuddered into ecstasy? With a brisk handshake? A kiss on the cheek?

'Good morning, Gareth,' she said instead, tying the satin ribbons under her chin with a jaunty bow and taking her time patting the curls at her temples into place.

'Good morning.' He sounded perfectly normal. A little cool, perhaps, although he smiled as their eyes met. 'You are very prompt.'

'I was thinking the same of you.' She picked up her gloves and reached for her reticule.

'I have taken the liberty of instructing my man of business to call upon you.' He picked up her pelisse and held it for her to slip into. His hands were efficient, adjusting it at her shoulders, and then he stepped back and lifted her vast muff, waiting while she did up the buttons.

'Thank you. But why?'

'I thought you would want him to start looking for a house for you. You can discuss which towns or parts of the country you feel might be suitable and he can start a search right away. You will want everything arranged in advance of the end of the Season, I am certain.'

'Of course. How thoughtful,' Jessica knew her tone was colourless and forced a polite smile. Inside, a hot ball of mortification gathered in her stomach. *He wants to make certain I leave as soon as this is over. After last night he wants to make certain I understand my place and am reminded of our bargain.*

'Not at all. His name is Wayman. Tell him everything you feel is important in the house you want—number of chambers, gardens and so forth.'

'Thank you.' Jessica led the way to the door. Gareth had not appeared the slightest bit discommoded by the sight of the *chaise* even. It just went to show that he placed no importance upon what had happened, other than as a warning that Miss Jessica Gifford had to be neatly, and generously, disposed of after the Season was over. 'Where shall we drive?'

'Hyde Park, I think. We want to make the maximum impact. That is a most fetching ensemble, if I may say so.'

'Isn't it?' She managed a much more creditable smile at his admiration. The outfit was cut far too tight in the bodice for comfort, had far too much ruching and laces around the neck and hem for modish restraint and the bonnet was positively pert. The overall effect was that

Mrs Carleton wished to attract as much male attention to her person as possible without actual indecency.

'What a handsome rig!' The rakish sporting carriage standing at the kerb had three black geldings harnessed unicorn in the shafts with a small tiger in red-and-blue striped jockey jacket at the head of the lead horse.

It attempted to bite him as they emerged and he dodged the big yellow teeth, grimacing at his employer. 'He's a right limb of Satan, this one, guv'nor. I told you how he'd be if you gave him lead position.'

'He will be fine, Jimmy.' Gareth handed Jessica up on to the buttoned leather of the seat. It was dyed deep blue to match the wheels, which were picked out in red like the rug he tucked around her knees. He got up beside her, gathered the reins into his left hand, took the whip in his right and nodded to the tiger. 'Let them go.'

With a muttered epitaph about the lead horse, the lad scampered round and swung himself up behind as they clattered over the cobbles down to Piccadilly.

Gareth had his hands full—even Jessica, with next to no understanding of horses or driving, could see that. The lead horse was, indeed, set on rebellion and the two behind were nervous of its plunging and head tossing. 'See, guv'nor?' Jimmy observed from his perch. His accent was pure London. 'Said you should put Nightshade up in lead.'

'If I thought this lady was interested in your observations, Jimmy, I would encourage you to continue to lecture me.' Gareth lifted his hand slightly and used the whip—the merest flick—and the leader settled. The turn right into the busy highway was accomplished safely and Jessica let out the breath she had not realised she was holding. 'As it is, you will kindly hold your tongue.'

There was a faint *humph* from behind Jessica. She glanced sideways and caught the twitch of a smile at the corner of Gareth's mouth. Not a tyrant with his servants, then. But, having seen him with his butler, she had not imagined that he would be. 'What is the name of the lead horse?' she enquired, grateful for a safe topic of conversation.

'Nero—not very original, given his colour. Although I am considering renaming him Beelzebub.'

'But Nero was a tyrant,' Jessica pointed out. 'It does indicate his character.'

'He is not tyrannising over me,' Gareth said with gritted teeth as the animal took vast exception to a sedan chair and did its best to get a leg over the traces. There was a short battle from which Gareth emerged the un-doubted victor.

'You drive very well.' It was a safe conclusion that any man would be gratified with female admiration for that skill.

'Flattery, Mrs Carleton?'

'Of course,' she teased demurely. The hot knot of mortification inside had dissolved slightly, although she still felt as though every nerve was exposed, she was so alert for the slightest hint that Gareth was thinking about last night and worrying about her feelings for him. But it was not flattery. His hand was strong and sensitive on the reins, his reactions almost supernaturally sharp as he assessed the crowded thoroughfare ahead for triggers for the horse's skittish bad temper.

'Here we are.' He guided the team between the park gates and up the long carriage drive a few yards before reining them in. 'Down you get, Jimmy.'

'Wait here, shall I, guv'nor?' The lad jumped to the raked tan surface and stood, head tilted up under his peaked cap, waiting for his orders.

'Yes. Don't get into any trouble.' Gareth drove off, apparently oblivious to the snort of derision from his tiger.

'He worships you,' Jessica observed.

'I rescued him from a back slum, had him scrubbed up, beat the worst of the swearing out of him and let him do what he adores, be with horses. Of course he worships me,' Gareth said cynically.

'How did you come across him?' she asked, ignoring the cynicism for the moment. She would not let him get away with that, but now was not the time to challenge it. 'Do you often frequent back slums?'

'I do in pursuit of cutpurses who knock a lady into the gutter and make off with her reticule. I drove straight into the rookery after them. The alleys are narrow—too narrow for a horse-drawn vehicle, as I rapidly discovered. I got in as far as I could, then jumped down and took the whip to them. By the time I got back Jimmy was holding the team, swearing at all comers and offering to black their daylights if they laid a hand on my prime 'uns. I can tell a natural with horses when I see one. He told me—in between biting the coin I'd given him as a reward—that he was an orphan. So after we got the team backed out I threw him up, brought him back and he's been with me ever since.'

'That was good of you,' she said warmly, putting a hand over his gloved fist on the reins. Gareth went still, his eyes steady on his team. With care, Jessica lifted her hand away and placed it in her lap. 'You are a generous employer.'

'It is in my own interests to be so.' Still refusing to warm to her praise, he steered the team right along one of the tracks.

'Indeed? As it is in your interests to chair that charity for orphans that I have heard about? The orphans who you invite down to your country house and allow to play cricket on your lawns?'

He smiled, accepting that her persistence had defeated him. 'Very well, I am a paragon amongst employers and the foremost philanthropist in the land.'

'Now I never said that!' Jessica laughed and suddenly all was right with the world again.

Chapter Sixteen

Gareth's grin broadened at her teasing and the shadows of the morning fled, leaving her relaxed and happy.

The timing of this show of harmony could not have been better. A barouche containing two heavily befurred matrons was approaching them and Gareth dropped his whip into its ring to be able to raise his hat to them. He was answered by two frosty nods and stares of penetrating disapproval. 'They are having a good look while they are about it.' She was not sure whether she was affronted or amused.

'Of course. The sight of a scarlet woman is always a source of titillation. Good morning, Lady Bathlomew!'

'They do not know that I am scarlet,' Jessica protested. 'I may be merely extremely forward or simply ignorant of correct behaviour.'

'They live in hope of a rich scandal broth,' Gareth said with a chuckle. 'Mere ignorance is not at all entertaining. Here come some of your gentlemen admirers— I expect you to exert your best efforts to make them extremely jealous of me.'

Or possibly the other way round, Jessica thought with a flash of rebellion. If he felt for her one iota of what she was beginning to feel for him… She removed one hand from the muff and waved coyly at Lord Chevering on his flashy bay. At his side Mr Sayle looked, in her opinion, far more the gentleman on a neat hack, his simple riding dress in contrast to the younger man's padded shoulders and nipped-in waist.

'Good morning, gentlemen! See how fortunate I am—Lord Standon is letting me drive behind his lovely team.' She distributed a sunny smile between them, but let her fingers rest fleetingly on Gareth's wrist. Two pairs of eyes followed the gesture.

'If I had know you wished to drive, Mrs Carleton, I would have called for you myself,' Lord Chevering declared.

'Driving what?' Gareth enquired with interest. 'Good morning Sayle.'

'I should have acquired a rig,' the young man blustered while his companion acknowledged Gareth's greeting.

'Oh. You don't have a carriage, Lord Chevering?' Jessica enquired with a little *moue* of disappointment. 'I suppose it would be very expensive.' She lingered a little on the last word.

'Perhaps you would care to ride?' Mr Sayle enquired diffidently. 'I have just acquired a very pretty grey mare you might like to try.'

'I shall be mounting Mrs Carleton myself,' Gareth interjected firmly. There was, of course, nothing wrong with the statement, unless one counted its proprietorial tone, but there was a certain something about the exchange of glances between the three men that left

Jessica feeling she had missed the point. And then she got it—and did not know how she managed not to turn beet red. He didn't mean mounting her on a horse, he meant mounting…. *Oh, outrageous!* And there was no way she could punish him for it without revealing that she understood the *double entendre*.

'Well, I would like Mr Sayle to show me his grey mare,' she said pettishly.

'Mrs Carleton, I have just said you will ride my horses.' Gareth's tone was ominous.

'I shall ride what I like,' she returned brightly, with a twinkling smile at the other men as if to invite them to admire her show of rebellion. 'You do not own me, my lord.'

That put the cat amongst the pigeons, she thought, suddenly enjoying herself, and knowing full well she was treading on dangerous ground, on the shifting sands between reality and their make-believe. 'Indeed not, ma'am,' Gareth said calmly, 'but just now I *am* in the driving seat. Good day to you, Chevering, Sayle.

'What in blazes do you think you are dong?' he demanded, the minute they were out of earshot. The sunshine seemed to vanish again. What was the matter with the man? He had seemed to welcome her teasing, they had agreed that she needed to flirt with the other men—now he was being a dog in the manger. Where had his sense of humour gone?

'I was shopping around,' Jessica replied in a sweet tone designed to infuriate. 'Don't you think it would be a little suspicious if I surrendered to the charms of your wallet without inspecting any others?'

'You are showing a suspicious talent for harlotry,' Gareth retorted. He sounded as though he meant it.

The amusement that had been bubbling up vanished. He was angry, and, suddenly, so was she. Presumably he was jealous, despite the fact that this was all a hoax. *Typical man*, she thought bitterly. She wanted to hurt him, but she did not understand why, although it was somehow connected with what had happened last night and the snub he had dealt her that morning.

'I am using my intelligence, my lord. That was one of the reasons you selected me, was it not? And I have listened to the advice of your cousins and your friends about how I should behave. Or do you think I have somehow misrepresented my character to you?'

'No, I do not,' Gareth said, breaking off to swear under his breath as Nero, sensing his driver was distracted, shied at a dead leaf blowing in the wind. He got the animal under control again. 'I said a talent for harlotry, not experience. After last night I am quite clear that I am dealing with a virgin spinster school teacher, if I ever doubted it.'

'Oh!' It was the exact truth—that was what she was. But it sounded like an insult—and when she thought about what had passed between them only hours before, Jessica decided it most certainly was one. 'Stop this carriage this instant, my lord!'

'Why?' His attention was still on the sweating horse, who had seen a yapping lapdog and was gathering his haunches under him for another display of temperament.

'Because I intend to get down.'

'What? You cannot do that here—' he took the whip out of its holder and caught the horse a glancing touch on the shoulder. At any other time Jessica would have admired his skill at missing the other horses.

'Yes, I can. And don't beat that poor horse.' She dropped her vast muff to the floor, gathered up her skirts and jumped, taking advantage of Nero deciding he was going to stand stock still in the middle of the carriage drive.

'Je—Mrs Carleton, get back here!' Something of his mood must have reached the team, for they suddenly stopped their tricks and stood placidly, as though butter would not melt in their mouths.

Jessica snatched her muff out of the carriage, thrust her hands into its snug depths and stalked to the pedestrian path at the side of the carriage drive, nose in the air. She had no intention of walking off out of the park and finding her own way home—even Mrs Carleton would not walk the streets of London unattended. No, she just wanted to teach Gareth Morant a lesson. She would find Jimmy and talk to him until Gareth turned the team—which, given the press of carriages, was going to take him a while—and came in pursuit.

The tiger was leaning against a tree, whittling a stick with an evil-looking knife and whistling tunelessly between his teeth while he watched the world go by. 'Jimmy?'

'Eh?' He dropped the stick and stood upright, staring at her. 'Where's the guv'nor, mam?'

'Coming.' Jessica waved a hand in the vague direction of the carriages. 'I felt like walking, but of course I cannot do so without a footman. Will you escort me?'

'Me, mam?' He tugged down his frogged jockey jacket self-consciously and produced a gap-toothed grin. 'Cor.'

'How old are you, Jimmy?' Jessica began to stroll along, keeping an eye out for Gareth. It wasn't that she wanted to provoke him to compete fury exactly...

'Not sure. Fourteen?' he hazarded, trotting along at her side.

'And what do you want to do when you grow up?' His brown eyes were sharp and intelligent and his movements alert; he was a bright child, she decided.

'Be head stableman for the guv'nor. Lord Standon,' he corrected himself. 'Old Franklin'll be past it by then, I reckons.'

Probably Old Franklin was a hale and hearty thirty-year-old, but Jessica refrained from saying so. Jimmy was proving an excellent distraction from having to worry about what Gareth was thinking and what she was feeling.

'Can you read and write, Jimmy? Do your figures?'

'No, mam.'

'Hmm. Well, you will need to if you are going to run a big stables.'

The lad pushed his lower lip out dubiously. 'Ain't no one to teach me.'

'I shall mention it to his lordship. There is sure to be someone on his staff who can teach you.' She wished she could do it herself, it would be a delight to work with such cheerful intelligence.

'Jimmy!' It was Gareth. The team, looking remarkably docile, was drawn up by the side of the path. 'What do you think you are doing?'

'Being a footman, guv'nor.'

'Naturally I could not walk in the park unescorted,' Jessica observed demurely, keeping a wary eye on his lordship's countenance as they walked over to the carriage. The lad helped her up, then scrambled to reach his perch. 'Jimmy has been very obliging.'

'The lady says I should learn my letters, me lord.'

'Mrs Carleton,' Gareth corrected. 'It is very kind of her to take an interest,' he added drily.

'Jimmy has ambitions. He will not achieve them without his letters and his numbers. Surely there is someone on your staff who can teach him? It need not interfere with his work.'

'You are quite correct, ma'am. Jimmy—you will tell Watson I said he's to teach you. And work hard, he's got a broad palm for slack lads.'

'Yes, guv'nor!'

'Get down here and run back to the house. I won't need you again today.'

He tooled the team out of Hyde Park, up Piccadilly and into Green Park. Watching his face, Jessica had the uneasy feeling she was in for a lecture. Well, if he didn't want her taking an interest in his servant, he only had to say so.

'Where are we going?' she ventured.

'Somewhere peaceful where I can be assured you will be attempting neither to seduce young gentlemen nor to tutor my tiger.' Gareth spoke with a satirical edge to his voice, which might have masked either amusement or irritation.

'I miss teaching,' Jessica said, suddenly discovering that it was true. 'He is a nice lad.'

'Yes.' There was a long pause while Gareth was apparently engrossed in pointing his leader precisely to enter a narrower track leading into a grove of trees. He reined in and thrust the whip handle into its stand before looping the reins around it and shifting in his seat to look at Jessica squarely. His face held the calm expression she had come to think of as typical of him, but there was something in the depths of his eyes she was not certain she could read. Puzzlement? Surely the very ordinary Miss Gifford was not a source of confusion for Lord Standon?

'What, exactly, was going on back there?' he asked. She opened her mouth to speak and he held up one hand. 'No. I know what we each did, what we each said. But why? We were both angry and I wish I understood why.'

'I was annoyed by your *double entendre*,' Jessica admitted before she had time to think about where that might lead.

'My—ah.' He grimaced. 'Providing your mounts?'

'Mounting me,' she corrected grimly.

'I did not think you would understand.' He was, at least, looking reasonably penitent.

'I may be inexperienced, but I am not quite the innocent you imagine Gareth. I can work things out without a diagram. And my business is words.'

'Yes. Apparently so.' He stared past her left ear for long enough for her to begin to fidget. 'My instinct is to warn them off,' he said abruptly.

'Because of our masquerade?'

'Because you are under my protection.' He grimaced. 'Not that I was doing a very good job of protecting you last night. Which I suppose is what is playing havoc with my temper,' he added thoughtfully.

'You hardly ravished me,' Jessica pointed out. 'It does take two.' What devil got into her she did not know, but she added, 'I enjoyed it. I would have liked to do it again.'

If she had hoped to take him completely aback, she

could not have succeeded better. For once, Lord Standon was deprived of a ready answer. 'That would be unwise,' he said at length, with the wary air of a man talking a dangerous lunatic down off the edge of a roof. 'It is not always easy to keep such things within bounds.'

'Oh, I didn't mean I thought it *wise*,' Jessica assured him. 'Or fair to you, of course—please do not think I am not very well aware of the extent of your self-restraint. I just meant it would be nice.'

'Nice.' For a moment she wondered if he was about to lecture her, then Gareth threw back his head and laughed, a full-blooded, genuine shout of amusement that had the horses sidling. 'Miss Gifford, I am beginning to wonder whether my life was simply very dull before I met you, or whether I simply did not understand how to enjoy it.'

Jessica's green eyes were amused but cautious as she watched him gain control of himself. 'I doubt it was dull, my lord,' she said drily. No, of course it hadn't been— he did not need her to remind him that he had a privileged and enjoyable life. But before he had not had the stimulus of Miss Gifford's cool regard, the novelty of being on the receiving end of unspoken disapproval or the delight of sparring with a woman who was not only intelligent but who held him in no awe whatsoever and who stirred his blood like none he could recall before.

Gareth made himself focus on Jessica's words and the feelings behind them and not on the ache of need settling low in his belly. She was, as they had discovered last night, a highly sensual young woman. It was no wonder she wished to explore that sensuality further. She trusted him; he did not flatter himself that she had been waiting for Prince Charming all her life and he was the answer to her dreams

'So nice that we had best be careful over the next few weeks,' he cautioned. 'It was not just pleasant for you. I enjoyed it.' The little smile that twitched at the corner of her mouth made him want to lean in and taste her. That taste had not left him, he realised, since their first encounter when the scent of her naked skin had filled his nostrils and his lips had touched her hair. He had kissed her and told himself that was the end of it; but last night had proved it was not. His reactions to the other men proved it too. He was jealous.

'Men are unreliable creatures, too driven by our base animal instincts to rely on.'

'I trust you,' she said simply, her dark lashes sweeping down to veil her eyes. He wanted to touch them with his tongue tip, was swaying towards her even as he thought it.

'Then your much-vaunted common sense is at fault, Miss Gifford.' Gareth sat bolt upright. 'We are close now; we will become closer. We must paint the picture of a couple who are not only on the verge of lovemaking, but who are lovers in fact. And the moment we are alone we must draw back from that, suppress the instincts that tell us to indulge in that sensual pleasure.'

'You are afraid that if we fail, then there is the danger of—' She broke off frowning, the fullness of her lower lip caught for a moment by a sharp tooth as she bit it in thought. 'Of an emotional attachment on my side.'

'I—' It was what he did fear. That and the fact that one

did not seduce innocent young ladies of good birth and then pension them off as one did a discarded mistress.

'I am an educationalist, Gareth. I thought I simply wanted the freedom to be my own woman and not be at the beck and call of an employer. Now I know I still wish to teach, but on my own terms. I am not looking for a lover or a husband.' That was said with surprising emphasis. 'But that does not mean I wish to renounce the company of men.'

'I did not think it was my company you desired,' he said, teasing, and was rewarded by a blush and a dimpling smile.

'Gareth! I meant that I am not asking that we become lovers—certainly not. I am just saying that if something like last night happens again, I am not going to go into a decline about it. Nor would I presume upon it to make demands.'

Her intention, he realised with a sudden insight, was to reassure him as much as herself. 'We are alert to the strains this strange playacting puts upon us now,' he said, choosing not to answer her words directly. 'Thank you for being so frank; we can act our roles more easily now, I think.'

'Providing you do not provoke any gentlemen into a duel,' she retorted tartly.

'I shall try not to,' he promised, gathering up the reins and heading the team back the way they had come. 'We had better give the impression that a liaison has begun as soon as possible then.'

'No one will dare to challenge you for what you have already claimed?' she asked.

'I would hope not.' Both Sebastian and Ashe had

fought duels. He never had and had no desire to do so. But if anyone harassed or insulted Jessica, he would have no hesitation in meeting them, he realised with a shock. 'The evening we met I was complaining of being bored,' he added inconsequentially, and beside him Jessica laughed richly.

Chapter Seventeen

'You have made an excellent beginning,' Eva said warmly. Far from the strict Grand Duchess who had ordered Mrs Carleton's presence that afternoon, she was lounging on a *chaise*, her hair down, clad in a sumptuous negligée and surrounded by fashion magazines.

'Are you unwell?' Jessica enquired, puzzling over why Eva appeared to be resting at three in the afternoon.

'No.' She placed a hand over her stomach and grimaced. 'Merely very sick this morning. I am fine now, but I am humouring Sebastian, who is flapping around as though the house were on fire. This is a man who climbs down sheer castle walls on the end of a rope and conducts knife fights in French alleyways, mind you. I thought it was women who became mildly addled with pregnancy, not their husbands, but Bel says Ashe is just as bad.'

'Lying on a sofa nibbling almond biscuits and reading *La Belle Assemblée* isn't such a sacrifice,' Jessica suggested.

'I don't know why I bother with fashion journals—

I won't fit into a thing soon. But never mind that, Bel and Maude will be here in a minute and we want to hear all about it.' On her words the boudoir door opened to admit the friends, Maude beaming. She dropped her muff and flew to embrace Jessica.

'You were wonderful! Papa is beside himself. He pressed a fifty-pound note into my hand this morning and told me to go and do some shopping to cheer myself up.' She sank elegantly into a chair and spoiled the effect by pulling off her bonnet, heeling off her shoes and curling her feet up under her.

'Yes, but you told me he said to buy something to dazzle Gareth in, so he hasn't given up,' Bel pointed out, entering more moderately and giving Jessica and Eva a peck on the cheek.

'No. Though he keeps moaning about how he was mistaken in him, and what a disappointment he is being and how he must take him in hand.'

'I'd like to see that,' Jessica observed appreciatively.

'I have talked him into inviting Gareth to the theatre tomorrow night. I suggested a nice party in our new box— you and Ashe and Eva and Sebastian and Gareth and me.'

'Would that be your new box at the Unicorn?' Eva asked. 'How did you persuade him to rent that?'

'I didn't. That's what I've spent my fifty pounds on.'

'So cheap?' Bel was peeling off her gloves, but looked up in surprise.

'Lord, no! I've had to raid my quarterly allowance as well. But it isn't the Opera House, after all.'

'And what will you tell your papa when he asks why his present has gone on that?' Jessica asked. She did not know if Maude had confided her infatuation with Mr

Hurst to the others, and realised she had not when she received a mischievous smile in return, but no mention of the theatre's owner.

'I told him I was taking a great interest in drama. He is too worried about Gareth to question it at the moment.' Maude helped herself to an almond biscuit and settled back. 'Anyway, we must warn Gareth to refuse on the grounds of an earlier engagement, and then he must take you. I have hired the box opposite for the evening.'

'An excellent plan,' Eva approved. 'What is the piece?'

'Goodness, I have no idea.'

Jessica picked up *The Times* from the table beside her and scanned the columns. 'Here we are. *The Duenna* with Mr Sinclair as Carlos and Miss Stephens as Clara. With a farce and other entertainments.'

'Oh, that's a Spanish romantic comedy. The men will hate it,' Bel observed. 'But it is a good plan. Now, Jessica, we are all dying to know—what happened last night?'

'You saw. I flirted with various men and then Gareth arrived and we were together and caused something of a stir and then we left.' Was she blushing? She hoped not.

'But what came over him?' Maude demanded. 'It was wonderfully effective, all that masterful stalking about, but that was not how we had planned it. I was completely taken aback.'

'Exactly. Everyone was taken by surprise, including me, so it seemed more realistic.'

'Realistic is certainly the word.' Eva sounded amused. 'And what happened after you left?'

'He took me home.'

'Indeed.' Eva narrowed her eyes and Jessica plastered

a bland smile on her face. 'Gareth appeared really quite…attracted.'

Bel cleared her throat and tipped her head warningly towards Maude, who caught the gesture. 'Are you asking if he seduced Jessica?' she demanded.

Now she was blushing, she could feel the heat. 'He kissed me goodnight,' she said repressively. 'It was to help get us in the mood.' The other three bit their lips, struggled with themselves and then burst into laughter. 'Oh, you know what I mean!' Jessica said crossly.

'Yes, of course,' Eva agreed, getting her giggles under control. 'Did you enjoy it?'

Jessica glared, on the point of refusing to answer. Then the urge to confide got the better of her. 'Yes.' They all stared expectantly. 'He was very good at it.'

'Goodness.' Maude stared at her. 'Gareth? I never thought of him like that.'

'Well, I suggest you do not start now,' Jessica said in her best governess tone. 'We can do without any further complications.' The stab of jealousy that shot through her at the thought of Maude in Gareth's embrace shocked her. If he ever stopped thinking about Maude like a younger sister, then why wouldn't he fall head over heels for her? She was so lovely. But should she encourage Maude or—

'I wouldn't dream of it. Gareth? I love him dearly, but he is so sensible,' Maude said firmly. 'And old.'

'*Old?*' Jessica stared at her. 'He cannot be thirty yet. I am sure he is no older than your Mr Hurst.'

'He has a loyal defender,' Bel observed. 'Maude, have you got the theatre tickets for Jessica and Gareth?'

'Oh. No, I left them in my reticule on the hall table.'

'Better go and get them now while we think of it.' Bel got to her feet. 'I wanted to ask Eva's housekeeper something, I've just remembered. I'll come with you.'

'Has Bel just tactfully removed Maude for a purpose?' Jessica demanded as the door shut behind them.

'I expect she feels I should give you a little warning about men.'

'Gareth has been a perfect gentleman,' Jessica said hotly, remembering with shame her fears about finding herself in the power of a nobleman.

'Of course. And you are a very intelligent and well-conducted gentlewoman. Which is exactly how I would have described myself before I first came into contact with a male Ravenhurst.' There was a reminiscent smile playing around Eva's lips. 'All I will say is that if you ever need any…assistance, I am here for you.'

Jessica sat staring at her own hands, which seemed to have twisted her handkerchief into a corkscrew. The knotted tangle seemed simple compared to the swirling thoughts that jumbled her brain. Ruthlessly she unpicked them. She was employed, for a generous fee, to impersonate Gareth's lover. *Impersonate, is the key word.* And she had discovered a strong physical attraction to him. In fact, if she were to be honest with herself, a *tendre* for him. And he had implied that he was not precisely indifferent to her. And now Lady Sebastian was implying that Jessica's situation was in some way comparable with hers when she met Lord Sebastian. *But they are married now…* What was Eva suggesting? That such a thing was a possibility? Or that she might let herself believe it and would need help in extracting herself?

The latter, of course. She had just been given a

friendly warning, not that she needed one. Governesses did not marry earls, even if they wanted to. Which she did not. Life was hard enough without idiotic daydreams.

'Thank you,' she said with a bright smile. 'I am very grateful for your support in all of this. I was saying to Gareth this morning that I miss teaching already; I am sure I do not know how I would get through to the end of the Season without your help, and Bel's, of course.'

'You miss teaching?' Maude came back into the room. 'Here are the tickets for the box before I forget. But teaching? Really? I would hate it—when I think of the trial I must have been to my poor governesses, I shudder at the thought of things being reversed.'

'I miss it so much I wish I could teach Gareth's tiger his letters.' Jessica tucked the ticket away safely. 'What should I wear tomorrow night?'

'Good God.' Gareth stood stock still in the middle of the drawing room and stared at her.

'What's wrong?' Jessica cast a harried glance at the mirror. She had thought the ivory moiré-silk evening gown rather lovely, although she was nervous about moving too abruptly or taking in a deep breath, the neckline was so low and her lacing so tight.

'Wrong? Nothing. You look spectacular.' He was stalking round her, inspecting every angle. 'Fantastic. I am going to have to go armed to keep off my rivals, I can see.'

'Nonsense.' Jessica felt quite flurried. True, the hairdresser had spent the afternoon on her hair and her dresser had exerted every trick in her considerable repertoire—Jessica had drawn the line at the attempt to pad out her bosom with what Mirabelle described as *chicken fillets*—but she knew she had none of the natural beauty that Maude or Eva or Bel wore so naturally. A silk purse may have been temporarily created out of the sow's ear, but she felt it was but smoke and mirrors.

'Jessica, truly, you look exquisite. Look at yourself.' He turned her to face the mirror, standing behind her so his face reflected back at her over her own shoulder. As she frowned, he frowned too. 'Stop looking doubtful! You have got to sweep into that box, utterly confident of your own beauty and your own powers. You have bagged me. I am at your feet. You have secured your earl. This is your moment of triumph.'

'I do not know if I can do it!' Panic, far worse than the nerves before the ball, swept through her. 'I do not know if I can sit in one of those boxes, lit up, stared at, the focus of everyone's attention and act that.' His hands, cupping her naked shoulders, tightened. 'I will go stiff, freeze, I know I will.'

'Then we had better unfreeze you.' Gareth turned her until she stood facing him toe to toe, the ruffles at the hem of her skirts brushing his shoes. 'We have spent all night and all day making love, I imagine. Let us see if we can look like it.'

He bent and took her lips before she could form the question. The word *how?* was swallowed up as, open mouth to open mouth, he drew her to him. There was no need to coax her lips open, no need to tease her tongue into playing with his. He filled her, bold and demanding, mimicking the ultimate possession that the pressure of his pelvis against her belly promised. And she answered him, all thoughts of freezing up banished. Her tongue moved with his, teased his as he explored her, then, boldly, licking past his lips into the heat of his mouth.

He had been drinking brandy. It flamed, hot, on her tongue as she flicked the tip against his teeth, then withdrew a little, teasing his lips. The needy sensation she had experienced before surged through her, stronger now, she realised, because she understood what it was demanding, what it would lead to.

They stepped back together, speaking together. 'I think—'

'We ought to—'

'Stop,' Gareth finished. She had succeeded in over-turning his usual amused calm. The man who faced her looked aroused, looked dangerous, for all that he had freed her when he must have known she was far too carried away by his kisses to have resisted him.

'Yes.' Jessica nodded vigorously, then grabbed for a loosened ostrich plume slipping from her elaborate coiffure. 'I imagine we look adequately, um...'

'Bedded?' he suggested with a grin, relaxing. The dangerous predator was still there, though, she thought with a delicious secret shiver. What would it be like to be kissed by Gareth if he truly desired you? If he loved you? 'Do you need any help with that feather?'

'No, I have it.' Jessica jabbed the pin in firmly, making her eyes water. 'Oh, I shall be so glad to let my hair down!' Was that a growl or was he simply clearing his throat? 'We had better go, don't you think? Maude thought it best if we enter our box just after they have got settled in theirs and she says they will leave her house just about now.'

* * *

They sat opposite each other in the carriage, chatting easily about neutral subjects as the wheels rumbled over the wet cobbles. It was hard to believe that only minutes before they had been in each other's arms. Jessica was beginning to feel she had regained her composure as they drew up and the flickering light from the massed torchères outside the theatre illuminated the interior of the vehicle.

Gareth stood, pulled her to her feet and pressed one hard, intense kiss on her lips, holding it until the groom threw open the door and let down the steps. Blushing, torn between indignation and bliss, Jessica tottered out and into the theatre on Gareth's arm.

'How could you! I can hardly walk, my knees have turned to jelly.'

'That's quite the nicest thing you have ever said to me,' he teased as they handed their cloaks to a waiting attendant. 'Is Lord Pangbourne here this evening?'

'Yes, my lord. His lordship has brought a small party—you have just missed them.'

'Perfect.' Gareth shepherded her through the foyer and up the stairs to the first floor.

'Have you been here before?' He seemed to know his way as he walked along the curving wall punctuated with numbered doors, checking against the pasteboard slip in his hand.

'Yes, when you told me about Maude's interest in Hurst. I wanted to check that this was at least a respectable theatre, if there is such a thing.'

'And is it?'

'It appears to be. And a very profitable one, by all

accounts. Here we are. Are you ready?' He opened the door, making as though to seize her again, and Jessica was laughing as she walked through into the box.

The light, the noise, the crowd hit her like a blow as she emerged from the shadowed passageway on to what seemed to be centre stage. It was smaller than the Opera House, and there she had been able to hide behind a curtain. Here, their box seemed to thrust out towards the tiers of others with their red and gilt and flaring lights. Heads turned, eye glasses glinted as they were lifted, a buzz of speculation went around, cutting through the clamour as people recognised Gareth.

Opposite, Maude started, her hand flying to her mouth, her gaze transfixed on Gareth's face. 'She should be in melodrama,' he murmured, amused, as he took his time arranging their chairs and seating Jessica. Alerted by his daughter's gesture, Lord Pangbourne turned from speaking to Bel, his jowls quivering with indignation.

'Oh dear, I do hope he is not going to have a seizure,' Jessica said, concerned.

'Not he. The man thrives on combat and indignation. It looks as though he is going to walk out—that really would make the gossip columns—no, Eva is being firm with him.'

Puffing indignantly, Lord Pangbourne subsided into his chair, folded his arms across his substantial stomach and proceeded to glare at their box. 'Everyone is looking at us,' Jessica hissed.

'Excellent.' Gareth lifted her hand and began to kiss her fingers elaborately. 'Could you possibly look as though you are enjoying this?'

'Oh, sorry.' Jessica ran her free hand through the

thick hair at his temples, then cupped his cheek, gazing at him adoringly. 'I want to giggle.'

'Then fan yourself vigorously and tell me how magnificent I was this afternoon in bed.'

'That, my lord, is taking playacting a little far.'

'What if there are lip readers out there?' he suggested, straight-faced.

'Oh, Gareth darling, you were magnificent in bed this afternoon,' Jessica gushed obediently. 'And you are teasing me.'

'Yes, but no one has said that to me recently.'

'Outrageous man!' She couldn't help laughing at him. 'I don't believe that for a minute.'

'I am flattered that you have such a high expectation of my performance.'

'I have a high expectation of what a mistress would expect to say to her paramour, whether she meant it or not.' Jessica snapped her fan shut and fetched him a reproving tap on the knuckles. *Expectation? He speaks as though* we *will become lovers.*

Gareth captured it, unfurled it and used it to shield their faces. 'Ouch, that was Miss Gifford, governess, at her most severe. And I do not have one just now.'

'No mistress?'

'No, not at the moment. Too much hard work, too expensive and I am too lazy.' He restored the fan to her as the snuffer men began to extinguish candles and dim lamps until most of the light was focused on the stage. Jessica bit her lip in thought. Was that why he was so passionate with her? Simple frustration? That was a flattering thought, to be sure! It was certainly one well suited to dampening down over-heated imaginings on the part of inexperienced ladies thrown into intimacy with London bucks.

And thinking of bucks… she squinted through the gloom at the box opposite as the door opened, admitting a tall figure and a fleeting shaft of light. 'Is that Captain Grahame?'

Gareth, who had bent and was trailing kisses along her neck, tilted his head to look. 'I think it is.' He went back to nibbling.

'Stop it! No one can see.'

'I can taste. And you will be nicely pink and flustered when the lights come back up.'

'I will be that without what you are doing now, my lord! Be sensible and think about Captain Grahame. Is he courting Maude, do you think? Because if so, I should warn her about his character. His conversation with me was positively warm.'

'No need, surely, given her infatuation with Hurst? No, he appears to be Pangbourne's guest—they have their heads together.'

'Does no one ever watch the play?' Jessica tried to concentrate on what was taking place on the stage. Gareth had abandoned her neck, but had taken her left hand in his and was playing with her fingers. 'Obviously not,' she answered herself, looking round at a burst of catcalling and waving from a group of rakes towards some of the more scantily clad members of the chorus. 'People are still staring at us.'

'Good. Just enjoy the play and gaze adoringly into my eyes from time to time,' Gareth recommended, cheerfully ignoring her unladylike snort.

Gradually she became less self-conscious, forgot the

raised eyeglasses and the gossip and relaxed into the play, whispering comments in Gareth's ear, clutching his hand at moments of high drama, finding again the easiness in his company she had found at the opera.

The curtain falling for the interval brought her to herself to find Gareth on his feet opening the box door. There was an exchange with someone she could not see, then he turned back, frowning, a folded paper in his hand.

'It is a note from Maude, asking me to met her urgently.' He peered at it in the dim light of the box. 'Dreadful scrawl, I hardly recognise her hand. She wants me to go to the balcony overlooking the main foyer.'

'She is still in her box.' Maude was talking with animation to Lord Sebastian.

'Probably waiting to see if I move—she won't want to stand there by herself. I had better go—goodness knows what Pangbourne is planning now.' He looked down at her. 'Will you be all right for a few minutes? Lock the door of the box, I'll knock.'

Jessica slipped the catch over and went to watch Lord Pangbourne's party. Maude was still in her box, although now she was standing towards the rear. Minutes passed; Maude stayed where she was, apparently unable to find an excuse to slip out.

A tap on the door made her jump. She had not realised how tense she had become without Gareth there. The catch was stiff under her kid-covered fingers. 'I don't think she was able to get away—' she began as Captain Grahame slid into the box, shut the door and leaned back against it.

'My dear Mrs Carleton. I must congratulate you upon

the speed of your conquest. Lord Standon is notoriously selective in his choice of *belles amies*.'

'What do you want?'

'Why, to deliver a message. And a warning.' His smile beneath the pencil-thin moustache held no warmth whatsoever.

Chapter Eighteen

'A warning, Captain Grahame? You mean a threat? I must ask you to leave—I have no wish to entertain you, and for your own sake I would strongly recommend that you remove yourself before Lord Standon returns.'

It was the same haughtily confident tone with which Jessica had faced down the tipsy husband of one of her employers, bent upon ravishing the latest unfortunate governess to cross their threshold. In that case he had retreated in confusion and had written her a glowing reference in the morning. Somehow she suspected the captain was not going to be so easy to handle.

'I have no intention of lingering—not now. I am sure we will have the opportunity for mutually profitable conversations in the future. But for now, I am bearing an offer from Lord Pangbourne.'

'He is rather older than I was looking for in a... friend,' Jessica said coolly.

Captain Grahame flushed with irritation. It seemed she was not being as compliant as he had expected. 'I would suggest you are not quite so flippant, ma'am.

Lord Pangbourne offers you two thousand pounds to leave London and Lord Standon and not return.'

How would Mrs Carleton react to that? I want to slap his face—but would she? 'Paltry,' Jessica drawled. 'He will need to do better than that Captain, and you may tell him so. What is your warning?'

'That two thousand pounds or not, leaving London would be good for your health—and for Standon's.' He handed her a rectangle of embossed pasteboard. 'My card. I suggest you do not think about it for too long, my dear.'

He was gone before Jessica could react, or fully take in the threat. She looked down at the calling card, then stuffed it into her reticule as the door opened again. 'I thought you locked this.' Gareth strolled in. 'No sign of Maude—I suppose she was unable to find an opportunity to slip out.'

'I did lock it.' Jessica sat down, feeling oddly flustered. 'I thought I heard you knock just now.' Why was she lying to him? Why not tell him what had just happened and have the satisfaction of seeing him punch Captain Grahame's unpleasant smile off his face? The offer of money doubtless came from Maude's father, but she doubted that bluff, direct, man would threaten a woman with violence. And Gareth?

'Captain Grahame is still over there,' she observed, gesturing towards the Pangbourne box. He must have slipped back in while she was talking to Gareth. 'He looks the sort of man who ends up getting called out by outraged brothers.'

'He does the calling out—you might almost call it a hobby of his.' Gareth sat down next to her, picked up her fan and began to waft it back and forth. 'You are quite flushed.'

'So he has fought many duels?'

'Four, to my knowledge.' He put down the fan and opened the programme. 'Wounded his opponents badly in all of them: he's a crack shot and a seriously good swordsman.'

'Oh.' Jessica managed not to gulp. 'How unpleasant. Do you duel?'

'Never have.' Gareth had found what he was looking for and was studying the cast list. 'Thought I recognised that man in the bad wig—saw him last week in something.'

'Why not?'

'Why not duel?' He smiled at her. 'You are very bloodthirsty all of a sudden, my sweet. I have never been provoked enough to issue a challenge and I appear not to have provoked anyone else sufficiently either.'

'Are you a good shot? Or better with a sword?' she persisted, trying to sound as though it were an idle interest.

'Adequate at both, I suppose. Sebastian is a better shot than I am and Dereham a better swordsman.' The curtain went up to the accompaniment of a drum roll from the orchestra and Gareth settled back in his chair, the question of duels apparently dismissed from his mind.

He was probably being modest, Jessica tried to reassure herself. Gareth was not the sort of man she would expect to boast of his prowess at anything; he would simply get on and demonstrate it. A flash of heat through her body reminded her just how effectively he had demonstrated his abilities at love-making. She forced her mind away from that seductive memory and back to the present.

Given what Gareth had just told her about Captain

Grahame's predilection for duelling, it seemed she was not mistaken in believing he was issuing a direct threat to Gareth. Should she warn him? But then he would probably go straight off and challenge Grahame for threatening her and that would trigger the very thing she wanted to avoid.

My sweet, he had called her. But then, *All of us Ravenhurst cousins seem to have an ability as actors*, she reminded herself of his words when they had been discussing Maude's fascination with Mr Hurst and the theatre. Why was she thinking about that now? Jessica shifted her position a little so she could watch Gareth's profile. He was smiling at something happening on the stage—she had lost all track of the entertainment, wild horses might be rampaging through for all she knew—his body big, powerful and relaxed.

There was a natural masculine elegance about him that came from inside as much as from the form of his body. He would be a powerful physical force if angered, but he did not spend his time picking fights like the captain, he used his wits to deal with difficult situations. Like her rescue from the brothel or the way he concealed Maude's presence when Lord Pangbourne had burst into the breakfast room.

Jessica could not imagine Gareth ever wanting to hurt anyone, let alone risk their life. Captain Grahame, on the other hand, must enjoy it. It was probably only the sanction of having to flee abroad if he killed his man that kept him from doing so. A hideous image of Gareth lying bleeding, his life ebbing out on to the crushed turf came to her, wiping away the reality of the man sitting beside her. *I love him. I can't—I must not—Oh my God, I love him...*

* * *

'Jessica?' Gareth turned at the sound of the gasp. 'Are you all right?'

'Hiccup,' she apologised, scrabbling in her reticule. 'My goodness, it has made my eyes stream.' She was being uncharacteristically clumsy with the strings of the purse. Gareth fished in his pocket and proffered his own handkerchief. 'Oh, thank you.' He could not see her face from behind the large linen square, but her voice sounded oddly muffled.

'Would you like a drink?' There were no more hiccups. Jessica finished mopping her eyes, blew her nose and folded up the handkerchief with great care.

'No, thank you. I was so nervous I was picking at my dinner, and then I thought I must eat, so I rather bolted it. I deserve indigestion for being so silly. I will have this laundered and returned to you.' She fidgeted with the reticule some more, finally succeeded in opening it and pushed the handkerchief inside.

The curtain came down, making her jump as the audience, despite their previous inattention, broke into applause and calls for the actors. 'Oh dear, I missed the end.'

'Never mind, we did not come for the play. I think that was quite a successful evening, don't you?' He clapped as the actors parted, revealing the tall, unsmiling figure of the manager who bowed to the audience. 'Is that Hurst?'

Jessica seemed to pull herself out of some abstraction and peered down at the stage. 'Yes, that is he.'

'Handsome fellow,' Gareth remarked, eying the tall, broad-shouldered figure with the austere, sculpted face. 'I can see why Maude is attracted.'

'He reminds me of you,' Jessica said.

'Me? Good God, my sweet, look at him! The man's off some classical frieze—you have noticed my nose, I assume?'

She smiled, faintly. 'There is nothing wrong with your nose—on a man. You are the same shape as he is. The same build. From the back I thought he was you that first time.' The smile vanished and was replaced by a blush.

Startled, Gareth looked down again. She noticed the way he looked? His figure? She compared him to the man on the stage and thought him as well built? A glow of purely masculine smugness ran through him and he grinned at himself for feeling it.

'I think you are all about in your head,' he said frankly. 'Are you feeling better?' She did not look it. The animation of earlier had gone and now Jessica looked strained and reserved. He was asking a lot of her, he told himself, filled with self-reproach. He was used to being stared at, gossiped about. She was not.

'Yes, I am fine. What would you like to do now?' Her head was up, her shoulders back, the smile on her face again. *My brave Jessica. I know what I* want *to do now.*

'Take you home. We have done enough for one night, I think.'

'Very well.' She placed her hand on his arm as they came out into the passageway, smiling and flirting with each other as they passed other couples on their way to the head of the stairs. She saw the Pangbourne party the moment he did, her fingers gripping on his forearm so tightly he thought she would be unable to relax them.

Breathe, smile he heard her murmur under her breath and the grip relaxed, her chin came up. Maude gave a theatrical start at the sight of them, them swept past, almost treading on Jessica's toes, eyes averted. Her father glowered at them both before escorting her down the stairs, his jowls quivering with indignation. Eva and Sebastian, Bel and Ashe followed, all four nodding coolly as they passed. And then he felt Jessica's grip tighten again. Captain Grahame, elegant in full regimentals, the insolent smile on his face that had Gareth longing to hit him, bowed.

'My dearest Mrs Carleton, how pleasant to see you again so soon. Standon, one must congratulate you upon setting society on its heels—so very unlike you, one would have said.' He bowed again and was gone, jogging lightly down the stairs to catch up to his party.

'What did he mean, *so soon*?' Gareth demanded, prioritising insults in his head and finding that Grahame's sniping at him was as nothing compared to the intimacy with which he addressed Jessica.

'I have no idea.' Jessica removed her hand from his arm and began to walk down the stairs. All the colour had gone from her cheeks and Gareth stepped across to take her elbow, anxious that she might faint. 'He was being provocative, no doubt. He appears to have succeeded. Thank you, I can manage.'

'Has he been pestering you?' Gareth persisted as they stepped out into the night. With the high collar of her velvet evening cloak up around her face, she seemed ethereal, fragile. Where had the strong-minded governess gone? This woman looked as though she would break in his hand, flinch at a hard word.

'No! Gareth, please do not hector me.' That was clear and decisive enough; perhaps appearances were deceptive. Gareth apologised, guiding her towards where his coachman had positioned the carriage. At times like this, in the midst of a jostling throng, the man was worth every penny of his generous wage.

'I did not mean to. The man sets my hackles up.'

'As he no doubt intends,' Jessica observed. It appeared she was once more back in control; perhaps whatever had ailed her had been set to rights by the crisp night air.

This time, instead of sitting opposite, he sat beside her on the soft plush. It would take almost half an hour to get back to Half Moon Street at this time of night, with frost on the cobbles and the streets full of the night-time crowds. Time to hold her in his arms, repeat those kisses that had so fired his blood earlier that evening.

He turned, just as the flambeaux outside the theatre illuminated the inside of the carriage like daylight. It only lasted a moment, but it was enough to see her profile: pure, pale and stark. She looked like a woman who had received the worst of news, something so bad that she was beyond crying out with the pain of it, but instead must sit still and silent, absorbing it.

'Jessica?' He reached for her in what was now virtual darkness.

'No! Please, I am not...we should not...' She got her voice under control. 'I am not in the mood for kisses, my lord. There is no one here for us to deceive.'

'You are tired,' he said, wanting nothing more than to wipe that bleakness from her eyes. 'I just want to hold you. Relax.' He put his arm around her shoulders and pulled her to him. 'There, now.'

For a moment he thought she would resist him, then

she came to him with a little sigh as though in surrender, curled against him, soft and trusting. And something inside him changed, welled up and gripped his breathing so that for a long moment he could only sit there, eyes wide open on the shadows, his senses full of the sweetness of her. It was like lemon blossom, he thought. Utterly fragrant, yet with the promise of a sharp tang behind it. *I love her.*

'Gareth.'

'Yes?' *I'll tell her; I must tell her. Surely she feels something for me? Surely she cannot lie so trustingly in my arms, surely she would not have shuddered into ecstasy like that if she did not feel something—?*

'When is your man of business calling? Mr Wayman, is it not?'

'You want him to call?' It was an effort to drag his mind away from the fantasies it was weaving to deal with this.

'Of course.' She sat up, leaving him feeling bereft. 'I need to have this settled—we discussed it and you were quite right. I think I will feel better when I know what I will be doing next—it will be easier to deal with the stress of this masquerade when I can be planning for getting back to normal.'

'Normal?' It was as though she had slapped him. 'What you said you wanted was very far from what has been normal for you up to now.'

'Yes, but I do need to work. I realised that, talking to Jimmy. This will give me the opportunity to be my own mistress, to choose who and when to teach.'

'This scheme of ours is so distasteful to you, then?'

She turned to him, surprise at his question in every line of her silhouette. 'Of course. I made a bargain and

I will fulfil it, but I never pretended that I thought it would be a pleasurable experience.'

Irrational and unreasonable anger at her, anger at his own foolish, emotional weakness swept through him. She had insinuated herself into his heart and his soul. His body ached for her. The fact that she had not intended to do so, had done nothing other than scrupulously follow his orders, did not matter. She had burrowed under his carapace of calm, his ordered world, his cynical observance of other peoples' emotional turmoil, without any effort at all. And he had invited her into his life—he had as good as commanded her to make him fall in love with her. He had, in fact, wished this upon himself.

Through a red haze that seemed to fill his vision, Gareth reached out and yanked on the check string. The carriage rumbled to a halt and the trap flipped open. 'My lord?'

'Home.' The trap shut and the carriage moved off.

'To your house? Why?'

'Because I have something I want to show you.' *Show her? Coward, you dare not risk telling her, dare you? She will throw the words in your face, demand to be taken back to Half Moon Street and drag those damned awful stuff gowns out of the wardrobe again. She'll plait up her hair and pick up her schoolbooks and flee and you'll never see those emeralds burning on her white skin, never... But I'll be damned if she can ever say again that these few weeks had not given her any pleasure.*

'Show me?'

'Yes.' He felt her withdrawal, as thought she understood what he intended, yet she did not move.

'Very well.' She sat in silence while the carriage

moved through the streets, her hand raised to hold the strap as it swayed around corners. 'Only once, to last for ever,' she murmured, so soft he would have thought he had imagined it, if it had not been for the puff of her breath on the cold air. So soft that he surely could not have heard the note of resignation in the six words.

The butler opened the door wide, ushering them into the warmth and light of the hall. 'Good evening Jordan.' The butler took their heavy cloaks and Gareth's tall hat.

'Good evening, madam. My lord?'

'Nothing, thank you. You may lock up and retire. I do not require Malvern either.'

'I will apprise him of that, my lord. The decanters are in the library.'

Jessica gazed at Gareth from under her lashes. His mood had changed abruptly during the carriage ride and now she could not read him, other than to understand quite clearly that he had brought her here to make love to her.

If she said *no*, he would take her back home, she knew. But she did not want to go: there was the rest of her life to sleep alone, the rest of her life to reach out in the dark and find no one there. And the rest of her life to remember what it felt like to make love to the man she loved.

Why he was doing this, now, she did not understand. Was it a reaction to Captain Grahame's sneering insolence, a male need to make her unequivocally his? Or had he sensed, perhaps at some level too subtle to realise with his conscious mind, that she was his now and would welcome him?

'Would you like a drink?' He was watching her,

something more serious in his eyes than she had ever seen before. It puzzled her—she had been expecting the heat and the desire she had seen before

'Dutch courage? No.' It was tempting, to drink a glass of wine to help her toss her hat over the windmill. But she wanted all her senses tuned to him with nothing to cloud them. She smiled at him and knew it was a poor, shaky effort. 'My legs are wobbly enough as it is.'

'In that case, you give me the perfect opportunity for some masculine showing off.' He grinned as he bent and scooped her off her feet. It seemed his mood had changed again. There was a note of recklessness in his tone as though he, not she, was the one taking the risk.

'Gareth!' Oh, but it was good, held so strongly against his chest. Despite her protest, Jessica let her head fall to his shoulder and relaxed into the grip of his big hands. 'I am not some skinny little thing—'

She broke off as he began to climb the stairs. 'Are you suggesting I am not strong enough? I am wounded. You are a very satisfying armful of woman, my sweet; I will not drop you.'

'I never feared you would,' she murmured as he shouldered open a door at the first-floor front and set her on her feet. It was unmistakably his bedchamber, she could tell that even with a quick glance round by candlelight. There were piles of books on the floor by the chair and on the bedside stand. The pictures that covered the walls were an eccentric mix of size and style and subject. The colour scheme was dove grey and a stormy bluish-purple that found echoes in his eyes and there was the faintest scent of Castile soap, citrus cologne and leather.

And against the wall, opposite the heavily curtained

window, stood a bed. The dark bedcover was turned down to reveal the stark white of linen, the pillows were heaped up as though ready for their owner to lie back comfortably with a book in his hand, the firelight played over the richness of the walnut headboard.

She was staring at it, the image of Gareth lying there so strong that when the real man spoke, just behind her, she jumped. He rested his hands on her shoulders so she could not turn and face him as he spoke. 'I want to make love to you, Jessica. I want to pleasure you, to show you how it can be. I will be very careful—you need not fear…consequences. But if you have any doubts, any at all, say so and I will take you home.'

'At any point?' she asked, testing him.

'At any point.' He was standing so close behind her that she could feel the heat of him down the length of her body. Deliberately she leant back so they touched and felt the shiver go through him.

'That is asking a lot of you. I understand that it is very difficult for a man to stop when things are…' she searched for a phrase, '…well advanced.'

'Difficult and uncomfortable,' he acknowledged, his mouth muffled in her hair. 'But this is you, Jessica. I promise.'

'Then show me,' she said simply, turning into his embrace and burying her face into the soft linen over his breast.

Chapter Nineteen

Gareth had shed his coat while she was staring at the bed and now, as her palms slid round his chest and down his back she could feel the shape of him clearly, the complex strapping of muscle over his ribs, the dip into the fluid line of his spine, the way his torso narrowed to slim, tight, hips.

'You are beautiful,' Jessica breathed, wondering at how good it felt just to touch him, to caress the man she loved.

His chuckle as his hands slid down her back made her smile. 'Deluded, poor creature,' he murmured, husky with desire. One hand flattened against the small of her back; the other came up to cup her breast. 'You are wearing too many clothes.'

'So are you.' The buttons came free with her tugging, the shirt slid back over his shoulders, leaving him golden in the firelight. 'Oh.' He looked so much bigger, broader, more powerful, standing before her half-naked. But there was not time to be alarmed; the urgency of his hands with the fastening of her gown distracted her and she wriggled and turned to help, feeling nothing but relief as it slid down to puddle around her feet. Her petticoats followed, then she was standing in front of him in corset and chemise, stockings and slippers. She must look ridiculous, Jessica thought, biting her lip.

Gareth did not appear to think so. He was staring at her. His lips moved soundlessly. *Thank you, God? Surely he did not just say that? One nervous, inexperienced school teacher is not much of a blessing...*

'What shall I take off next?' she asked into the silence. Instead of answering, he reached out one hand and touched her cheek as though to reassure himself she was still there. It unnerved her, that Gareth should suddenly appear so tentative, so uncertain. She had relied upon him sweeping her off her feet before she had time to think.

A log shifted and fell, sending up a shower of sparks. Jessica kicked off her slippers. 'Gareth—you are making me nervous.'

'Relying on me to sweep you off your feet?' he asked with uncanny perceptiveness. 'Give me a moment to recover from the shock of being given what I wished for.'

She frowned at him, puzzled, and then he had gathered her up in his arms and she had no time to explore his words, only to gasp as he set her down by the bed and set to work on her corset strings. They came free in seconds, the boned garment tossed aside as the chemise was whisked over her head, and then she was on the bed. The slither of the satin bedcover under her bare bottom was a shocking reminder of the brothel, but the momentary panic vanished at the sight of Gareth standing beside the bed, naked and—

Jessica shut her eyes. Tight. He was *magnificent*. Terrifying—but magnificent. She wanted to touch him. She wanted—utterly immodestly—to kiss him, kiss him *there*.

'Don't be frightened.' The bed dipped, she was pulled against him. She realised he was using her own body to shield her from the sight of his arousal. That had the equally disturbing consequence that she was pressed to it, to all of its heat and hardness.

'I'm not,' she protested, wondering if he would be unutterably shocked if she reached between their bodies and held him as she wanted to do. 'I'm…impressed.'

That surprised a snort of laughter from him.

'I'm sorry. Are virgins supposed to shriek at the sight of a naked man—or faint dead away?' she enquired, worried now, although it was becoming difficult to hold any thought but that she wanted Gareth very badly indeed and that if he did not do something in a minute, *she* was going to have to.

'I don't know—I have never been to bed with a virgin.' His hands began to move again, stroking down the length of her back, down over the curves of her buttocks, then cupping them, pulling her against him. *Oh, thank goodness, at last.* 'You may shriek if you like.'

'I would rather you kissed me.' He took her mouth on her words, rolling her over so he was above her, his weight on his elbows, his knees pressing her legs apart so her body cradled his. *We fit so well*, she thought hazily, sinking into the whirlpool of sensation that his mouth, the teasing brush of his chest hair on her nipples, the outrageous, demanding pressure at the junction of her thighs, all threw at her.

He shifted, moving lower, and she gave a gasp of complaint until his mouth found her nipple and his hand eased between their bodies to caress into the damp tangle of curls. He nipped and licked and then one long finger slid into the wet, hot folds and touched her, insistent, demanding. 'Come for me,' he said, the words vibrating against the hard, aching peak of her nipple and the world splintered, only this time with an intensity that broke her, tossed her limp and gasping on to some foreign shore where she had never been before.

She came to herself to feel him sliding up her body, cupping her face in his hands so he could kiss her trembling, parted lips. 'Have you any idea how arousing it is, the way you respond to me?' He was pressing against her, down there where the whole core of her being was opening for him, and she moaned against his lips.

'Gareth, please.'

It felt so strange, and yet so inevitably right. He was too big, yet she never doubted he could sheath himself safely within her. The pain, when it came, made her arch to take him deeper into her heat and when she opened her eyes to see him poised above her, his eyes closed, his face rapt, even that sharp pang vanished in awe. 'Gareth?' *I love you, I love you…I cannot tell you…*

His eyes were dark and stormy and fierce as his lids lifted. She saw his Adam's apple move as he swallowed once, hard. 'Jessica?'

'I'm all right. Rather more than all right.' His face relaxed, just a little, at her earnest tone and the corner of his mouth twitched. 'May we move?'

'Oh, yes. We may.' He kept his eyes open on hers as he began, the rhythm slow and powerful and achingly deep. Jessica shifted beneath him, searching for the perfect angle, seeking to become totally one. A building ache made her gasp, move restlessly against the steady discipline of his movements .

'Slowly, my sweet.'

'Yes…no. *Gareth*.' This time she came to herself to find him still moving within her, his eyes intent as he gazed down into her damp, stunned face.

'Come with me this time,' he asked her, beginning to drive the pace, spinning the sensations through her. Weakly she shook her head; surely nothing more was possible? 'Oh, yes, again Jessica.' He shifted slightly, his weight greater as he moved one hand, sliding it between their bodies again, finding that small, desperate core that ached for him, reaching it as he drove harder until she cried out, arching upwards, her fingers raking his shoulders her breasts crushed to his chest.

She was aware, just, of him leaving her body, of him pressed to her, shuddering, and then of sinking, drifting down within Gareth's embrace, deep into a velvety blackness and peace.

Gareth lay on his back, Jessica's sleeping form held snug against his side, and tried to think practically. It was hard—all his mind wanted to do was revel in what they had done and join his body in utterly relaxed abandon. But it had to be done. Cautiously he sat up, adjusting her against his shoulder, smiling at the complaining grumble before she burrowed in again and slept.

He loved her. If he had believed it before, he was certain now. He had lain with many women, but he had never felt that it was anything but a mutual exchange of pleasure. This, for him, had been an exchange of hearts. But would she feel the same? Even to think not was painful; then he looked down at her, confidingly wrapped around him, and smiled. No, Jessica would never have come to him like this if she did not feel for him what he felt for her, surely?

That just left the practical obstacles that stood between him and happiness. They had to marry—anything else was unthinkable. He knew nothing about her family, but she had obviously been raised as a gentlewoman. Noblemen married actresses and weathered the storm; he could marry his respectable governess with no more harm than a few raised eyebrows.

But. But society knew her not as modest, hard-working Miss Jessica Gifford, mistress of the harp and the Italian tongue. They knew her as brazen Mrs Carleton, adventuress. To admit who she really was would involve them all in scandal—Bel and Eva, their husbands, the Maubourg court and Maude. Goodness knows what it would do to Maude's reputation if it became known he would install a false mistress rather than marry her.

There was an answer, of course, he just had to think of it. Gareth slid down the bed again, reaching to pull more covers over the two of them. As his eyes closed, he wondered how he had ever managed to sleep before without the warm weight against his shoulder of the woman he loved. He imagined her response in the morning when he told her how he felt, drifting off with the image of her smile, of the wide green eyes gazing into his, of how she would tell him of her feelings for him.

Jessica woke, not slowly as she usually did, but all of a piece, knowing exactly where she was. Her back curved warm into the long male body holding her protectively. Yet even as she smiled at the safety Gareth's strength offered her, she caught her breath at the evidence of such blatant masculinity hard against her softness. He was asleep, she could tell from his breathing—was it normal for him to be so aroused?

Not sure whether to be alarmed or flattered, Jessica closed her eyes again and tried to drift off again into this perfect dream. The creak of a floorboard, the subdued rattle of fire irons, had her eyes snapping open again. There was a servant in the room making up the fire. In Gareth's room. She was in Gareth's bed, had slept there all night after they had made love. This was not a dream, this was not a fantasy. This was real life and now she had to pay the penalty of last night's indulgence.

The floorboard creaked again as she cringed under the covers, half-expecting a shriek of outrage. But, of course, in an earl's household no one would turn a hair if his lordship chose to spend the night with a troop of opera dancers and a performing bear in his bed.

Dare she get up? Better not, not until she had her mind clear, she was sure to wake him. Jessica wished she could move away from his heat, the warm sleepy scent of him; it made it so hard to concentrate on the right things.

I love him. I have lost my virginity to him and last night it seemed the world was well lost for love—but of course it isn't. The world would certainly have something to say about it if it knew—and I have to live in the world again now. This is not some romance. He likes me and desired me and now he has had me. He was very careful and considerate about it. Probably, like all males, he is going to feel awkward about last night's sins this morning, so I have to show him it is no great matter. I am not going to make demands, become hysterical.

Behind her Gareth shifted, nuzzling his mouth against her neck, his morning beard rasping with a pleasurable, almost painful, friction against the soft skin.

He is going to wake up in a minute. Think what you are going to say. Gareth sighed and turned over, his imprisoning arm lifting from around her waist. Jessica slid carefully out of bed and found that the servant had picked up her scattered clothing and laid it carefully over a chair back. Was it going to be possible to leave without seeing the staff? She would sink through the floor, she knew it.

Where were her garters? Jessica scrabbled on the floor and found them under the trailing hem of the coverlet. Shift, corset. She gritted her teeth as she struggled to tighten the laces by herself. Petticoat, gown, shoes. Decent, covered, shielded against temptation.

Gareth turned again, throwing back the covers until they tangled around his feet. What was temptation if it were not this? Jessica crept up to the bed, reached out her hand, palm down, hovering just above his heart, her eyes aching with unshed tears as she tried to imprint this image on her mind. No, she could not talk to him when he woke—she was too vulnerable to her own weakness here in his bedchamber. With sudden resolution she turned, scooped up her cloak and let herself out on to the landing.

As she crept down the stairs into the hall, Jordan stepped out of the shadows. 'Miss Gifford?'

'Call me a hackney, please, Jordan.'

'Is his lordship awake, Miss Gifford?'

'No. I do not wish to disturb him.'

'He would wish me to apprise him of your departure, ma'am.'

'In which case I will be out on to the street, trying to call a hackney myself before you reached his bedchamber, Jordan,' she said steadily.

'I see. I will do as you request in that case.'

By the usual alchemy of butlers a cab materialised within minutes of him stepping outside, despite the empty streets. Jessica slipped down the steps and into the vehicle unobserved except by a hod carrier delivering coals, two interested maids scrubbing area steps and a porter with a basket of vegetables on his head.

'I have paid the cab.' Jordan closed the door, carefully tucking in her trailing skirts. 'He knows where to take you.' He hesitated, one hand on the ledge. 'What shall I tell the earl, ma'am?'

'Why, that I have gone home and will await his instructions on which further events he wishes me to attend.' She smiled with a brightness designed to hide any distress. The butler bowed his head in acknowledgement and signalled to the cabby to drive on.

Goodness knew what Jordan made of all that. He must have known she had spent the night in Gareth's bed and he would know, too, that under no circumstances would Gareth have let her leave the house without his escort, at least as far as the front door. His lordship was not going to be pleased about any of this.

Not that she could be described as happy either, although whenever she thought about last night Jessica's mind seemed to become fuzzy and a treacherous warmth spread through her. It had been magical. And, like all things magical, it must vanish in the harsh light of dawn.

The cabby set Jessica down at her own door step. It was still a wildly unfashionable hour for any lady to be about, which was why the presence at the kerb of a vehicle she recognised as the Pangbourne's town carriage had her frowning in indecision. It surely was not Maude, which meant Lord Pangbourne must have decided to deal with this personally. Walking round to the mews and sneaking in through the kitchen door was tempting.

Jessica took two rapid steps up the street, then turned and marched up the steps. She was not going to be brow-beaten. She would tell Lord Pangbourne what she thought of his tactics and his unpleasant messenger.

The door was ajar and she pushed it open as Hedges was saying, 'I am afraid that madam is not yet at home to visitors, Lady Maude.' His expression as he took in the sight of her would, under other circumstances, be amusing, but Jessica realised suddenly that she was still dressed in an opera gown and a velvet evening cloak and the ready tarradiddle of an early morning walk was completely unsustainable.

'Good morning, Hedges. Good morning, Maude. Will you take breakfast? In the dining room as soon as possible, please, Hedges—my apologies to Mrs Hedges.'

Leaving her cloak in the butler's hands Jessica ushered Maude through into the dining room. 'Yes, I have spent the night with Gareth before you ask,' she said flatly, sitting down at the head of the table. 'For the first and last time.'

Maude, who had been staring wide-eyed, found her voice. 'Was it nice?'

Her question so startled Jessica that her 'Wonderful!' was out before she could bite it back. 'I am not going to talk about it.'

'No. Of course not.' Maude tried to look prim and failed utterly. 'But why aren't you going to do it again?'

Because I do not wish to end like my mother, was one very honest answer. One that she was not prepared to give. *Because I love him and it would hurt too much to be just a mistress*, was another, just as unsayable. *Because being with me puts him at danger from your father's unsavoury minion*, was another. She shook her head firmly. 'No, Maude, I am not discussing anything to do with it. Why are you here? Look at the time.' To underline her point the clock struck eight with clear thin chimes.

'I wanted to warn you about Papa.' Maude was stripping off her gloves with nervous jerks at the thin kid. 'He has some sort of plan; I heard him muttering to Captain Grahame last night, just before the captain went to your box. What did he say to you?'

For a moment the idea of telling Maude everything was powerfully attractive. She would rush home and berate her parent, shame him into calling Grahame off. But it was not the money that was the issue. Jessica could, and would, ignore that. It was the threat and that, she was certain, was the captain's own embellishment, not Lord Pangbourne's idea at all.

'He offered me money to leave London and Gareth,' she said, calmly dismissing it. 'The obvious ploy and the usual solution in such matters, I believe.' Mama had received a very nice 'gift' on one occasion, shortly before they moved temporarily to Cheltenham and visits from a youthful sprig of the nobility ceased abruptly. She thought of explaining to Gareth just how they had survived in the years after her father had died and shuddered. Better heartbreak than humiliation and the sight of his face changing as he realised just who his respectable governess was. There were reasons enough why she could not continue an intimate relationship with him without needing to go into that.

'Oh.' Maude had obviously been expecting something far more Machiavellian. 'What did you say?'

'No, naturally. I am sure that will be the end of it. Maude, I would appreciate it if you would not tell anyone about this morning.' She stared down at her own reflection, hazy in the highly polished mahogany surface. 'I do not regret it, but I have no wish to confide in anyone upon the subject.'

'Cross my heart and hope to die,' Maude swore, her face solemn despite the silly schoolgirl oath. 'I will not tell a soul, and I won't ask you any questions now. But when I want to seduce Mr Hurst, may I ask your advice?'

'No!' Hedges, entering with a salver, almost dropped it at the vehemence of Jessica's reply. 'Thank you, Hedges. A very large pot of coffee, if you please.' She waited until the door shut behind the butler again. 'And for goodness' sake, do not try to flirt with Hurst—that man is dangerous, I am certain of it.'

It was probably the worst possible thing to say to Maude, whose interest was piqued enough, without Jessica idiotically portraying the theatre owner as some sort of Byronic hero. As it was, breakfast was enlivened sufficiently by hissed exchanges on the subject of choosing the man of one's dreams, the inadvisability of flouting one's parent's wishes and the hypocrisy of one unmarried lady lecturing the other on modest behaviour while still warm from a man's bed, for Jessica to be able to ignore the lump of lead that was establishing itself heavily just under her heart.

Chapter Twenty

Jessica and Maude had bickered themselves back into friendship by the time the last of the toast and strawberry jam had been consumed. 'What are you going to do this morning?' Maude asked, cupping her pointed chin in her palm. 'Wait for Gareth?'

She ought to, of course—anything else was cowardly. They should have a civilised talk about what had happened. If only she felt civilised. 'No. I am going shopping, I need all kind of trivial things.' *All of which can wait*, she chided herself.

'I wish I could come with you,' Maude grumbled. 'But I hardly suppose we can be seen so much as smiling at each other. In fact, I think I must go before anyone sees me here.' When she had whisked out of the door, Jessica sat regarding the remains of breakfast, then got to her feet. She must get changed and prepare to deal with Gareth—once she had done her shopping. Dealing with him would be easier if she had some time to think about what to say about last night.

The sound of the knocker just as she was donning her

half-boots and picking up her pelisse had her starting in alarm. 'Are you all right, madam?'

'Mirabelle, please run down and tell Hedges that I am not at home if his lordship calls.'

The dresser was too well trained to allow her feelings to show on her face, but the very speed with which she scurried off showed she knew there was something afoot.

'It isn't his lordship, Mrs Carleton, it is another gentleman,' she reported back, panting slightly.

'Who?' Not Captain Grahame, surely?

'Oh, I'm sorry, ma'am, I didn't ask. Mr Hedges has shown him into the drawing room.' The dresser patted her hair into place, recovering her breath. 'Shall I run down again?'

'No, here is Hedges.'

The butler stood in the half-open door. 'Mr Wayman, ma'am, sent by his lordship.'

It was Gareth's man of business, with the house details. Jessica put down her pelisse. 'Excellent. Thank you, Hedges.'

His timing was a relief, she realised as she opened the drawing-room door. She could not sit here and brood, thinking of nothing but Gareth, and an inner core of self-knowledge warned her that wandering around the shops with nothing more to distract her than the exact shade of silk stocking to buy was likely to see her giving way to tears in the middle of Harding and Howell.

Mr Wayman was brisk, cheerful and businesslike. And, despite her fears, he did not appear to think he was dealing with a pensioned-off mistress or some other disreputable female beneath his touch. 'His lordship has given me a free hand to find exactly the property that best suits your requirements Mrs Carleton. Shall we start with the area where you would like to reside?'

'Winchester.' She had given it some thought and the cathedral town seemed perfect. She had visited it briefly to see the cathedral on her way to a new post eighteen months before and it was just the right size to provide comfortable society for a respectable single woman, just far enough from London that she need not worry about meeting anyone who might recognise her and with all the right contacts to identify suitable poor children who she might help with free schooling. That, she had decided, would be the most satisfying and useful way of spending her time.

'Excellent. I see you are a lady of decision, Mrs Carleton.' Mr Wayman produced a folder, a sheet of paper and a travelling ink well. 'Now, let us discuss the details of the accommodation and I will send a reliable man off tomorrow to establish what is available.'

Gareth woke slowly, knowing he was happy before his sleepy consciousness provided him with the reason why. Jessica. 'Mmm.' He stretched luxuriously, remembering the night before, the way she had turned to flame in his arms, the scent of her, roused and feminine, filling his nostrils, her innocent, instinctive reaction to his caresses, her passion. His love.

Eyes closed, he stretched out a hand, his imagination already shaping the warm, sensual curves it would find. Nothing. He froze—only his hand moved, fruitlessly searching the cold dent in the mattress where she should be. Then he dragged his eyes open. The bed was empty, the room was empty and all her clothes had gone.

'Jordan!' He was out of bed, the bell pull clenched in his fist as the butler appeared, far too soon. The man had known she had gone and had been lurking on the landing, awaiting this summons. In some rational part of his brain Gareth could only admire the butler's *sang-froid*, confronted by a naked, and incendiary, employer. 'Where the hell is she?'

'Mrs Carleton left at half past seven, my lord.'

'You just let her walk out of the house?' Gareth ground out between clenched teeth.

'I was not aware, my lord, that wrestling young ladies to the ground to prevent them leaving your lordship's establishments was amongst the requirements of my position, my lord.'

'Damn it, Jordan—' This was bad enough without being confronted with one's butler's manifest disapproval and frigid 'My lords'.

'I hailed a hackney carriage for Mrs Carleton and, acting upon her instructions, paid the man and directed him to take her to Half Moon Street.'

'Thank God.' He sat down on the bed. For a moment there he thought she had run away.

'Mrs Carleton said that I might tell you that she was awaiting your further instructions on which social events you wished her to attend, my lord.'

'Did she, indeed?' Jordan was not rash enough to answer that. 'I will take breakfast in half an hour and I will require my carriage immediately I am finished. Send Malvern to me. And water for a bath.'

Gareth sat on the edge of his bed, his hands braced

on his thighs, head bowed in thought. So Jessica had gone home. Why? Had he scared her? He did not think so. It must be modesty about facing him in the morning, or perhaps anxiety about the difference between their stations. Well, that was easily taken care of by a declaration of his feelings and his intentions. She would be anxious about that. He stood up and began to pace as his valet entered.

'The new-sage green coat and the cream pantaloons, Malvern.' The man bowed and began to open drawers as the footmen entered, lugging the hip bath. Gareth continued to pace, unselfconscious of his nakedness. He needed a tangible statement of his intent. Why the devil had he not thought to buy a ring when he was buying the other jewellery? *Because you didn't know you loved her then. It took you long enough to work it out*, his inner self supplied. So best to call at Thomas Grey's or Rundell and Bridge on his way to Half Moon Street.

'My lord?' His bath was ready. Absently Gareth climbed in and took the soap while footmen and valet effaced themselves. He was not a man who expected others to scrub his back for him, even if Jessica probably assumed he was. He was aware as he lathered the soap and began to rub it into his torso that he was washing the scent of her from his body. But it would soon be engrained again, he could not doubt that.

Clean, Gareth laid his head back on the rim of the bath and looked round the room, remembering it last night. How right Jessica had looked in it, the firelight catching the emerald flames in her eyes. *Emeralds!* 'Malvern!' The valet's head popped out from behind the dressing room door. 'Get that emerald parure out of the safe.' Time to make this serious with a serious gift. No woman confronted with that was going to doubt her suitor's intentions.

The morocco leather case was tucked under his arm as he ran up the steps and beat a tattoo on the knocker. 'Good morning, my lord.' Hedges stood squarely in the door opening.

'Good morning Hedges. Is Mrs Carleton up yet?'

'Madam is not At Home, my lord.' Behind the butler's arm, Gareth could see a tall hat and a pair of gloves on the side table.

'Yet she clearly has a visitor, so you appear to be mistaken, Hedges,' he said, aware from the sudden narrowing of Hedges's eyes that his smile had been nothing but a baring of teeth. He moved his left foot so that he was standing squarely on the threshold, breast to breast with the other man. *Grahame?* The wave of sheer territorial possessiveness that swept through him was almost shocking, it was so primitive.

'I am quite clear about madam's instructions, Lord Standon.'

She is not at home to me*? What the hell is going on?* 'Please do not make me get past you forcibly, Hedges.'

'I should like to see you try, my lord,' the butler said gamely, squaring his shoulders.

The encounter was brisk, short-lived and surprisingly satisfying. Leaving Hedges puffing on the floor, recovering from the effects of a neat cross-buttock throw, Gareth deposited his own hat next to the one on the table, took a firm grip on his cane and strode into the drawing room without knocking.

'My lord!' Wayman was on his feet instantly, bowing and smiling. Beside him Jessica rose more slowly.

'Good morning, my lord. Did you by any chance see Hedges on your way in?' Her tone was chill, her back ramrod straight; if he had not come to know her very well by now, he would have missed entirely the look of blank panic in her eyes.

'The poor man slipped on the marble,' Gareth said, placing his cane and the morocco jewellery case on a side table and stripping off his gloves. 'I believe he is recovered now, though.' Behind him the door opened.

'Madam—'

'Thank you, Hedges, that will be all for now.' So, whatever it was that was wrong, Jessica had enough self-control to preserve a calm face before Wayman and her staff. In fact, Gareth was coming to think, she had enough self-control to captain an artillery crew.

'I did not expect to see you here, Wayman.'

'No, my lord? I must have misunderstood your instructions. However, we have had a most productive meeting and I am sure I will soon be able to meet Mrs Carleton's requirements.' Something about Gareth's steady regard must have penetrated his efficient good cheer, for he began to gather up his papers. 'I will be in touch, madam. No, please do not trouble to ring, I will see myself out. Good day. My lord.'

The silence as they each waited for the front door to close was almost tangible. Gareth had the illusion that if he put out a hand and touched the air between them there would be a twang like a harp string.

'You left,' he said curtly into the stillness.

'Yes. I thought it best.' She walked away from the

table and went to stand on the other side of the room, one hand resting on a chair back. 'After last night, I feel I should make it clear that I do not see that what occurred should affect our agreement in any way.'

'I took your virginity,' he said, trying to make sense of the way this conversation was veering wildly away from the way he had rehearsed it.

'I gave it to you,' she corrected gently. 'I was curious, and I was attracted and perhaps I should not have done it if I did not trust you as I do.' A faint smile played around the lips that last night he had kissed until they were swollen.

'So just what—' To his horror Gareth heard his voice begin to crack, cleared his throat and tried again. 'So just what are you expecting to happen now?'

'Why, nothing. We go on as we did before.' Jessica moved gracefully to sit down. 'Please, Gareth, do sit.'

Bemused, he did as she bade him, feeling like an awkward seventeen-year-old, not the experienced man he was. Obviously the panic he had seen in her eyes was an illusion.

'You will forgive me if I had other ideas, Jessica.'

'Other—' She broke off, biting her lip. 'Yes, of course. I realise that you might well expect that I would become your mistress after such a wanton display. But that is out of the question. I have every intention of completing this assignment as we agreed and then retiring to the country. Last night was just an…aberration.'

'Aberration?' He felt she had kicked him in the gut and the groin simultaneously. 'Jessica, I came to give you this.' He stood, lifted the morocco case and held it out to her.

She took it and sat with it unopened in her hands, a frown between her brows. 'This? Why?'

'To show you my intentions.'

There was a long silence after she opened it, while she stared down into the fitted interior and its contents. Gareth thought he could see the reflection of the emeralds in her eyes as she raised them to meet his. Then she shut the case gently, laid it on the table beside her and got to her feet. There was colour in her cheeks and for a moment her lower lip trembled. *Thank God, she realises at last...*

'It is all my fault, I realise that,' Jessica said, forcing herself to stand just in front of Gareth. 'I behaved very immodestly, led to you make assumptions. I did not think, though, that you would attempt to pay me for what happened last night. I am justly rewarded for my behaviour by that insult. I behaved like a...a loose woman and you recompense me as such.'

She felt her lip quivering and bit it savagely before she could disgrace herself. Mama had done this, but to live, so that her daughter could live. She, Jessica, had no excuse whatsoever other than her weakness for this man. Loving him was no justification.

'It was just lust, then?' he asked, his voice hard.

'What, did you think I had fallen in love with you?' she asked. The mocking laugh was a triumph of acting, she thought from somewhere inside the cold, hard shell that was growing around her like frost on a window pane. 'My lord, I am a professional, although not a professional whore. And now, if we have finished with this subject, perhaps you would be so good as to tell me which event we are attending tonight?'

'Is that it?' he demanded. The vein in his temple throbbed with suppressed emotion—anger, rigorously controlled. 'Jessica—'

'The hairdresser is coming this afternoon—it would be helpful if I know how I will be dressing this evening.'

'For the Eversheds' ball.' He picked up his cane and gloves. 'You will oblige me by wearing the emerald parure.'

'But—'

'That is an instruction from your employer, Miss Gifford. I will collect you at nine.'

The case seemed to burn her hands as she lifted it to carry it upstairs. She had thought he would understand that last night had been a single moment of recklessness, not the abandonment of everything she had worked so hard for in exchange for the gaudy insecurity and disgrace of a life as a kept woman. Had she been so very wrong in thinking he understood her, or was it all a delusion? Perhaps loving him was a delusion too.

'Madam?' Mirabelle eyed the morocco case with interest and Jessica realised she must have been standing in the middle of her bedchamber, unspeaking, for several minutes.

'His lordship has lent me this to wear to the ball tonight. What will be the best gown to complement the stones?'

The dresser gasped as she opened the box. 'Madam, these are heirloom-quality gems!' She hurried to the dressing table and picked up the goldsmith's loupe that she used when cleaning Jessica's jewellery. 'But they are new—this is not a family piece.'

No, of course not. You give your wife the family pieces,

for your mistress you buy new. 'Will the pale green silk and net go? Emerald is such a hard green to match.'

Mirabelle lifted down the large box and folded back the silver paper so Jessica could lay the necklace against the bodice of the gown. 'It is perfect. Exactly the right shade, just many tones lighter. With such a parure you will need nothing else—in fact, I think I will remove the lace trim.' She looked up for approval and Jessica nodded, remembering to smile.

How many days before we can end this? She would talk to Eva and Bel, explain that she was finding it increasingly difficult to sustain the role and asking them when they thought Lord Pangbourne would be sufficiently convinced of Gareth's unsuitability for Maude. But it would not be yet, not if he was trying to buy her off.

Another week? Another month? How was she going to bear to be with him, acting the part of his mistress, loving him and yet knowing he thought her at best a foolish, confused creature who did not know what she wanted, at worst a tease and a wanton?

Chapter Twenty-One

Gareth arrived that evening not alone, but in company with Bel. 'Poor Ashe is laid low with a shocking head cold,' she apologised, as the footman helped Jessica into the carriage. 'So I sent Gareth a note to ask if he would pick me up too.' Mercifully she seemed inclined to chat. Jessica had been dreading the ride to the ball, being alone with Gareth.

'Which gown are you wearing?' she asked, hoping Bel could not sense the chill reserve that seemed to her to roll off Gareth like mist off a frozen lake.

'A new blue one with blonde lace and a French hem. What about you?'

'Pale green silk with a gauze overskirt in a slightly darker shade. There is plaited detail at the neckline and hem and the sleeves are puffed.' Jessica chattered on, her hand clasping the throat of the crushed silk evening cloak to keep the hood up over her elaborate hairstyle. 'I had my hair done again this afternoon; I believe I am growing used to the colour.'

'Will you wash it out again, once this is all over?'

Bel asked, glancing, for some reason, at Gareth's still profile against the lights outside.

'Oh, certainly. Beside anything else, it is so distinctive; I am sure that once it is gone no one will recognise me if they should see me.'

There was the usual crush of carriages in the straw-strewn street, the usual crowd jostling politely for their places on the wide red carpet laid between the flambeaux and the lines of footmen.

Both women vanished into the retiring room to remove their cloaks and repair the damage to coiffures their hoods had caused. 'My dear!' Bel stared wide-eyed at the emeralds that emerged from Jessica's swathing layers of taffeta. She drew her to one side and whispered, 'Wherever did you get those?'

'Gareth produced them and ordered me to wear them.' Jessica made a business of tweaking her hair into order to show off the emerald clips holding up all but one trailing curl. The earrings quivered against the whiteness of her neck, the necklace lay heavy on her breast and both wrists were clasped with emerald cuffs over the long white gloves.

'Ordered?' Bel was still staring. 'They are fabulous. What a statement of intent! He might as well pin a large *Private Property Keep Off* notice on your gown.'

'I imagine that was in his mind when he bought them. I am not…happy, wearing them.'

'Well, you may give them to me in that case,' Bel said, half-laughing, half still shocked by the magnificence of the gems. 'I have nothing so splendid.'

Jessica was smiling at the frank envy in Bel's voice

as they emerged into the hallway where Gareth was waiting to escort them up the stairs to the receiving line.

'I had better go up alone,' Bel said. 'Gareth? Did you hear what I said?'

'Yes,' he said vaguely. Bel rolled her eyes at Jessica, picked up her skirts and began to edge into the line, smiling and waving at acquaintances. 'Jessica?'

'My lord?'

'You look—' He shook his head. 'Words fail me.'

'It's these wretched stones,' she said in a whisper, walking to his side and taking his arm. 'Come on, we are holding up the line.'

'No. It is you. You look...' he tried again. 'Utterly ravishing.'

Jessica tried to tell herself that it was the effect of Mirabelle removing all the lace trim at the bodice, thus creating an almost indecent expanse of bosom on which to display the trembling stars of the necklace, but the heat in his eyes was producing too extreme a reaction inside her for common sense to have much effect.

She had not realised how it would feel to be so close to him again, to feel the heat of his arm under hers, sense the discreet fragrance of oriental spice and citrus overlying warm, clean man, to glance up at the hard-cut line of his chin and the familiar, beloved crookedness of his broken nose.

This is so hard. I love you, she murmured under her breath. Gareth glanced down, but she merely smiled and, remembering to play her part, brushed an almost invisible fleck of lint from his lapel.

People moved aside slightly as she passed, skirts drawn back from the courtesan's contaminating touch.

Jessica felt the colour mounting in her cheeks and moved closer to Gareth. 'They are staring at me.'

'I'm not surprised. Jessica—' Something had changed. The anger that had gripped him that morning seemed to have evaporated, leaving the old Gareth behind. Imperceptibly she relaxed; she had hated being at odds with him.

'Shh! Someone might hear.' They had reached the head of the stairs. The Marchioness of Evershed stood, formidable and frosty, awaiting them. Jessica braced herself for the *cut direct*.

'Aunt Hermione, what a quite fabulous gown.'

His aunt? Jessica attempted to melt into the background as Gareth was kissed on both cheeks, then had his wrist slapped with a large lacquer fan.

'You are a very naughty young man—still, I don't blame you. That Maude Templeton is a flighty little thing.' She fixed Jessica with a hard stare. 'Is that a family set, Morant?'

'No. It is new,' Gareth said politely—Jessica could hear the mingled exasperation and amusement in his voice.

'Good. I congratulate you, young woman. Hold tight to your Maubourg protector, though, and remember, all men are bastards.'

Jessica was still gasping as they reached the end of the receiving line. 'Did she really say that?'

'Oh, yes. Aunt Hermione worked her way through two husbands and four lovers that I know of, before netting Evershed. Jessica—'

'Yes?' He was looking at her with a sort of rueful tenderness that made her heart twist painfully. 'I only want you to be happy, you know. You must do as you wish.'

It undermined her determination more than his expectation that she be his mistress had done. He would miss her, that look said. He wanted her, but he would let her go.

'Thank you,' she said firmly, with a hard-won smile. 'I believe you, Gareth. Now, we must not look so serious or people will think we are quarrelling. Look, there is Eva and Lord Sebastian. Who is that in the blue uniform?'

The tall, distinguished officer in pale blue and silver lace was standing, head cocked to one side, listening to Eva. 'That is the Maubourg uniform,' Gareth said. 'He didn't come over with Eva—he must have come with messages from the Regent.'

They stood for a moment, watching the magnificently dressed throng passing to and fro. Most of the men greeted Gareth, their eyes running over Jessica with carefully shielded assessment. The ladies nodded coolly to him and ignored her. It was strange to be treated as though she were invisible, or a curiosity, but she was becoming used to it; if she had Gareth by her side she did not care. It was not for much longer; she needed to hoard the memories for the long, lonely years.

Cross with herself, she gave her head a little shake, setting the earrings swinging. Not *lonely*, she corrected. *Independent*. It was what she had worked for, what Mama had sacrificed upbringing and morality for. She could not, must not, allow a man to make her weak. This, with Gareth, was for days. She had the rest of her life to be prudent for.

'Penny for them?' he asked, smiling, and her treacherous pulse beat hard.

'Do you think the world would be well lost for

love?' she asked lightly, expecting him to make a teasing response.

'Yes,' he said bleakly. 'I do. But you have to find it first, do you not?' Then, as quickly as the darkness had entered his eyes, he was smiling again and sweeping her on to the dance floor as a waltz struck up.

They danced until Jessica's feet in her glacé kid slippers were aching, dance after dance together, both of them smiling and talking and, to any onlooker, she was certain, enthralled in their own private world.

But she was hiding herself from him and he was guarding his inner thoughts from her, she could tell. Being in his arms, the rhythms of the music, the heat and the heady scent of flowers heightened her awareness of him as a male animal and an insidious pulse began to beat low down and inside, where he had filled her, she ached, missing him.

Gareth felt it too, she sensed. His eyes were hooded, his hands when they touched her were firm and possessive, and when those grey eyes lifted and met hers, the heat in them scorched her.

'I must go to the retiring room for a minute,' Jessica confided as they walked off the floor after a vigorous country dance. She stood on tiptoe and whispered, 'One of my garters is loose.'

'Come out on to the terrace and I will tie it for you,' Gareth suggested wickedly.

'Certainly not.' She hesitated as she turned, one hand spread on the breast of his coat as she smiled up at him. 'We know where that sort of thing leads.' It was a risk, alluding to last night so lightly, but his mouth quirked and he smiled as she had hoped he would. Thank goodness—perhaps they were finding their way back on to solid ground again.

'I will fetch champagne and wait for you here,' was all he said as Jessica began to weave her way towards the door leading to a withdrawing room. It would, she thought, give her a short cut to the corridor where the ladies' retiring room was situated.

It was empty. People were beginning to leave the dance floor for the supper room and it was a little too early for weary dancers to be wanting to rest their feet. It would only take a second to tie her garter and if she did it here she would not have to run the gauntlet of supercilious feminine stares in the retiring room .

Jessica put one foot on a low table and pulled up her skirt to her knee. The garter knot had pulled tight and she had to wrestle with it before she could free it and retie the ribbon to secure her stocking. As the door opened behind her, she tossed down her skirts and put both feet on the floor with more haste than grace.

'Tying your garter in public? Tut, tut, Mrs Carleton.' It was Captain Grahame in uniform, the formality of a dress sword by his side.

'An empty room is hardly public, Captain, and a gentleman would have taken himself out again the moment he saw a lady who obviously wanted privacy.' Jessica smoothed down her skirts with a steady hand, the baleful gleam of the emeralds at her wrist lending her courage.

'But then you are not a lady, are you, Mrs Carleton? You are a light heeled wench, one who prays on her back.'

'I have no intention of listening to your smutty talk, Captain. Kindly take yourself off.' She should turn and walk out of the door in the far corner of the room, but she was damned if she was going to give him the satisfaction of routing her.

He grinned, a feline smirk that made her want to slap him, and moved close, so close that she could give way to that temptation very easily. She should have walked away, she realized, as his hand came up and he gripped her right wrist, forcing the metal of the emerald cuff painfully against the narrow bones.

'No wonder you sneered at a paltry couple of thousand pounds,' he remarked, turning the cuff back and forth, twisting her arm with it. 'I must tell Lord Pangbourne to raise his offer.'

The pain brought tears to her eyes and she bit back a cry of distress. She would *not* give him the satisfaction. But she could box his ears. Jessica clenched her left fist and raised it, catching him sharply.

'You little slut!' Jessica found herself yanked hard against his chest, her ears filled with a stream of obscenities. He was furious, as big as Gareth and as strong and she was being shaken like a rat by a terrier. Then as she staggered, breathless, he took her mouth in a hard, wet kiss.

She bit his tongue and he pushed her away. She should scream, she knew it, scream the place down before he really hurt her. But if she did that Gareth would know and would challenge him and that was what Grahame wanted, the chance to wound, perhaps to kill.

'Whore!' He was following her across the room as she backed away from him, her eyes searching for something, anything to use as a weapon. Then the backs of her knees came up hard against an obstacle and she stumbled, threw out a hand to save herself, found something, gripped it and crashed to the ground in a great shattering of porcelain.

There was water everywhere, flowers, something hard and metallic hit her on the head and rolled away to crash against a table covered in bibelots.

'My God!' That was Eva, her voice carrying, and the room was suddenly full of noise. A man bent over her, brushing away the flowers.

'Are you hurt, *madame*?' His accent was foreign; she shook her dizzy head and tried to focus. Blue and silver: the officer from Maubourg.

'No, just shaken, thank you.' He helped her to her feet and she stared round the room in horror. In falling she had taken down a tripod with a vast flower arrangement perched on top; the results appeared to cover half the floor. Eva, a young couple she did not recognise, a distinguished elderly man with the ribbon of some order across his chest and Lady Evershed were all staring with horror at her. Captain Grahame, his face white, one ear scarlet, stood in the middle. The officer in blue kept his hand under her arm. The door into the ballroom was, thank God, shut.

'I tripped,' she explained, trying to sound as though the only thing on her mind was the demolition of her hostess's best Worcester. 'I am so sorry about the vase.'

'Madame did indeed trip,' the man beside her said. 'She was fleeing this…person.' He gestured at Grahame, who began to bluster.

'How dare you, I was attempting to assist Mrs Carleton—'

'Liar.' The officer added something in French, which Jessica did not understand, but Grahame obviously did.

'You will meet me for that,' he stormed.

'But certainly, *monsieur*. Name your—'

The door opened and Gareth walked in with a champagne bottle and two empty glasses dangling from the fingers of one hand. It was obvious he had heard nothing, but had simply come in search of her.

Eva made as though to put out a hand and then stopped, arrested as Jessica was by the expression on his face as he took in the scene.

'My darling, there is blood on your wrist. Who put it there?' He might have been discussing the weather, but there was rage in his eyes.

'Mrs Carleton fell—' Captain Grahame began.

'*Silence, cochon,*' the Maubourg officer snapped. 'My lord, this pig was assaulting the lady as I entered the room.'

'Then I thank you for your assistance, Colonel. You...' he stalked forward until he was almost nose to nose with Grahame '...will name your friends. Should you have any.'

'I regret, my lord,' the Colonel said, 'I am before you. This creature has challenged me. However, should you wish, I am more than willing to merely wound him so you may have your satisfaction in turn.'

'I would not put you to so much trouble,' Gareth said with an awful politeness, bunching one formidable fist and punching Grahame squarely under the chin. His fall completed the demolition of the bibelot table.

Gareth did not stop to look at what damage he had inflicted, nor did any of the onlookers move to help the captain. No one spoke as Gareth lifted Jessica's hand in his and stared down at the red marks that stained her white gloves. 'My love. Let me take you home.'

Home. My love. The room was spinning. Eva seemed to be coming towards them, very, very slowly. But someone else was moving. 'Gareth! Behind you!'

He spun round and Grahame's dress sword ripped through the fabric of his coat. She saw him wince, then he completed his turn with total control, seized the other man's sword hand and bent it back. There was a small disgusting noise like twigs snapping and the captain screamed.

'Her Serene Highness says this would be a good moment to faint,' the Colonel whispered in Jessica's ear. 'I will catch you.'

She did not need the suggestion. Jessica fought against it, but blackness was pressing in, her view of the room was getting smaller and smaller and she felt herself falling and being held. 'Gareth. My love...' But it was not his arms that supported her and it was not his voice that murmured reassurance as she slipped into blackness.

'Jessica?' That was not Gareth either. She dragged open her eyes to see Eva sitting by the bed she was stretched out upon. The room was totally unfamiliar.

'Gareth?' She sat up and the chamber spun. 'The sword—'

'He is alive,' Eva reassured her briskly. 'He has a nasty scratch all along his right side, that is all. Now lie down. You are in one of Lady Evershed's guest chambers. The Marchioness is explaining to the witnesses of that little scene that both she and I are relying upon their utmost discretion. Colonel de Arnheim is removing Captain Grahame to a surgeon while explaining to him that he, as a gentleman, has no intention of meeting someone who draws on an unarmed man and attempts to run him through from behind. The Colonel is pointing out to the Captain that the resignation of his commission, coupled with a speedy retreat to his country estate, would be the healthiest option open to him.'

There was a tap at the door and Bel peeped in. 'Oh, good, she is awake. Look, I have warm water and bandages, I think we should do something about that wrist.'

Bel was inclined to fuss, Eva to use the same technique that Jessica used with small children who had fallen over: speak firmly and calmly and they will conclude there is nothing to worry about. The only problem with that approach was that it only worked if the recipient was not aware of it.

Jessica submitted to having her glove cut off and her wrist bandaged by Bel. Over the top of her friend's bent head she met Eva's dark gaze squarely. 'How much of a mess are we in?'

'Less than one might expect.' Eva kicked off her shoes and put her feet up on the bed with a sign of relief. 'That's better. Goodness knows how one is excepted to stand about when the baby gets any bigger, my ankles are swelling already. This episode has brought forward my strategy to have you run away back to Maubourg by a few weeks, that is all.'

'But it is too soon. Maude—'

'Maude having got wind of what has occurred—naturally I told her—has informed her father that she is utterly humiliated by his attempts to buy you off so that Gareth would return to her and marry her. Pangbourne has finally grasped that the match would be a disaster and has promised her he will not pursue it.'

'Thank heavens for that,' Jessica said with feeling.

'Indeed. Now, unless you are enjoying playing, Mrs Carleton—no, I thought it was beginning to pall—I think you have been frightened and disgusted by the demonstration of masculine violence you have just been the focus of. Colonel de Arnheim, who was not the officer I had in mind, but who will do very nicely, will take advantage of your feelings and bear you off to Maubourg tonight. Gareth will be left broken hearted and will, no doubt, retreat to his estates to lick his wounds.'

'How very neat,' Jessica said faintly. 'But I cannot go to Maubourg.'

'You are very welcome, but I understand Gareth's man of business is busy finding you a nice house in Winchester, so you can go and stay with Bel's second cousin who lives just outside the city. She is elderly and almost blind, but I dare say you will not mind that for a week or two until your house is ready.'

'No, it is so kind of you, if the lady does not mind,' Jessica said faintly. It was very strange being organised like this.

'Cousin Mildred will be delighted,' Bel said. 'If you do not mind reading to her and walking her lap dog, it would be appreciated, I am certain. It will help establish your credentials in the city, for she knows everyone and can introduce you all around.'

'Excellent, thank you so much.' Jessica smiled, finding to her horror that the thought appalled her. Respectable society in a cathedral city, chatting politely to well-bred and staid ladies. She could get herself a pet dog. She would certainly need to hire a lady companion. There would be useful charitable work to be done. Only a few weeks ago she would have seen that as the height of her ambitions, the fulfilment of her dream of independence—now she rather thought she would rather run away to the Grand Duchy with Colonel de Arnheim.

Life without Gareth was insupportable, she realised that now. And she was probably never going to see him again.

There was a knock at the door. 'May I come in?' It was Gareth.

Chapter Twenty-Two

'We are just going.' Eva and Bel were on their feet and out of the door before Jessica could protest.

Gareth stood aside for them, then closed the door and stood with his back to it, watching her. He looked paler than usual. He was without his coat and waistcoat and his shirt, presumably borrowed, was open at the neck. He seemed to need the silence and the stillness, so she did not speak, only wished she could smooth back the hair that was falling across his forehead and massage away the line between his brows.

'How badly hurt are you?' he asked abruptly. If she had not known him so well, she would have thought him curt; now she knew he was controlling himself with some difficulty.

'I have a graze on my wrist,' she said temperately, ignoring the fact that it was raw and burning like fire. 'And I expect I will have bruises in unmentionable places after landing on the floor like that. I have no need to be lying upon this bed, other than to stop Bel fussing; it is you who should be lying down.'

'My ribs are sore, that is all. You fainted. I should have killed him.'

'And would have had to flee abroad,' Jessica snapped, relief making her irritable. 'A very sensible reaction, my lord.'

'Let us be sensible at all costs.' Gareth smiled faintly and came to sit on the end of the bed. 'And I have to admit, it was very satisfying, hitting him on the spot rather than having to hang around for a meeting.'

'Good. I wish I had punched him myself, but he is rather large. I did box his ear, though.'

'You should not have needed to, I should not have left you.'

Oh dear, he is going to be very male *about this*, she thought, trying to steady her nerves with some inner humour. But it was not working. It was touching that he cared and his anger and his response when he had hit Grahame were shamefully arousing. And his words when he had seen her…

'You could hardly escort me to the ladies' retiring room,' she pointed out prosaically. *We are not going to make a drama out of this.* 'Eva has been telling me about her clever plan for me to appear to run off with the colonel. I am afraid it will make you appear to have been—what is the word for losing your mistress to another man?'

'Outbid?' Gareth chuckled. 'My pride and my dignity will stand it. Eva thinks I should retreat to my estates and brood, but I think I will walk around town looking brave and broken hearted for a week or so.'

'All the young ladies will try and comfort you.' It was hard to produce the little laugh and the smile to accompany her teasing.

'I will not need comforting.' He lifted her uninjured hand and looked down at it, playing with her fingers. 'Jessica, I realised something last night, something I should have seen days before. I love you. I want to marry you.'

For a moment she thought she was going to faint again, she who had never fainted in her life before this evening. The emotion that swept through her was so complex that she did not know what she was feeling. Joy? Love? Despair? Yes, all of those, because, of course, it could never be.

'Gareth.' His fingers closed tight around hers and she made herself look at him, at the strong face and the deep eyes and the freckle on his cheekbone and the dark sweep of his lashes. 'It is impossible.'

'It is if you do not love me,' he agreed. 'Tell me the truth.'

'I love you.' To deny it would be to deny herself. His eyes closed and against her fingers his pulse thudded, hard. 'But it cannot be.'

He did not answer her with words, simply pulled her into his arms and lowered his mouth to hers, parting her lips, thrusting slowly, possessively, into the heat of her mouth, stroking the softness into desire. When he lifted his head, his eyes were dark. 'It can be. You are worried that society knows you are Francesca Carleton and that will be a challenge to overcome, but we will overcome it somehow, I just have to think of some stratagem.'

'No. That is not why.' She had hoped never to tell him, but whatever else happened this evening she was not going to lie to him. 'I am not a suitable wife for you.

It has nothing to do with this masquerade we have been acting out.'

'You are a gentlewoman, a lady of accomplishment and grace. You have obviously been gently reared. There is no disgrace in your profession,' Gareth said fiercely. 'If anyone thinks to slight you—' He would have gone on, but she put up a hand and pressed her fingertips to his lips, silencing him.

'My mother was the daughter of a banker, a prosperous, respectable man. My father was the younger son of the Buckinghamshire Giffords, an ancient family. They do not seem to go about much in society, but I believe they have connections to many of the great families.'

'That is perfectly eligible, Jessica. I do not see—'

'You will if you let me finish,' she said quietly. 'Papa was a captain in the infantry. He was handsome, charming, wonderful fun and completely feckless in his private life, although I understand he was an excellent officer. He and Mama eloped, for her father would never countenance such a match. Then he sold out and lived on his wits—he was a gambler. I suspect, a sharp.

'Sometimes we had money to burn, sometimes we found ourselves sneaking out of lodgings in the early hours because of the rent. It was feast or famine.' She smiled, reminiscent, and Gareth did not try to speak. 'They were so much in love, so happy. It was always fun. And then he died.'

'And there was no more money?' Gareth lifted her hand and kissed the knuckles, lingeringly. Jessica rubbed her cheek against the back of his hand.

'No. Mama's family would not help, she had been cast off. Nor would the Giffords. If I had been a boy, perhaps, but I was just a girl. So Mama used what she had, her looks and her charm and her wits. She found a protector—a string of them, in fact. She never spoke of why they gave her money, only that Mr this and Lord that were so kind, so generous. She knew, as I got older, that I knew, but we never spoke of it.

'What happened?' Gareth asked. He was still holding her hand, he had not recoiled in disgust yet. But he would know, now, that this was impossible. Earls might marry bankers' granddaughters, but they do not marry the daughters of barques of frailty, or whatever nice little euphemism you used to indicate that a woman sold her body.

'She died of a summer fever when I was seventeen. The protector of the moment made me an offer which I refused, politely. I sold everything, buried her decently, and resolved to never have to be ashamed of how I earned my living.'

Gareth put down her hand and got up from the bed. Jessica tried to read his face, but he looked merely thoughtful as he wandered round the room, fiddling with the books that lay on a side table, adjusting the lamp slightly. When he spoke she realised that he had been giving himself time to control his voice. 'And are you ashamed of last night?'

'No! I wanted you and I love you and I needed that night to give me a memory for the rest of my life. I would never feel shame for that.'

'Nor should you feel shame for what your mother did. If anyone should it was your grandparents, all of them, for their lack of charity and their intolerance. Jessica, I love *you*. I do not care if your father was a card sharp or a bishop, I do not care if your mother was a duchess or a courtesan.'

'But society will care, and someone will remember and will talk. As a governess no one noticed me—even if an employer had once been royally rooked by James Gifford, why should he connect him with me? And if he once shared Miranda Gifford's favours, he would not connect her with the governess. But the marriage of an earl is news and the eyes of all society will be on your bride. What will you do—call out every man who mentions my mother?'

'If that is what it takes,' Gareth said steadily. 'I love you, Jessica. Marry me.'

'I love you too.' She got up and went to stand in front of him, her hands flat on his chest, his warmth and the beat of his heart under her palms. 'And I will not marry you.'

'I can make you.' His voice was rough as he took her in his arms, pushed her back so she sprawled on the bed. 'I will make love to you until you say yes, until you have no will left to resist me.' His weight on her was heaven, his mouth on hers, bliss. Her body knew his now, knew how to arch into his, knew what the heat and hardness stroking against her belly meant. She wanted him. If he lay with her again, she would go up like dry leaves at the touch of his flame and if he asked her to be his mistress she knew, to her shame, she would say yes. But she could never marry him. Never.

'I cannot resist you, you know that perfectly well.' He had lifted his head to watch her face as he moved against her and she saw his triumph at her capitulation. Her breathing was all over the place, but she managed to say the words. 'I will be your mistress, Gareth.'

'No!'

Oh, but it was cold and lonely without him, even though he was only feet away where his instinctive recoil at her words had taken him. Jessica sat up, clutching her knees for want of anything else to hang on to. 'Yes. Or nothing. There is no other way for us to be together without disgracing your name and you know it. I would have no shame in being your mistress, because I love you.'

'Take it or leave it?' he asked harshly. She nodded. 'Then I leave it. Wayman will be in touch; our former agreement stands.'

She bit down hard on her lip, determined that she would not cry until the door closed behind him. But when it did, they would not come. There was no relief to be had that way, only a future where her consolation had to be that she had done the right thing.

'Thank you, Lucy. Will you go and make some tea now please?' Jessica sank down on a packing case and watched the May sunlight streaming through the window making the dust motes dance. There was plenty of dust and a lot of sun streaming through the uncurtained windows.

One housemaid, one footman, a cook and a tweeny made up her new household and all of them seemed to have spent the last week covered in dust. But the little house was coming together now, the curtains and the carpets would be delivered soon and she almost had enough parlour furniture in place to invite old Mrs Chivers, Bel's cousin, and her equally elderly friends to tea.

In the weeks since she had left London, Jessica had

felt she was watching a play in which a character representing her had moved upon a stage, smiling, talking, organising. She, the real Jessica, had sat in her box, her cold, dark and empty box, and watched the fictitious Jessica acting out her life.

People had been so kind. Winchester was everything she had hoped it would be. The house was a gem, the garden a delight. She rinsed the dye out of her hair and braided it up neatly. She had bought a puppy, all feet and tail and lolling tongue and its soft warmth gave her something to hold against her breast and a reason to put on her bonnet and take exercise, greeting her new neighbours, just as though she was a real person and not a ghost.

Mr Wayman had sent a young man to make sure everything was just as it should be, to help hire servants and to escort her to the furniture warehouses and the upholsterers. Her elderly friends all adopted him and made a great fuss of that nice young Mr Peters, and he showed no sign of having to rush back to London, but ran errands for them and was fattened up on cakes and scones. He mentioned Mr Wayman frequently, but never Gareth, and Jessica assumed he knew nothing of her background.

She looked around the dining room, absently wiping one grubby hand across her damp forehead. The mouldings around the ceiling were charming, but a perfect dust trap, and she and Lucy had spent the morning taking it in turns to steady the stepladder while the other wielded the feather duster. She should have waited until the tweeny, twelve-year-old Gertrude, had finished helping Cook to scrub the scullery, but hard physical work seemed the only thing these days that made her feel real.

The knock at the front door was unexpected. Her small circle of new friends knew she was not receiving yet, so it must be a delivery. She waited a moment, but there was no patter of feet along the hallway; Lucy was obviously still in the kitchen.

There was a second knock. Jessica twitched her apron into place and pushed back her hair as she went to answer it. Pansy the puppy skittered out of the drawing room as she passed, claws clicking on the polished boards, tail flailing. Jessica reached down for her collar as she pulled open the door. The last time Pansy had managed to escape it had taken three of them to catch her again, much to the amusement of most of the inhabitants of the square.

'Sit!' Jessica ordered, squinting upwards from her doubled-up position at a pair of well-muscled thighs in buckskin breeches, a broad chest and a very familiar chin.

'I will sit if you order me to so firmly, but these steps are likely to be cold,' Gareth said, managing to sound pained while grinning at her.

'I didn't mean you!' Jessica scooped up the puppy and stood upright, hanging on to it until it squeaked in protest. 'Gareth, what are you doing here?'

'Collecting my bride,' he said, ignoring her gasp of shock. 'Peters, come and deal with the household—my orders are clear, I hope?'

'My lord.' It was Mr Peters, nice helpful Mr Peters who wasn't supposed to know anything about her, tipping his hat as he slid past her and into the hallway.

'Gareth, you cannot walk in here and take control like this!'

'It is my house,' he pointed out reasonably. 'And

you, my love, are about to become my wife now I have worked out how to do it without causing a scandal to distress you. Come along.' There was a travelling carriage at the kerb, there were trunks strapped on behind and a greatcoat-clad driver up on the box.

'Come along? I can't just *come along*, for goodness' sake! I told you I cannot marry you and why—Gareth! No!' He bent and picked her up, puppy and all, with as little effort as she had picked up Pansy. The puppy, with her usual promiscuous affection, licked him on the nose.

'I hope she's a good traveller. I made no allowance for puppies in my abduction plan.' Gareth strode down the steps and bundled Jessica and Pansy into the carriage, following them in before Jessica could reach the far door handle. The carriage moved off and he sat back, smiling at her.

'I had no idea you were such a messy housewife,' he observed.

'What?' Jessica put the squirming puppy on the floor where she promptly started to lick Gareth's boots. 'Oh, for goodness' sake, look at me!' She was swathed in a vast apron that had begun the day white and was now streaked with dirt, her front hair was in her eyes and her hands were filthy. No doubt her face was too.

'I am looking, my love,' he said, leaning forward and removing a cobweb from her hair. 'I rather like my prim and proper governess like this, all hot and bothered. It brings on an urge to make you even more flustered.'

'I am as flustered as I need to be,' Jessica said, striving for control. But this was Gareth; he was here, and suddenly she was real again. 'Gareth, what are we *doing*?'

'Driving to my estate near Romsey—you see how

very convenient it was of you to choose Winchester? We will be there easily by dinner time. Tomorrow we will be married in the parish church by special licence and the day after that, my love, the Earl and Countess of Standon will depart secretly for the Continent on my yacht from Southampton.'

'But—'

'Which is where everyone thinks I am at this moment.'

'But—'

'In the course of my travels—nursing my wounded pride and broken heart over Mrs Carleton—I shall meet the charming Miss Gifford, educationalist, who is making a study of French art. She is somewhat like Mrs Carleton in looks, as people will notice when we return to London after our prolonged honeymoon. Miss Gifford is a lady of elegant restraint, of course—not at all like the other lady everyone will be too polite to mention—and society will be too kind to remark upon Lord Standon's obvious partiality for blonde ladies with green eyes.'

It was inspired. It would work, of course it would. People saw exactly what they expected and she had hardly exchanged a word with anyone except Gareth's cousins. But… 'Gareth—my parents.'

'No one will remember,' he said gently. 'And if some gentleman saw something of your mama in you, would he want to hurt the daughter of such a sweet lady? I do not think so.'

He was right. It was going to be all right. She was going to marry Gareth. Tears were welling up; the only way to fight them was with briskness. 'I have been here *weeks*. Where were you?'

'It has taken me weeks to work this out, make all the arrangements, be seen brooding darkly around town. I sent Peters to keep an eye on you—some days I have had to make do with reports that simply said *Miss Gifford is undecided upon the colour of the drawing-room curtains. It rained today, so she has purchased an umbrella.*'

'I thought my heart was broken,' she managed and then she was in his arms, her hands tangling in his hair and she was kissing him as she had dreamt of kissing him through the long, lonely nights. 'But now you have mended it.'

'Then let us go home, my love, because I have a very pressing need to carry you over my threshold, up the stairs and into my bedroom.'

'Not before we are married,' Jessica said firmly. 'We will shock the servants.'

'Very well.' He reached for the blinds, jerking them down. 'Let us shock one impressionable puppy then, because, my love, I need, very badly, to show you how much I love you and have missed you.'

An hour later Jessica became vaguely aware of the sound of muffled chewing as she lay, bare and hot and slicked with perspiration in Gareth's arms on the cramped seat. She slid up his chest, provoking a sleepy male grumble, and peered down over his shoulder. Pansy, blissfully happy, was chewing the tan top of one of Gareth's beautiful boots. It had all been rather too much excitement for one barely housetrained puppy: Gareth's breeches were not going to be wearable and his valet was going to be very unhappy indeed.

'Gareth,' she murmured into his ear. He grunted,

nuzzling his face into her neck. 'I'm afraid Pansy has demolished your clothes. We are going to end up shocking the servants after all.'

He opened his eyes and regarded her severely. 'Then, madam, I suggest you ensure I am in a very good mood by the time we get to Standon Hall.' His pocket watch was hanging by its chain from a hook on the squabs. 'I think you have about three-quarters of an hour.'

'Oh.' Jessica contemplated some of the things she had dreamt about doing to the long hard body stretched beneath her. 'Very well, my lord.' She began to slide down his body again. 'Would this put you in a good mood, my love?'

'It puts me in Heaven,' he murmured huskily, reaching out to play with her hair as it flowed over his chest. She stretched out a hand to link her fingers through his, feeling the strength and the tenderness, and knowing, with all the years ahead, that it was only going to get better.

* * * * *

THE DISGRACEFUL MR RAVENHURST

In the course of their courtship Ashe Reynard informed Belinda Felsham (*The Outrageous Lady Felsham*) that she should stop matchmaking for her bluestocking cousin Elinor because what Elinor needed was an intellectual, someone who could match her intelligence.

The problem was, where could Elinor, firmly on the shelf, find such a man? One who would see past the drab gowns and meek studiousness to the warm, loving, adventurous woman inside? Especially when she was convinced she did not want a man at all.

And then there was Theo Ravenhurst, in disgrace and, so his mother kept insisting, off on the Grand Tour. Only I had my suspicions that Theo was not pursuing a blameless course around the cultural sights of Europe but was up to something altogether less conventional. What would happen if these two cousins met, I wondered?

I hope you enjoy finding out and, if you have the first three Ravenhurst novels, meeting again Eva and Sebastian, young Freddie and the indomitable Lady James.

Coming next will be *The Notorious Mr Hurst*. Lady Maude Templeton, having escaped marriage to Ravenhurst cousin Gareth Morant (*The Shocking Lord Standon*) has already fallen for the entirely inappropriate attractions of theatre owner Eden Hurst. She knows what she wants, and is not used to being thwarted, but this time it looks as though everyone, from society to the gentleman himself, is set on her not getting her heart's desire.

Chapter One

August 1816—Vezelay, Burgundy

The naked female figure danced in timeless sensual abandon, revelling in the provocation of her blatant sexuality. The face of the hapless man watching her was etched with mingled despair and lust as he reached out for her, blind and deaf to the imploring prayers of the holy man who watched the scene unfold from behind a pillar.

It was hard to see the detail clearly in the shadows, and having to crane her neck upwards did not help, but the scene was unmistakable—and who was at fault, equally plain.

'Honestly! Men!' Exasperated, Elinor stepped backwards, furled parasol, rigid sketch book, sharp elbows and sensible boots, every one of them an offensive weapon.

'Ough!' The gasp from behind her as she made contact with something solid, large and obviously male, was agonised. 'I beg your pardon,' the voice con-

tinued on a croak as she swung round, fetching the man
an additional thwack with her easel.

'What for?' she demanded, startled out of her cus-
tomary good manners as she turned to face the
doubled-up figure of her victim. 'I struck you, sir. I
should apologise, not you.'

As he straightened up to a not inconsiderable height,
a shaft of sunlight penetrated the cracked glass of the
high window, illuminating a head of dark red hair that
put her own tawny locks to shame. 'You were express-
ing dissatisfaction with the male sex, ma'am; I was
apologising on behalf of my brothers for whatever sin
we are guilty of this time.' His tone was meek, but she
was not deceived—there was strength in the deep voice
and a thread of wicked amusement.

Yes, said a voice inside Elinor's head. *Yes. At last.*
She shook her head, blinking away the sun dazzle and
whatever idiocy her mind was up to, and stepped to one
side to see her victim better. He was smiling, a conspiratorial twist of his lips that transformed a strong but
not particularly distinguished face into one that was
disarmingly attractive. Somehow he had succeeded in
charming an answering smile out of her.

She was not, Elinor reminded herself sternly, given
to smiling at strange men. It must be part and parcel of
hearing things. The voice had gone away now; no doubt
it had been some trick of an echo in this cavernous
place.

'I was referring to that capital.' Hampered by her
armful of belongings she dumped them without
ceremony on a nearby pew, keeping hold only of the
furled parasol, partly as a pointer, partly because of its
merits as a sharp implement. All men, her mother was

apt to warn her, were Beasts. It was as well not to take risks with chance-met ones, even if they did appear to be polite English gentlemen. She gestured with the parasol towards the richly carved column top, Number 6B in her annotated sketches. 'It is a Romanesque capital; that is to say—'

'It was carved between 1120 and 1150 and is one of a notable series that makes the basilica of Vezelay an outstanding example of religious art of the period,' he finished for her, sounding like an antiquarian paper on the subject.

'Of course, I should have realised that, if you are visiting the basilica, you must understand architecture,' she apologised, gazing round the wreckage of the once-great church. Outside of service times no one else was going to enter here on a whim. 'Are you a clergyman, sir?'

'Do I look like one?' The stranger appeared mildly affronted by the suggestion.

'Er…no.' And he did not, although why that should be, Elinor had no idea. Many men of the cloth must have red hair. Some must also possess smiles that invited you to smile right back at a shared, and slightly irreverent, joke. And, without doubt, tall and athletic figures graced pulpits up and down the land.

'Thank goodness for that.' She noticed that he offered no explanation of himself in response to her question. 'So…' He tipped back his head, fisting his hands, one of which held his tall hat, on his hips to balance himself. 'What exactly is it about this particular scene that merits your ire, ma'am?'

'It shows, as usual, a man succumbing to his own base animal instincts and lack of self-control and blaming his subsequent moral downfall upon a woman,' she said crisply.

'I must say, your eyesight is excellent if you can deduce all that in this light.'

'I have been studying the capitals for a week now with the aid of an opera glass; one gets one's eye in.' Elinor stared round at the nave, littered with crumbling masonry, broken pews and rubbish. 'I have had to go round at least three times in an attempt to interpret as many as possible when the light is at its best. It is still possible to do that, but unless something is done very soon, I fear they may all fall or be damaged beyond repair or study. See the holes in the roof? The carvings must be exposed to the elements, even in here.'

'You are a scholar, then?' He was squinting upwards, his eyes fixed on the carved figures, frozen in their eternal masque of temptation and yielding. 'Researching the iniquities of the medieval male mind, perhaps?'

'My mother is the scholar, I am merely recording the carvings for her detailed study. She is an authority on the early churches of France and England.' Elinor could have added that the medieval male mind probably differed little from its modern counterpart when it came to moral turpitude, but decided against it. It was not as though she had any experience of turpitude to base the assertion upon.

'Indeed?' The man switched his attention from the carving to her face and this time the smile lit up his eyes as well. They were green, she noticed. An unusual clear green, like water over pebbles, not the indeterminate hazel that looked back at her whenever she spared a glance in a glass to check that her bonnet was at least straight and there were no charcoal smudges on her nose. 'I feel sure I should meet your respected parent. May I call?'

'You are a scholar too?' Elinor began to gather up her things, stuffing pencils, charcoal and paints into the battered leather satchel and swinging it over her shoulder. 'I am joining her now, if you would care to accompany me.'

'Let's just say I have an interest in antiquities.' He removed the easel from her hands, folded its legs up, lashed the straps around it with a competence that suggested he used one himself, and tucked it under his arm. There was a short struggle for possession of the stool, which he won, and for the parasol, which Elinor retained. 'You are staying in Vezelay?'

'Yes, we have been here seven days now. We are making our way down through France, visiting a number of the finer early cathedrals. Mama intends that we will remain at Vezelay for several weeks yet. *Merci, monsieur.*' She smiled and nodded to the verger, who was wielding a broom and stirring up the gritty dust in the porch. 'Sweeping seems pointless, he would be better employed on the roof with a tarpaulin.'

She dropped a coin into the outstretched hand of the beggar by the door and headed diagonally across the open space before the basilica, glancing up at her companion as she did so. 'We have lodgings just down the hill here.'

There was something vaguely familiar about him, although she could not place it. It certainly made him easy to talk to. Normally Miss Ravenhurst would have contented herself with a polite inclination of the head and a murmured *good day* when she came across a male countryman to whom she had not been introduced. It would never have occurred to her to invite one back to their lodgings to meet Mama.

Perhaps it was the red hair, somewhat extinguished now as he clapped his hat back on his head. Being one of the red-headed Ravenhursts, she saw a less spectacular version of it every time she looked in the glass. It was generally considered to be a handicap in a lady, although if hers was less a good match for a chestnut horse and more the flame of well-polished mahogany by firelight as his was, she might have felt more reconciled to it. He seemed to have avoided freckles as well, she noticed with envy, but then, his skin was not as fair as hers was.

'Here we are.' It was only a few minutes' walk down the steep main street, although it always took rather longer to toil back up the slippery cobbles to the basilica. The door was on the latch and she pushed it open, calling, 'Mama? Are you at home? We have a visitor.'

'In here, Elinor.' She followed her mother's voice through into the parlour, leaving her belongings on the hall bench and gesturing to the tall man to put the easel and stool down, too. At the sight of him, Lady James Ravenhurst rose to her feet from behind the table, its chequered cloth strewn with papers and books.

'Mama, this gentleman is a scholar of antiquities who wishes to meet—'

'Theophilus!' Lady James lifted her quizzing glass to her eye and stared, for once clearly out of countenance.

Elinor stared, too. 'Cousin Theo?' Her disgraceful

and disgraced cousin Theo? Here? 'I haven't seen you for years.'

'Not since I was twelve, fifteen years ago,' he agreed. 'You must have been about seven. I wondered if it was you, Cousin Elinor.'

'The hair, I suppose,' she said, resigned to it being her most memorable feature. 'I was ten,' she added, ruthlessly honest. It was nice of him to pretend he thought she was only twenty-two now, and not an on-the-shelf spinster of almost twenty-six.

'What are you doing here, Theophilus? I under-stood from your mama that you were undertaking the Grand Tour.' Lady James gestured impatiently towards the chairs set around the stone hearth. 'Sit.'

'I am, you will agree, Aunt Louisa, somewhat old to be undertaking the Tour with a tutor to bear-lead me.' Theo waited until the two women were seated, then took the remaining chair, crossing one long leg over the other and clasping his hands together. He appeared quite tame and domesticated, although a trifle large. If Elinor had imagined a dangerous rakehell, which she had been informed her cousin was, he would not look like this.

'Mama uses the Tour as code for *sent abroad in disgrace,*' he continued. 'I am earning my living, avoiding English tourists and generally managing to keep my doings from the ears of my sainted papa.'

'Your father, even if Bishop of Wessex, may not be a saint,' his aunt said tartly, 'but you have certainly tried his patience over the years, Theophilus. Where were you when the Corsican Monster returned from exile last year, might I ask?'

'Oh, here in France. I became a Swedish merchant

for the duration of the troubles. I found it interfered very little with my business.'

Elinor found she was grappling with unsettling emotions. Of course, she was pleased to see her cousin. Any cousin. The Ravenhursts were a large and friendly clan. But something—the memory of that unsettling little voice in her head, perhaps?—replaced the calm contentment that was her usual internal state with a cold knot in her stomach. If she did not know better, she would think it disappointment.

'What are you frowning about, Elinor?' her mother enquired. 'Nothing is more productive of lines on the forehead.'

'A slight headache, that is all, Mama.' She had met an intelligent, attractive man—Theo was certainly that, even if he was not exactly handsome—and he turned out not to be an intriguing stranger, but one of the Ravenhurst clan. A relative. So what was there to be disappointed about in that, other than the fact he would treat her like they all did, as Mama's bluestocking assistant? An hour ago she would have said she wanted a man to talk to about as badly as she wanted to be back in London, sitting with the wallflowers in the chaperons' corner through yet another hideous Season.

Whatever Cousin Theo's business was, it appeared to be flourishing. She might not know much about fashion, but she knew quality when she saw it, and his boots, his breeches and the deceptively simple cut of his riding coat all whispered money in the most discreet manner.

'Did you say *business*, Theophilus?' Mama, as usual ignoring her own advice, was frowning at him now. 'You are not in *trade*, I trust?'

'One has to live, Aunt Louisa.' He smiled at her. Elinor noticed her mother's lips purse; he had almost seduced an answering smile out of her. 'My parents, no doubt rightly, feel that at the age of twenty-seven I should be gainfully employed and cut off my allowance some time ago.'

'But *trade*! There are any number of perfectly eligible professions for the grandson of the Duke of Allington.'

'My father has informed me that I enter the church over his dead body. It is also his opinion that I was born to be hanged and therefore a career in the law is ineligible. I find I have a fixed objection to killing people unless absolutely necessary, which eliminates the army and the navy.'

'Politics? The government?' Elinor suggested, smiling as much at her mother's expression as Theo's catalogue of excuses.

'I am also allergic to humbug.'

Lady James ignored this levity. 'What sort of trade?'

'Art and antiquities. I find I have a good eye. I prefer the small and the portable, of course.'

'Why of course?' Careless of deportment, Elinor twisted round on her seat to face him fully.

'It is easier to get an emerald necklace or a small enamelled reliquary past a customs post or over a mountain pass than a twelve-foot canvas or six foot of marble nude on a plinth.' The twinkle in his eyes invited her to share in his amusement at the picture he conjured up.

'You are involved in smuggling?' his aunt asked sharply.

'In the aftermath of the late wars, there is a great

deal of what might be loosely described as *art* knocking about the Continent, and not all of it has a clear title. Naturally, if it sparkles, then government officials want it.' Theo shrugged. 'I prefer to keep it and sell it on myself, or act as an agent for a collector.'

'And there is a living to be made from it?' Elinor persisted, ignoring her mother's look that said quite clearly that ladies did not discuss money, smuggling or trade.

'So my banker tells me; he appears moderately impressed by my endeavours.'

'So what are you doing here?' Lady James demanded. 'Scavenging?'

Theo winced, but his tone was still amiable as he replied, 'I believe there is an artefact of interest in the neighbourhood. I am investigating.'

There was more to it than that, Elinor decided with a sudden flash of insight. The smile had gone from his eyes and there was the faintest edge to the deep, lazy voice. The coolness inside her was warming up into something very like curiosity. She felt more alive than she had for months.

'Where are you staying, Cousin Theo?' she asked before her mother insisted upon more details of his quest, details that he was most unlikely to want to tell her. Once Mama got wind of a secret, she would worry it like a terrier with a rat.

'I've lodgings down in St Père.' Elinor had wanted to visit the village at the foot of the Vezelay hill, huddling beneath the towering spire of its elaborate church. She would have enjoyed a stroll along the river in its gentle green valley, but Lady James had dismissed the church as being of a late period and less important to her studies than the hilltop basilica. They could visit it later, she had decreed.

'Rooms over the local dressmaker's shop, in fact. There's a decent enough inn in the village for meals.'

And now he is explaining too much. Why Elinor seemed to be attuned to the undertones in what he said, while her mother appeared not to be, was a mystery to her. Perhaps there was some kind of cousinly connection. She found herself watching him closely and then was disconcerted when he met her gaze and winked.

'Well, you may as well make yourself useful while you are here, Theophilus. Elinor has a great deal to do for me and she can certainly use your assistance.'

'But, Mama,' Elinor interjected, horrified, 'Cousin Theo has his own business to attend to. I can manage perfectly well without troubling him.'

Her cousin regarded her thoughtfully for a long moment, then smiled. 'It would be a pleasure. In what way may I assist?'

'You may escort her to St Père to make some sketches in the church there. I will review your preliminary drawings of the capitals tomorrow, Elinor, and see what needs further detailed work. I doubt St Père will prove of interest, but you may as well eliminate it rather than waste a day.'

'Yes, Mama.'

Theo watched Elinor, puzzled. Where was the assertive young woman from the basilica? It was as though the presence of her mother sucked all the individuality and spark out of his cousin. Sitting there, hands neatly folded in her lap, clad in a slate-grey gown that might have been designed to remove all the colour from her face and disguise whatever figure she might possess, she looked like the model for a picture of a dowdy spinster. He had been flattering her when he made the remark about her age when they last met; she looked every bit the twenty-five she admitted to.

He reviewed his agreement to take her to St Père. Was there any danger? No, not yet. It was probably too early for his client to have become restless over the non-appearance of his goods and, so far as he was aware, none of the opposition had yet appeared on the scene. If they had and he was being watched, escorting his cousin would be a useful smokescreen.

'At what time would you like me to collect you and your maid?' he enquired.

'Maid? There is no need for that,' his aunt rejoined briskly. 'We are in the middle of the French country-side and you are her cousin. Why should Elinor require chaperonage?'

He saw the faintest tightening of Elinor's lips and realised that she was sensitive to the unspoken assumption behind that assertion—that she was not attractive enough to attract undesirable attention.

'I will walk down the hill, Cousin, at whatever time suits you,' she offered. 'There is no need for you to toil all the way up, simply to escort me.'

That was probably true; she seemed to know her way around the large village well enough, and it was a respectable and safe place. But he felt an impulse to treat her with more regard than she obviously expected to receive.

'I will collect you here at ten, if that is not too early. The weather is fine; I have no doubt the inn can provide a luncheon we can eat outside. The interior is not really fit for a lady.'

'Thank you.' Her smile lit up her face and Theo found himself smiling back. Those freckles dancing across her nose really were rather endearing. If only her hair was not scraped back into that hideous snood or whatever it was called. 'You will not mind if I am out all day, Mama?'

'No, I will not need you,' Lady James said, confirming Theo's opinion that she regarded her daughter in the light of an unpaid skivvy. Her other children, his cousins Simon and Anne, had escaped their mother's eccentricities by early and good marriages. His late uncle, Lord James, had been a quiet and unassuming man. Theo's father, the Bishop, had been heard to remark at the funeral that his brother could have been dead for days before anyone noticed the difference.

Elinor was obviously fated to become the typical unwed daughter, dwindling into middle age at her mother's side. Although not many mothers were scholars of international repute as well as selfish old bats, he reflected.

She might be a dowdy young woman, and have a sharp tongue on the subject of male failings, but he found he was pleased to have come across her. Sometimes life was a little lonely—when no one was trying to kill him, rob him or swindle him—and contact with the family was pleasant.

'Is there any news from home?' he enquired.

'When did you last hear? I suppose you know about Sebastian and his Grand Duchess?' He nodded. He had been in Venice at the time, pleasurably negotiating the purchase of a diamond necklace from a beautiful and highly unprincipled contessa. But even on the Rialto the gossip about his cousin Lord Sebastian Ravenhurst's improbable marriage to the Grand Duchess of Maubourg was common currency. He had even glimpsed them together on one of his fleeting and rare visits to London, while their stormy courtship was still a secret.

'And Belinda has married again, to Lord Dereham.'

Now what was there in that to make Elinor's lips twitch? he wondered. 'Yes, I had heard about that, too. I met Gareth and his new wife in Paris and they told me.'

'Your cousins are all settling down in a most satisfactory manner,' his aunt pronounced. 'You should do the same, Theophilus.'

'Should I find a lady willing to share my way of life, then I would be delighted to, Aunt. But so far I have not discovered one.'

'Really? I wonder if perhaps the ladies who were *willing* were among the reasons your parents disapprove of your way of life,' Elinor murmured with shocking frankness, so straight-faced he knew she had her tongue firmly in her cheek. She had a sense of humour, did she, his dowdy cousin?

'They would most certain disapprove if I wanted to marry one of them! Perhaps you will be a good influence upon me,' he countered. 'Having heard a little of your views on male moral decadence, I am sure you can guide me.'

Fortunately his aunt was too busy ringing for the maid to notice this exchange. Theo refused the offer of tea, which he was assured had been brought from England in order to ensure there need be no recourse to inferior foreign supplies, and took his leave. 'Until tomorrow, Cousin.' He smiled a little at the heap of sketching gear and scholarly tomes in the hall; yes, this would prove an undemanding way to pass the time until all hell broke loose.

Chapter Two

Theo was conscious of a familiar presence behind him as he made his way down the steep hill, but the follower at his heels made no move to speak to him until they reached the square at the bottom where the gig was waiting.

'Picking up ladies again?' the other man said, swinging up beside him as Theo guided the horse out and down the St Père road. 'Not your usual style, that one. Dowdy little hen. Still, expect she'll be grateful for the attention. Got some trinkets to sell do you reckon?'

'That *little hen* is my cousin Miss Ravenhurst, so keep your tongue between your teeth and your light fingers off her trinkets,' Theo said mildly.

'Right. Sorry, guv'nor.'

He allowed Jake Hythe, his groom, factotum, valet and right-hand man, a long leash, but he knew that one word was enough to ensure obedience. When you rescue a man from a well-deserved place on the gallows it tended to ensure an uncommon degree of devotion.

'And keep an eye on her, if you see her about,' he added. 'Her mother's mighty careless of her.'

'As if it was your own self,' Hythe assured him. The man had killed before now to protect Theo's back—it was to be hoped for their own sakes that no local bucks attempted any familiarities with Elinor while he was around. 'There's no sign of *them* at their place on the hill,' he added cryptically, jerking his head back towards Vezelay. 'I reckon you're going to have to get yourself invited to the chateau. How are you going to do that, then?'

There were, perhaps, advantages to having interfering, overbearing and well-connected aunts. Theo smiled to himself. 'Do you think the Comte de Beaumartin would like my aunt, the daughter-in-law of the Duke of Allington, as a houseguest?' he enquired. 'Because I believe I am going to engineer a meeting.'

'Cunning bastard,' his companion said, in a voice of deepest respect. 'You always thinks of something.'

Elinor was ready and waiting, opening the door the moment Theo laid his hand on the knocker. 'I was watching for you to make sure you didn't knock. Mama is deep in a letter to the Antiquarian Society, disputing claims of the Reverend Anthony's about the development of the ogival arch, and must not be disturbed.'

'Good God,' he said faintly as he took her easel and satchel. 'Ogival arches? Doesn't it drive you insane?'

'Not often.' Elinor shut the door quietly behind them and fell into step beside him, not pretending to misunderstand. 'Compared to being the companion to some old lady with a smelly lap dog in Bath, or being a general dogsbody for my sister and her six *interesting* children, it is a positively desirable existence.

'I get to use my brain and what creative skills I possess. I can read five languages you know, including Ancient Greek. And I have a remarkable degree of freedom. In fact,' she pondered, ducking under a pole with washing on it that protruded into the street, 'I probably wouldn't have this degree of freedom until I was in my forties under any other circumstances. Unless I was a widow, of course. But one has to be married first for that.'

Theo did not reply immediately. Elinor glanced up at him. Today he was dressed in buckskins and boots, a broad-brimmed straw hat on his head. He looked far less English and considerably more formidable for some reason.

It seemed to her that the relaxed, polite and slightly deprecatory young man in the parlour yesterday had been an act. All the Ravenhursts were good actors—there was a family joke that there must have been a scandalous actress in the family tree at some point in the past—perhaps in his line of business that was a useful ability.

'Mama is a very considerable scholar, you know,' she added. 'It is not as though I am spending my time pandering to some pointless pastime. And it is better than sitting at home being a meek wife to some self-important gentleman who thinks women have no role except as mothers and housekeepers.'

'That is not the sort of marriage I imagine our three cousins have lately embarked upon,' Theo observed, fielding a ball aimed inexpertly at him by a small boy. He tossed it back, making sure it was catchable.

'No. Those are real love matches. Marriages of equals, I truly believe.' Elinor shrugged. 'It was extraordinary luck for them, I suppose.'

'Then you do not have much faith in men, Cousin, if you find three happy marriages extraordinary. But I gathered that up at the basilica yesterday.'

'Some of you are perfectly all right,' Elinor said with a smile. 'I suspect men are as much a victim of society as women are; it is just that you seem to have much more fun. Look at you, for example—all over the Continent chasing antiquities and having adventures, I dare say. Just imagine what would happen if I tried it.'

Theo gave a snort of amusement. 'It is a dangerous world out there. Even your valiant parasol would not be much protection.' There were more weapons in her armoury than the sharp ferrule of a sensible sunshade, but Elinor did not judge it prudent to reveal them. Under his unconventional exterior her cousin could well turn out to as easily shocked as most men.

'Here we are.' He led the way to a neat gig drawn up in the shade of a lime tree and helped her to climb up, stowing the easel and the rest of her paraphernalia under the seat. 'Would you like to drive?'

'I've never tried.' No man had ever suggested such a thing and she found herself quite taken aback. But Theo did not appear to be joking; he sat with the reins in his hands, the horse standing quietly, tail flicking against the irritation of the early summer flies.

'I'll show you.'

'Thank you.' Warily she held out her left hand and allowed him to arrange the reins in it. To her relief he kept hold of the whip.

'Now, say *walk on*.'

'In English?'

'It appears to be bilingual.'

Elinor laughed, then stopped abruptly as the animal, obviously hearing the command in Theo's more familiar voice, set off towards the lower road. 'Ah! What do I do?'

'Nothing. Keep contact with its mouth and wait until we need to turn off. Just relax.' He seemed very relaxed himself, for a man who had handed over control of his vehicle to a complete amateur. The horse seemed relaxed too, as did the entire local population of dogs, chickens and small children who might have been expected to rush out and cause the creature to bolt, throwing them both into the ditch and killing them.

Elinor decided it was unfair that she was the only tense one. 'So why, exactly, are you so in disgrace?' she asked.

'Nameless sins,' Theo said with a sinister smile.

'I refuse to believe it. Tell me.'

'Very well. By the time I was sixteen I was disappearing over the school wall every night, bent on a ruinous course of drink, wenching and gaming.'

'And were you ruined?' He did not appear very dissipated—not that she was too certain what a rakehell looked like.

'Morally? Undoubtedly. Financially, not one whit, which was what, I suspect, most infuriated my father. I was buying and selling even then. Buy from one dealer, sell to another. Scavenge around market stalls and pawn shops, clean things up and sell them on to the right person. I found early that I had an aptitude for cards and I was happy to take payment in objects, not coin. By the time I was sent down from university for running a faro school, I was able to support myself financially.'

'I can quite see why that made the Bishop so cross. You should have gone creeping home, all penitence and desperate for him to keep up your allowance and instead you— Ooh! Where is it going?'

'It knows the short cut.' To her alarm Theo left the reins in her hand as the horse turned off the road and began to amble along a track. 'Yes, I came home, announced my independence and I have been living off my wits ever since. I go home occasionally to give Papa the pleasure of delivering a thundering good lecture and for Mama to fuss over the state of my linen and to try to find a nice young lady for me.'

'Without success?'

Theo grinned. 'I run a mile in one direction at the thought of all those simpering misses while their mamas are sending them running in the other direction to escape my polluting influence.'

'Aren't you ever lonely?' She had become so lulled by his relaxed manner and lazily amused smile that the question escaped her before she could catch it.

'Lonely?' The amusement vanished from his eyes, although the smile stayed on his lips. 'Certainly not. Remember all those willing ladies you mentioned yesterday? And what about you? Aren't you lonely?'

'With all those fascinating antiquarian meetings to go to?' Elinor responded lightly. It was no business of hers how Theo lived his life or whether or not he was truly happy. She could not imagine what had come over her to loosen her tongue so.

She was puzzling about it when the reins, which had

been sitting so comfortably in her hand, were suddenly jerked forwards violently. Instinctively she tightened her grip and held on, only to find herself falling towards the horse's rump. Then a solid bar slammed into her stomach and she was sitting back in the seat with Theo's left arm still out-flung across her midriff. With his right he dragged on the reins to remove the horse's head from the particularly lush patch of grass it was munching.

'Relaxed is right, total inattention is perhaps taking it a little too far,' he remarked while she jammed her straw hat inelegantly back on the top of her head.

'Indeed. I can see that. Thank you. Walk on.' They proceeded for a few steps. 'You may remove your arm now.'

'What? Sorry.' It had felt warm and hard. He must be both exceptionally fit and very fast to have caught her like that, Elinor reflected. She had no idea how much she weighed, but she knew that, propelled forwards so abruptly, her body would have hit his arm with considerable force. Was the rest of his body as hard?

She caught the thought and felt the blush rise. What was she doing, having such improper thoughts about a man she hardly knew? She flapped her free hand in front of her face. 'My, it is warm, is it not?'

'Unseasonably so, and odd after the shocking summer we have been experiencing.' Theo did not appear to notice anything amiss in her demeanour. 'Turn left down that lane.'

'How?'

Patiently he leaned across and covered her hands with his, looping the reins between her right-hand fingers as well, then using the pressure of his grip to guide the horse. Elinor made herself concentrate on what he was showing her, not how it felt, nor how the sharp scent of citrus cologne cut across the smells of a warm summer day in the countryside.

'Turn again here.' There were houses on either side now, but he left her to manage on her own.

'I did it!' Then, honesty got the better of her. 'But he would have turned anyway, wouldn't he?'

'Probably. You have nice light hands, though. We must try another day on a less familiar road so he will have to be guided by you.'

'Another day?' The church with its towering spire and vast porch was looming before them.

'I expect to be in the area for some days. A week or two, perhaps. Pull up on the far side at that gateway. You can see the ruins of the old church.'

Distracted by the news that there was an older church, one that might perhaps be of interest to her mother, Elinor handed the reins back and jumped down without waiting for Theo.

'Oh, there is hardly anything left.' She leaned on the gate, peering into the jumbled mass of stones, leaning tombstones and brambles.

'You don't want to go in there, do you? It'll wreak havoc with your gown.'

'This thing?' Elinor gave a dismissive twitch to the skirts of her drab brown walking dress. 'But, no, there doesn't seem to be anything to see of any significance. Let's look inside the other one.'

To her amusement, Theo offered her his arm as they walked the few yards to the great porch, big enough to put some of the village hovels into entire. He was an odd mixture of the gallant and the matter of fact, and she found it both pleasant and a trifle disconcerting. Gentlemen did not flirt with Elinor. They treated her with politeness, of course, but she was used to being regarded almost as if she were not there, an adjunct to her formidable mother.

Cousin Bel had made a spirited attempt at pairing her off with Patrick Layne. But he had been attracted to Bel, not knowing she was having an outrageous and secret *affaire* with Ashe Reynard, Viscount Felsham. The two men fought a duel over Bel in the end and naturally Mr Layne had no thought of turning his attentions to Bel's bluestocking cousin after that.

It was as though being able to read Greek and Latin somehow labelled you as unfit for marriage. Not that she wanted to get married, but it might be nice, just sometimes, to be treated as a lady, not as a shadow, not as a mere companion.

And Theo, while definitely not flirting, *was* treating her like a lady, which was an interesting novelty. He was also acting as though he realised she had a brain in her head and did not blame her for using it—and that was delightful. She turned her head and smiled up at him and he smiled back, a smile that turned into a fleeting frown. Then he was opening the church door for her and she forgot to wonder what had caused that change of expression.

'This is lovely.' The church was full of light, clean, in good repair. Slender columns lifted towards the high roof and the air was full of the scent of incense.

'It is, isn't it? Do you want to sketch? I'll get our things.'

Theo was gone before she could respond, leaving

her to wander about the wide side aisles. Light streaming in illuminated an ancient stone statue of a saint in
a niche. It might have been old and battered, but it was
obviously much loved. A bunch of wild flowers had
been placed in a jar on its plinth and many candles had
burned out in the stand at the foot of the column.

Elinor found a stool and dragged it across to a
position where she had a good view. Footsteps behind
her announced Theo's return. 'A good subject. May I
use it too?'

'Of course.' She let him set up her easel while she
emptied her satchel and found her watercolours.
Mainly pencil, she decided. Soft greys with a little
white chalk and colour just for the flowers, a splash of
poppy red and the deep, singing blue of a wild delphin-
ium.

Beside her Theo was humming under his breath
while he flipped open a camp stool and spread a large
sketchbook on his knee. There were pencils stuck
behind his ear, a long thin brush in his teeth and he
looked at the statue through narrowed eyes while his
hands unscrewed the top of his water pot. He was definitely an artist, Elinor realised, recognising the concentration and seeing the well-worn tools. She just
hoped he would not find her efforts laughable.

It was strange sitting sketching next to someone
else. Theo had not done so since his tutor had given him
his first drawing lessons and he was surprised to find
it so companionable. He rinsed his brush and sat back,
biting the end of it while he studied the results of an
hour's work. Not bad. A little overworked, if anything.
The habit of producing precise drawings to show to

possible clients was too engrained now to easily throw off.

His eyes slid sideways to where Elinor was also sitting back, her head on one side as she frowned at the sketchbook propped on her easel. It was turned so he could not see her work; instead he looked at her profile, puzzling over his rediscovered cousin.

She was tall for a woman, slender, as far as one could tell from that badly cut gown. There had been softness, but also firmness against his outstretched arm when he had checked her fall. Her hair, which ought to be her crowning glory, was bundled ruthlessly into a thick net at her nape, presumably to disguise it as much as possible. Doubtless she had grown up being made to feel it was a handicap. His own sisters, Jane and Augusta, had escaped the family hair, and left him in no doubt about what a tragedy it would have been if they had not.

Her hands, unprotected by gloves, were long fingered, strong and ink-stained, her walk a stride that easily kept up with his. He suspected she was unused to gentlemen paying her much attention and found that rather endearing. But why on earth did she dress as though determined to appear a frump? The hair he could understand, even though he deplored it. But why sludge brown and slate-grey gowns that seemed to have been badly altered from ones made for a larger woman?

She tipped her head on one side, her lower lip caught in her teeth, then leaned forwards and touched her brush to the paper once more. 'There. Finished.'

'May I see?' Jane or Augusta would have blushed and dimpled, pretending to be too modest to let a gentleman look at their work, while all the time waiting for praise. Elinor merely leaned forwards and turned her easel so he could look. 'That's incredible.'

'It is?' She was rather pleased with it herself, but she did not expect such praise.

'You handle the drawing with such freedom. And the way you have so simply touched in the flowers with colour lifts the entire composition. I am envious of your talent.'

'Thank you.' She could not think of what else to say. She was unused to being praised and thought her work merely competent. 'Recently I have been experimenting with a looser style. I must admit to being influenced by Mr Turner. He is very controversial, of course. It does not do for the sketches of record for Mama, of course, but I am enjoying experimenting. May I see what you have done?'

Wordlessly Theo handed her his sketchbook. The drawing was precise, focused, full of tiny detail she had not noticed. It should have been cold, yet he had changed the position of the flowers so they wreathed the ancient figure with a tender beauty.

'But that is lovely. You saw things that I never knew were there.'

'I am used to having to be very precise.' He shrugged and she realised she was embarrassing him.

'I can see that. No, I mean the way you have used the flowers to echo the curve of the mantle and highlight the sweetness of her smile.' She handed the book back. 'I shall look more carefully in future for the emotion in what I am drawing.'

Now she had really done it. Men did not enjoy being

accused of emotion, she knew that. Theo was packing away his things somewhat briskly, but he looked up and his eyes smiled. 'Perhaps we can learn from each other.'

I expect to be in the area for some days. A week or two perhaps, he had said. They could go sketching together again.

'I am sure we can, if you have the time.'

'I hope so. My plans are uncertain.' Theo folded her easel and his own stool. 'Shall we explore some more?'

They wandered through the church, peering into corners, admiring carvings. 'Is your mother interested in domestic architecture as well?' Theo asked.

'Yes, although she has not made such a study of it. Why do you ask?' Elinor moved a moth-eaten hanging to one side and sneezed as she disturbed a cloud of dust.

'There is a very fine and ancient chateau in the village of St Martin, beyond St Père. I have…business with the count. Perhaps she would care to visit with me when I call. I would not be surprised if he did not invite us all to stay.'

'Really?' Elinor had clambered up on to a rush-seated chair to study the stained glass more closely. 'Staying in a chateau sounds fascinating, but why should he ask us?'

'Count Leon spent much of his life in England with his father during the French wars. They were refugees. I am sure he would welcome English visitors.'

'You must mention it to Mama,'—who would not have the slightest qualms about moving into a chateau full of complete strangers if it interested her, Elinor knew full well. 'Have you—?' The ancient rush work sagged beneath her feet, then began to give way. 'Theo!'

'Here, I've got you.' He swung her down easily and set her on her feet.

'Thank you—you have saved me again.' Elinor began to brush down her skirts. 'I have been scrambling over the wreckage in the basilica for hours without so much as a turned ankle and today I am positively accident prone.'

'Cousin—why do you wear such frightful gowns?' Theo said it as though it was a pressing thought that had escaped unbidden.

She could still feel the press of his hands at her waist where he had caught her. Shock and indignation made her voice shake, just a little 'I...I do not!' How *could* he?

Chapter Three

'Yes, you do,' Theo persisted, seemingly forced to speak. He did not appear to be deriving much satisfaction from insulting her dress sense. 'Look at this thing, and the one you wore yesterday. They might have been designed to make you look a fright.'

'Well, really!' A fright indeed! 'They are *suitable*.'

'For what?' he demanded irritably. 'Prison visiting?' Although what *he* had to be irritable about she had no idea. She was the one being insulted.

'Suitable for the sort of life I lead. They are practical. I alter them from old ones of Mama's.'

'A well-tailored gown in a colour that suits you would be equally practical. Green or garnet red or amber.'

'What business have you to be lecturing me about clothes?' Elinor demanded hotly. Theo looked equally heated. Two redheads quarrelling, she thought with a sudden flash of amusement that cut through the chagrin. She was not ready to forgive him, though. He might think her a dowd—he had no need to say so.

'If you were my sister, I would—'

'I am not your sister, I am thankful to say.'

'You are my cousin, and it irritates me to see you dressing so badly, just as it would irritate me to see a fine gemstone badly set.'

'A fine gemstone?' she said rather blankly. Theo was comparing her to a *gemstone*? Some of the indignation ebbed away to be replaced with resignation. He was quite right, her gowns were drab beyond description—even tactful Bel had told her so.

'As it happens, I have a couple of walking dresses that Bel bullied me into having made. I will wear one of those if we call at the chateau; I would not wish to embarrass you in front of your friends.' She was willing to concede he had a point, although she could not imbue much warmth into her agreement.

'That was not what concerned me—I am sorry if I gave you the impression that it was.' He regarded her frowningly for a moment, then smiled, spreading his hands in a gesture of apology. 'I truly am sorry. I spoke as I would to an old friend, out of bafflement that a handsome woman would diminish her looks so. But you rightly tell me to mind my own business; a chance-met cousin has no right to speak in such a way. I did not intend to hurt your feelings.'

And he had not, she realised, disregarding the blatant flattery of him calling her *handsome*. If she was honest with herself, she recognised in his outburst the same exasperation that sometimes led her to blurt out frank, or downright tactless, comments. She could remember demanding outright of a drooping Bel if she and Ashe were lovers. In comparison with that, a blunt remark about clothes was nothing.

'I know you did not. Let us go and have our luncheon,' she suggested. 'I am starving.'

Theo ducked his head in acknowledgement of her gesture. 'I will take the gig and our painting gear round to my lodgings first. It is on the way.'

A gangling youth came to take the reins as they led the horse up to a substantial village house. Theo lifted down the pile of easels and stools and opened the door while Elinor waited. From the exchange of words, it seemed his landlady was at home and after a minute she came out, a piece of sewing draped over her arm, a needle and thread trailing from the bodice of her crisp white apron.

'*Bonjour, madame.*' Elinor inclined her head and was rewarded by a flashing smile and an equally punctilious acknowledgement. Theo's landlady was a handsome woman in her late thirties. Her abundant brown hair was coiled on top of her head and her simple gown showed off a fine figure. It could not, Elinor reflected wryly, be much of a hardship for him to lodge there. She was also, if the cut of her own gown and the fine pleating around the hem of the sewing she was holding were anything to judge by, a fine sempstress.

'The inn is over here.' Theo took Elinor's arm and guided her towards the bridge. 'We can sit under that tree if you like.'

The food was good. Plain country fare, and all the better for it in Elinor's opinion, which she expressed as she passed the coarse game pâté across the table to Theo. 'Do you keep house for Aunt Louisa?' he asked, cutting them both bread.

'Me? Goodness, no! I am quite hopelessly undomesticated. I do not have any of the proper accomplishments for a young lady.' She glanced down at the lumpily-hemmed skirts of her offending gown and added, 'As you have already noticed.'

'Why should you, if your inclination is not in that direction?' Theo took a long swallow of ale. 'I have no inclination for any of the things I ought—I know nothing of estate management, my knowledge of politics is limited to keeping a wary eye on the international situation, it must be years since I went to a play…'

'But I am a lady and for me not to have accomplishments is disgraceful, whether I want them or not. You are a man and may do as you please.'

'True. A gratifying circumstance I must remind myself of next time Aunt Louisa is informing me that I am a scapegrace or Papa is practising one of his better hellfire sermons on me. Do you ride?'

'Papa taught me when I was little, but I could never keep my seat on a side saddle. When I reached the age when I could not possibly continue to ride astride, I had to stop.' Elinor sighed with regret. 'Perhaps I will persevere with trying to drive instead.'

'I knew a lady who rides astride,' Theo remarked. 'She has designed a most ingenious divided garment that looks like a pleated skirt when she is standing or walking. It was necessary to have the waistline made unfashionably low, of course, near the natural line. But it would be more suitable for your activities in the ruins, I imagine. It certainly appeared to give her considerable freedom.'

There was a faint air of masculine nostalgia about Theo as he spoke. Elinor bit the inside of her lip to repress a smile—or, worse, an indiscreet question. She would hazard a guess that the lady in question enjoyed more freedoms than simply unconventional dressing and that her cousin had enjoyed them with her.

'That sounds extremely sensible,' she observed, visited by an idea. 'Do you think your landlady could make me such a garment if you were to draw it for her?'

'But of course. From what I have seen on her work-table and her stocks of fabrics, she makes clothes for most of the ladies in the area, including those at the Chateau de Beaumartin, I imagine.' Theo set down his glass and sat up straighter, reaching into his pocket for the big notebook he seemed to take everywhere. 'Let me see what I can recall.'

What he recalled proved beyond doubt that he had a far more intimate knowledge of the garment in question than he should have. Elinor preserved a straight face as diagram followed diagram until she could resist no longer. 'How clever of you to deduce all of that from the external appearance only, espe-cially, as you say, the garment is designed to conceal its secrets.'

'Ah.' Theo put down his pencil. 'Indeed. And I have now revealed a situation that I should most definitely not discuss with my sisters, let alone you, Cousin. How it is that I do not seem able to guard my tongue around you, I do not know.'

'Was she one of the willing ladies I most reprehen-sibly referred to yesterday?' Elinor enquired, not in the slightest bit shocked, only slightly, and inexplicably, wistful. Her newly rediscovered cousin was nothing if not a very masculine man. Doubtless he had to beat the ladies off with sticks.

'Yes, I am afraid so. Rather a dangerous lady, and willing, very much on her own terms.'

'Good for her,' Elinor retorted robustly. It sounded rather a desirable state, being dangerous and dealing with men on one's own terms. 'May I have those?'

She reached for the little pile of sketches, but Theo held them out of reach. 'On one condition only.' She frowned at him. 'That I choose the colour.'

'Certainly not! I cannot go and discuss having gowns made with a man in attendance, it would be quite shocking.'

'Gowns plural, is it?' He grinned at her, still holding the papers at arm's length. 'I am your cousin, for goodness' sake, Elinor, and she is my landlady. All I want to do is help you pick colours.'

'Dictate them, more like,' she grumbled, trying to maintain a state of indignation when truthfully she found she was rather enjoying this. It had been a long time since she had allowed herself to think about clothes as anything but utilitarian necessities. 'Very well. And, yes, gowns plural if it will save me from being nagged by you.'

'I am forgiven for my plain speaking, then?' He moved the sketches a little closer to her outstretched hand.

'About my clothes or your mistress?' Elinor leaned forwards and tweaked them from his fingers.

'Your clothes. And she was never my mistress—a term that implies some kind of arrangement. I am too careful of my life to entangle myself with that dangerous creature.'

'Tell me about her.' Elinor folded the sketches safely away in her pocket and regarded him hopefully.

'No! Good God, woman, Aunt Louisa would have my hide if she had the faintest idea what we are talking about. I don't know what has come over me.'

'We are becoming friends, I think,' she suggested. 'I find you very easy to talk to, perhaps because we are cousins. And I am not the sort of female you are used to.'

'That,' Theo observed with some feeling, 'is very true. Would you like anything else to eat? No? Then let us go and consult Madame Dubois.'

After five minutes with Madame, Theo was amused to observe that Elinor stopped casting him embarrassed glances and dragged him firmly into the discussion, even when he judged it time to retreat and began to edge towards the door.

'Come back,' she ordered, sounding alarmingly like her mother for a moment. 'My French is not up to this, I do not have the vocabulary for clothes.'

'What makes you think I have?' he countered. She slanted him a look that said she knew all to well that he had plenty of experience with French *modistes* and turned back to wrestling with the French for *waistline*.

Between them they managed well enough and Madame grasped the principles of the radical divided skirt very quickly. 'You could start a fashion, *mademoiselle*,' she remarked, spreading out the sketches and studying them. 'Your English tailors say we French cannot produce riding habits to their standard—let us see!'

They agreed on the riding skirt with a jacket and a habit-shirt to go beneath it, a morning dress and a half-dress gown. 'Now, this is the fun part.' Theo began to poke about in the bales of cloth and had his hand slapped firmly away by Madame.

'Zut! Let *mademoiselle* choose.'

'No, I trust Monsieur Ravenhurst's judgement,' Elinor said bravely, apparently only half-convinced of the wisdom of that assertion.

'That for the riding habit.' Decisive, he pulled out a roll of moss-green twill. 'And that, or that, for the morning dress.' Elinor submitted to having a sprigged amber muslin and a garnet-red stripe held up against her. Madame favoured the amber, he the red. Elinor wrinkled her nose, apparently unhappy about pattern at all.

'No, look.' Theo, carried away, began to drape the cloth around her. 'See? Pinched in here to show your waist off, and here, cut on the bias across the bosom—' He broke off, finding himself with both arms around Elinor, his nose not eight inches from where her cleavage would be if it was not swathed in fabric.

'It is *my* bosom,' she pointed out mildly. He felt heat sweep through him, dropped the fabric and stepped back abruptly. She caught the falling cloth, plainly amused at his discomfiture. 'I like this garnet stripe, I think, and I agree with Monsieur Ravenhurst's suggestions about the cut.' She tilted her head provocatively, disconcerting him by her agreement.

'*Alors.*' Madame appeared to have become resigned to her mad English clients, or perhaps she was simply used to him and inclined to be indulgent. 'The evening gown. Amber silk I have. A nice piece.'

'Violet,' Theo said, pointing. 'That one.'

'With my hair?' Elinor asked in alarm. He grinned at her. There would be no hiding in corners in a gown of that shimmering amethyst.

'Definitely.' She was not going to prevail this time. And he felt as though he had found a ruby on a rubbish tip and had delivered it to a master jeweller for cleaning and resetting. It was really rather gratifying.

A price and a startlingly short delivery time having been agreed, Elinor found herself outside with Theo, feeling somewhat as though she had been caught up in a whirlwind and deposited upside down just where she had been originally standing. 'I came out to look at a church,' she observed faintly, 'and now I've driven a gig, had my clothes insulted, eaten at an inn and bought three outfits.'

'You may express your gratitude when you see the effect.' Theo placed her hand in the crook of his elbow and began to stroll. 'A walk along the river bank before we go back?'

'I did not say I was grateful!' Elinor retrieved her hand, but fell into step beside him.

'Admit that was more fun than drawing capitals all day.' He turned off the road and began to walk upstream.

'It was *different*,' she conceded. 'Oh, look, a king-fisher.' They followed the flight of the jewelled bird as it fished, moving from one perch to another. The water was clear with long weed streaming like silk ribbons over the mosaic of pebbles and here and there a weir broke the smooth surface into foam and eddies.

There did not seem to be any need to speak. Some-times Theo would reach out and touch her arm and point and she would follow the line of the long brown finger up to where a buzzard soared overhead or down to a yellow butterfly, unnoticed almost at her feet.

She picked a tiny bunch of wild flowers—one sprig of cow parsley, one long-stemmed buttercup, a spray of a blue creeping thing she had never seen before—and tucked them into his button hole. He retaliated by capturing her straw hat, which she had been swinging by its ribbons, unheeding of the effect on her complexion, and filling it with dog roses, won at the expense of badly pricked fingers.

The path began to meander away from the riverside. Then Theo pointed through a tangle of bushes to where a shelving stretch of close-cropped grass ran down to the water. 'Rest there a while, then walk back?' he suggested.

Elinor nodded. 'I could wander along here all afternoon in a trance, but I suppose we had best go no further.' It was the most curious sort of holiday, this day out of time with the almost-stranger she could recall from her childhood. Restful, companionable and yet with an edge of something that made her not *uncomfortable* exactly…

'You'll have to duck.' He was holding up a bramble. Elinor stopped pondering just how she was feeling and crouched down under a hawthorn bush, crept under the bramble and straightened up. 'Careful—too late, stand still.'

Something was grasping her very firmly by the net full of hair at her nape. Impatient, she shook her head and felt the whole thing pull free. 'Bother!' She swung round, her hair spilling out over her shoulders, only to find Theo disentangling the net from a blackthorn twig. 'Thank you.' Elinor held out a hand.

'Torn beyond repair, I fear.' Theo scrunched it up in his hand and tossed it into the river where it bobbed, forlorn, for a while, then sank, soggily.

'Liar!' Elinor marched up until she was toe to toe with him. 'It was fine. It is just like my gowns.'

Theo dropped to the ground, disconcerting her as she stood there trying to rant at him. 'I wanted to see your hair. Would you like a drink?'

'Yes, I would, but I'm not drinking river water—look, cows. And you did not have to throw my hairnet away.'

Theo was fishing in the satchel she had thought contained only sketching equipment, emerging with a bottle, a corkscrew and two horn beakers. 'I did. What would you have said if I'd asked you to let your hair down?'

'No, of course.' Exasperated Elinor sat down too, hugging her knees. Hair was in her eyes and she blew at it.

'I rest my case. Here, try this. It really ought to be cooler, but never mind.'

'Do you always get what you want?' Elinor took the beaker resentfully. The first mouthful of wine slid down, fruity and thirst quenching. She took another, her irritation ebbing away. It seemed impossible to be cross with Theo for very long.

'I try to.' He was lying back, his beaker balanced on his chest, hat tipped over his eyes. 'There's a leather lace in my bag somewhere if you want to plait it.'

'And a comb, no doubt.' Elinor began to rummage. 'Honestly! And men complain about all the things women keep in their reticules. You could survive for a week in the wilds on what you have in here.'

'That's the idea.' Theo sounded as though he was dropping off to sleep.

Notebook and pencils were the least of it. There was

rye bread folded in greased paper, a water bottle, a red spotted handkerchief, a fearsome clasp knife, some coiled wire she suspected was for rabbit snares, the comb, a tangle of leather laces, some loose coins... 'Ouch!'

'That'll be the paper of pins. Have you found what you need?'

'Thank you, yes.' Sucking a pricked finger, Elinor bundled everything back into the satchel and began to comb out her hair. Thanks to the careless way she had stuffed it into the net that morning it was full of tangles now and the task took a good ten minutes.

Finally she had it smooth. Her arms ached. Plaiting it seemed like too much trouble. She reached for the beaker of wine, found it empty and refilled it. As though she had called to him, Theo picked the beaker off his chest, sat up and pushed the hat back out of his eyes. 'Finished?'

'I have to plait it yet.' The late afternoon sun was warm and the burgundy, unaccustomed at this hour, ran heavy in her veins. Sleep seemed tempting; Elinor straightened her spine and tipped the unfinished half of her wine out on the grass.

'I'll do that.' Theo was behind her before she could protest, the weight of her hair lifting to lie heavy in his hands. 'Give me the comb.'

He seemed to know what he was doing. Elinor reached up and passed the comb back over her shoulder, then wrapped her arms around her drawn-up knees and rested her forehead on them. It was curiously soothing, the sweep of the comb through her hair from crown to almost her waist. Soothing to sit there in the warmth with the birds chattering and the river splashing and her own pulse beating...

Chapter Four

'Time to go.'

'Mmpff?' Elinor woke up with a start to find the shadows lengthening over the meadows and Theo on his feet, stretching hugely. 'I've been asleep?'

'For about half an hour. Me too.'

As she moved her head, the weight of her plait swung across her shoulders and curls tickled her cheeks. 'What have you done to my hair?' Reaching up, she found he had braided it, not from the nape, but elaborately all the way down from the crown, leaving wisps and curls around her forehead and cheeks.

'Plaited it. Isn't it right? I did it like I would a horse's tail.' Elinor eyed him, unsure whether this was the truth or whether she had just been given some other woman's hairstyle.

'Thank you,' she said at last, settling for brief courtesy and wishing she had a mirror to check it in. She ran a cautious hand over her head, half-expecting to find he had woven in buttercups while he was at it.

Theo was moving about now, stooping to pick up

the wine bottle and the beakers, fastening the satchel. He moved beautifully, Elinor realised, the image of his body elongated in that luxurious stretch proving hard to dislodge from her mind. Long legs, long back tapering from broad shoulders to narrow hips—all those markers of perfect classical proportion it was acceptable for a lady to admire, provided they were depicted in chaste white marble.

She seemed to have spent the past few months surrounded by men acknowledged to be the best looking in society—some of them her cousins, one Bel's new husband—and she could honestly say she had felt not the faintest stirring of interest in anything other than their conversation. Why she was noticing now that Theo's boots clung to his muscular calves in quite that way was a mystery. It was not as though he was good looking.

Elinor got to her feet, brushed off her skirts and catalogued all the ways in which he was not good looking. His nose, though large and masculine, was undistinguished. His jaw line was strong, but his chin had the suspicion of a dimple which somewhat diminished its authority. His eyebrows were much darker than his hair and he showed no tendency to raise one in an elegant manner. His mouth was wide and mobile and he seemed more prone to cheerful grins than smoothly sophisticated smiles. Yes, she could quite see why Cousin Theo would not fit in to London society.

He was ducking under the treacherous brambles again, holding them up for her with one hand, the other outstretched. Elinor took it, crouched lower and was safely through. Somehow her hand remained in his as they turned back along the path towards St Père and somehow it felt remarkably normal to have those warm fingers wrapped companionably around hers.

'I will come at ten tomorrow and see if Aunt Louisa would like to call on the Count.'

'It is her writing day tomorrow, it may not be convenient. She will probably wish to make it the day after.' And tomorrow would be a free day for Elinor, unless she was required to redraw her basilica sketches. If Theo was not going to make his call…

'It is, however, the day on which I am calling on him, so I am afraid your dear mama will just have to fit in with someone else's convenience for once.' She blinked, startled by the thread of steel in Theo's tone. 'I will come in with you when we get back, if you would prefer not to pass on that message.'

'No, no, please do not trouble yourself. I will make sure she understands that any other day would not be possible.' His chin, elusive dimple or not, suddenly looked really rather determined. Elinor shrank from the thought of finding herself in the middle of a confrontation between her mother and Theo.

'Does she bully you?'

'No. Not at all.' He made no response to that. Elinor walked in silence, well aware that her mother did not bully her for the simple reason she never had any occasion to stand up to her. Given that she was on the shelf, and the alternative ways of life were so unappealing, she simply went along with whatever Mama wanted. What would happen if she ever did find herself in opposition?

'We are nearly back; you had best put on your bonnet again.' Theo fished another lace from his satchel and gathered her prickly roses into a bunch so she could tie on the flat straw hat again.

'That,' he remarked, flipping the brim, 'suits you. We will save it from the bonfire.'

'What bonfire?'

'The one for your gowns and any other garment you possess that is sludge coloured.'

'You are just as much a bully as Mama,' Elinor remarked, climbing into the gig and waving away his offer of the reins.

'Am I?' Theo's mouth twisted into a wry smile. 'Say *no* to me, then, and see what happens.'

'Very well. I will not burn my old gowns.'

'What will you do with them?'

'Give them to my maid, who will probably sell them.'

'An excellent solution. See, no opposition at all.'

'You are all sweet reasonableness, in fact.'

'Of course.' The horse toiled up the hill to the square below the long steep street to the basilica while Elinor tried, and failed, to come up with a retort that was not thoroughly unladylike. Theo guided it towards the hitching post in the shade.

'No, I can walk from here, honestly.' He looked doubtful, then clicked his fingers at a burly man lounging against the tree trunk.

'Hey, you. Carry this lady's things up the hill for her.' The man caught the coin tossed in his direction neatly, then came to lift the sketching paraphernalia from the gig, shouldering the easel and waiting for Theo to hand Elinor down.

'Tomorrow at ten, then? Thank you for my day.'

'And for the new gowns?'

'I reserve judgement on those until I see what they look like.' She laughed back at his smile and set off up the hill, her porter at her heels.

* * *

Theo caught Hythe's eye and nodded almost imperceptibly before the man set off in Elinor's wake. He tipped his hat over his eyes, leaving just enough room to see under the brim, and leaned back against the backboard, apparently asleep. It was a useful trick, and had served him well in the past.

That had been an unexpected day. Unexpected, different and quietly pleasant. It had left him with the desire to set a match to the entire contents of his aunt's study, though. Poor Cousin Elinor. No—he had started out feeling sorry for her, but that, he acknowledged, was not the right emotion.

She was intelligent, amusing, artistically talented and really rather lovely, if she could ever be brought to see it. On the other hand, her very unconsciousness of her looks was part of her charm.

Or was it just him? Certainly no other gentleman had shown her overt attention in the past or she would not have been so completely relaxed in his company. It seemed she vanished at will behind a mask that disguised her as *spinster bluestocking* and both she, and all the men she came in contact with, accepted that.

When he thought of the liberties he could have taken with her—probably *would* have taken with someone of more sophistication—he shuddered. The feel of her, her waist trim between his palms as he lifted her down from that chair in the church. Her hair, glossy under his hands as she let him handle it. Her total relaxation as she slept on the riverbank beside him. And her warm, long-fingered hand trusting in his as they walked back.

Through his narrow viewpoint Hythe came into sight, striding down the hill. 'That the same cousin, guv'nor?' he asked when he was up on the seat and Theo was lifting the reins.

'The same. Why?'

'Thought her a bit of a drab piece yesterday. Different today, bit of a sparkle about her.'

'She needed some fresh air,' Theo said. Fresh air, a change of scene and someone to appreciate her. Perhaps Count Leon would take a fancy to her; that would distract him nicely.

Was there any danger, taking his aunt and cousin into that chateau? No, surely not. Even if it were the count who had robbed him of the ch—the *object*. Even to himself he did not name it. It seemed hard to believe that he was the culprit, the man who had struck Theo down and murdered the old count, his father. If he was innocent, then the danger would come when whoever did have it attempted to sell it back to the count. Theo could send the women packing as soon as that happened.

His hand went to the small of his back where the pistol was wedged into his belt and then down to check the knives slipped into his carefully made boots. Things were safe enough now. His mouth settled into a thin smile that did not reach his eyes.

'Good afternoon, Elinor.' Lady James hardly glanced up from her work table as Elinor came in, a rustic jug with the wild roses in her hands. She looked around for a free flat surface, then gave up and stood them in the hearth.

'Good afternoon, Mama. Did you have a good day?'

'Passable. Those sketches of yours are acceptable, I do not require any of them redone. What was the church at St Père like?'

'Of as late a date as you supposed,' Elinor said indifferently. At least she did not have to spend any more time squinting into shadows in the basilica. 'There are the ruins of the old church next to it, but nothing of any interest remains.'

'You were a long time.'

'Cousin Theo and I went for a walk. I found the exercise invigorating after so much time spent drawing.'

'Very true. A rational way to spend the day, then.' Lady James added a word to the page, then looked up, apparently satisfied with the sentence she had just completed. 'What have you done to your hair?'

'Oh.' Elinor put up a hand, startled to find the softness against her cheek. 'My hair net caught on a twig and was torn. I had no hair pins, so braiding it seemed the best thing to do.' In for a penny... 'I ordered some new gowns while I was in the village. Cousin Theo's landlady is a dressmaker.'

'Nothing extravagant, I trust. There is plenty of wear in that gown for a start.' Clothing, especially fashionable clothing, was not just an unnecessary expense, but a drug for young women's minds, in Lady James's opinion.

'They are well within my allowance, Mama—a positive bargain, in fact—and they are practical garments.' She had lost her mother's attention again. Elinor half-stood, then sat down again. Normally at this point she would retreat and leave Mama in peace, but today, after the experience of spending hours with someone who actually understood the concept of a reciprocal conversation, she felt less patient.

'Mama, Cousin Theo tells me that there is a most interesting chateau in St Martin, a village beyond St

Père. He has an introduction to the count and thought you may like to accompany him tomorrow and see the building.'

'Hmm?' Lady James laid down her pen and frowned. 'Yes, if that is the Chateau de Beaumartin, I have heard of it. I believe it has an unusual early chapel, a remnant of an earlier castle. Tomorrow is not convenient, however.'

'It is the day Cousin Theo will be visiting. That and no other, he says, so I am afraid we will have to be a little flexible if we are not to miss the opportunity.'

'Flexible? He obviously has no concept of the importance of routine and disciplined application for a scholar. Very well. I never thought to see the day when I would have to accommodate the whims of a scapegrace nephew.'

'I believe he is calling on business, not for pleasure, Mama. And he is a most accomplished artist,' she added, feeling the need to defend Theo in some way. He would be amused to hear her, she suspected. Somehow he seemed too relaxed and self-confident to worry about what one eccentric aunt thought of him. 'He will be here at ten, Mama.'

'Indeed? Well, if we are to spend tomorrow out, then we have work to do. Those proofs will not wait any longer, not if I am to entrust them to what passes for the French postal system these days. It pains me to find anything good to say about the Corsican Monster, but apparently he made the mails run on time.'

'Yes, Mama, I will just go and wash my hands.' It did not seem possible to say that she would rather spend the remainder of the afternoon while the light held in working up some of the rapid sketches she had made during the day. The one of Theo drawing, for example, or lying stretched out on the river bank with his hat tipped over his nose, or the tiny scribbled notes she had made to remind her of the way that blue creeping flower had hugged the ground.

Never mind, she told herself, opening the door to her little room on the second floor. They would still be there in her pocket sketchbook, and her memory for everything that had happened today was sharp. All except for those soft, vague minutes while Theo had been plaiting her hair and she had fallen asleep. That was like the half-waking moments experienced at dawn, and likely to prove just as elusive.

She splashed her face and washed her hands in the cold water from the washstand jug without glancing in the mirror. She rarely did so, except to check for ink smudges or to make sure the parting down the middle of her hair was straight. Now, as she reached for her apron, she hesitated and tipped the swinging glass to reflect her face. And stared.

Her nose was, rather unfortunately, becoming tanned. Her cheeks were pink and her hair... She looked at least two years younger. Which was probably because she was smiling—not a reaction that looking in the mirror usually provoked. Or *was* it that?

Elinor assumed a serious expression. She still looked—what? Almost pretty? It must be the softness of those ridiculous tendrils of hair escaping around her forehead and temples. Looking pretty was of no practical use to a bookish spinster. On the other hand, it was rather gratifying to discover that her despised red hair could have that effect. And the unladylike tan at least disguised the freckles somewhat.

What would have happened five years ago during her disastrous come-out if she had dressed her hair like this instead of trying to hide it? Nothing, probably. She was still the younger daughter, destined to remain at home as Mama's support. And she had always been studious, which immediately put men off. It took a long time, and numerous snubs, before she realised she was supposed to pretend she was less intelligent than they were, even when their conversation was banal beyond belief. But she never could bring herself to pretend. It was no loss; she would be bored to tears as a society wife.

The apron she wore when she was working was still in her hand, the cuff-protectors folded neatly in the pocket. She looked down at the sludge-coloured gown and tossed the apron on to the bed. The gown was going, it might as well go covered in ink spots.

Elinor ran down the twisting stairs, humming. Even the waiting proofs of *A comparison between early and late eleventh-century column construction in English churches* did not seem so daunting after all.

'Pink roses?' Lady James levelled her eyeglass at the crown of Elinor's villager hat, decorated with some of yesterday's roses. 'And ruby-red ribbons? Whatever are you thinking of?'

'The ribbons match my walking dress, Mama. And I think the roses look charming with it. The dress is one of those Cousin Belinda persuaded me to buy, if you recall. I thought I should make an effort for our call.'

'Hmm. Where has that young man got to?' As the clocks had not yet struck ten, this seemed a little harsh.

'He is just coming, Mama.' Reprehensibly Elinor

had her elbows on the ledge of the open casement and was leaning out to watch the street. 'Good morning, Cousin Theo. You are very fine this morning.'

'And you, too.' He swept off his tall hat and made a leg, causing a passing group of young women to giggle and stare. Biscuit-coloured pantaloons, immaculate linen, a yellow silk waistcoat and a dark blue coat outshone anything to be seen on the streets of Vezelay on a workaday Wednesday morning. 'Has the bonfire occurred?'

Jeanie, their Scottish maid who had travelled with them from London and who was proving very adaptable to life in France, came down the stairs, opened the door with a quick bob to Theo, then vanished down the street with a large bundle under her arm.

'Unnecessary, as I told you.' Elinor whispered, conscious of her mother behind her gathering up reticule and parasol. 'Jeanie's on her way to the used-clothes dealer right now.'

'Do you intend to converse with your cousin through the window like a scullery maid, Elinor, or are we going?'

'We are going if you are ready, Mama.'

'I am. Good morning, Theophilus. Now, then, who exactly are these friends of yours?'

'Good morning, Aunt. Not friends, I have never met the family. I did business with the count's late father earlier this year, just before his death. There are…complications with the matter that I need to discuss with the son.'

Lady James unfurled her parasol, took Theo's arm and swept off down the hill, leaving Elinor to shut the door and hurry after them. 'Count Leon is about my

age and lived almost entirely in England since just
before the Terror.'

'His father obviously had the sense to get out in
time.'

'The foresight, certainly. He moved his money to
English banks and his portable valuables he placed in
hiding in France. The estates and the family chateaux
were seized, of course. Most of the furnishings and
paintings were dispersed.'

'And your business with the late count?'

'*Mama!*' Elinor murmured, cringing at the blunt-
ness of the enquiry. Theo was hardly likely to answer
that.

'Why, helping him retrieve the missing items,' he
answered readily. 'I had some success, especially with
the pictures. They are easier to identify than pieces of
furniture.'

'Ah, so you have located some more items,' Lady
James said, apparently happy now she had pinned down
Theo's precise business.

He did not answer. Which means, Elinor thought,
studying the back of his neck as though that singularly
unresponsive and well-barbered part of his anatomy
could give her some clue, Mama is not correct and his
business with Count Leon is something else entirely.
How intriguing.

Waiting at the bottom of the hill was a closed
carriage. Theo's own? Or had he hired it especially?
Determined not to be as openly inquisitive as her
mother, Elinor allowed herself to be handed in and set
to studying the interior.

Dark blue, well-padded upholstery. Carpet under-
foot. Neat netting strung across the roof, cunningly

constructed pockets in the doors and pistol holders on either side. Theo's own, she was certain. Her cousin was a man who enjoyed luxury and valued practicality, she deduced, her gaze on the swinging gold tassels of his Hessian boots and her memory conjuring up the contents of his sketching satchel. But what sort of life encompassed carriages of this quality and the need for rabbit snares?

She lifted her eyes to find him watching her, one dark brow raised. She had been wrong to think he would not do that, she thought. Today, far from the comfortable cousin of yesterday, he was a society gen-tleman and a rather impressive one at that.

'I was admiring the appointments of your carriage,' she said calmly, in response to the raised brow. 'Although I cannot see the container for the game you snare.'

He gave a snort of laughter, the gentleman turning back into Cousin Theo again. 'You guessed it was mine?'

'I am coming to know the style,' she said, and was rewarded by a smile and an inclination of the head. He looked rather pleased at the compliment.

'Whatever are you talking about, Elinor?' Lady James did not wait for a response, but swept on. 'How far is it, Theophilus?'

'Another five miles, Aunt. I do not suppose I can prevail upon you to call me Theo?'

'Certainly not. I do not approve of shortening names. Most vulgar.'

Under cover of brushing his hair back he rolled his eyes at Elinor, almost provoking her to giggles. She frowned repressively and set herself the task of talking her mother into a good humour before they arrived. 'Do tell me about this chapel, Mama. I am sure I will not appreciate it without your guidance.' This time Theo crossed his eyes, making her cough desperately and be thankful that the interior of the carriage was dim enough for Mama not to notice.

He was back to being the perfect gentleman again by the time they rolled past the outlying farmhouse, through the gatehouse and into the courtyard of the chateau. 'I sent ahead yesterday to apprise them of our visit; we should be expected.'

As he spoke the great double doors at the top of the steps swung open and a young man stepped out, two women dressed in mourning black just behind him. Elinor did not like to stare and with the fuss attendant on having the steps let down, retrieving her mother's reticule from the carriage and following her up the steps, it was not until she was within arm's length of the count that she saw his face.

It was only the tightly tied garnet ribbons under her chin that stopped her jaw dropping: the Comte Leon de Beaumartin was quite the most beautiful man she had ever seen.

Chapter Five

The pain in his right hand recalled Theo to the fact that he needed to be making introductions, not reacting to the look in Elinor's eyes when she saw the Count. He relaxed his grip on his cane and removed his hat. His cousin was once more demurely composed; he doubted anyone else had noticed her widening eyes. The count had been looking between them as though to assess their relationship. Now a polite social smile replaced the assessment.

'Monsieur le Comte?'

'Monsieur Ravenhurst. I am delighted to meet you at last. My father, unfortunately, told me so little about you.'

I'll wager he did, Theo thought grimly. 'Aunt Louisa, may I introduce Comte Leon de Beaumartin? *Monsieur,* Lady James Ravenhurst, my cousin Miss Ravenhurst.'

The count switched his attention to the ladies, and more particularly to Elinor. Theo was close enough to see his pupils widen. *And, of course he has to kiss her hand.* Lady James received an elegant bow, Elinor the full flourish ending with a kiss a fraction above her gloved hand. *Why the hell does she have to look so damnably pretty this morning? And she doesn't even realise.*

'Lady James, Miss Ravenhurst. Allow me to introduce my mother, the Countess Christine, and Mademoiselle Julie de Falaise.' Theo bowed, the countess and Lady James bowed, the younger ladies curtsied. It was all extremely proper. Now all he had to do was engineer an invitation to stay for the three of them and he would be able to search the chateau from garrets to cellars for his property. It was what he needed to do, yet suddenly his appetite for it was waning. Surely that beating he got when the *object* was taken hadn't shaken his nerve?

'We will take coffee,' the countess pronounced, leading the way across a stone-flagged hallway.

'My aunt is a notable scholar of ancient buildings,' Theo interjected smoothly, pulling himself together and following the ladies. 'As I explained when I wrote, the purpose of our visit is largely that I had hoped you would be willing to show her your famous chapel, ma'am.'

The countess stopped, turned to Lady James and positively beamed. 'But it is our family pride and joy, *madame,* I would be delighted to show it to you.' Her English, like her son's, was fluent, although accented. Hers was a heavier accent; the count's, Theo thought darkly, was precisely the sort that sent impressionable English ladies into a flutter. Elinor, of course, was made of sterner stuff. Or so he would have said half an hour ago.

'Excellent. Kindly lead the way.' Aunt Louisa thrust her parasol into the hands of the waiting footman, produced a notebook from her capacious reticule and stood waiting.

'Before coffee?' The question seemed rhetorical, the countess recognising single-minded obsession when she saw it. 'This way, then.'

Theo followed them as they went through a small doorway and began to climb a spiral staircase. 'If you don't mind?' he said over his shoulder to the count. 'I would be most interested.' And taking advantage of every legitimate opportunity to study the layout of the chateau was essential. He had no intention of creeping about in the small hours with a dark lantern any more than he had to.

He did not stop to see what the other man's response might be, but ducked through the doorway in the wake of Mademoiselle Julie's slight figure. There was silence behind him for a second, then the sharp snap of booted feet on the stone floor. Count Leon was coming to keep an eye on him, or was it Elinor?

The turret stair wound up, passing small doors as it went. At one point Aunt Louisa gave an exclamation and pointed to a change in the stonework. 'Interesting!' Then, when they had reached what Theo estimated must be the third floor above the ground, the countess opened a door and led them through into a dark, narrow passageway, through another door and into a tiny chamber blazing with coloured light.

Even Theo, who had some idea what to expect, was startled by the rose window filled with red and blue glass that occupied almost the entire end wall. On either side ranged columns with richly carved heads.

'They are so like those at Vezelay!' Elinor exclaimed, darting across to study one. 'But in such good condition, and low down, so we can see them.'

Lady James, for once in her life, appeared speechless. 'I must study this,' she pronounced finally. 'In detail.'

Theo strolled across to Elinor's side and stooped to whisper, 'Do what you can to engineer an invitation to stay. For all of us.' She looked up, startled, then nodded. 'I would appreciate it.'

The count was standing in the middle of the room, unmoved by Lady James's ecstasies, his eyes on Theo. 'Are you really interested in this, Ravenhurst?' he enquired, his voice puzzled. Theo chose to treat the question as a joke, smiled warmly and continued to study the walls of the chapel. No cupboards, no niches, no apparent changes in the stonework to indicate a blocked-up hiding place. But then, he had not expected to find it here. It would take an atheist, or someone with a careless approach to their faith, to hide that thing in the family chapel.

There was another door on the far side from where they had entered. He strolled across, passing the count. 'Shall we leave the ladies? There is something I would appreciate discussing with you. Through here, perhaps? I would prefer not to have to spin round another tower.'

Silently Leon led the way, opening the door on to a broad corridor. Theo followed as slowly as he dared, looking about until they reached a panelled door and passed through into what was obviously the study.

Theo suspected it had been the old count's and hardly changed by his son in the month since he had succeeded. He took a chair on one side of a vast desk, noticing he was not offered refreshment.

'To what do we owe the pleasure of this visit? Your letter was somewhat lacking in detail beyond your aunt's interest in architecture,' Leon remarked, dropping into the chair with its carved arms and high back. Darkly saturnine, he looked like the wicked prince in a fairytale as he frowned across the wide expanse of desk.

'You will know I assisted your father in recovering some of the family artefacts lost during the Revolution?' The other man nodded. 'There was an item I wished to purchase from him, something that had remained in hiding throughout the family's exile from France.'

Theo watched the count's face for any betraying sign that he knew that Theo had in fact purchased that item and had lost it, in violent circumstances, a week after the transaction. He rubbed the back of his neck as he waited. The bruising and the torn muscles had healed, but the pain of having been taken completely off his guard still lingered. He had had not so much as a glimpse of the person who had struck him down. Was he facing him now?

'If you speak of the object I assume you are, it has vanished.' Leon's frown deepened, his well-modelled lips thinning. 'My father was murdered the day after he arrived in Paris, having removed it from this chateau in circumstances of extreme secrecy. No sum of money equivalent to even a tenth of its worth was found on him, nor in the Paris house, nor with our bankers.' He shook his head, his face grim. 'I still find it hard to believe he could ever have sold it—it was an heirloom. And yet it is gone.'

'Indeed? I can assure you he intended to.' Either the man was a damn good actor or he did not know that Theo was the purchaser. 'What use is an heirloom so shocking that you could never openly admit you had it? An heirloom that none of the ladies of the house must ever catch a glimpse of? Your father intended to sell it because he needed the money. I wish to buy it as the agent of an English collector who will pay hand-somely.'

Who had, in fact, paid very handsomely indeed and was expecting the arrival of his purchase days ago. No one else knew about the sale except three rival treasure seekers, one of whom had been sharing his bed. He had not believed Ana, or the English couple, had realised why he was in Paris, his security had been so tight.

'Perhaps he *had* already sold it,' he ventured, probing. 'Was there no receipt?' Theo had certainly ex-changed them with the count. His had been taken along with the item as he had lain unconscious on the inn floor.

'There was no receipt in my father's papers or on his person.'

'How did your father die?'

'A blow to the head. We hushed it up as the result of a fall. He was found across the hearth, the back of his skull against the iron fire basket. It *may* have been an accident,' Leon conceded as though it caused him pain to do so. 'But I want the Beaumartin Chalice back.' He regarded Theo through narrowed eyes. 'You think I killed him, don't you?'

That was precisely what Theo thought. That the count had quarrelled with his father, had taken back the Chalice and was now pretending it had gone to cover his actions.

'Indeed, that had seemed the most logical explanation to me. That you quarrelled with your father when you discovered that he had sold the Chalice, that there was a terrible accident.' It seemed odd to be naming the thing out loud after months of secrecy, code words and whispers.

They sat looking at each other in silence, contemplating Theo's cool suggestion. It was the count whose eyes dropped first. 'I disagreed with him about this. Violently. But we exchanged words only, before he left Beaumartin. I did not kill him, even by accident.'

'Of course,' Theo said, injecting warmth into his voice. Now he spoke to the man he was inclined to trust him. Leon had been raised in England—did that mean he shared the same code of honour as Theo? Perhaps.

'Why do you want it back—other than the fact you cannot trace the money that was paid for it if it was sold and not stolen?'

'Do you imagine I want that thing out there, bearing our name? It has taken years for the rumours about the family to die down.'

'It is a work of art and was no doubt destined for a very private collector.'

'It is an obscenity,' Leon snapped.

'Indeed. And a valuable one. Too valuable to melt down and break up.'

'When I get it back, it will go back into safe keeping, in the most secure bank vault I can find. My father, and his before him, kept it hidden here, in this chateau. After his death I checked—it had gone.'

It is not going into any bank, not if I can help it, Theo thought grimly. His client had paid Theo for the Chalice. It was now his, however much the count might deny it.

His lordship would not even accept the return of his money. He wanted that Chalice, and what he wanted, he got.

It was an impasse. He thought the Court believed Theo did not have it, had not bought it in the first place and was here now attempting to locate it. Count Leon was convincing, too, when he said that it was missing and that he had not harmed his own father, but Theo had not been in this business so long without learning to trust no one. It could be an elaborate bluff to remove all suspicion from the family and keep the money.

And if the man did have it, he had no belief in Leon's announcement that he would put it in a vault. Leon was a traditionalist—it would stay here, in hiding, as it had been for hundreds of years. He was still going to check. 'Shall we rejoin the ladies?'

'Of course. Your cousin is most striking. Are you all redheads in your family?'

Theo bit back a demand that the count refrain from discussing Elinor if he did not want to find his elegant nose rearranged, and shook his head. 'Some are brown-headed, some dark. But in most branches of the family there are redheads.'

'With tempers to match?' The count led the way down a broad staircase into the front hall. The place was a rabbit warren.

'We learn early to control them that much better, *monsieur.' But don't chance testing mine...*

The ladies were sitting in a room that was pure eighteenth century—white and gilt and mirrors in startling contrast to the medieval parts of the building. Wide glazed doors opened on to a terrace with lawns sloping away down towards the river. Elinor turned as they came in. 'Cousin Theo, it is so delightful, the Countess has invited us to stay next week. There is to be a house party.'

'Delightful indeed,' he said enthusiastically. 'I, for one, accept with much pleasure.' The countess had her face under control in an instant. The younger woman had less experience; Theo, plainly, had not been included in the invitation. But no one could say so now. He smiled sunnily at the count. 'Delightful.'

There was an awkward moment while Mademoiselle Julie plastered a smile on her face, the count looked like thunder and the countess recovered herself. 'It will be quite an English party,' she declared. 'Sir Ian and Lady Tracey are joining us. You may know them? I met them in Paris, soon after my poor husband's death. They were such a support until dear Leon could reach me.'

The Traceys? Here? So they *do not have it either. Have they followed me or will I come as a nasty surprise to them?* If he did not have it, and Leon did not have it and the Traceys did not, then that left only one person in the game. He would let the houseparty run its course, satisfy himself that the Chalice had not come home and that this was not some complex manoeuvre on the part of the English collectors, and then he would find Ana. And wring her very lovely neck.

'I have met them,' he conceded. The last time had been just before he had bribed their coachman to take the wrong road south to Paris from the coast and then, when they were well lost, to engineer a broken axle. He was sure Sir Ian was going to be just as pleased to encounter him again as he was to see them. 'It will be most interesting to become reacquainted.'

Elinor was watching him, her head tipped a little to one side. She knew there was something going on beneath this polite surface chatter, something beyond the odd fact that he had asked her help in securing an invitation to stay in a chateau where he already had an entrée of sorts.

'Is anyone else coming?' she asked now, gazing directly at the count. If it did not seem too bizarre a phrase to use in connection with Elinor, she was positively batting her eyelashes at him.

'Some relatives of ours,' he answered, strolling over and taking the place next to her on the sofa. 'This is a large house, we can accommodate a lot of people.' He shot Theo an unreadable look as he said it, then turned to smile at Elinor. Behind their back Mademoiselle Julie bit her lip and began to make brittle conversation with Lady James. *The paid companion? A poor relation? Whichever it is, she does not like the count paying attention to another woman. And neither do I. Not that one.* Which was strange. He supposed it was because he was used to keeping an eye out for his sisters. But Elinor was not his sister.

Aunt Louisa was drawing on her gloves. 'Until Monday afternoon, then. I shall look forward to it. Come, Elinor, there is much to do.'

'Packing?' Mademoiselle Julie ventured.

'Packing? No, I have my work on the basilica to complete.' The poor girl looked daunted, but she did not return the conspiratorial smile that Elinor directed at her.

'Well, that is most satisfactory,' Lady James pronounced, settled back in the carriage. 'Four days should see a considerable advance in my researches. The chapel will provide a most valuable addition to chapter four.' She took up her notebook and began to scribble, frowning as the carriage lurched over a rut.

'You timed that announcement very neatly, Elinor.' Theo was not smiling, however. He looked almost grim, she decided, puzzled. She had done what he had asked, hadn't she? And the prospect of a house party at the chateau was something to be looked forward to, surely?

'Thank you. I decided the only option to ensure they could not exclude you was to gush like that. Why did you assume they would not invite you? You knew the late count, after all.'

'His son does not like me.' It appeared to be mutual.

'Really? I did notice a certain tension, but I assumed it was business matters.' Tension was an understatement. The count had looked like the demon king and Theo positively dangerous. 'He is very charming, and incredibly good looking.'

Her cousin regarded her through narrowed eyes for a long moment, but all he said was, 'Who is Mademoiselle Julie?'

'I am not entirely certain. A distant connection of the countess, I think. She seems to act as her companion.'

Theo lapsed into silence and Elinor recalled something she had noticed on their arrival at the chateau and had no opportunity to mention. 'The driver of this coach is the man you hired to carry my things up the hill yesterday.'

'Yes.'

'He was waiting for you.'

'Yes.'

'And he is already in your employ?' He nodded. Elinor opened her mouth to demand to know why Theo's employee was hanging around the town pretending to be a stray loafer looking for casual work and then closed it again. *Not in front of Mama*. He nodded again in recognition of her tact, the glimmer of a smile touching his mouth. It was the first genuine sign of pleasure she had seen from him since they arrived at Beaumartin.

'You could stop now and have a fitting for your new gowns,' Theo suggested as the carriage rolled into St Père. It was far too early for even the most industrious sempstress working alone to have anything ready for a first fitting. He knew it and she knew it. Only Lady James, loftily above such trivia as gowns would not think it strange. Perhaps Theo was going to confide in her at last.

'What a good idea.' Elinor sounded suspiciously bright and breezy, even to her own ears. 'Will you drive me back to Vezelay later in the gig?'

'Yes, of course. Aunt Louisa, that will be all right, will it not?'

'What? Oh, yes, whatever will waste least time on fripperies.' Lady James went back to frowning over her notebook.

Theo stood watching the carriage vanish round the bend, leaving a cloud of dust and two yapping dogs in its wake, then fished a key out of his pocket and opened the door into the dressmaker's shop.

'Madame is not even here, is she? So, are you going to tell me what all the mystery is about?'

'There is no mystery.' Theo ignored her sceptical

expression. 'Just a confidential business matter. However, I need to talk to you about the count. It had not occurred to me that he may not be a suitable person for you to associate with. You should keep your distance from him throughout the stay. I could wish I had not involved you now.'

'Why ever not?' Elinor demanded, perplexed. 'He is quite charming...'

Theo shrugged. 'If you like that sort of all-over-you hand kissing.'

'And extremely good looking.' He merely snorted. 'And delightful to talk to.'

'The accent, I suppose. Really Cousin, I am surprised you, of all people, would fall for such facile attributes.'

'*Facile?* Well, and if he is, what is the harm, pray? I am sure he will be a delightful host.' Theo was frowning. 'And unless you give me a good reason why he is not a *suitable person*, I have every intention of associating with him as much as I please. I am going to be his guest—to oblige you—after all.' She glared at his unresponsive face, then remembered another grievance. 'And what do you mean, *you of all people*?'

'I thought you were past the simpering débutante stage—'

'Too old, you mean? A spinster?' Elinor enquired, her voice dangerously quiet. 'I should not enjoy conversing with an attractive and charming man? In effect, I would be making a fool of myself and would appear to be angling for his attention?'

'Damn it!' Theo's hands were on his hips, his expression a mixture of frustration and anger.

'And do not swear at me, if you please,' Elinor said,

with the deplorable intention of infuriating him further. 'I am certain Count Leon would not do so, however annoyed he might be,' she added sanctimoniously, throwing oil on the flames.

'But he would do this,' Theo snapped, taking her by the shoulders and kissing her, his mouth hard, hot and angry on hers.

Chapter Six

As first kisses went, it was a lamentable disappointment.

Elinor bit Theo's tongue which was, to her alarm, between her lips, stamped on his instep and fisted her right hand in his hair, giving it a violent tug. 'And if Count Leon did assault me in that manner, that is what I would do!' she spat, wrenching herself free to stride to the door and throw it open.

She was out on to the quiet street before he could reach her. The door banged back against the frame and she took three strides away from it, shaking with humiliated shock. Two small children playing on a doorstep with a puppy looked up at the noise, a woman leaning out of a window to shake a rug stopped flapping it for a moment to stare and the rider on the raking bay horse walking down the middle of the street reined in as the animal tossed its head and snorted.

'*Excusez-moi,*' Elinor apologised, struggling to find her French, blinking against the light. The bright sun was the reason her eyes were blurry with unshed tears, of course. That, or anger.

'It is nothing.' The rider spoke with a heavy accent. It took Elinor a moment to realise that she had been identified as English, which was disconcerting, and that the speaker was a woman, not French, and was riding astride. Riding astride, moreover, in a skirt just like the one Theo had sketched.

She was not paying Elinor any further attention. '*Teó, mi amor.*' She smiled over Elinor's head. *Spanish?* It was not one of Elinor's languages, but she could work it out from Latin.

'Ana.' He sounded less than delighted to see her, but Elinor could not bring herself to turn round and look at him. Not yet. Possibly being addressed as *my love* by one woman, in front of another who has just bitten and kicked you when you kissed her, was enough to strain any man's temper. Well, hers was most uncertain also, just at this moment. 'What the devil are you doing here?'

'Following you, Teó, all the way from Picardie. You did not make it easy. You have sold the object back to the new count?'

'I have not got it, and if I had, it is not, as you very well know, mine to sell.' They were talking in riddles, but this must have something to do with Theo's secretive behaviour and his wish to stay at the Chateau de Beaumartin. Elinor kept her eyes on the woman. 'You are telling me *you* do not have it?'

'But, no, I do not! You thought I had? This is enchanting.' She laughed, a throaty chuckle. Elinor's fingers curled into her palms. 'So someone has taken it from you, my poor Teó. By force, one assumes? Were you hurt, *mi amor*?'

'My skull is thick and has recovered. I thank you for your concern.' His cold voice sounded anything but grateful.

'Do, please, introduce me, Theo,' Elinor asked, flicking a glance over her shoulder and managing to sound as though they had all just met in Green Park.

'Yes, please do.' The other woman smiled, plainly relishing the awkwardness of the situation. Elinor moved slightly so the sun was no longer behind the horse and she could see her more plainly. Tall, whip-cord slim, with honey-gold hair coiled elegantly under a broad-brimmed hat. And older than she, older than Theo. Thirty-five? More? She found she was shocked, which was ridiculous. Men took lovers and wives ten years their junior—why should women not have younger lovers?

'Marquesa, may I introduce my cousin, Miss Ravenhurst. Elinor, this is the Marquesa Ana de Cordovilla.'

'Marquesa.' Although it seemed bizarre in the middle of a dusty French village street, Elinor produced a curtsy fit for the wife of an English marquis, which she assumed was correct. The Marquesa inclined her head graciously.

'Charming. A family party, in effect.'

'You have just missed my mother, Lady James Ravenhurst,' Elinor said politely. She was damned if she was going to be goaded into discourtesy, although she rather thought that by introducing her as his cousin, Theo had surprised the Marquesa. Doubtless she had thought she was embarrassing him in front of a new lover. 'We are staying in Vezelay.' After a moment she added, 'With our household.' The fact that the household consisted of one maid was neither here nor there. This woman appeared, shockingly, to be travelling quite alone.

The comment did not provoke her into any form of explanation; she was obviously far too self-assured for that. 'And where are you staying, Teó?'

'Why, in Vezelay, with my aunt,' he lied easily. 'In fact, we must be getting back as Elinor's dressmaker does not seem to be at home.' He took Elinor's arm. For a moment she tensed, unsettled by his touch, which sent strange ripples of sensation down her arm. She wanted to free herself, then thought better of it. 'And you, Ana?'

'Why, at Beaumartin, of course.'

'You have been invited, too?' Elinor said, then caught herself up before she could blurt out anything more.

'Not yet.' The Marquesa produced that throaty chuckle again. 'But I will be. I have letters of introduction. So, we will meet again.' She looked down at Elinor. 'And you will be another relative of Lord Sebastian Ravenhurst, of course. Such an *interesting* man.' She touched her spurs to her horse's flanks. *'Hasta luego.'*

'Well!' Momentarily distracted from her own preoccupations, Elinor watched the horse and rider vanish round the bend. 'Do you think she and Sebastian—'

'Probably. He had a…lively life before he met Eva. She never mentioned him when we were—I mean, she has never mentioned him before.'

'She is a good ten years older than you.' Elinor tried to sort out her emotions—anger over that kiss, curiosity about the Marquesa, her need to find out exactly what

Theo was up to. She could hardly remonstrate over the kiss, not in the middle of the village street, but somehow that woman was tangled up with the way she felt about it: shaken, angry and very confused.

'So?' He raised one eyebrow.

'It's disgusting!'

'Nonsense.' He appeared amused by her reaction, not shamed as she had expected. 'What a little prude you are, Elinor.'

'I am not.' Did he also think her a prude because she would not let him kiss her like that? If that was prudish, then the cap fitted indeed. He was strolling towards the stable and she followed. 'But you said she was dangerous, did you not? And she appears to have been Sebastian's lover once, and she is mixed up with whatever is going on between you and the Count.' He pulled out the gig and began to harness the horse, his movements practised and economical. The stable smells of straw and hay and warm horse were oddly soothing. 'You cannot tell me you loved her?' she asked.

'*Love* is not why one has affairs, Elinor.'

'So it was just sex, then?'

'Elinor!'

'You cannot accuse me of being a prude and then come all over mealy-mouthed yourself.'

He gave a snort of amusement. 'Let us just say that it was an exciting experience. You have heard about female spiders who eat their mates? One does not remain the lady's lover for long, not if one has any sense.' He backed the horse into the shafts, fastened the traces and led it out. 'Come on. We need to talk.'

'Indeed we do. About all sorts of things,' she added crossly to the broad shoulders in front of her. It was not until she was sitting next to Theo that it occurred to Elinor that she should be having the vapours and refusing to have anything more to do with him.

She wondered if she had been to blame for him kissing her. Had he sensed the way she had looked at him, fooling herself into believing it was simply aesthetic appreciation of his long, fit body? Surely not? Surely they had just been friends and now… Now they weren't. Obviously she was completely lacking in sensibility, because all she wanted to do was understand. Understand why he had kissed her, why it had been so horrid and disappointing and why, despite that, she felt so disturbingly, pleasantly, confused inside.

Damn, damn, double—no, make that triple damn. Theo let the horse find its own way. Beside him Elinor was almost radiating emotion. The trouble was, he was not certain he could read it. She must be furious with him about that kiss. Upset as well—she was a virgin, he reminded himself, rubbing salt in the wounds. But he was not ready to discuss that kiss yet—not until he worked out why he had done it. On the other hand, that left very little else to safely talk about. The fact that he had lost his temper and kissed her was like having an elephant in the gig with them—it somewhat dominated both their thoughts.

There was a flush on Elinor's cheeks and her lower lip looked swollen. *Hell, did I do that?* Probably. He had kissed her with temper, not gentleness, for God knows what reason other than that to see her responding to the count was more than he could stand.

And it was not, he admitted to himself with painful honesty, simply because he did not trust de Beaumartin. His bluestocking Cousin Elinor was getting under his skin in a way he did not recognise and was very sure he did not like. It was not lust, exactly. He knew what that felt like perfectly well. This was different.

He shot her another glance, less obviously this time. She was sitting, apparently composed, but with a faint frown line between her brows. Then it came to him, like a blow to the solar plexus: that had probably been her first kiss.

It was not that she had retired to sit on the shelf and be a comfort to her mother because after three lively Seasons she had failed to secure an offer. No, Elinor had never come out, not in the way his sisters had, with parties and all the expectation that they would secure husbands. The whole extended Ravenhurst clan appeared to accept from the start the fact that 'poor dear Elinor' with her red hair and her freckles, her alarming scholarship and intelligence and her inability to pretend she was a brainless butterfly, was destined for spinsterhood amidst the dusty splendour of her mother's library. Had any man so much as flirted with her before?

'I should not have kissed you,' he said abruptly as they came into the square that sat on the saddle of land a third of the way up the Vezelay hill.

'No,' she said quietly. Out of the corner of his eye he could see that her hands were knotted in her lap, but her face was composed. Was she so used to swallowing insult and neglect then?

'Not like that,' Theo pushed on in the face of her lack of response. 'I was angry with him, and frustrated by not being able to see my way through this problem I have concerning him.' He reined in. From the far side of the square Hythe got up from the wine shop under the lime trees and begin to walk across. 'That is not an excuse, you understand.'

'No,' she agreed again, her voice colourless as she began to gather up her skirts in one hand so she could climb down.

On an impulse Theo shook the reins and the horse moved forwards. He waved Hythe away and they continued across the square and down the hill on the other side. The road turned as it went, so they were out of view of the houses almost immediately, passing between small trees and bushes, the farmland opening out in front of them. Theo turned the gig into a wide, flat opening that must once have been a small quarry, reined in and wrapped the reins around the whip in its stand.

They were in a small green amphitheatre, quite alone. A skylark was singing overhead. Beside him Elinor sat silent; at least she was not scrambling down in alarm to escape him.

'Had you ever been kissed before?' Theo asked abruptly, a way of asking tactfully escaping him.

'No, I have not. And if that is a sample of what to expect, I am not sorry.' The tartness in her voice made him smile, despite his guilty conscience. Elinor was not about to succumb to maidenly hysterics. He rather wished she would, he could deal with those.

'It was an extraordinarily inept performance on my part,' he apologised. 'I would like to believe I usually do better than that.' She was silent, but he could almost hear her mind working. 'Shall we get down and talk? You aren't in a hurry to get back, are you?' *That might have been better put, you idiot.*

'This is a lovely spot.' Elinor jumped down without waiting for him—or commenting that she was quite naturally anxious to get out of his company and into her mother's protection as soon as possible—and went to sit on a grassy bank spangled with daisies. She wrapped her arms round her knees defensively and watched him as he walked across to stand before her. 'I *think* I understand. You really wanted to box my ears, didn't you Theo?'

'Yes, I wanted to box your ears. But I also wanted to kiss you.' He dug deep for complete honesty. 'I wanted to do both because I did not want *him* kissing you. Does that make any sense?'

'Dog in the manger?' Elinor suggested, untying her bonnet and dropping it on the grass beside her. She tipped back her head and watched him, her expression open and candid and curious. She seemed strangely relieved by that explanation.

'In a way. It was territorial, certainly. I'm afraid men do tend to react that way when women are involved. If you were my sister I could stand over you and frighten off any man showing an interest. But—'

'I am not your sister and so other…instincts come into play?' She was interested, he realised, intellectually interested in how he and de Beaumartin were interacting. 'And I was not meekly doing what you wanted, so you did the male equivalent of stamping your foot.' And now she was laughing at him; he could see it in her eyes despite the puzzlement on her face.

'How very unflattering, the strong light you hold up to my primitive thought processes,' Theo said wryly. He shouldn't be feeling better, but he was. Her very lack of feminine wiles was refreshing.

'So, we have come here so you can apologise, or so you can show me what a proper kiss is like?' Elinor enquired, taking him aback.

'Would you like me to?' he asked, looking down at her, his hat in his hands.

'I thought you would never ask,' she said with such startling frankness that he burst out laughing. 'I am dying of curiosity now. And stop laughing—I am sure you can't do it properly if you are laughing.'

'Oh, yes, I can.' He set his tall hat on the grass and dropped down to sit beside her, stripping off his gloves. 'But laughing while kissing is an advanced lesson.'

The pupils of her eyes were wide and dark as she watched him, but she did not seem apprehensive. Theo cupped her shoulders with his hands, feeling the fine bones through the cloth, conscious, as he had not been in his anger, of her warmth and the faint, innocent, scent of soap. He wanted to kiss her very much, he realised, pulling her towards him as he bent his head and found her lips, careful, aware that they would be tender.

Elinor came against him with no resistance, her hands clasping his elbows as if to steady herself. He let their own weight carry them down until she was lying on the turf, eyes closed, mouth still pliant under his. The curves of her body were distracting, sending his own body messages he had no intention of listening to. Theo moved, careful not to let her become aware of his instant state of arousal, and concentrated on making love to her mouth.

If Elinor had thought about kisses before, she had imagined sensation purely on the lips. A pressure, warmth, possibly distasteful moistness. This, the thing Theo was doing to her, involved her whole body and every sense, even though he was touching only her mouth and her shoulders.

Distantly she could still hear the birds, almost drowned by the hammering of her heart. Her nostrils were filled with the scents of crushed grass and warm man. Theo smelt of clean linen, of leather, faintly, and not unpleasantly, of hot man and subtly of something she could only guess must be his own, indefinable scent.

His mouth was certainly moist. She had not expected to find that exciting, nor had she expected the heat and the way his lips moved gently over hers, caressing them. Then she felt his tongue running along the seam of her lips, pressing, and understood that he wanted her to open to him. Why? He was not angry with her as he had been before, when she had perceived the invasion of his tongue as an assault, not a caress.

Now the intrusion made her gasp with the sensual shock, the sound swallowed up as his tongue probed, found her own, caressed the sensitive flesh. Then he was sucking, nibbling, at her lower lip and the gasps became moans and she found her body was arching, shockingly, against the weight of his chest as he hung, poised, over her.

And then he had released her, was lying beside her, his weight on one elbow while he stroked the hair back from her flushed face. 'Now that, Nell,' he said with a smile that was oddly tender, 'was a *proper* kiss.'

Elinor shut her eyes hastily, unable to meet his. Not yet. From behind closed lids she tried to come to terms with her body, which, alarmingly, was not returning to normal now he had stopped. Her breasts ached, there was heat in her belly and lower. She felt restless and agitated and—

What did he call me? She opened her eyes on to the bright sunlight and pushed herself up on to her elbows. Theo's eyes were dark and heavy-lidded and suddenly she did not want to speculate about what he might be feeling.

She had asked him to kiss her out of curiosity, pure and simple, because she was never going to get the chance to be kissed again and he was, after all, just her friend and the only man she could possibly ask such a thing of. And now… Now she realised she had started something that she could not stop, for herself at least. You could not put that sort of knowledge back in the bottle and forget you did not know what a man's mouth felt like on yours, how his body felt, so intimately close. How he tasted, smelt. How *this* man felt. And there, at the back of her mind, was the nagging doubt that it had not been simply curiosity, that she had wanted him to kiss her because…

'That was very interesting.' Elinor sat up abruptly. It was essential she gave him no clue how this had affected her. If he thought she was a little idiot for naïvely asking him to kiss her, so much the better. 'I can quite see why young ladies are not supposed to do it.' She made herself look at him again and was surprised to find that he was still Theo, large and friendly and smiling at her, the dimple appearing in his chin. If she leaned forwards, she could just reach it with her lips. *No! No, this wasn't the same. He had not changed, but she had.*

'Thank you,' she added, sounding stilted to her own ears. Knowing how she felt, guessing how she must look, Elinor had a sudden recollection of a number of occasions when she had seen Cousin Bel looking just like that. *Goodness, that must have been when she was meeting Ashe!* Hastily she shut down her imagination and concentrated on smoothing her skirts.

'It was my pleasure, I'm glad you enjoyed it,' Theo said, as though she had just thanked him for carrying her easel. 'I did,' he added, making her blush.

'I said it was *interesting*,' Elinor said, speaking sharply in her anxiety least he think she would want him to do it again. 'I certainly will not allow Count Leon to do any such thing,' she added.

'I should hope not. Save all your kisses for me,' Theo teased. At least, she supposed he was teasing— they would not do this again, of course. His expression became suddenly serious. 'You now know so much about why I am here that it is probably more danger-ous, for both of us, not to tell you the whole.'

Elinor caught her breath. *At last he is going to confide*. And whatever it was, however dreadful, at least it would be something she could deal with in-tellectually, not some emotional puzzle she could not understand.

Chapter Seven

'I told you that I make my living buying and selling antiquities.' She murmured assent, forcing her scattered wits to focus on this and not on what had just happened. 'I often work for collectors, on commission. Sometimes for a specific object, sometimes simply to keep my eyes open for whatever it is that interests them—early Italian paintings, small Roman ceramics and so forth. In the case of the late Count de Beaumartin, it was to track down the dispersed furnishings and paintings from his Paris house and the chateau.

'I had some success and gained his confidence. He hinted that he had an object of great worth he wished to sell, but it was for a specialised market. Finally I managed to tease out of him that it was a piece of seventeenth-century metalwork of a highly erotic nature. I need not go into detail—'

'For goodness' sake, Theo, you may as well. I am not going to faint away.' It was completely unladylike, but now, with her body still singing from his kiss, she was more than a little curious about what a *highly erotic* item might look like.

'Very well, don't blame me if you are shocked. Two hundred years ago the then count was highly dissolute, positively depraved in fact. He, and like-minded friends, formed a club of sorts to indulge these tastes.'

'Like the Hellfire Club,' Elinor interrupted. 'Sir Francis Dashwood. Don't look like that,' she added as Theo stared at her. 'Mama does not censor my reading and there are books on every sort of subject in the library. I think we have something on him because of the architectural interest of the temple and catacombs at West Wycombe that Dashwood built.'

'This was very much worse than Dashwood's play-acting at monks and nuns with his friends,' Theo said grimly. He did not sound even faintly titillated by the tale he was unfolding. 'Dashwood employed prosti-tutes, but de Beaumartin took the women he wanted by force, and the more innocent they were, the better. He died mysteriously and the rumours were that outraged local peasants, tired of their daughters being de-bauched, rose up and murdered him.'

Elinor felt a sudden chill. This was not amusing any more—they were talking about a seriously unpleasant man. 'A revolting person—but surely that is not why you are warning me about the present count?'

'No. The family has spent a century and a half trying to live down the association of their name with de-pravity. But rumours still persist, amongst them the tale that objects of great value and artistic merit were created for the fellowship to use in their rituals. The finest of them was a chalice and that was what the late count offered to sell me. He needed the money and it is not an object that could ever be shown publicly.'

'But you have seen it?'

'Yes. I saw it, drew it and went back to England to discuss it with a certain connoisseur—let us call him Lord X—who collects objects of that nature. He owns some of Dashwood's paraphernalia as well, but this far surpasses them in quality.'

'May I see the drawings?' she asked, interested in the craftsmanship more than anything else. She knew nothing about early seventeenth-century goldsmiths' work.

'Certainly not! I returned, with a very substantial amount of money and the authority to negotiate with the count. I purchased the Chalice from him at their Paris house, we exchanged receipts, I left for the coast. An hour from Dover I stopped at an inn to eat and change horses and I was attacked, knocked unconscious and the Chalice and the count's receipt stolen.'

'You have no idea by whom?' Elinor found she was leaning forwards, her fingers clasped tightly together, completely caught up in the tale.

'I thought at first it was Count Leon. He is very unhappy about the scandalous object being out of their family control. However, when I heard that his father had been found dead the next day, his head split open on the hearth, I did wonder. Would he go to such lengths to avert even the hint of scandal? But sons have killed fathers before now and it may have been an accident in the course of a quarrel.'

'So you have come back to find it?'

'I have told him I want to buy it, not revealing that I already have. He says he does not have it, that it has been stolen, but I do not know that I believe him. There were others I suspected, but they are all converging on Beau-martin. Why should they do that if they have the Chalice?'

Elinor gave an unladylike whistle. 'No wonder the atmosphere was tense. From the way you spoke to the Marquesa, is she one of the suspects?'

'She is in the same business as I am. Whether she was ever married to the Marqués de Cordovilla, or even if that gentleman existed, I have no idea. We met, acted upon a certain mutual attraction, and I can only guess she found my notebooks. So she is a possibility. She certainly has the cold-blooded determination for theft, to hit me over the head and possibly even to murder. And there are the two English collectors, man and wife, Sir Ian and Lady Tracey, who appear to have become aware of the Chalice from a leak at Lord X's end of things. I had thought I had disposed of them neatly with a harmless trick. I would not suspect them of the violence, to be honest, but they owe me a grudge, and I cannot afford to dismiss anyone.'

'And they are attending the house party, too. Goodness.' They were silent. Elinor digesting what she had just heard while Theo picked daisies and began to pull the petals off, his expression one of brooding thought. Doubtless he had gone over and over the conundrum, all to no avail. 'I can understand why you started to become alarmed that you had involved Mama and me. Never mind, I am sure I can be a great help,' she reassured him.

'You will be no such thing,' he said hotly. 'You will be a perfect English miss.' Elinor snorted. When had she ever been one of those? 'You will pretend this is a normal houseparty and—'

'Steer clear of my host who may be a parricide, my fellow guests who may also be murderers, one of whom was your lover and the other two who are your deadly rivals?'

'Exactly.' He ran his hands through his hair. 'No. Put like that, it is clearly impossible. We must write and decline, say you have been taken ill or something. I will find some other way of searching the place.'

'I do not agree; anyway, I would have to be at death's door, otherwise Mama will simply leave me with Jeanie. She is not a clinging parent.'

'I had noticed.' Theo turned to look at Elinor, the frown even more pronounced. His indignation on her behalf gave her a twinge of pleasure. It felt strange to have a friend who defended you. 'I try to imagine my mother abandoning one of my sisters if she was ill in a foreign town, and failing.'

'Mama has even less sensibility than I.' It was too late to start feeling hurt about it. Mama, if challenged, would simply look puzzled and explain patiently that it was simple common sense and that hovering about her daughter when she felt unwell was not going to assist her recovery. One should call the doctor and get on with one's work. That was the rational approach.

The trouble was, the rational approach was beginning to feel a very cold thing to Elinor. Was that the result of one kiss? Surely not? Perhaps it was that Theo was making her see her mother, and her own situation, through his eyes. It was not a very comfortable picture.

'I want to go to Beaumartin,' she said, meeting his eyes squarely and putting all the conviction she could muster into the statement. 'Mama can be in no danger—I doubt very much if she would notice a full-scale orgy taking place when she is working—and I am forewarned. I will just keep out of the way and let you get on with your search.'

There was a long pause while he thought about it. Elinor concentrated on looking as much like a meek and biddable young lady as was possible under the circumstances. 'I am forewarned,' she repeated as the silence lengthened. 'And I know who to avoid.'

'Very well,' Theo surrendered with a frown. 'It is going to be thoroughly awkward if we pull out now. But, Elinor—you stick to Aunt Louisa and concentrate on drinking tea and drawing interesting architectural features. Absolutely nothing else. You promise?'

'I quite understand.' Elinor nodded earnestly. *And that is not a promise.*

'Then we had better be getting back. Even Aunt Louisa is going to notice that you could have tried on an entire wardrobe of clothes in this time.'

Theo got to his feet and stood looking down at her. She was aware of a moment of hesitation before he held out his hand to draw her to her feet. Against the light his body was reduced to a powerful male silhouette. Elinor placed her hand in his, conscious of the strength of the long fingers as they clasped hers, and was pulled easily to stand in front of him. The temptation to sway towards him and see what could happen was powerful. No, her curiosity, if that was what it was, had got her into enough trouble already, and Theo, she was sure, was regretting that kiss, even if she could not bring herself to. She applied some self-control instead and stepped briskly towards the gig.

'You did not tell me about your man, the one who carried my things and drove the carriage.'

The big watchful figure was waiting still when they came back into the square. 'All you need to know about Hythe,' Theo said as he reined in, 'is that if anything happens and you can't find me, you may trust him with your life.'

He tossed the reins to the man. 'I am going to walk Miss Ravenhurst back. Wait for me.'

The next day they saw nothing of Theo and Elinor could only guess what he was up to. She and Lady James worked hard at the draft chapters on the basilica, visited three very ancient local antiquaries and the prior and got up to date with their letter writing. With Lady James engrossed in more academic correspondence, writing to her siblings was left to Elinor. As she wrote, trying to make an interesting narrative of their researches and the visit to the chateau, she wondered if everything that had passed with Theo had been a dream.

Then a little shiver ran down her spine and that pooling heat deep in her belly reminded her that, yes, she had been kissed and held in those strong arms. And if truth be told, she wished very much it would happen again. She sat back, biting the end of her pen and thought ruefully that the legend about Pandora and her box was something she should have attended to.

On Friday morning a local lad brought a note from Madame Dubois telling her that her clothes were ready for the first fitting. 'Is there a horse and gig to be hired in the town?' she asked the boy. 'A very quiet horse?'

'*Mais oui, mademoiselle.*' He nodded earnestly. 'Jean le Grand down in the square has a livery stable, he will have something for *mademoiselle*. He is not busy just now, I know, for I help him. Shall I run down and ask him to make one ready?'

He was hoping for a tip from both ends, Elinor guessed, smiling at the slightly grubby face upturned to hers. 'I will come down now. You run ahead and talk to Monsieur le Grand for me. A quiet horse, remember!' she called after him as he took to his heels.

'Mama, I am going down to the dressmaker. I expect I will be back later this afternoon—there are all the gowns to try on.' And she might meet Theo and have luncheon at the inn. Or walk by the river again. And try to pretend that kiss never happened.

'You are walking?' Lady James looked up from her work.

'No, driving, Mama.'

'Good.' The rigidly coiffed grey head bent over the table again. *She hasn't even remembered I cannot drive,* Elinor thought, snatching up her hat. She hesitated over her bulging satchel, wondering if she should take just her reticule, then lifted it and slung it over her shoulder. There might be an opportunity for some sketching.

The lad, whose name, he informed her, was Pierre, had been as good as his word and the stable owner was standing in the square, holding the head of a placid-looking grey mare harnessed to an equally elderly gig. 'As quiet as you could wish, *mademoiselle,*' he assured Elinor, helping her up. 'She will give you no trouble.'

'Thank you.' She leaned down and handed the lad a coin and he doffed his cap, informing her that he, above all the other boys, was at her service for any errand. The reins felt stiff and awkward in her hand, and she did not risk trying to hold the whip as well. 'Walk on!'

The mare pricked her ears and set of at a reassuringly steady pace. Elinor took a deep breath and tried to look as though this was not the first time she had ever driven a carriage all by herself.

By the time they had reached St Père her back was aching and her arms were weary, but the little mare had been as good as gold and she felt sure she could drive back after a rest. 'Good girl!'

Stretching, she led the mare into the lean-to stable and found the gig and Theo's horse. He was here. With a smile of anticipation she tied up the mare, pulled some hay into the manger in front of her and lugged over a water bucket before lifting down the satchel and going to the shop.

The door was ajar, so she tapped and pushed it open. Garments in fabrics she recognised lay on the work table, white basting stitches all over them and the hems raw. A tape measure and a big pincushion were on top and the stool was overturned.

'Madame?' No answer. Puzzled, Elinor righted the stool and wondered if she should sit down and wait here, or go outside and watch for the dressmaker.

There was a thump from overhead, the sound of something heavy landing on the boards, a man's voice muffled and then abruptly cut off. She could make none of it out clearly, but it sounded like violence. *Theo?*

She might be making a complete fool of herself, but she was not going to risk ignoring it. Elinor delved in her satchel and came out with two objects that she eyed with some misgiving. She untied her bonnet and set it on the table and kicked off her shoes. There was another thud from upstairs. Cautious on the old boards, the pulse pounding in her throat, she began to climb the winding stair in the far corner.

It emerged on to a dark landing, lit only by a small window at the far end. The door leading to the room over the shop was ajar. She hesitated, wondering if she was imagining things. Then a voice that she realised after a moment was Theo's said, 'How many times must I tell you? I haven't got the damned thing, and I haven't got the money either.' It sounded odd, as though he was speaking with no air in his lungs.

'His lordship isn't going to like that,' said another voice, also speaking English, closer to the door and much clearer. It was a man and he sounded profoundly unimpressed by what he was hearing. 'His lordship is going to be very unhappy indeed.'

'I gathered tha—' Theo's voice was cut off in a grunt. The sound of the blow made Elinor flinch. The silence that followed was broken only by Theo's gasping breaths. 'I am trying to find out who took—' This time she heard a body hit the floor and the sound of retching. Her stomach churned. *Theo*.

'If anyone did take it.'

There had to be two of them, the one who was hitting and the one who was talking. And Theo was not going to stand around to be hit without fighting back, so at least one of them must have a firearm. Elinor swallowed hard and edged the door open, then slid through the gap.

One man was standing with his back to her, a shotgun in his hands, blocking her view into the room. He was about Theo's height and build with strands of greasy black hair slicked over a bald head. His companion she could just glimpse, a great bruiser of a man, his attention on something at his feet. She had to duck down to see Theo lying on the floor, his body curled up protectively as the man drew back his booted foot to kick. There was a great deal of blood on the boards, on Theo's shirt, on what she could see of his hands raised in front of his face.

Anger washed through her, driving away her fear and the shock of the violence. Elinor gripped the object in her right hand and pressed it firmly into the small of the bald man's back, right into his spine. 'Tell him to stop. Now.' She could feel her voice shake and steadied her diaphragm as though she were singing to try to stop it.

'What!' The man half-swung round and she jabbed harder, nauseated by the stink of sweat, blood and violence emanating from him.

'Stand still. This is a pistol, it is loaded and I am holding it at half-cock. My thumb is not very strong; I suggest you do not make me lose my grip.'

'It's only some gentry mort,' the other man said, his attention distracted from Theo for a moment. 'Where would she get a pop from? Just a bluff—you get her, Bill, and we'll have some fun with her. That'll make him talk.' Theo moved convulsively and was kicked in the head.

'It is no bluff, and neither is this.' Trying not to think about what was happening to Theo, Elinor lifted her left hand and pushed the point of the old kitchen knife she kept in her satchel for sharpening pencils against the man's throat. 'Put down the gun carefully and tell your bully boy to step away from him.'

'That's a chive right enough, Bill,' the big man conceded.

'I know it is, you jolterhead. It's my throat the silly girl is sticking it into.' The bald man bent his knees slowly and Elinor followed him down as he laid the gun on the floor. She put out a foot and kicked it across to Theo, praying he was conscious.

'Theo!' He stirred and looked up, his face a mask of blood. 'The shotgun.' He pushed himself up with one arm and reached for it with the other and then all hell broke loose.

The man in front of her turned so fast that she lost her footing. The pistol in her hand went off, the explosion deafening her, and spun away into a corner of the room. Elinor felt herself falling and struck out with the knife, found flesh without knowing what she had hit, then was knocked away with a backhanded blow to her jaw.

The big man was roaring, the words meaning nothing, then there was sudden, shocking, silence. 'If she is hurt, you are dead,' Theo said in a voice she hardly recognised and Elinor opened her eyes to see him leaning against the wall, the shotgun in his hands and the two men huddled together in the opposite corner. 'Nell?'

'I'm fine,' she said firmly, managing to stand up, dizzy with her ringing ears. It was true, you did see stars…

'Come round here, don't get between me and them. My satchel is on the bed—take out some of those leather laces. You two, turn around.' He waited until they obeyed him before he moved, and as he began to walk towards them Elinor realised why: he could hardly stand. 'Kneel down, hands behind you.'

They went down on their knees and she approached cautiously from the side, looped the leather around first one and then the other, pulling it as tight as she could, making herself concentrate on the knots.

'Guv'nor?'

The voice from below had her spinning round in alarm, but Theo called out, 'Jake!' as feet pounded up the stairs.

'Oh hell.' Hythe burst through the door and stopped at the sight of Theo, then saw Elinor, 'Saving your presence, ma'am. Who are these two?'

'His lordship's men. I have not been able to convince them that I have neither the object nor the money.'

'Yeah, they look a bit thick. What'll we do with them, then? Nice deep river out there.'

'Go and get the carriage. You can drive them over to our friend in Avallon—I'm sure he'll keep them snug for a week or two.'

'Yeah.' A broad grin spread over Hythe's face. 'I'll do that thing—the carriage is outside, I haven't taken the team out of harness yet. You all right, guv'nor?'

'Fine. You know what head wounds are like for blood. Nothing we can't take care of.'

Elinor wrestled the shotgun out of his hands and gave it to Hythe, then followed the man down the stairs, pistol in hand, until she was sure he had the two helpless in the back of the carriage. 'One of them's bleeding, I got him in the arm.'

'He'll live, miss.'

'It is Mr Ravenhurst's carpet I am worried about,'

she retorted, earning herself a broad grin and a wave of the hand as he whipped the horses up.

When she got back upstairs Theo was still leaning back against the wall, apparently keeping himself upright by sheer willpower. 'Lie down this instant!' Something inside her seemed to clutch at her heart, something primitive and fundamental. Something to do with the fact that here was her…her friend and he was hurt and he was brave and he was very, very male and she wanted…

'Come here.' He waited until they were toe to toe, then focused painfully on her. One eye was cut across the brow and almost closed, the other caked in blood. 'Are you all right, Nell?'

'Perfectly. It was a glancing blow, he caught me off balance. Now you—' he was not going to be sensible, so she had to be. *Think, Elinor. Bandages, a doctor, should I give him brandy? No, that is bad for head injuries…*

'Oh God, Elinor. They could have ra— killed you.' *Thank God.* He had her in his arms and was kissing her with a sort of desperation before she could get any of her sensible words out. The desperation of his kiss echoed the way she felt, the wave of emotion that had run through her when she had seen him on the floor, battered, in pain and yet defiant. It was shocking that they should be clasped in each other's arms like this, but nothing else could express what she felt.

Hazily Elinor was aware that they were holding each other up, and then they were not and she was tumbling on to the bed to end up sprawled on Theo's chest.

'Theo!' Then she found his mouth and was kissing

him back. It was clumsy, instinctive and the smell of blood and sweat was making her dizzy, but the heat of his mouth under hers and the thud of his heart against her breast told her that they were both alive, both so thankful to be alive. *Mine,* that echo in her mind said. *Mine...*

Chapter Eight

Theo's head fell back on to the pillows and Elinor stared down at him, realising how battered he was, realising she should be tending his wounds, not behaving in an utterly wanton manner with a man who was barely conscious. Just because she felt like this about him did not mean he wanted her throwing herself at his injured, battered body.

'God, Nell, where the hell did you get that pistol? I thought you were bluffing when I heard you.'

'Mama and I carry one each. Mama says one can never rely on having a man to hand when one needs one, so we must be self-reliant.' *Mama had obviously never met this man in a crisis!*

'I can hear her saying it.' He closed his eyes. 'Have you ever fired it?'

'No.' Elinor swallowed. 'But I would have done if they hadn't stopped hitting you.' She slid off his body and got, somehow, to her feet. 'Now, you stay there—' he gave an amused snort, apparently at the thought of doing anything else '—while I find some water and bandages.'

Where was Madame Dubois? Elinor called out her name as she opened the door at the back of the shop and found herself in a kitchen. There was no response. She filled a basin with cold water and carried it back. Over one end of the work table was a clean sheet, apparently used for covering sewing in progress. Elinor put it over her shoulder, hooked her finger through the handle of the cutting shears and went back upstairs.

Theo was sitting on the edge of the bed. He had pulled the shirt off over his head and was dabbing with the stained cloth at the cut over his eye. His torso was streaked with blood and covered in reddening marks that were obviously about to become bruises.

'Are you hurt below the waist anywhere?' she asked briskly to cover the fact that she wanted to put down the basin and weep. She never cried. *Never.* 'He didn't kick you in the kidneys or anything?' Could she touch him? Dare she? She wanted to, so much. But that was self-indulgence. It would do him no good, it would satisfy only that jumbled mass of emotions she did not properly understand. He was her *friend* and he was hurt. That was enough.

'No, I was rescued by a dragon before he got to those.' Theo looked up and dropped the shirt. 'Thank you, Nell. That was so brave.'

Now she *was* going to cry. Elinor bit her lip until she recovered her composure. 'I could hardly leave you, could I?' she demanded. 'And why are you calling me Nell?' She knelt down and began to cut up the sheet. 'Let me see your eyes.'

Somehow he kept from flinching as she washed and dabbed. 'Nell suits you. Elinor wears dust-coloured gowns and bundles her hair into a net and has her nose stuck in a book all day. Nell lets her hair out and walks by the river and has fun.'

He had only started calling her Nell after he had kissed her. She did not point that out; she didn't know what it meant. She made him bend his head so she could search through the thick red hair for any cuts on his scalp, running her fingertips carefully through the springing mass, trying not to think about how sensual it felt. There were some vicious lumps, but the skin was not broken.

Obedient to the pressure of her hands, he bent further and she found herself staring down at the nape of his neck, the tendons supporting the skull, the recent scar that must be the result of the last attack when he had lost the Chalice. Her fingers hovered over it, a fraction of an inch from the skin, then she snatched them back, her breathing quickening.

Theo reached for a piece of cloth, wet it and began to clean the blood off his chest. 'Less dramatic than it looks,' he said lightly. 'Most of that blood's from the cut over my eye. I'll be fine in a minute.'

'Yes, of course you will,' she agreed to keep him quiet, dipping another piece and beginning to work on his back. She had heard those muffled blows that must have landed solidly in his stomach. 'There, no cuts on your back.'

Theo straightened cautiously and she put one hand on the bands of muscle just above the waistband of his breeches and pressed. He drew a sharp breath as though she had stuck in a knife.

'I thought so. Fine, indeed! Lie down.'

'I *am* fine.' She shifted her hand to his chest and pushed. He resisted and she saw his lips tighten as the abused muscles were forced to work to counter her lesser strength.

'Liar.' He met her eyes and shook his head. 'Theo, if you do not lie down and rest, I am going to fetch Mama. I mean it—I cannot think of any other threat you might pay attention to.'

It worked; he lay down and smiled at her, turning her insides to jelly. 'That's the trouble with an intelligent woman—you know how to terrify a man.' There was a moment's silence while they looked at each other. Was he going to say anything about that kiss just now?

No, of course not. She was an *intelligent woman*, a *dragon* who just happened to have become over-emotional for a moment. Theo would dismiss those crowded moments, when he had kissed her with fervour and she had returned the embrace with just as much passion, as due to shock, relief, thankfulness they were both safe. She acknowledged the truth of all of those emotions. But there had been something more, something she sensed but did not understand.

'Take your breeches off and get into bed.'

'Not with you in the room! And don't try to threaten me with Aunt Louisa again—I'm even less likely to undress in front of her. You go and ask Madame for some coffee. Where is she?'

'I don't know. She sent me a note to say she was ready for my fitting, that's why I'm here. You don't think they hurt her?'

Theo tried to sit up and she pushed him down again ruthlessly. 'I'll go and look—and you get into bed.'

It took ten minutes, but eventually Elinor found the dressmaker in the woodshed, tied and gagged, furious but unharmed. She freed her and helped her back to the kitchen, explaining that Theo had been attacked by two men who thought he was carrying a considerable sum of money.

'*Cochons!*' Madame spat out. '*Monsieur* is unhurt?'

'No. He is somewhat battered, I am afraid; fortunately, his man arrived and is taking the miscreants to the authorities.' Elinor skated as lightly as she could past her own part in all this. 'May I make us some coffee?'

'I will make it. You go and make sure he is all right and I will bring it up. Then we fit your gowns.'

'But, *madame*, after the experience you have had—'

'You think I allow these creatures to interfere with my business? Huh!'

Sunday morning found Elinor filing papers and her mother collating notes. Elinor suspected that the absence of a Protestant church for miles was no hardship for her mother, whose views on religion were somewhat relaxed. She enjoyed listening to a good sermon, largely to engage afterwards in vigorous debate with the clergyman, but otherwise seemed inclined to call upon the support of Greek gods in an emergency. Elinor had become used to quietly reading her prayer book to herself if no Anglican congregation was within reach and then treating Sunday as if it were any other day.

But they rarely had callers on a Sunday. Even fewer who caused Jeanie to scream and drop the tray of dishes she'd been balancing on one hand as she opened the door.

After Friday's drama, Elinor was prepared for anything. She had the paperknife in her hand as she ran out into the hallway to find Jeanie scrabbling amidst the potsherds and Theo, his face sporting dramatically black, blue and purple bruising, attempting to reassure her.

'Cousin Theo, good morning.' Somehow she got her breathing under control. It was doubtful the girl heard anything other than irritation in her tone. 'Jeanie, fetch a brush and a bucket and clear this up and stop crying, then bring coffee to the front parlour. Mama is in the back room, I am sure she would like a cup, too.'

She led the way, smiling brightly until Theo closed the door. 'What in Heaven's name are you doing?' she scolded. It was easier to rant at him like a fishwife than to do what she wanted, which was to kiss those bruises better—or turn and flee. She was not sure which. 'You should be in bed. I told Mama you had fallen down some stairs; she assumes you must have been drunk at the time. I did not disabuse her of that opinion.'

'You didn't come to look after me,' he said with an unconvincing attempt to sound pathetic. 'So I had to get up.'

'*Madame* has been looking after you very well, I make no doubt. It would have been highly improper of me to visit you in your bedchamber.'

Theo attempted to raise one brow quizzically, winced and grimaced. He did not have to say it. What they had been doing last Friday in that very room was beyond improper. No wonder he seemed so uncomfortable. How could he look on her as his friend if this kept happening? 'Why are you brandishing that knife?'

Elinor realised she was gesticulating with the paper-knife and put it down. 'Jeanie screamed. For all I knew it could have been more of Lord X's henchmen. I do wish you would tell me who he is.'

'So when you get back to England you can go and tell him off? I think not.'

As that was exactly what she had been brooding darkly about doing before he arrived, there was really no answer to that. She studied the man in front of her critically. Leaving aside his face, which completely justified Jeanie's screams, he was moving more easily than she could have believed possible. Her hands tingled with the desire to run them over his chest again. It had felt so good. So hard and smooth and deeply disturbing. Did that make her wanton? Or merely a very inexperienced virgin in intimate contact with an attractive man for the first time? The latter no doubt, as it was certainly the least interesting option.

'He deserves horsewhipping,' she said, 'but I will leave that to you. Theo—how are you?' She felt her voice wobble and controlled it. 'Truthfully?'

'Truthfully?' Neither of them had taken a seat. Now he walked forwards until he was standing in front of her, took her right hand and laid it against his midriff. Elinor caught her breath and made herself stay passive as one fingertip slid between the buttons and touched flesh. Reprehensibly she left it there. 'Sore. You want me to be even more frank? I was humiliated that I had to be rescued by a woman—'

'He had a shotgun! What could you possibly have done against that?'

'Let me finish,' he said mildly. 'My first reaction, when I got over being thankful we were both alive and more or less in one piece, was to feel humiliated. My next was to be angry with myself for that thought—I would not have been shamed to have been rescued by Hythe, just profoundly grateful. That was what I was hanging on to, the hope he would be back soon from the blacksmith's.

'Hythe would have barrelled into that room, yelling his head off, fists flying. Someone would probably have got killed. You used courage and cunning and we're all alive. I'm just very thankful that you are on my side. You *are* on my side, aren't you, Nell?' he added, his voice dropping into an intimate, husky whisper.

Elinor looked down. He had taken her hand in his, her fingers feeling very small within the strong grip. She swallowed. What did he mean? What did he want? What did she want, come to that? She had been perfectly content until Theo had come into her life and now everything was a jumble: her mind, her emotions, her body.

'Of course I am. I am your friend. We Ravenhursts stick together, don't we?' *The safe answer. Pretend there is no ambiguity, pretend I understand what is happening here.*

'Your sense of family duty is strong.' He lifted his hand, apparently studying the tips of her rather inky fingers.

'Not particularly,' she admitted. 'Only for the relatives I like.' The silence seemed to stretch on. 'Why are you here, Theo?'

'Because this morning, when my head finally stopped aching, it occurred to me that if Lord X has sent any more—minions, was it?'

'Henchmen,' Elinor supplied.

'What *do* you read? Sensation novels? I'm shocked.

Henchmen, then. You are staying here quite openly using our own name and I should be taking better care of you.'

'I don't think he would have. Sent any more, I mean.' She freed her hand and went to perch on the edge of the big chestnut wood table. His close proximity was too confusing. 'Two would seem adequate and they'd have to find you and report back. If I were he, I would not be concerned about not hearing from them. Not yet.' Theo nodded and leaned against the window frame, his eyes on the street outside.

'You don't think—?' she began, then broke off, shaking her head. 'I did wonder if he had had it stolen himself, but there would be no advantage, would there? He might have had the count murdered to get back the money, but you were bringing him the Chalice.'

'You are talking about a highly respected member of the peerage.' Theo sounded amused by her speculation.

'The man's a pornographer.'

'A collector of erotic art,' Theo corrected her. 'When it costs that much money, it is art, believe me.'

'Anyway, by tomorrow we'll all be safely inside the chateau.'

'Oh, yes, all the suspects in a murder case tucked up within nice thick walls with the portcullis down. Your idea of *safe*, Nell, is unique.'

The door opened on Jeanie with the tray, Lady James at her heels. 'Theophilus, I am appalled. What your poor mother would say if she could see you now I shudder to think. Let that be a lesson to you to foreswear strong drink.'

'Good morning.' Theo took the onslaught with admirable calm. 'Thank you for your concern, Aunt Louisa. I am not in any great pain now.'

'Huh! You should be suffering from a hangover, if nothing else. Why are you here, other than to alarm Jeanie and cause her to break the china?'

'To offer you my escort to morning service, naturally, Aunt.'

'I do not chose to attend the Roman rite, I thank you, Theophilus. However, it shows more sensitive feeling in you to have offered than I would have expected.'

'I also brought a copy of a plan of the chateau, which I thought might be of interest to study before we arrive.' He removed a package from his satchel and handed it to Elinor. 'How accurate it is I do not know, it appears to date from the middle of the last century. I found it in a bookseller's in Avallon.'

'I will make a copy.' Elinor spread it open on the table. 'I am sure Mama would like to have one to make notes on.' If they had several copies she and Theo could mark each chamber and passage as they searched it— once she had persuaded him to let her help, that was. It showed the chateau from cellars to roof, floor by floor, each part numbered in a crabbed hand. Down the edge, in the same hand, ran the key.

Theo came to stand close beside her while she ran her forefinger down the list, squinting to try to decipher the writing. 'Looking for a chamber marked *orgies*?' he murmured.

'There might be some clue,' she whispered back, refusing to rise to his satirical tone. 'The group must have called themselves something, and this is an old plan. With a key apparently written by a drunken spider,' she added, depressed.

'I will leave it with you,' Theo said. 'Until tomorrow, Aunt.'

* * *

One did not have first cousins who included a duke and an earl, an uncle who was a bishop and numerous titled relations by marriage, without having stayed in many fine and historic mansions. But this was the first time Elinor had ever found herself in a castle complete with battlements and turrets, and, according to the plan, dungeons as well.

She rested her elbows on the sill of the window in her allotted bedchamber and looked out. Below her the hillside sloped down through parkland, into fields and ended at the river, out of sight behind its fringe of trees. The shadows were lengthening now, the long summer dusk making the valley mysterious and tranquil.

On either side of her window the wings of the chateau stretched away. It seemed to have grown over the centuries without any coherent plan, each count adding and adapting to suit his needs. She and her mother were in rooms that dated from the seventeenth century, with fine panelling and great chestnut beams overhead. From the window she could see the medieval part with its turrets to her right and the incongruous eighteenth-century wing to her left, overlooking the formal gardens.

Lady James had a room next door and Theo was opposite. Where the marquesa was lodged, she had no idea. Doubtless she had secured a chamber close to Theo, Elinor thought, fighting a losing battle trying not to think about Theo's relationship with the woman.

It was none of her business and she shouldn't be thinking about such things in any case—the love life of an adult male was a highly unsuitable subject for speculation by an unmarried lady. But this was Theo, and he had kissed her, and now her overactive imagination was visualising him kissing the marquesa. Only she, of course, knew exactly what she was about and he would enjoy it very much indeed and—

'And nothing.' Elinor pushed herself upright and stalked into the room. He had kissed her for a number of reasons, none of which had anything to do with why a respectable young lady should wish to be kissed by a man. And Theo was her friend and should not be the focus for her romantic daydreams. If *romantic* was quite the word to describe the odd, shivery, yearning feeling that kept washing over her when she thought about touching Theo. Or Theo touching her. And it was more than touching, more than the vague and disturbing things that haunted her dreams. She wanted to be close to him with her mind as well as her body.

The only thoughts she should be having about her cousin were schemes to involve herself in his quest to find the Beaumartin Chalice, and that was likely to be difficult enough to banish all other considerations from her mind. Elinor smoothed down the skirts of her new evening dress and went next door to see if her mother was ready to go down.

The door diagonally across from hers opened at the same time. Of course, the marquesa had managed to secure a chamber next to Theo's. Why was she not surprised?

'Ma'am.' Elinor curtsied, realising as she did so that her punctilious behaviour was a way of subtly pointing out the other woman's seniority.

'My dear Miss Ravenhurst—Elinor, is it not?—call me Ana. We are going to be friends.'

'I am sure we are.' Elinor managed a warm smile of

utter insincerity. 'I look forward to discovering what interests we have in common.'

The other woman's brows drew together sharply, then she laughed. 'Interests in common besides Teó? Indeed, yes. And I look forward to meeting your esteemed mother.' She swept off down the corridor, a tall, slender lesson in elegance, her mass of golden brown hair coiled at her nape, her severe gown emphasising her figure with every step.

'Ouch,' Elinor muttered as she opened her mother's chamber door. She had hoped to be subtle and had been neatly countered by the other woman's alarming frankness. She saw Elinor as a rival for Theo—a pitiable one, no doubt—and she was quite prepared to make that clear.

'I have just met the Marquesa de Cordovilla, another of the guests,' she remarked, wondering whether to say anything about the woman. The marquesa would go through a polite drawing room like a shark through a school of fish. Her mother might be amused. On the other hand, like a ship of war, she might simply train her powerful guns on the other woman and fire a broadside.

'Indeed? What is there in that to amuse you?' Lady James settled a handsome toque on her grey curls and nodded decisively at her reflection in the mirror. When she chose to dress up, she did it with a vengeance and usually with an ulterior motive.

'She is somewhat unconventional. And she does not like me.'

'Indeed? Why is that? It appears extreme on a fleeting encounter.'

'I met her in St Père when I was with Theo. I believe she is…attracted to him and thinks I am a rival.'

Elinor expected her mother to give a snort of amusement, probably encompassing both disbelief that any titled lady might desire her nephew and that anyone should see Elinor as competition. Instead she fixed her daughter with a disconcertingly direct look. 'One of Theophilus's past lovers?' she enquired.

'Mama!'

'Do not be namby-pamby, girl. He's a man; a lady of your age is not ignorant of these matters, she simply pretends not to see them. What is the woman doing here? Or was she invited to distract Julie from Theophilus and keep her attention on the count, for whom I assume she is intended?'

She had thought her mother too absorbed in the chateau's antiquarian curiosities to have done more than notice its inhabitants in passing; this degree of cynical insight was fascinating. She had not thought it worth commenting on the possibility that the marquesa saw Elinor as any kind of rival. That, of course, was too ridiculous. But the marquesa would soon see that for herself once she realised that Theo saw her merely as his friend and relative.

'I believe the marquesa came to visit the chateau in passing because of her interest in art and antiques and was invited to join the party. She is in much the same business as Theo, I understand.'

'The company promises to be reasonably congenial,' Lady James commented, picking up her fan and reticule and getting to her feet. 'Is that one of your new gowns, Elinor?'

'Yes, Mama. I think madame has done excellent work with it.'

'Hmm. Where are your pearls?'

'I did not bring them, Mama. I thought it unlikely I would need jewellery on our journey.'

'Jeanie!' The maid emerged from the dressing room with her mistress's stole over her arm. 'Fetch out my jewellery case again.' She removed the key on its long chain from her reticule and opened the box. 'The amethyst and diamond set, I think.'

'I thought you did not believe in unmarried girls wearing diamonds or coloured gem stones, Mama.' The ornaments glittered and sparked as Lady James lifted them out and laid them on the dressing table.

'I do not. But you are past the age where one need worry about that, Elinor. The earrings and necklace, I think—this is merely a family dinner.'

'Yes, Mama.' Elinor hooked the drops into her ears, feeling the unfamiliar cold caress as they swung against her neck. Jeanie fastened the necklace, rosettes of amethysts interspersed with diamonds, and stood back to admire the effect.

'You look very fine, Miss Elinor.'

'Yes, I do.' Startled into agreement, Elinor looked into the mirror. Theo had been quite right about the colour of the silk: it made the pale skin of her neck and shoulders gleam. The softness of her hairstyle continued to work its magic on her face and the sophistication of the jewels gave her a confidence she had never felt before.

'It would have been better if you had kept your hat on and had not burned your nose,' her mother added, flattening her mood somewhat. 'Still, you do not appear a complete hoyden.'

Exchanging a wry smile with Jeanie, Elinor followed

her mother to the door. Burned nose or not, she felt suddenly more confident of holding her own with the marquesa.

Chapter Nine

'Mademoiselle Ravenhurst, *enchanté*.' Count Leon bowed over her hand, and this time he actually kissed it. Elinor bit the inside of her cheek to stop herself ginning. That she, of all people, should be having her hand kissed was too ridiculous. Still, it would not be long, once he had discovered she had no talent for social chit-chat nor a tendency to sit gazing at him admiringly whatever he said, before he was treating her as simply her mother's companion. It was to be hoped that, in the meantime, Theo did not become territorial again.

'Lady James.' He bowed. 'May I introduce you to our other guests? The Marquesa de Cordovilla, an authority on art.' The marquesa bowed, Lady James inclined her head. Elinor struggled with the precedence in her head: the daughter of an earl, daughter-in-law of a duke versus the widow of a Spanish marquis. Yes, Mama had it right.

'Sir Ian and Lady Tracey. English connoisseurs of the fine arts.' Elinor curtsied, her mother nodded and smiled, the Traceys made their bows. He was an athletic-looking man in his late thirties, she was tall for a woman, slim and dark with an alertness that intrigued Elinor. Could these two really be conniving adventurers? Her antipathy towards the marquesa inclined Elinor to suspect her, but it could be dangerous to overlook other possibilities.

The countess took over the introductions, presenting an elderly cousin, whose name Elinor did not catch, Monsieur Castelnau, the countess's widowed brother-in-law, and two girls, five or six years Elinor's junior, who were introduced as nieces. 'Laure and Antoinette. I am sure you young ladies will have much to talk about,' the countess said firmly, leading Elinor over to where they sat side by side on a sofa opposite Julie.

Mademoiselle de Falaise appeared as pleased to find herself sitting next to Elinor as Elinor was, and rather less adept at hiding the emotion. Elinor smiled brightly and did her best with small talk in French. There was no sign of Theo.

The large room was arranged with sofas grouped facing each other. Out of the corner of her eye Elinor could see her mother was talking to Sir Ian while Lady Tracey was chatting animatedly with Monsieur Castelnau. The count could be heard discussing Venetian painting with the marquesa while his mother watched them. In her corner the elderly relative appeared happily engaged with her tatting.

'Yes, I have been out for several years,' Elinor answered Laure's question. Or was it Antoinette? They appeared indistinguishable: both blonde, both blue eyed, both animated. 'Did you both remain in France during the Revolution?'

It appeared they had spent the years of the Terror in Scotland with relatives, but had learned very little English. Elinor told herself it was good for her to practise her French and soldiered on. Beside her she was conscious of Julie, her eyes on the count, while his attention was fixed on the marquesa.

Then the door opened, drawing every eye in the room, and Theo walked in. *'Madame.'* He went straight to the countess. 'My apologies for my tardiness; I have to confess I became completely lost and had to be rescued by one of your footmen. What a fascinating building this is.' He turned and regarded the rest of the company. 'I must apologise also to the ladies for my somewhat battered appearance—I fell down the stairs two days ago.'

Elinor was conscious of a subtle shifting of attention in the room. Both the young ladies beside her sat up and smiled brightly at the sight of another man, even one who was black and blue. Julie stared at the count, a small smile on her lips. The marquesa turned her head languidly and directed a smile of unmistakable intimacy at Theo and the count got to his feet, bowed to Theo and made his way over to stand beside Elinor.

Sir Ian rose slowly. 'Your sense of direction deserting you again Ravenhurst? The directions you so kindly gave to my coachman on the last occasion our paths crossed led us sadly astray.'

'I am sorry to hear that.' Theo strolled across and bowed to Lady Tracey. 'My apologies, ma'am, although the instructions I gave him were clear enough—what did he have to say for himself?'

'As he vanished into the countryside five minutes after our axle broke, I have no idea.' To Elinor's surprise, neither of the Traceys appeared as angry as one might have expected. Almost there was a sense that they had been beaten fair and square at a game. *How very English*, she thought with amusement. Perhaps her instincts were correct and they were not the villains of the piece.

Theo, apparently happily unconcerned by the fact that eight of the nine women in the room were watching him, drifted across the vast Aubusson carpet, took a seat next to the elderly cousin and began to compliment her on her tatting in loud, clear French.

The youngest ladies pouted, Lady Tracey went back to her conversation, Julie directed a look of spiteful amusement at Elinor and the marquesa smiled a sphinx-like smile that made Elinor uneasy. Irritated with her company, she got to her feet and went to sit next to Sir Ian. 'I did not realise you knew my cousin,' she began, crossing her fingers at the untruth.

'Oh, yes, we are rivals of old,' he said readily. 'Having been outwitted once recently, I am hoping that I can even the score eventually.'

Elinor asked him about his particular field of collecting and realised with surprise ten minutes later that they had been having a perfectly sensible and intelligent conversation without him once patronising her.

Theo was still deep in the intricacies of tatting, his elderly companion having had the amusing idea of teaching him how it was done. The sight of a large flame-headed man in impeccable evening dress with his big hands wielding a shuttle and a mass of fine white thread gradually drew the attention of everyone.

Eventually the marquesa got up and went over. 'Teó, show us what a tangle you are making.'

Theo looked up and smiled. 'How could I make a tangle,' he said in French, 'when I have such a skilled teacher?' He opened his hands and there, hanging from the shuttle, was an inch of fine lacy tatting. Amidst general applause he handed the shuttle back to the old lady.

'Oh, Monsieur Ravenhurst, will you give me your tatting?' It was Laure, blue eyes wide.

'But, no, it is unworthy to trim your handkerchief, *mademoiselle*. Here, take my seat and allow *madame* to show you how to do it yourself.'

'Wicked,' Elinor murmured as he stood by her side to admire the sight of a petulant young lady trying to look pretty whilst getting in a tangle.

'Aren't I just?' he murmured back. 'How are you getting on with Tracey?'

'I can't believe it is he.' Theo raised a brow. 'He is too sporting about your ruse.'

'And he treats you like a human being with sensible opinions,' Theo countered. Apparently his attention for the last half-hour had not been entirely on learning tatting. 'Don't be flattered into dismissing him, Nell.'

Irritated that he did not accept her judgement, Elinor turned away, only to encounter the marquesa's interested stare. Impulsively she turned back, laid her hand on Theo's sleeve and looked up into his eyes. 'I am sure you are right,' she said softly, holding the green gaze for a long moment.

Unholy amusement flickered in the depths of his eyes. 'Just be guided by me, Nell,' he said, adding under his breath. 'Now go and make friends with her.'

'Who?'

'Lady Tracey. Not Ana, not unless you have all your

wits about you.' Under her gloved hand his arm was steady and warm. She bit her lip and saw his pupils widen. Inside, something reacted to that look. Something primitive and female. 'You look very lovely in that gown and with those jewels.'

'Thank you.' She was not sure what devil possessed her, but she turned—slowly, with a lingering smile over her shoulder—and went across to take the seat next to Ana. What was the matter with her? She never flirted. If anyone had asked, she would have said she had no idea how to. And here she was exchanging lingering glances and fleeting touches with...with her friend Theo, that was who.

'Marquesa. May I sit here?'

'But of course.' Ana fanned herself, gentle, sweeping movements. 'Why are you here, Miss Elinor?'

'Miss Ravenhurst,' Elinor corrected with a smile. 'I am the eldest unmarried daughter.'

'Of course you are. The oldest *and* unmarried. I am so sorry...for my mistake.'

I walked right into that one, Elinor thought grimly. 'Why am I here? This is an unoccupied seat and I wished to sit down.'

'Here at the chateau, with Teó.' There was a slight snap in the richly accented voice. Obviously young ladies were supposed to wilt before her barbs.

'I am here with my mother. Meeting Theo was completely unexpected. But I am so pleased we did.'

'*Por qué?*'

'I am sorry, I read five languages, but Spanish is not one of them. Let me guess—was that *why*?' She did not wait for Ana's sharp nod. 'Theo was able to introduce us to the count and it will be so useful for Mama's researches to study the chapel here.'

'So that is why you are here? To study architecture?'

'Oh, yes,' Elinor said, allowing her gaze to linger on Theo's beautifully tailored back. 'To study...form.'

Fortunately, given the hiss of indrawn breath from the woman at her side, dinner was announced before she could add any further kindling to the fire. This really was an amusing diversion, pretending they were rivals for Theo's affections. She seemed to be convincing the marquesa; doubtless the family talent for acting was coming to her rescue.

The rest of the evening provided less challenging entertainment. Dinner was excellent and both Sir Ian and Monsieur Castelnau, her partners on either side, proved to be lively conversationalists. Coffee in the salon with the ladies afterwards was duller.

Ana announced that she had the migraine and retired, looking more like a cat setting out on an evening's prowl than someone suffering from a headache. The younger women chattered amongst themselves, Julie brooded and the countess made brittle conversation with Lady Tracey, Lady James and Elinor until the men joined them.

Watching the door, Elinor saw Theo's eyes as he scanned the room, then frowned. *So, he is looking for her is he?* Unaccountably irritated, Elinor got to her feet. She did not want to pay games. 'Do excuse me, *madame*, Mama. I think I will retire now. Goodnight.'

An hour later Elinor sat up straight and stretched, yawning. A copy of the plan of the chateau was spread on the table before her, coloured now to show the ages of the different parts. She could see clearly which areas remained from the time of the wicked count and his orgies.

But was that any help? She pushed the chair away from the table and began to walk up and down. It would be logical to assume that the original hiding place for the valuable artefacts was close to where the orgies had been held, but that did not mean that later de Beaumartins had not hidden the things elsewhere. Or that part of the chateau may have been demolished to make way for the eighteenth-century additions. Had she wasted her time? Perhaps, although Mama might find it useful.

From the corridor outside she heard the sound of footsteps, doors shutting. Everyone, it seemed, was going to bed. Elinor stood up to close the lid of her paint box and swirl the brushes in the water pot, then stood, dripping brushes poised in mid-air. Now was probably as good a time as any to corner Theo and persuade him to let her help in his search. She would give it half an hour to let everyone else settle down. Elinor reached out to trim a guttering candle and settled down to study the plan again.

Theo padded around his room, studying its furniture and pictures with automatic professional interest while his mind sifted through the impressions of the day. Either the Traceys were very, very good at dissembling, or they were exactly what they seemed: keen amateurs with the money and leisure to indulge their interests and the temperament to regard rivalry as an amusing sport.

Ana would not be here, surely, if she already had the

Chalice? On the other hand, she had all the instincts of a cat and nothing would appeal to her more than to see him threshing around looking for the thing when she knew she had it safe. He arrived in front of an ornate baroque mirror and realised that he was still stark naked, distracted when he had finished washing by the sight of an interesting Italian Primitive hanging by the door.

The mirror was one of the items he had tracked down for the late count. Now he stood in front of it and studied himself critically. The swelling on his face had subsided, but the cuts and bruises did nothing to enhance his looks. Not that his face was something he ever paid much attention to. His body was another matter—he relied on that to function well and to keep him out of trouble. He sucked in his stomach muscles and winced, then flexed his shoulders, critically studying the way the muscles moved, identifying each twinge of discomfort. That was better, less pain there now and the bastards had not got round to kicking him in the kidneys.

The heavy silk dressing gown lay across the end of the bed and he pulled it on, enjoying the slither of cool silk over warm skin. He would sleep for an hour, perhaps two, then dress again and begin the systematic search of the castle that would take him several nights to complete. If Leon was bluffing and had the Chalice, he would find it.

He left the candles burning, lay back on the heaped pillows and closed his eyes. Outside his door a board creaked. He had noticed it that evening, registering it as something to be avoided on his nocturnal wanderings. Now he opened one eye a fraction and slid his right hand up under the pillows beside his head until he could grip the butt of the pistol.

The door opened. Even in the dim light the figure was unmistakeable. He did not relax his grip on the weapon. 'Teó? Are you asleep?'

The champagne silk négligé was familiar, he could remember buying it for her. It was an elegant confection and not one that could conceal as much as a stiletto. He removed his hand from under the pillow and sat up warily. 'What do you want, Ana?'

'Such a warm welcome.' She sat on the end of the bed, her back against the post, and arranged herself languidly. It was no surprise to find a warm foot caressing his instep. Nor was he surprised at the way his groin tightened or by the heavy ache of arousal. She was a beautiful woman and he knew very precisely what she was capable of in bed. What was new was the complete indifference of his mind to the promise of her body.

'Poor Teó, were you so injured in your—fall, did you say?—that you cannot please a woman?'

'No, it was not a fall and I have no desire to have my back raked by your talons, Ana. Tonight or any night.'

She showed no sign of displeasure at his rebuff, nor did the caressing foot stop its sensual slide over his calf. The heavy silk slithered off his knee, exposing the length of his leg, and her eyes narrowed as her foot moved higher. 'Your patron is unhappy not to receive the Chalice, then?'

'Yes. He is not a patient man.' He concentrated on regulating his breathing and not flinging off the bed away from her. It was what she wanted, a reaction from

him, any sign she was hurting him. Men did not refuse
Ana de Cordovilla, she rejected them.

'And if you cannot retrieve it?'

'Then I will have to repay him.'

'Can you afford to?'

'Yes.' It would clean him out; he would probably
have to sell some of his own carefully selected investment collection and the carriage as well if he was to
retain the resources to travel, earn again.

'You are a richer man than I realised. But better not
to have to. Better by far to deliver the Chalice and to
earn your fee, which must be substantial. Big enough
to share, perhaps?'

'Is that an offer of help?' Her toes had reached his
groin, slipping under the edge of the robe, the lovely
taut line of her leg fully extended. Theo closed his
hand around her ankle and lifted her foot away. He had
no intention of gratifying her with the evidence of the
effect she was having on his body. If she was angling
after a cut of the fee, then she did not have the Chalice.
Or was it simply a bluff to distract him while she ne-
gotiated with the count for some other pieces?

'Why not?' Ana curled her legs under her, a still
golden figure in the candlelight. 'We are a formidable
team. I will begin by seducing Sir Ian—perhaps he
knows something.'

'We were never a team, Ana, and, no, I do not
require your help. And leave the man alone, he loves
his wife, they do not need your meddling.'

'Love?' A flicker of anger passed over her face.
'Foolishness. What is the use of love? You are too sentimental, Teó.' Before he could move she had uncurled
herself from the end of the bed and was in his arms, her

mouth hot and hungry on his, her long fingers curling around him in a blatant caress. It was so very different from the last pair of lips that had pressed themselves to his.

He made himself lie still until she lifted her head, staring down haughtily at his unresponsive face. 'Embracing chastity, Teó?' Her hand moved, sliding expertly down his aroused flesh. 'Difficult, is it not? Or perhaps you are saving yourself for your virginal spinster cousin. I am sure she would appreciate your... interest.'

Theo lay still until he heard the door close behind her, his eyes on the underside of the bed canopy. He reached down and flicked the skirts of his robe back across his legs, despising himself for reacting to Ana in any way, uncomfortably aware that her jibe about Nell had focused that tense ache on her image.

My virginal spinster cousin. He had polished the gem stone a little and now she sparkled, but it was not simply her looks that had attracted him. He knew it was her humour and her stoicism and her intelligence and that gleam in her eyes when she looked at him and the trust of her hand in his and her mouth under—

'Theo?' Nell was inside the room, the door closing behind her, and he had not even heard her opening it. He was hallucinating—he had fallen asleep and was dreaming.

Chapter Ten

'What the hell are you doing in here?' Theo sat bolt upright, appalled. Inappropriate thoughts about a young lady were one thing, finding her in his bed-chamber, quite another.

'Shh! I knew you were awake, I saw the marquesa leaving.' She perched on the end of the bed on the rumpled patch of cover where Ana had coiled her long body and regarded him critically. 'Are you sure that it is a good thing, becoming intimate with her again?' She blushed. 'I mean, of course…trusting her?'

'I—' Theo snapped his mouth shut. He'd been within an inch of explaining that he had rebuffed Ana's advances, being defensive as though there was something between Nell and himself, something beyond friendship. 'What the devil were you about, watching my door? Is there a queue out there?'

Disconcertingly Nell snorted with laughter. 'I am sure Laure and Antoinette would be there if they dared. I was watching because I wanted to talk to you about searching the chateau.'

'This is not the place, nor the time. Have you any idea what would happen if you were discovered in here?'

'It would be all right, you are my cousin,' she began, for the first time sounding doubtful. He saw her eyes flicker to the robe he was wearing and to his bare feet and ankles. All he had to do was to reach out, push her down on to the bed and use his strength and his sensual expertise and she would be his. She was too innocent not to yield, he thought, disgusted at himself, fighting to make sense of his impulses. What was the matter with him? He had just repulsed a sensual and experienced lover and here he was contemplating seducing an innocent.

Self-recrimination made him snap, 'I am a *man*, you idiot girl. Do you want to end up married to me? Because I am damned sure I don't want to find myself in that situation.' What, he asked himself savagely, finding reasons to push her away, would he do with a wife?

He realised he could not interpret the expression in her eyes. Shock at how indiscreet she was being? Alarm at finding herself in a man's bedchamber? She slipped off the bed and went to the door. Theo felt the breath he had been holding sigh out of his lungs, then she turned the key in the lock and padded back and sat down. 'Now no one can walk in and surprise us,' she said prosaically. 'You are quite safe.'

Which was more than she was. 'You look about seventeen,' he said crossly. It was not what he had intended to say: *Get back to your room this minute* being the highest on the list. She was valiant, his Nell. But she was regarding him candidly from those wide hazel eyes, clad from head to toe in a plain cotton nightgown of utter respectability with her hair in a heavy plait over one shoulder. A greater contrast to Ana it would be hard to imagine. And yet he was aroused. Painfully, embarrassingly and inconveniently aroused in both body and mind by a virgin bluestocking with no experience except a few kisses.

'I do not think that was a compliment,' she observed severely. 'Theo, listen, I have been studying the plan. It will take ages for one person to search alone, but if we do it together—'

'And if we are found?'

'We will think of something. Two brains are better than one.' He shook his head, feeling control beginning to slip away from him in the face of her certainty. 'Well, in that case I will search by myself, which is not a rational way to proceed.'

Silence. Theo regarded Nell, wondering what would happen if he took her by the shoulders and shook her. He rather thought he could not trust himself to touch her. But he believed her threat to explore by herself. And somewhere in all of this mystery was the person who had knocked him unconscious and taken the Chalice.

'Very well. If you are still awake at two, then get dressed and we will search.' Once upon a time, before he met his cousin Elinor, he had thought himself in control of his life. At least if she was with him he would know what she was up to. 'We will start in Leon's study.'

'I agree,' she said, nodding approval of the plan as though they were equal partners in this. 'The old count may have left some clue to its traditional hiding place. Until two, then.'

She went out as quietly as she had come in. Theo listened, but the board did not creak, which meant that she had deliberately avoided it. No fool, his cousin. No fool, but one hell of a complication.

Elinor sat down at the table in her room and stared unseeing at the plan. She had got her own way, she should be happy, not feeling hurt and confused and thoroughly hot and bothered.

It was not until she was inside Theo's bedchamber that it had occurred to her there might be any awkwardness in marching into a man's room two minutes after his mistress had left it. He could have been unclothed. He would certainly not be in any mood for a chat about hidden treasure.

But it did not seem as though Ana *was* his mistress any more—unless lovemaking was a much faster, tidier and less strenuous activity than she had been led to believe.

But it was different, being alone, both of them in their nightclothes, in a darkened bedchamber late at night. Different from that sunlit quarry where he had kissed her, different from his room at St Père where she had dressed his injuries and held him out of sheer thankfulness he was still alive. The shadows had hidden his face from her, veiling both the bruises and the familiar features.

Without his face to focus on, she had been burningly aware of his body under that exotic robe, of his hands, of his bare feet. And she had wanted to touch him. Was this desire? It seemed that being a confirmed spinster did not protect you from such feelings, nor could the application of common sense and intelligence stop you fantasising about a man. A man who might be quite willing to kiss her—men appeared to be thoroughly undiscriminating in that respect—but who certainly would not see her as a lover. Or anything other than a friend.

And then he had snapped at her, warned her quite clearly that he did not want to be found in a compromising situation with her. It hurt and she could not work out why. He was perfectly correct, it would be terrible to have to marry someone because you had compromised them. It was certainly no basis for a marriage. And she knew she was never going to marry, knew that those kisses had been all she was ever going to experience. She was a rational, educated, intelligent female—so why did Theo's words wound her so much?

You should be glad he is not a silver-tongued hypocrite, the voice of common sense chided. *And you should be very glad indeed he has no idea that you are lusting after him.* Because that was what she was doing, there was no hiding it from herself.

Elinor looked at the clock. Half past midnight. An hour and a half. Time to search this room thoroughly. The count was hardly likely to hide his indecent treasure in a guest room, but she might as well be thorough. Elinor removed her remaining old gown from the press and got dressed again. It was a deep bottle green, ideal for skulking about in the shadows, and was not such a bad fit as the others, so she might escape a lecture from Theo on how dreadful it was.

Theo's scratch on the door panels was so faint she would not have heard it if she had not been listening for him. He stepped back abruptly, straight on to one of the creaking floorboards, when she opened the door, knife in hand.

'Shh!'

'What are you doing?' he hissed.

'Searching my room. My painting knife is excellent for getting between floorboards, but none of them are loose.'

It was hard to see in the dim light of the dark lantern he carried, but she thought he cast up his eyes. 'Come on.'

The chateau was an eerie place at night. Sections of it were decorated and furnished to match their period, so one moment there was the comforting bulk of long-case clocks and armoires with vases on top, the next a suit of armour would loom out of the shadows or the mounted head of a wild boar would appear silhouetted against a window. Elinor resisted the urge to clutch Theo's coat-tails and padded along behind him in her light slippers, the knife still in her hand.

He found his way easily through the passageways to the study door. Elinor had thought she had committed the plan to memory, but she had become lost after the first staircase. He crouched down, removed something metallic from his pocket and began to pick the lock. It was a skill that Elinor did not think the average anti-quities dealer would have. Could she persuade him to teach her?

They were inside faster than she would have believed possible. 'Check the curtains,' Theo whispered, unshuttering the dark lantern only when he was happy no chink of light would show.

They worked their way systematically around the room, testing panels and searching cupboards, Theo opening locked drawers and relocking them. 'How big is it?' Elinor asked, sitting back on her heels and pushing her hair off her face.

'This big, top to bottom.' Theo held his hands about eighteen inches apart. 'It is heavy too.'

'That just leaves the floor.' Elinor began to wriggle her knife blade between boards, but nothing shifted. It took twenty minutes to work across it, prizing at each long board with no result. 'Ouch!'

'Splinters?'

'In the heel of my hand.' She flapped it back and forth, muttering.

'Let me see. Theo opened the dark lantern and took her hand. 'One nasty big one. If I can just get it—hold on—there. Better suck it in case there are any little ones left.' He lifted her hand to his mouth and sucked on the swelling at the base of her thumb.

His mouth was hot and wet and the suction was strong and should have hurt—only instead it seemed to go straight to the pit of her belly, straight down to where that hot disturbing ache had started when he had kissed her. She looked at his bent head in the yellow light and felt a wave of fierce tenderness wash through her, so intense that she trembled.

Elinor was not aware of placing her other hand on his cheek, of cupping it gently against her palm, only of seeing it there and of Theo turning his head into the caress. Did she kiss him or did he kiss her? How did they get here, on the wide dark boards, limbs tangled, mouths hungrily together?

This time she knew the taste of him on her tongue, his scent familiar and arousing in her nostrils and she was aware for the first time of his body against hers, of the size and solidity against her softness, of the hard thrust against her belly that should have terrified her, but only added to the ache and the needing.

They rolled, bumping into furniture, too intent on each other, on exploring, to care. Her breast fitted into the palm of his hand as though it had been made for it and his mouth left hers to nuzzle down over the shrouding cloth. Her nipples were hard against the friction of her chemise and she wriggled, frustrated, wanting her flesh against his, needing his mouth where his fingers were rubbing in maddeningly slow circles until she thought she would scream.

Some rational thought surfaced, telling her that this, here, now, was madness and they should stop, and then his hand left her breast and she sighed, a great shuddering exhalation of relief and disappointment, not knowing which was which. And she lost that thread of rationality again when Theo's mouth sealed over hers, his tongue filling her with slow, heavy thrusts that made her clasp his shoulders for some anchor in this whirlpool of sensation.

The scrape of metal in the lock cut through her senses like a surgeon's knife. One moment there had been nothing but the delirium of his kiss, the next she was staring wild eyed at Theo as he pushed her towards the deep kneehole under the desk. Elinor scrabbled for it, finding the knife, scooping it up as Theo followed her, his fingers pinching out the wick of the lantern as he jammed into the space. It was a partners' desk, she realised, deep enough for two people to work opposite each other. Unless whoever was opening the door sat down and stretched out their legs, or bent to look, they were out of sight.

Theo's arms came around her, holding her tight so they were facing each other, knees drawn up, backs curved protectively towards the openings on either side. Her body was still shaking, her mind was reeling, but his calmness helped her keep still, breathe slowly and quietly. The door was open now. Over Theo's shoulder she could see the light of a candle, perhaps a branch— it seemed quite bright.

What time was it? What on earth was the count doing? In answer a clock struck the half-hour. It must be past three. Perhaps he had been unable to sleep and had come down to read. Then the quality of the foot-steps struck her. Even a man in slippers should not be that quiet, surely?

As she thought it, she saw pale skirts pass and then stop. There had been a large inlaid box on top of the desk which they had left untouched because it was too small to hold the Chalice. The woman was opening that. Papers rustled, there was a soft exclamation, then the sound of the lid closing, the scrape of a key—or was it a picklock?

Who was it? She could tell nothing from the skirts, which looked like those of a heavy satin night robe. It could be any of the women who were staying. She was standing still as though in thought. Or was she listen-ing? Could she hear them breathing?

Then, with a swish of skirts and the light tread of kid slippers, she was moving towards the door again. It opened, closed. Darkness, there was the scrape of metal again, then silence.

Theo's hand pressed against her mouth. Elinor counted in her head and reached twenty before he began to wriggle back out of their tight confinement.

'Who was that?' she asked, getting to her feet as he lit the lantern again. Her legs were shaking. 'It was a woman.'

'I have no idea.' He took out the picklocks and began to work on the box. 'She was using picklocks, or a hairpin, on the door.'

'Ana, then? Surely the countess would have a key.'

'Not necessarily.' He had the lid open, the papers in his hand. 'It's an inventory. My God—it is the wicked count's inventory for his secret society. See, here's the Chalice.'

He spread the crackling sheets of parchment on the table, Elinor struggling to read the ancient handwriting in the poor light. 'And a platter from the same goldsmith. Chains of gold and silver…whips of horse hair and leather… What is that, I don't recognise the word?'

Theo folded the list and put his hand on it. 'I'm glad to hear it and I have no intention of telling you.' He put the inventory back and closed the lid. 'So, there are more things to find. Whoever she is, she is welcome to it. All I want is to locate the Chalice and get out of here.'

'The inventory gave no hint about the hiding place?'

'Not exactly. It has given me an idea, though, for where to look. I must study the plan again.'

'We'll look tomorrow.' Now all she wanted to do was to curl up in her own bed, by herself, and try to sleep. Sleep and not think or feel or want. And somehow to subdue the heated intimate ache that Theo's kisses had aroused.

'We will not,' Theo said sternly, working on the door. He shuttered the lantern and opened it a crack, listening. 'Come on.'

'Why not?'

'Why not?' He looked up from relocking the door, his face grim. 'Because for some reason I cannot seem to keep my hands off you and I must. We are playing with fire, Nell.'

'Just then—before she came in—what would have happened?'

'Nothing more than a kiss,' he said abruptly, taking her arm and turning back towards the wing where their rooms were. 'I am still enough of a gentleman to be sure of that. But it isn't easy, Nell, not when what I want is to take you to my bed. To take your virginity.'

'Why?' she asked, determined to work this out. She had no idea what she felt, what she thought. But he was experienced, he understood, surely, what was going on? 'We are not in love. We are both intelligent, rational people. I do not understand why I am so confused, why I want to...to touch you, to have you kiss me.'

They were passing a deep window embrasure with seats built into the thick stone. Theo sat her down firmly, then sat opposite. *At a safe distance,* she thought, distractedly. 'It is desire—impure, but very simple, Nell. It is easy to stir into life, difficult to damp down.' He leaned forwards, elbows on knees, and ran his hands through his hair.

'I see.' Elinor tried to work it out. 'I can understand why I want to kiss you—you showed me how, I like you and I trust you.' *And I want you, but I must not say that. I shouldn't even think it.* Theo groaned. 'You seem to like kissing me,' she ventured.

'Men like kissing women, full stop,' he said brutally, flattening any hope that somehow she was special. 'Nell, stop trying to apply your intellect to this. It isn't a set of grammar rules you have to learn and which then apply every time. Desire is very powerful, not logical and rarely convenient. It is not voluntary. It is especially inconvenient for ladies. Men can find mistresses. For ladies to take lovers and not lose their reputations into the bargain is almost impossible.'

'Bel—' she began and then clapped her hands over her mouth, horrified that she had almost said it.

'Bel and Dereham? Before they were married?' Theo, momentarily distracted, looked up. 'Really? Well, good for her after that prosy bore she was married to. But widows are different, Nell.'

'But I don't want a lover,' she said, trying to make herself understand as much as him. 'And you certainly don't want me, not when you can have experienced mistresses who don't need teaching and won't cause a scandal. So why can't we just—' She waved her hands about, frustrated at not being able to find the right expression.

'Turn it off like a tap?' Theo was smiling. It was a rather strained grin, but at least he was no longer frowning at her. 'Because it keeps surprising us and it is a very powerful instinct. You see why I don't want you in my bedroom?'

'Yes, indeed.' Her emphatic agreement had him smiling in earnest. He got to his feet and held out his hand. Elinor put hers in it and managed to smile back. 'It is such a...*crowded* feeling. I think it makes the Greek myths a lot easier to comprehend.'

Theo gave a snort of laughter, hastily choked back. 'Shh! We are getting close to the bedchambers. Do you want to explain to Aunt Louisa that we have been discussing mythology?'

On the threshold of her room he stopped and looked down at her for a long moment. 'I am not going to kiss you goodnight, Nell.'

'Very wise.' She put one hand on his shoulder, stood on tiptoe and touched her lips to his cheek. 'Goodnight, Theo.'

'Goodnight, Nell.'

The clock struck four and Elinor yawned, her jaw cracking, as she dragged off her clothes and stumbled into bed. Theo was wrong, she decided as she began to drift off to sleep. It *was* possible to understand this physical desire intellectually. The trouble was, it seemed impossible to make her body understand as well.

Chapter Eleven

'I don't remember you wearing this dress yesterday, Miss Elinor.'

Elinor looked up from her sleepy contemplation of her cup of chocolate to find Jeanie holding up the green walking dress, crumpled and dusty. The chateau's staff did not dust under desks, she thought, then caught herself before she said so. 'I couldn't sleep, so I got up and walked about,' she explained, stifling a yawn.

'What, in this spooky old place?' Jeanie shuddered dramatically. 'I wouldn't set foot outside my door in the dark, that's for sure, no matter what I heard outside.'

It took a moment or two for that statement to penetrate Elinor's drowsy brain. 'You heard something in the night? What, exactly?'

'Footsteps, and knockings and sounds like stones shifting,' the maid said, eyes wide, clothes brush suspended in mid stroke.

'Really? How odd. But then old buildings always sound odd if you aren't used to them,' Elinor said, suddenly no longer tired. She set her cup down. 'Where exactly are you lodged?'

Jeanie proved to have a poor sense of direction and even poorer descriptive skills. Eventually, with the help of the plan, Elinor pinpointed her room. 'You are on the ground floor?' That was odd for servants' rooms. Then she realised that it was part of the oldest wing and was immediately over the ancient cellars and dungeons. Presumably all the family and guest rooms were in the more modern parts of the building.

'Is Mr Ravenhurst up, do you know?' She slid out of bed and went to look out of the window. The sun was already brilliant; Mama would probably want to spend all day in the chapel.

'I saw him as I was bringing your hot water, Miss Elinor. He pinched my chin and told me I was looking too pretty for a man to stand at that time in the morning.' Jeanie tossed her head, obviously delighted with the compliment. 'Cheek, I call it.'

'That's men for you,' Elinor replied, from her wealth of recent experience.

It seemed Theo and the count had been for a ride, for they were both in the breakfast parlour when she came down, both slightly windswept and apparently in better humour with each other. She had not known what to expect when she saw Theo again. Surely the fact that they had been so...intimate would show somehow? Would she even be able to meet his eyes?

And then, miraculously, it was all right. Theo was just her friend and cousin again, his hair tousled, his smile when he saw her, wide and uncomplicated. Or was he feeling like she was, very different inside? No—

as he had implied, men hardly regarded a kiss as significant.

Elinor dimpled at the count, biting her cheek at Theo's comically raised eyebrows and took the opportunity to hiss as she paused beside his chair, 'Jeanie heard noises last night in the cellars. Someone else is searching.'

'It's a miracle we didn't bump into all the rest of the guests,' he murmured back, the scraping of chair legs as he resumed his seat covering the exchange.

'And what would you like to do this morning, Miss Ravenhurst?' the count enquired, placing a plate of very English-looking food in front of her. 'I still enjoy my English breakfasts,' he explained, sitting down to his own dish of kedgeree.

'Thank you. I will assist Mama, I expect. She will want to spend time in your lovely chapel, I am sure. The light will be good with so much sunshine.'

'And I cannot tempt you outside into that sun?' He was so hopelessly good looking, she thought. Those long lashes, those dark, stormy eyes, that beautifully chiselled jaw. And the intense way he focussed on her. It sounded as though his day would be ruined if she did not join him in the grounds.

'Oh.' Elinor tried fluttering her lashes. Her sister seemed to be able to do it to effect. She felt a complete idiot. On the far side of the count Theo raised his eyebrows, apparently in agreement with that assessment. 'That sounds lovely. But what I would *really* like to do is to see your dungeons. I *love* Gothic romances and they must be *so* atmospheric.'

Theo stopped pulling mocking faces and nodded approval. *Clever,* he mouthed.

'The dungeons?' The count looked wary. 'They are not very exciting these days, just cellars now full of wine barrels and old furniture. No hideous instruments of torture or skeletons in chains to send a *frisson* down your spine.' He did not seem exactly eager to take her, but then what host would be delighted at a request to tour his cellars on a bright sunny day?

'Please, Count?' Elinor tried wheedling. 'I am sure you could make it seem so exciting.' Theo, his mouth full of coffee, choked alarmingly.

'I cannot promise that,' he said, his eyes suggesting he lied. Elinor felt herself turn pink. Lord! Her inept flirting must be having an effect. 'But I will do my best. And you must call me Leon.'

'Oh, thank you—Leon.' Elinor reached for the toast, suddenly finding herself incapable of any more of this and terrified of meeting Theo's mocking gaze. 'I will come and find you when Mama no longer requires me, shall I?'

To her relief the others began to trickle into the room. Julie sat next to Leon, sending Elinor a cool, warning glance as though she had overheard her exchange with him. Laure and Antoinette fluttered in and sat down either side of Theo, exclaiming over the changes to the dramatic colouring of his bruises and managing to sound as though he had been injured in the course of some knightly endeavour. Elinor wondered about engaging him in conversation and then wickedly decided to leave him to deal with them as best he could.

His tactics appeared to be to treat them both as though they were about fifteen and he an indulgent and elderly uncle, an approach that won him an approving nod from his aunt when Lady James appeared.

The Traceys announced their intention of riding out and persuaded Monsieur Castelnau, and, to Elinor's surprise, Ana, to join them. Julie, she noticed, waited until Leon's refusal before refusing herself. *She's in love with him,* Elinor thought. *Poor soul, he sees only his mother's companion.* And companions, as she knew all too well, were so often invisible. But Julie was striking, with a slim dark elegance that matched the count's, and she hardly seemed lacking in self-confidence. They would make a handsome couple.

She waited for her mother to finish, sipping a third cup of coffee and crumbling a roll while she attempted to engage her hostess in conversation. The countess seemed heavy-eyed and strained. No doubt, Elinor thought compassionately, she was finding sleep hard to come by. Her husband had died in mysterious circumstances only a little while ago, after all. In fact, it was odd that she chose to entertain at all—perhaps she did so only at her son's insistence. Her gaze rested thoughtfully on Leon. He did not have the air of a man whose father had only recently died so tragically— had he and the previous count been on bad terms?

Lady James did not keep her waiting long. 'Come, Elinor, we have work to do.' Elinor turned to smile her thanks at Monsieur Castelnau, who had pulled back her chair for her, and blinked in sudden confusion. Who was that woman? Then she saw it was herself reflected in a long glass. She stared. Yes, of course it was her, only…

'I will just fetch my sketching things, Mama,' she said, leaving her mother to ask the countess about the key to the chapel.

* * *

Jeanie was folding clothes in her room and looked up with a smile as Elinor came in. 'Jeanie, do I look different?'

It was a bizarre question, but the maid did not seem to find it odd. 'But yes, Miss Elinor. You've got colour in your cheeks and your hair makes your face so much softer and you are wearing those pretty colours now.'

She stared at the mirror. She looked younger, or at least she looked her proper age and not years older as she sometimes felt. And if not pretty exactly—she did not have that sort of face—she might honestly claim to look quite attractive. She knew she had looked nice last evening, but then she had been wearing her lovely new gown and the jewels. But now... 'How odd. I suppose I have been getting more fresh air, and the new gowns and hairstyle, of course.'

'All those,' Jeanie agreed, coming to look over her shoulder. 'But its being in love that does it. Works every time.'

Elinor stared at her and Jeanie smiled back into the mirror, apparently unaware that she had said anything to shock her mistress. It took several attempts to make her voice work. 'Jeanie, I am not in love.' That did not seem emphatic enough. 'Not at all. Not with anyone.'

The girl actually winked! 'Of course, if you say so, Miss Elinor. You can rely on me not saying anything to her ladyship, we don't want to worry her, do we, not with all the things she's thinking about, what with her books and everything. It's ever so convenient over here, isn't it? Not like London. You can go around with him, just as you please.'

'Over here?' Elinor said faintly. 'Oh, yes. Very convenient.'

'And he's a lovely gentleman, isn't he? Not what you'd call handsome, not like the count. But what I'd call *manly*. And he's got lovely hands—' She broke off, looking thoughtful. 'Yes, miss, you definitely won't be disappointed in *him* for a husband.'

'Jeanie.' Elinor pulled herself together and spoke clearly, slowly and firmly, desperately ignoring the image of how Theo would not be a disappointment as a husband. 'I am not in love with Mr Ravenhurst. He is my cousin and my friend, that is all. There is nothing to keep secret from my mother.' *And may I not be struck down for lying!* she thought. *Lying about there being nothing to keep secret,* she amended. There was no secret about her feelings for Theo. It was ludicrous to think she was in love with him. That was not a rational emotion for her to have. And she was a rational female. Very rational, if unable to control the stirrings of physical desire. Nothing more than a kiss…that was no reason to fall in love.

'Yes, Miss Elinor.' Jeanie, not the slightest bit chastened, returned to her folding while Elinor, considerably flustered, snatched up her satchel and a folded copy of the plan and fled.

I am not in love with him, I can't be. 'Here I am, Mama—goodness, those stairs are steep! What would you like me to do?' *I desire him. That is a perfectly natural physical reaction over which I have no control. But I can control my actions and my thoughts.* 'Check the capitals for similarities with the basilica? Yes, of course.' *Falling in love is intellectual, surely? I do not want to fall in love, therefore I cannot. I have not.* 'This one, Mama, and that one there. I think they might be by the same hand.'

Falling in love turns your brain upside down. Look at Cousin Bel when she fell in love. Distracted, poor thing. I am perfectly in command of my emotions. I am perfectly normal.

'Elinor! What are you doing standing there, gazing into space? You have been looking like a moonstruck noddy for a good two minutes.'

'Sorry, Mama. I was trying to recall the basilica columns in detail.' *Focus, think.* She was terrified, she realised. Terrified by the emotions she did not understand, terrified that perhaps Jeanie was right, that she was in love with Theo. Because if she was, it was hopeless and it would hurt. It would hurt terribly and she had schooled herself to live life calmly, not expecting anything and never being disappointed. That way nothing wounded her any more, nothing was going to leave her raw and vulnerable and exposed. But this was going to, because it was quite hopeless, he had said so.

'Do you want me to draw, Mama?' she asked, praying the answer would be *no*. Her hands were shaking. 'Because I thought I would check for masons' marks, see if any match the ones in the basilica.'

'An excellent idea,' Lady James approved, beginning to pace out distances between columns. There, she could pull herself together and function after all. Elinor began to scan the walls closely, noting the cryptic signs the medieval masons had scratched on each block so their work could be identified and they would be paid correctly each day. It needed careful study and it meant she could check the walls for any sign of a hiding place as she went.

* * *

By the end of the morning her notebook was full of marks, her head was spinning and every inch of wall had been looked at. There was nothing in the least suspicious to suggest a secret.

A footman arrived with the message that luncheon was served, earning a frown from Lady James and a sigh of thankfulness from Elinor. 'Mama, can you manage without me this afternoon? I have such a headache. I could collate the marks against the ones for the basilica later if you like.'

'Very well. Come along, I suppose we must eat.'

Elinor wrestled with her problem throughout luncheon before she came up with a solution. She was seeing too much of Theo, and under circumstances that were so intense, it was no wonder she was becoming—she sought for a word—*engrossed* with him. All that was needed was contact with another man.

And there was an admirable candidate to hand. 'Miss Elinor?' The count was waiting to see if she was still hoping for a tour of the cellars. Yes, he would do perfectly. He was attractive enough to be diverting, sophisticated enough not to mistake her intentions or feelings.

'Leon.' She smiled back. 'I am relying upon you for some thoroughly spine-chilling stories.'

'Let me see what I can do to produce a *frisson*.' He took a lantern from a stand beside a small door off the great entrance hall and lit it. 'The dungeons date from the first castle, built by my ancestor, the Chevalier Guy de Beaumartin. He was a powerful war lord and needed somewhere to keep his many captives. Mind how you go on these narrow steps. Here.' He took her hand and led her down the spiral stairs.

It was no different from the way Theo helped her, his light grasp was quite impersonal, but Elinor freed herself with a murmured word of thanks as soon as they arrived at the bottom of the stairs. They were in a wide, stone-flagged passageway, vanishing into darkness and shadows and, on either side, small doors that she would have to stoop to enter. 'Cells?' she queried.

'Certainly.' Leon pushed one open with a rending creak of rusted hinges and shone the light inside for her to see. 'No windows, the damp runs down the stone walls. See the bolts in the walls that held the shackles? Imagine the despair of being chained here in the darkness, month after month, with only the rats for company.'

Elinor could imagine it only too vividly, and she did not find that sort of medieval barbarity romantic. But she had to maintain her excuse of wanting to see the Gothic horrors, so she produced an exaggerated shudder. 'Ghastly indeed.' Something scuttled across the edge of the pool of light: a vast spider. She gave an involuntary gasp and jumped backwards, to find herself being supported by Leon's arm.

'It is only a spider,' he said reassuringly, making no attempt to remove his arm. Elinor stiffened, but he did not try to take advantage of the situation either.

'Thank you. I have to confess to hating the things— so foolish.' She stepped aside as though to allow him to proceed and he dropped his arm away. The count's manner as he led her through the maze of underground passages and chambers was perfectly correct and yet

Elinor was left in no doubt at all that he saw her as an attractive woman and that he wanted her to see him as a man, not just as her host.

How he achieved that intrigued her and she began to watch closely to analyse his technique. Leon touched her, fleetingly, always with a good excuse, always somewhere unalarming, such as her elbow or her hand, but frequently. His voice was husky, soft enough that she had to move a little closer to him to hear, and, when he spoke, he kept his eyes on her face as though hanging on her every word of response. He was, in effect, flirting in the most unexceptional manner.

Elinor decided to try responding. She laughed at anything he said that could be considered even faintly amusing, she leaned a little when he offered her support on the steps, she gasped in admiration when he told her tales of his ancestors' deeds of chivalry. In fact, by the time the narrow passageways opened up into a great chamber with a vaulted ceiling, they were both thoroughly at ease with each other and, she suspected, he might very well try to kiss her at any moment.

Oddly, Leon did not seem to want to linger, but took the direct path across the imposing space. 'Oh, please wait,' Elinor implored. 'What a strange room. Was it a guard chamber?'

'I have no idea,' Leon said, a trifle shortly. He wanted her out of there, she realised, staring round. The chamber was like a chapel with bays at intervals along the walls and rusted flambeaux holders. There were small metal hooks high up that she recognised as suspension points for tapestries, although the walls were stark stone now. There was a small stone platform at one end. It was too low for an altar.

Then she saw the ring bolts at all four corners of the platform and more on the pillars. She measured them by eye, cold chills running up and down her spine. They were the right height to tie the wrists of a woman to, if she stretched up. This, surely, was the room the wicked count used for his depraved orgies. And where better to house the ritual objects and the Chalice?

Leon set down the lantern, sending wild shadows flickering across the walls. As he walked towards her, smiling, his dark, lean features seemed devilish in the gloom. 'Do you find this gives you the thrill of horror you were seeking?' he asked her. And it seemed the light, bantering tone had been replaced with something more sinister. Almost she could believe he was the re-incarnation of his ancestor.

'Oh, yes.' She tried to laugh. 'See, I am all of a tremble.' She held out her hand, surprised to see she was speaking the truth, and he took it, drawing her in to him. It seemed impossible to resist, as if he, or the strange atmosphere of the chamber, was mesmerising her. He was going to kiss her, she realised, almost fatalistically.

'Oh, Elinor, how I would like to make you tremble,' Leon murmured and lowered his mouth to hers.

Chapter Twelve

Think, Elinor told herself fiercely, *see how this is no different from kissing Theo? See, all it is, is physical passion and my lack of experience.* She opened to the pressure of Leon's insistent lips, let his mouth mould hers, let his tongue explore, let him brace her hard against his lean body so she could feel his arousal. And she felt nothing, nothing but surprise that she could do this and feel only detachment.

But detached though she might be, this was enough. More than enough. Elinor put her hands on Leon's shoulders and pushed. It did not make him loosen his hold, but it threw her off balance. She took a step, the backs of her knees met an obstacle and she fell, Leon coming with her, to the low stone platform. He threw out a hand to take their weight, then let them both subside slowly on to the hard surface.

Now Elinor did start to feel uneasy. Surely he would not persist? He was a gentleman, her host—but she had held out her hand to him, gone willingly into his arms. Perhaps he thought that her unconventional lifestyle

meant her morals were loose. With an effort she freed
her mouth, pushing against the upper part of his chest
with her left palm. From a distance of inches Leon's
dark eyes burned into hers.

'No,' she managed. 'Enough!' Her outflung right
hand met metal, grasped it, and she found she was
holding one of the rings set at the corner of the
platform. It was as though the panic and fear of those
women from so long ago flowed into her body, lending
her strength. She shoved harder and Leon stood up,
catching her hand in his and pulling her to his feet as
he did so.

He seemed neither put out by her rejection nor particularly agitated by what had just occurred. 'I am sorry
we fell. Are you hurt?' he asked solicitously.

Elinor bit back the retort that it was rather late in the
day to ask that and managed a bright smile. She did not
want to expose her own inexperience, nor did she want
to let him glimpse her fear, not of him, but of the place
where they stood.

'I am quite all right, but I am afraid that this wildly
romantic atmosphere has led us both further than we
meant to go.' She heard her own voice sounding as cool
and emotionless as though she was disputing a footnote
in a learned journal. What was the matter with her? Her
heart was pounding, but it was not the same as the way
she felt after Theo kissed her. What did she feel? More
than a little embarrassed, in the aftermath of that
embrace, but not even slightly stirred by it. Shouldn't
she be? He was an attractive man, his technique seemed
perfectly assured. Wasn't she supposed to be aroused
by what they had just done?

All she wanted, she realised, was Theo. She wanted

to be in his arms and have him sooth away the terror that seemed to ooze from the stones; despite that, she wanted to join him searching the place, certain that here they would find the Chalice.

'Elinor!' Even distorted by the echo in the maze of underground corridors, his voice was unmistakable.

Leon smiled tightly. 'It appears your cousin desires to chaperon you. He does not like you being alone with me, I think.'

That was all she needed. The two men were prickly enough around each other without them circling like two dogs over a juicy bone. The thought of herself in that light, when previously the best analogy would be to a rather overcooked and dried-up mutton chop, made Elinor's lips twitch in wry amusement.

'That makes you smile?' Leon asked. 'It amuses you to have two men desiring you?'

'My cousin most certainly does not—Theo! You have found us. Is this not the most atmospheric place? I swear I am going to try my hand at writing a Gothic novel, I am so inspired.'

'Aunt Louisa would have kittens,' Theo observed, smiling. In the light of the lantern his eyes looked like cold obsidian, utterly at odds with his voice and the curve of his lips. 'She is wondering, loudly, where you are. I gather you are supposed to be in your room, recovering from a headache.'

'So I am,' Elinor said. 'But it is much better now.' It seemed politic to move to Theo's side. 'You found your way down here all by yourself? How clever, I would be lost in an instant if it were not for Leon. Shall we go back the way you came?' She tucked her hand under his elbow, looking back over her shoulder at the count. Faintly, there was the sound of a low growl, then she realised it was Theo. Her smile was becoming somewhat fixed, she realised, urging Theo in the direction of the door. *'I've found something,'* she hissed. *'Can we please get out of here?'*

He had taken a shorter route and they emerged through a door into the inner courtyard of the chateau. The countess and Mademoiselle Julie were sitting in the shade, sewing. Elinor felt their speculative scrutiny and moved closer to Theo. 'How wonderfully atmospheric!' she exclaimed. 'Thank you so much, Count. I have to confess I would have been terrified to find myself down there alone—those spiders.' She gave an exaggerated shudder. 'Now I had better go and help Mama again. Theo, could you come and carry my easel, please? I left it in my room.'

When they reached the door she pulled him in, ignoring his protests about propriety and the damage she was doing to his sleeve. 'Theo, I think I know where it might be.'

'Sit over there.' He pointed a long finger at the window seat and took a stool by the door. 'If Aunt Louisa comes in, I want to be at a very safe distance from you. Now, tell me, what have you been doing, besides making love with the count.'

'I have not,' she began indignantly.

'The back of your gown is dusty, there is a slight red mark on your cheek. He needs to shave twice a day if he is kissing women.'

'He did kiss me, but that is all.' She had nothing to feel defensive about. Theo was not her guardian, certainly not her brother. Which was how he was sounding.

'Lying down?'

'I tripped. Theo, *listen.* You know I went down there with him to explore, so stop being so…sanctimonious. And why should I not kiss him if I want to? He is a very attractive man.'

Theo seemed to be counting silently. Eventually he said, 'So what have you discovered?'

'The room where you found us is very strange. Did you notice?' He shook his head and she felt a strange twinge of satisfaction that he had been so focussed on her. 'Look at the plan.' Her copy was still spread on the table and she went to trace her route. 'See? Like a chapel, with lots of deep alcoves, like side chapels. And there are rings on the walls.' She felt herself go pale and kept talking. 'And a low platform, like an altar, with rings at all four corners. That's what I fell back on to and I realised that it was probably used for…for…'

Standing on the other side of the table, looking down at the plan, Theo's face was grim. He probably knew, far better than she in her inexperience, the sort of activities that room had witnessed. 'You think it would be the place to hide the Chalice?'

'Surely there would have been somewhere to keep the silver and so forth, in the days when it was in use?'

'I think you are right. And look, the chamber is almost directly below the servants' lodgings.' He tapped a finger thoughtfully on the curling edge of the parchment. 'What do you think—someone searching, or someone checking it is still there?'

'Checking,' Elinor said, uncertain why she was so sure. 'What time shall we go tonight?'

'We?' Theo raised an eyebrow. Elinor mimicked

him, earning herself a grin. 'You are not going anywhere, certainly not down into nasty, spider-infested dungeons.'

'Theo, if we don't go together, then I will go by myself,' she warned.

She thought he muttered, 'Give me strength.' Then, 'Very well. I will collect you at two. If you scream at spiders, I'll gag you.'

'Yes, Theo,' Elinor murmured with mock meekness. She liked the way he did not try to order her to do things simply because he said so—or, at least, he did *try* ordering her, but when she refused he did not bluster and get indignant, which she had observed was so often the male way when confronted with obdurate females.

Theo began to fold the paper and she watched his hands, wondering why she had an ache inside. He folded it meticulously, with exaggerated care, running his thumb down the creases, then standing with it in his hands, looking at it. Then he tossed it on to the table, took three long strides around it to her side and pulled her against him with one arm around her shoulders.

'Did he frighten you?' he asked, his voice gruff.

'No.' She shook her head, certain. 'No, it was very odd. There was something about that chamber, the atmosphere. When he kissed me I felt nothing from him, but I did feel fear—almost as though it was another woman's emotions.' Elinor gave an exaggerated shiver. 'Foolishness.'

'Perhaps.' Theo kept hold of her. She felt a pressure on the top of her head as though he rested his cheek there. 'Something is very wrong in this place, Nell, but I do not think it is ghosts from the past.'

Elinor let herself lean, indulging herself, realising that it *was* an indulgence and that revealed some truth about her feelings. And suddenly she did not care. Perhaps she was in love with him. What if she was hurt? Perhaps it was better to feel strong emotions than to go through life on a safe, dull, even keel. She lifted one hand and laid it on Theo's chest, just above his heart, feeling the strong beat pulse through her.

Yes, said the voice in her head. *Yes, he is the one. At last.*

'Nell? Are you all right? You sighed.' He let her go, setting her back a pace and holding her by the shoulders to look into her face. 'You know, you are damnably pretty in that colour.'

'For which you may take all the credit,' she said, making light of it. 'I freely acknowledge that my wardrobe was full of dreadful gowns. But you should not lie to me, Theo—I am not pretty.'

'No, you aren't, are you?' He frowned at her. 'That's too lightweight a word. I am no sure what you are, I will have to think about it.' He bent, kissed her on the lips with a fleeting pressure and turned abruptly to the door.

'Theo!' It came out as a somewhat strangled gasp, but at last she could still articulate. It hadn't been a proper kiss. It had been, she supposed, just a friendly gesture. No doubt he had got whatever *desire* he had felt for her out of his system with that kiss in the study and now she was just a friend to be reassured, and protected from the count. 'My easel? Mama will be waiting.'

'Lord, yes. I was forgetting, she wanted me to measure something high up—string courses, I think. Come on.'

At two in the morning Theo watched Elinor as she walked softly along the passageway in front of him, a lantern in her hand. They had decided to go the longer way to the chamber, the way she had gone with Leon in the afternoon, rather than risk opening an external door into the courtyard in the dark.

He had spent the rest of the afternoon balancing on stepladders holding measuring rods, while his aunt tried to make the dimensions of the chapel fit some mathematical formula dreamt up by a scholar whom Theo had no trouble stigmatising as being as daft as a coot. She had failed, something that appeared to give her great satisfaction, and had dismissed him until dinner, leaving him ample time to brood over what, exactly, was the right word to describe Elinor now.

She never had been plain, he had realised, his soup spoon halfway to his mouth during the first course, just smothered by drab colours and scraped-back hair and a life of dull regularity. Like the uncut gemstone he had likened her to, or perhaps a painting, languishing under layer after layer of ancient varnish.

The countess addressed a question to him and he answered her, half of his mind still on Elinor. Then it came to him as he saw her turn, laughing at something Sir Ian had said, her face lit up with amusement and intelligence and the lovely line of her upper body silhouetted against the baronet's dark evening coat. *Comely,* that was the word. And she always would be, even in old age, he realised, finding he was smiling.

He was still thinking about that revelation as he followed her into the hall, his eyes on the pool of light cast at her feet by the dark lantern. Distracted, he bumped into a chest. The sharp edge dug into his thigh, the lid lifted and banged down with a loud thud that seemed to echo round the great hall. He stopped, cursing under his breath and rubbing his leg.

'Does it hurt?' Elinor came back and held up the light to see.

'Damned chest.' The long-case clock they were standing next to chimed the half-hour, making her jump. 'We had better get a move on.' Elinor nodded, lifted the light and turned. 'Wait!'

'What?' She came back and looked where he was pointing. The great tapestry hung from floor to ceiling. It was in poor condition, moth-eaten and dusty from long years hanging close to the fireplace, but it was possible to make out that it showed the Chateau of Beaumartin in an earlier age. Around the borders were trails of vines, hunting scenes, vignettes of harvest and feasting. And in the middle of the left-hand border, the image of a chalice, half-hidden by a drapery.

'Is that it?' Elinor put the lantern on a side table by the sofa that stood in front of the tapestry and climbed up onto the upholstered seat. 'I can't see very clearly.'

'It is the right general outline. It doesn't show the detail, of course—that would probably scorch a hole in the fabric.' He could remember the effort it had taken not to react when the late count had finally taken the thing out of its case and handed it to him and he was able to study it for the first time. He had thought himself sophisticated and had been astonished to find himself shocked, enlightened and shamefully aroused, all at once.

Theo joined Elinor on the sofa seat, making it dip and forcing her to clutch at his sleeve to steady herself. 'If I lift this edge away from the wall, can you shine the light behind and see if you can see any kind of wall cupboard or opening?'

It took some doing. The tapestry was heavy, and without moving the weighty sofa, it was difficult to pull away from the wall. Sneezing from the dust, Elinor managed to get both the lantern and her head into the gap he created.

'Nothing, just smooth wall.'

'Good—I did not relish trying to drag this sofa out and then get it back in the right spot,' he said with some relief, helping her tuck the rucked tapestry back down behind the high upholstered back again.

It was smooth at last, and the two of them panting with the effort of doing it while balancing on the squashy and rather mobile cushions, when Theo froze. 'Someone's coming.'

It was just on the edge of his hearing, but it was definitely movement, the sound of someone trying to be quiet, and coming from the direction they had entered from. 'Hell, where can we hide?'

The heavily shadowed hall stretched out before them, singularly free of tables with heavy cloths over, cupboards or windows with floor-length curtains. It was quiet again. Theo had just decided he was imagining things when the door at the far end burst open.

It was too late to run—there was nowhere to conceal themselves. Theo fell on to the sofa, pulling Elinor down into his arms. 'Kiss me.'

He saw her grasp his intentions as fast as he spoke. With a ruthless hand she pulled open the top three buttons on her old gown, scattering them, then attacked the neck of his shirt. By the time he had her flat on her back his shirt was open to the waist and her hair was tumbling out of its pins.

It sounded as though half the village had erupted

into the room. Theo sat up, pulled Elinor protectively against his chest and demanded, 'What the hell is going on?'

It might not have been the village, but it was certainly the entire house party, hastily bundled into night robes, candles in hand. 'I might ask you the same thing, Ravenhurst,' the count retorted, stepping in front of his mother and Julie as though to shield them from the shocking sight.

To one side Lady Tracey put her hands over her mouth and her husband appeared to be fighting the desire to laugh. Laure and Antoinette were agog, their hair in curling papers, their eyes wide at the sheer, wonderful, horror of what was occurring. From the shadows Ana looked on, smiling. When he caught her eye, she licked her lips like a cat delicately relishing a mouse she had just eaten

'Theophilus!' It had been too much to hope that Aunt Louisa was absent from this mob. 'What do you think you are doing?'

'I should have thought that all too obvious, *madame*,' the countess interjected in freezing tones.

'We were going outside. For a walk. But I am afraid our passion got the better of us before we got to the door,' Theo said, improvising rapidly in an attempt to come up with a convincing story. Crushed beneath him, he could feel Elinor shift. He tried to take some his weight off her without standing up. The image he wanted firmly in everyone's mind was one of lovers caught *in flagrante*, not of two people dressed to be creeping about the chateau on some clandestine errand. And the warm curves pressed against him were decidedly inspiring. 'Aunt Louisa,

I had hoped to speak to you about this before now, but I fully intend—'

'You most certainly do,' she said. There was something in her tone that alerted him. She was not reacting as he expected her to. The others would not notice, they did not know her. But Theo knew that he could have expected to have been hauled off the sofa by his ear while she sent for a pair of blunt scissors, not subjected to a quelling stare down her imposing nose and utter, chilly, calm. 'You will attend me in my room at once. Both of you.' She turned to regard the others. 'Thank you, Count. I am sure there is nothing here to keep anyone else from their beds.'

Theo stood up and turned his back on the room, giving Elinor time to compose herself a little while the sounds of the retreating party diminished. Finally the door shut. She looked up at him, her face white. 'Theo, she is going to say I am compromised and insist—' Her fingers fumbled with the bodice of her gown and she looked up again. 'I do *not* want to marry you, Theo.'

'You don't?' He did not want to marry her, either, of course he didn't. The last thing he needed was a wife. But it shook him to realise his spinster cousin was just as adamantly unwilling to wed him. *Coxcomb* he jeered a himself for his reaction. *You are hardly God's gift as a husband, are you? A red-headed adventurer in disgrace with his family? Sensible woman.* 'All right, we will tell her the truth.' And that would be an act as courageous as any he had ever performed, explaining to his formidable aunt that he was involving her daughter in a perilous search for a pornographic artefact.

Chapter Thirteen

'What on earth were they all doing here?' Elinor asked, following Theo along the corridor as he tried to restore his shirt to some kind of order.

'I haven't the slightest idea—that damnable trunk lid banging down did not make so much noise it would rouse them from sleep, that's for sure.'

'Well, they were hardly likely to all be up recreating one of the famous orgies,' she said, shakily attempting humour. 'Not with Mama there. Can you imagine?'

'That was an image I am going to regret you placing in my imagination,' he said with feeling as they reached Lady James's door. 'Ready, Nell?' Elinor put back her shoulders and shook her hair out of her eyes. She felt as though she was going to face a firing squad.

'Ready.'

Mama was seated at her writing desk, her chair half-turned so she could scrutinise them as they came to stand in front of her. She did not ask them to sit down. 'Well, Theophilus?'

'I can explain, Aunt.' He did not appear either cowed or abashed by the situation. 'But first, tell me—how the dev—how on earth did everyone come to be in the hall at this hour of the night?'

'Those two idiotic girls decided it would be *fun* to creep around the chateau after dark in search of the Gothic horrors Elinor was foolish enough to speak of. They are addicted to sensation novels, it appears. They heard a loud bang as they approached the hall, assumed it was burglars—or a headless fiend, they are confused on that point—and rushed back, hammering on everyone's door and shrieking the place down.

'Normally I would have allowed the search to take place without me—most irrational and foolish, it merely needed the count to summon his male staff to search for the intruders. However, I was surprised to see neither of you coming out in response to the racket and looked in your rooms. Expecting the worst, I joined the group.'

'Mama, it was not what it seemed—' Elinor began.

'Nell.' Theo took her arm and guided her to one of the wing chairs by the fireside. 'I'll explain, you sit down.' She could not help but feel it was feeble of her to obey him. They had both got into this mess, she should be standing up to Mama at his side. But he looked cool and very confident and the smile he gave her was reassuring. Perhaps he could manage Mama better than she could.

He turned the other chair to face his aunt and sat down, uninvited. It was a good start—if she thought he was standing there to be carpeted like a naughty schoolboy, she was much mistaken.

'I have involved Elinor, and you, in an assault, a

theft and a murder,' he began. The full frontal attack had the desired effect: Lady James's eyebrows rose, she reached for her eyeglass, but she did not speak. 'It began when I was commissioned to negotiate for the purchase of a unique, and utterly indecent, piece of precious metalwork…

'…and if you think I, or any other man, can stop your daughter when she decides to involve herself in something, then I am afraid you are much mistaken, Aunt,' he finished half an hour later.

Elinor could sense that Theo was making himself sit still in the silence that followed. Her mother looked at Elinor through her eyeglass, then turned it on Theo. 'I collect you two do not wish to marry?' she said calmly.

'No, Mama, I—'

'No, we do not.' Lady James opened her mouth to utter her next question, but he answered it before she could speak. 'Nor is there any pressing reason why we must. That scene in the hall was pure theatre.' He was, Elinor thought blankly, extremely convincing.

'Indeed? I am relieved to hear it.' She let the eyeglass dangle on its black cord and watched it swing for a moment or two while Elinor contemplated her toes and wondered just how crimson she was blushing. 'It would be prudent, I believe, to allow the impression that you are now betrothed. You will no doubt suffer considerable embarrassment for the remainder of your stay here, which I can only say is your just desserts. Once we are back in England, no more need be said—no one here moves in the same circles as we do.'

She waited, apparently for them to comment, then

added with a certain malicious relish, 'It will certainly put your mistress's nose out of joint, Theophilus.'

'Mama!'

'Don't be mealy mouthed, Elinor. That unprincipled creature is one reason I was quite confident that Theophilus's amatory inclinations were directed elsewhere and not towards you.'

Had anyone ever tried to strangle the old witch? Theo wondered. But say what you might about her adder tongue, her attitude was an enormous relief. Or it should be. He was feeling unaccountably flat, but that, no doubt, was due to the shock of what had just occurred. Somehow he had been braced for an argument about marrying Elinor.

'Mama, Theo must find this Chalice or repay Lord X a great deal of money,' Elinor said, cutting across his musings. 'Even then, if he does not get the Chalice, there is no knowing what Lord X might do.' Lady James's gaze came up to scrutinise his bruised face.

'I did not suggest you stop looking for it,' she said. Theo's jaw dropped before he shut his mouth with a snap. Most of the time he felt confident he was in command of himself and of the situation—encounters with his aunt were a definite exception. 'One cannot allow murder and theft to go unpunished. As for his lordship, I suggest you tell me his name, Theophilus. I have powerful friends.'

'I do not break my clients' confidentiality,' he said, wishing he could in this instance. Goodness knows what, or who, Lady James Ravenhurst could summon to her aid if she wanted revenge upon someone. He shuddered to think, imagining a blood-crazed mob of Greek scholars pelting his lordship with heavy tomes.

'I intend helping Theo,' Elinor said firmly. He turned in the chair and smiled at her. Her chin was up and she was looking determined, despite the dark shadows under her eyes. He lov... He *admired* her courage.

'Of course,' Lady James said, startling them both. 'We are Ravenhursts, we do not abandon each other in times of trouble. However, I warn you, if she is harmed in any way, Theo, I will have your hide. Now, off to bed, both of you. I have work to do in the morning.'

'She called you Theo,' Elinor whispered as they stood outside in the corridor looking rather blankly at each other.

'I think we're dreaming,' Theo said, shaking his head. Elinor was still looking at him, the frown line between her brows furrowed. 'And don't do that.' He reached out and smoothed it with his thumb. 'Remember what your mother says about frowning.' Her skin was warm and soft and he ran the ball of his thumb along one arching eyebrow, feeling the elegant vault of the bone beneath. 'Goodnight, Nell.'

'Goodnight, Theophilus,' she said, suddenly grinning at him. 'I had better learn to address my be-trothed with suitable deference.' She was through the door before he could respond, although he thought he could hear her chuckle, floating behind her on the air.

Coming down to breakfast required a considerable amount of courage. The flash of amusement that had made her tease Theo evaporated as soon as she was alone in her room, leaving Elinor to toss and turn all night, al-ternately turning hot and cold with embarrassment.

It had never, ever, occurred to her that she might find herself compromised. Before Theo, men had not wanted to be alone with her for any other reason than to prose on about their translation from the Greek, to argue with her about Mama's latest controversial paper or occasionally to tell her at great length how miserable they were because their suit of some lady was not prospering.

Now—post-Theo—she did at least have the confidence that she looked well enough, and he had seemed to enjoy kissing her. But that they might find themselves caught, apparently locked in a passionate embrace... Every time her churning imagination presented her with the image of how they must have looked, she curled up tighter in bed and buried her head further into the pillows.

For some reason their exposure that night in a sham, and relatively mild, situation, was worrying her far more than the risk they had run kissing passionately— and very genuinely—in the study when they had been so nearly caught.

At this point Elinor got out of bed and began to prowl up and down, unable to lie still any longer. Her feelings in the study had been fuelled by ignorance, and the disorientation caused by the havoc Theo had wrought on her body and her emotions. This time they had been caught, and the appearance was everything. And it had just been appearance. He had been pretending; yet for her, even in the middle of that confusion and embarrassment, she had revelled in the feel of his hard body, his quick thinking, the instinctive way he had shielded her.

If Mama had insisted he marry her! She tried to

imagine being married to someone she loved and who did not want to be married to her. It was too ghastly to contemplate. Ruin was infinitely preferable—after all, how much worse off would she be in disgrace than she had been before she bumped into Theo in the basilica?

Pride made her pinch her cheeks when she looked in the mirror in the morning and she sent Jeanie off to find rice powder to cover the shadows under her eyes. It was hard to find a manner pitched between shame-faced and brazen when she found the entire party gathered in the breakfast parlour, all apparently determined to make their meal last as long as possible in the hope that the errant couple would make an appearance together.

Theo, deep in conversation with Sir Ian on the subject of horses, got to his feet when she entered, walked to her side and kissed her cheek. 'Courage,' he whispered before turning and leading her to the chair beside his. 'Good morning, Elinor.'

Laure and Antoinette were staring. Elinor smiled warmly at them, making both drop their eyes to their plates in confusion, then extended the smile to take in the rest of the table. 'I am so sorry we disturbed you all last night, but I know you will all be happy for us—we are betrothed.'

That at least had the effect of taking the wind out of their sails. If they thought she was going to creep around, blushing and humiliated, they had another think coming. Elinor gazed up at Theo and tried to look like a woman in love. It was apparently more convincing than she expected. Lady Tracey gave a sentimental sigh, Mademoiselle Julie looked pleased—presumably

because she would no longer take any notice of Leon—
and even the countess's severe expression softened
somewhat.

'When do you intend to wed?' Monsieur Castelnau
enquired.

'We have not decided—' Elinor began, but Theo
cut in smoothly.

'It will be a while. Naturally we want my father, the
Bishop of Wessex, to marry us and I would hope our
cousin the duke will be able to attend, although he
rarely travels south. And her Serene Highness, the
Grand Duchess of Maubourg, who has recently joined
our family, is naturally subject to many commitments.'

'A large Society wedding, then?' Sir Ian asked.

'Huge,' Theo said expansively, warming to his
theme. Elinor sat quietly eating while he talked. If
anyone there had not fully comprehended just who
Theo was, and how well he was connected, they knew
now. And, as his cousin, they must realise this applied
equally to her. He was taking out insurance, she
realised, making it very clear that anyone who harmed
or insulted them would have the entire Ravenhurst clan
to deal with.

She allowed herself to fall into a daydream of
walking down the aisle of the cathedral on Theo's arm,
as his wife. The organ would be filling the space with
joyful sound, the entire family would be beaming, she
would be looking beautiful in cream silk with almond
trimmings. The scene ground to a shuddering halt at
this point, as though the actors had been turned to
stone. She was never going to make a fairytale bride,
the bishop would never agree to marry them, the
family would be aghast at Theo making such a poor

match as a spinster bluestocking. And, above all, Theo did not want to marry her anyway and this was all pretence.

To her horror, tears began to well up in her eyes. 'Oh. Oh, forgive me, I feel a little—' She bolted from the room, hearing Ana's voice, rich with mock concern, just as the door closed behind her.

'I *do* hope she is not feeling sick.'

Oh my God, she means morning sickness. Elinor found herself in the inner courtyard and sat down, trembling. *Well, they'll see, I'll be fine every morning after this.*

'Elinor?' It was Theo. 'What is it? You were doing so well.' He sat down and took her hand. The warm, familiar grasp made the tears gather again and she jerked it away, furious with herself.

'Have you got a handkerchief?' Wordlessly Theo produced a large white square and she blew her nose.

'I am just tired and I do not feel very…very…' She ran out of inspiration and sat twisting the linen between her hands, forbidding herself to produce one more sniffle.

'Oh, that,' Theo said calmly. 'I've got sisters, I'm quite used to regular, um, moods.'

He thought she was having her courses! Elinor was not sure whether to simply melt into the ground with embarrassment or seize thankfully on the excuse for her loss of control. Theo seemed to be taking it in his stride, so she decided to simply ignore the whole thing. She blew her nose again, conscious that it had probably turned pink, and folded the handkerchief away. 'What are you going to do today? We cannot search during daylight hours.'

'I was going to take advantage of the count's invitation to browse in his library. There probably isn't anything there, or he wouldn't be so open about it, but there might be some volumes of value I might be able to persuade him to sell.'

'Can you afford it?' Elinor asked. 'If you have to repay Lord X, that will be very expensive won't it?'

'Very,' he agreed grimly. 'I won't be able to afford a wife, I'm afraid.'

He was joking, of course, despite his very straight face. 'Well, that will give us a good excuse to break it off,' she said. 'I don't wish to figure as a jilt—not that anyone would believe I would be so foolish.'

'Really?' Theo looked bemused. 'Why on earth should anyone imagine I would be a good catch?'

'Don't fish for compliments,' Elinor said, her lips twitching, amused despite herself that she had made a pun.

Theo grinned back. 'Go on, flatter me, my morale needs boosting.'

'You are very well connected, healthy, intelligent, well-off—provided you do not have to repay Lord X—and moderately good looking, assuming one discounts the hair of course.'

'I suppose I should be glad of the *moderately*,' he said with mock gloom. 'Go on—is there anything else on the plus side of the account?'

'You are a talented artist, have good taste and a sense of humour. And you—' She broke off, confused at where her list was taking her, and bit her lip.

'And I what?' Theo was watching her mouth.

'You kiss very well.'

'Thank you,' he said gravely. 'And might I ask what basis for comparison you have, Miss Ravenhurst?'

'None, except Leon, but I do not think he can be very good. He kissed me and I did not feel a thing.'

'Indeed? Excuse me for a moment while I fight the urge to feel smug. But I feel bound to point out that he was kissing you in a dark and gloomy dungeon, which might well have dampened your feelings of ardour.'

'You kissed me on a study floor,' Elinor pointed out. 'And that was very stimulating.'

'For both of us.' Theo got to his feet. 'Are you going to stay here and rest?'

'Rest?' It took Elinor a moment to remember he thought her to be feeling delicate. 'Goodness, no. I think I will escape for a walk before Mama finds me and gives me something dreary to do indoors. Those woods look beautiful. I thought I would climb up through them and see if there is a view of the basilica from the top.'

'May I come with you? The library can wait for a wet day, if one ever comes. The weather is so beautiful it seems set to be like this for ever.'

'I will see you at the front door in fifteen minutes,' Elinor said. 'How lovely to get out of here and away from all those sharp tongues and prying eyes.'

She was before him, hurrying through the hall, enjoying the freedom of her new divided skirt and not noticing the other figure standing there until she was almost upon them.

'Marquesa.' Ana was wearing the original of Elinor's garment.

'Miss Ravenhurst. And where did you find the pattern for your habit, might I ask?'

'Theo drew it for me,' Elinor said cheerfully. 'He was able to describe it in detail.'

'So I should hope, he has removed it often enough.'

'Were you his mistress for very long?' Elinor enquired, refusing to gratify the woman by showing any embarrassment.

Ana drew in her breath in a sharp hiss. 'He is my lover—I was never his mistress. There is a difference.'

'I am sure there is.' Elinor gave no sign that she noticed Ana's use of the present tense, although a sharp stab of jealousy knotted her inside. 'What fun for you, to find a man so much younger than yourself.'

'Comparing fashion tips, ladies?' It was Theo, his satchel over one shoulder. He reached out and took Elinor's easel. 'Come on, my love, let's take advantage of this light.'

He nodded to Ana as he swung the heavy door open and Elinor went through, not looking at the other woman, but hearing her indrawn hiss of angry breath.

'*Not* tactful to call one woman *my love* in front of another who has just declared you are her lover. Present tense.'

Theo swung the easel on to his back and grimaced. 'She isn't.'

'You don't have to justify yourself to me.' Elinor walked through the arch under the gatehouse and turned uphill along a steep track. She was feeling decidedly flustered. She had stood up to Ana on instinct; now she was realising that she was way out of her depth, sparring with a woman of the marquesa's experience. 'We aren't betrothed. Remember?'

'What you think matters to me.' Surprised, Elinor looked back over her shoulder and slowed her pace. 'I respect your opinion and your judgement.'

'She is a beautiful woman and an intelligent one. I

imagine she is stimulating company.' Elinor tried to be fair. 'You must enjoy the freedom you have. I imagine it exceeds even what a gentleman might expect in England.'

'Yes.' Theo climbed beside her in silence for a while. 'Freedom, of course, is everything.'

Elinor was about to retort that it was not, that, precious though it was, there were other equally important things in life, and then the edge of bitterness in his voice struck her. How many lovers, how short a time with each? So much intimacy of the body—how much of the mind? No ties, no responsibility. No one to care about and no one to care about you.

'I don't agree,' she said. 'Not at the price of love.'

'Who do you love?' he asked harshly.

'My mother. I loved my father. I love my friends and our cousin Bel.' *I love you.* 'Don't you love anyone?'

He was silent so long that she thought he was not going to reply. They climbed on, up through the woodland, past a group of foresters stacking logs, up the last steep pull and out on to open scrubby meadow.

'I do not intend ever to marry,' Theo said abruptly. He stood still, shading his eyes, apparently orientating himself, then strode off along the crest.

Confused, Elinor stared after him. He had not answered her question. But that statement was clear enough. Why not? She bit her lip, watching him. It could only mean he loved someone he could not marry.

Chapter Fourteen

Elinor watched Theo walk away. Should she follow him? Did he want to be alone with his thoughts? So he was in love. Not with Ana. Not with herself, obviously. A hopeless love, then, one that was not returned. Or perhaps she was a married woman. No wonder he sought companionship from lovers and felt no attachment to any of them. It was lonely, unrequited love, she was discovering. At least Theo was not being tormented by daily contact with the object of his affections as she was.

It was better, she decided, not to marry at all rather than to marry someone one didn't love, while all the time there was someone you did care for and could not have. No wonder he had reacted so strongly when she had come to his room, and had been so clear about their present masquerade being merely for convention.

He had stopped, dumped her easel and his satchel on the ground and was standing, hands on hips, looking out over the view. Elinor straightened her back, adjusted her own bag on her shoulder, and walked to join him, indulging herself with the opportunity to study the tall figure unobserved.

When she reached him, she realised he had found a fine view out towards the basilica perched on its hill. 'Do you want to sketch?' he asked without looking at her.

What she wanted was to talk. But did he? She studied his unresponsive profile. 'Not just yet. That was a steep climb, I think I'll sit over there on that outcrop of rock and enjoy the view for a while.'

It took almost quarter of an hour before he joined her. Elinor lifted her chin from her cupped hand and smiled at him. 'Hello.'

'Hello.' He folded down on to the turf at the foot of her perch, presenting her with the unreadable back of his head. 'I must apologise.'

'For what?'

'Brooding. You did not come up here to put up with me moping.'

If she reached down, she could run her fingers through his hair, smooth it down where the breeze had caught and tossed it into disarray. If she slid down the smooth rock, she could be in his arms. Elinor sat still and made herself smile so her voice would sound cheerful. 'I would hardly call that moping. Or brooding. I'm your friend, Theo, we can talk to each other about things that matter to us, or we can be silent in each other's company. It doesn't matter.' His shoulders dropped, as though he had relaxed. 'There is someone, isn't there? Doesn't she love you? Or can't she marry you?'

'Doesn't love me, doesn't want to marry me,' he said,

tipping his head back against the rock. 'Not that I'd ask.
Can you imagine the sort of married life she would have
to put up with, stuck in England while I'm away so
much?'

'Naval wives put up with it,' Elinor said. 'And in any
case, why wouldn't she travel with you? I would.' Theo
went very still. 'If I was in love with you, that is. Or
wanted to marry, for that matter.'

'You, Nell, are unique. I can't imagine any other
woman I know living out of a trunk for months at a time
or pulling a pistol on a pair of thugs. And what about
the children?'

'You would just have to get a bigger travelling
coach,' she said robustly. 'Or a second one for some of
the children and the nurse, so they could rotate with
you. Of course, as the children got older, you'd need a
schoolroom coach as well.'

'So you wouldn't put all the children together to
give my wife and I some peace and quiet?' He sounded
as though the fantasy was cheering him up. 'I thought
you didn't like children.'

'I'm not over-fond of my nephews and nieces, they
have been thoroughly spoiled and indulged. I wouldn't
mind mine, and I'm sure yours would be delightful.'
*And ours would all have red hair and tempers to match
and would be a complete handful in a coach! But such
fun...* This was edging into dangerous ground. 'I think
I'll draw now. Can you pass me my things? Not the
easel, I'll just use my sketchbook.'

Theo found himself a rock to sit on and balanced his
own sketchbook on his knee. God! That had been dangerous and painful and very illuminating, that flash of

realisation at the top of the hill. *Of course* he loved Nell, his red-headed cousin who just wanted to be his friend. Why hadn't he realised it sooner? Perhaps he had and had simply denied it to himself. She was perfect for him, in every way, but she was not in love with him, did not want to marry him.

Was it worth risking asking her? What would happen if he told her the truth, convinced her he meant it and it was nothing to do with compromising her? But she would say *no,* and their friendship would be spoiled and he would lose even that. He glanced across at her and found Elinor was sitting biting the end of her pencil and looking at him. She grinned, tossing back the heavy plait that hung over her shoulder.

There was no point in entertaining false hopes. If she felt anything for him, she would never have reacted so violently to the suggestion they might have to marry and she would never have discussed his love for another woman with such frankness. Nor would she be so open with him about sex—it was obvious that she had none of the self-consciousness on the subject he would have expected if her feelings for him were involved.

He squinted at the landscape and found no inspiration there. Then he began to doodle in one corner, the image taking shape with speed under his hand. After a few minutes he moved to another part of the sheet and began another sketch, then another, aware that his spirits were lightening, too focused to see any danger in what he was doing.

Soon the pages were filling with a procession of travelling carriages of all shapes and sizes, luggage piled on top and falling off behind and from each window a child was hanging, dropping toys, waving, fighting with a sibling. The top of two adult heads were vaguely discernible in the chaos and a pack of dogs ran behind, barking madly. In the middle was his self-portrait looking desperate, his arms full of precariously piled precious objects while infants rampaged around his feet.

'Show me what you have done.' It was Nell, somewhat tousled from having slid down the rock.

'No.' He flipped his book shut, realising he must have filled five or six pages with his fanciful sketches.

'But I want to see.' She tried to tug it out of his hands, but he held firm, pulled it free and sat on it.

'No,' he said, reaching to pick up her sketch book.

She too had been caught up in the foolish fantasy. There, on the first page, was Elinor's impression of his travelling family, a circle of carriages drawn up like a gypsy encampment. Children of all ages had been sketched in, noses in books, playing with kittens, chasing each other in a wild game of tag over and under a collection of scantly draped classical statues, the subjects of which looked on in frozen marble hauteur. In the middle, in front of a camp fire with a kettle suspended over it, was a woman drawn from the back, her sun bonnet tipped back, her feet on a box, a fan in her hand. A wickedly accurate sketch of himself showed him sitting in one of the carriages, head in hands.

He flipped the page and found the children sitting in a circle, solemnly listening to Elinor herself, perched on a box while she read to them from a book. Her hair was dishevelled, she was wearing the divided skirt and she had dotted in a fine array of freckles across her own nose.

'Give me that back!' She made a grab for her sketchbook and missed as he held it over his head. 'I thought perhaps you would employ me as a governess,' she explained.

'They seem to be paying you a great deal of attention,' he said, finding his voice was, inexplicably, not quite steady. 'Elinor.'

'Yes?' She was a little pale, but that was probably explained by the time of the month. He shouldn't have let her come on this strenuous walk, he wanted to wrap her up and cosset her. Even as he thought it, he realised that she would hate it, that what she wanted was freedom, the freedom he had. The freedom he could give her. Hell, he would risk it.

'Elinor, why don't we get married. Really get married?' He dropped the sketchbook and pulled her to him. 'There is no one else for us. We are friends. We have this.' She was so still in his arms that she seemed frozen.

Her mouth under his was warm, tremulous. He coaxed with his tongue, slid his lips across hers, trying to show her how he felt without saying the words that would place such an emotional burden on her.

For a moment she melted, swaying into his body, her lips parting to let him in and he was dizzy with triumph, then she pulled back so she was straining against his grip. 'No, Theo. No. I do not want to marry you. I told you, I meant it.' He let go and she took three steps away from him, her back turned. 'There has to be love, Theo,' she said over her shoulder. 'I am a fool to be such a romantic when I thought myself rational, but there you are.'

All the laughter had gone from her, all the trust, replaced by regret and wariness. He should have listened to his head, not to his heart. Listened and settled for what he had, not what he hoped for. She could give him friendship and laughter and her courage. But not her love.

And now she was miserable and he was lonely again. So lonely. He had not realised how wide and deep that hole had been until she had come into his life and filled it. Now it gaped blackly under his feet.

'I'm sorry, Nell.' She did not move. 'Compromise is not right for us.' A nod. 'I just thought it would be companionable, you and I together. Can we be friends again? Have I ruined things?'

'No. No, of course not.' She turned and walked back to him, put her arms around as much of him as she could manage and hugged hard, then stepped back and smiled. *Well, that settles it. Hugged like a brother.* The smile was a little wary, but it was genuine, he saw it in her eyes.

'What have you got to eat in that bottomless satchel of yours?' she asked. 'Or do we have to snare a rabbit if we aren't to go hungry?'

'I went and charmed some food out of the cook. That was why I was late,' Theo confessed.

'Good.' She nodded towards a dense thicket. 'I'll just go and, um…'

Theo knelt down and began to unpack the food. Nell's sketchbook lay open where it had been dropped. He reached across and tore the sketches clean out, looked at them for a long moment, almost hearing the ghost of the children's laughter, then slipped them inside his own book, tying the strings into a knot it would be impossible to open without a knife. All the portraits of their children who would never be.

* * *

Elinor reached the shelter of the bushes before her legs gave way and she sank down on the turf. To have a good weep was tempting, but pointless. She would have to emerge, nose red, eyes bleary—and what could she say? *I love you, of course I'll marry you, even if you love someone else? I'll marry you because you want a companion and feel sorry for me so I'll do?* She prided herself on common sense and stoicism; now was the time to exercise those qualities.

After all, she was no worse off than she was a few weeks ago, she told herself, selecting a nice dense bush and checking for thistles, adders and stinging nettles.

Adjusting her clothing again, she decided that actually she was worse off. Much worse. If you had never eaten strawberries, you had no idea what you were missing. But once you had, you never forgot the taste and always yearned for them. Theo was strawberries and cream and every sensual pleasure she had ever experienced and he was here, now. Not safely out of the way, but a constant reminder, a constant temptation.

There was only one way to get through this and that was to stiffen her backbone and just endure until they parted company. 'Well,' she said brightly as she emerged from the thicket, chin up, shoulders back, 'I hope you did well with the cook, because I am starving.'

They ate chicken legs and crusty rolls, cheese and apples, all washed down with cider. 'I'm sleepy,' Elinor confessed.

'Sleep, then.' Theo took off his coat, rolled it up and set it down as a pillow. 'Go on.'

'You, too.' Elinor stretched out on the short grass in

the shade of the big tree where Theo had laid out the food. 'We both need our sleep if we are to search that chamber in the cellars tonight.'

Theo stopped, halfway into a sprawl, and propped himself on one elbow, looking at her. 'I am searching alone, you are not…well.'

'I am perfectly well. It isn't an illness.' Elinor shut her eyes and snuggled into the Theo-smelling soft wool. 'And it certainly isn't an excuse for missing the fun.'

'Fun?' She could hear him yawning. Perhaps he had managed as little sleep as she had last night. 'And what are we going to say if we are caught down there, pray?'

'That we are rather, er, sophisticated in our tastes and wanted to make love at the scene of the infamous orgies?' she suggested sleepily.

There was a gasp of laughter from Theo. 'Now that is another image you have put into my imagination that I really, truly, did not want there.'

A person would need to be not sophisticated, but downright perverse, to want to be anywhere near this chamber, let alone making love in it, Elinor decided, shivering in the semi-darkness at two the next morning. Theo was pacing, muttering under his breath; she was perched on the unpleasant stone slab, waiting to do something useful.

'If I was conducting a semi-ritualistic orgy,' he announced at length, 'I think I would want as much drama as possible.'

'I agree,' Elinor nodded vigorously, trying not to speculate about what was making scuffling noises in a far corner.

'So—I produce the Chalice and all the other items of plate with a flourish. From where?' He frowned at her. 'Would you mind very much lying down?'

'As the sacrifice?' He nodded, looking as happy about it as she felt. 'All right. Like this?' Elinor lay down and stretched up her hands to catch the iron rings. Theo seemed to tower above her in the flickering light, the shadows making a mask out of his face and the focused light from the dark lanterns setting his hair aflame. It took an effort of will to remember that this was play-acting. He threw up his arms dramatically as though commanding an audience.

'Now what? I wouldn't bend down, that loses impact. There is nothing in front of me...' He spun on his heel, coat tails flaring out behind him, and flattened his upraised palms against the stonework. There was silence. 'Elinor, come and help me—there is something here.'

She came and stood beside him, the two of them feeling the stone, running their fingertips along the mortar lines. He was right—there was something odd about the feel of that patch of wall, but whatever it was, it was well hidden.

'I give up,' Elinor said after ten minutes, standing back to suck at a torn nail.

'Damn it.' Exasperated, Theo thumped the wall with his clenched fist, then swore with the pain of it. There was an odd grinding noise and there, in front of him, was wood. 'That's a keyhole.'

She saw the gleam of his teeth as he smiled at her, then the picklocks were clinking in his fingers and she stepped back to give him room. It seemed to take for ever, and it seemed too that the ghosts of the chamber were crowding in behind them, eager to see their treasures again, rustling and breathing in the darkness.

Fighting her lurid imaginings, Elinor kept her gaze firmly on Theo's hands until the panel swung open on to the gleam of precious metals, the sparkle of gemstones and the dull sheen of leather. 'Is it there?' She craned to see past his shoulder.

'Yes. You should not look at it.' He sounded oddly breathless.

'Well, I am going to! For goodness' sake, Theo, you cannot expect me to close my eyes now.'

'Very well.' He reached in and lifted it out, a vast vessel that took both his hands to bear, and set it down on the stone platform. 'Just don't ask me to explain anything.' Elinor crouched down and studied it.

From the square base four columns, uneven and yellowish white in colour, rose from pairs of great oval opals to support the silver cup itself. There were six sides, each etched and chased and each with a scene in almost full relief of small figures sculpted in gold, The arched lid rose above it, ribbed, with sprawling figures tumbling down in utter abandon.

Elinor reached out a hand and touched the supporting shafts. 'Ivory, with a pair of opals at the base of each.' The shafts were oddly veined and ridged and she ran her hand down one, marvelling at the tactile finish. 'It's a—' She got a grip on her voice, even as she snatched her hand back. 'They are all male, er... members.'

'Yes.' She could not look at Theo, but neither could she tear her eyes away from the object. The tiny, perfectly detailed figures were men and women and—animals? Some scenes she could understand, some, as she turned the object slowly around, mystified her. It was arousing, disgusting, beautiful and beastly. She wiped her fingers on her skirts as though they were sticky. The sound of Theo's breathing was harsh.

'Are the receipts there?'

'Yes.' He had gone back to the cupboard and was staring into it, some papers in his hand.

Elinor ducked under his arm. There were cups, a great platter, coils of leather she realised with a jolt were whips, and more ivory objects. 'More male members?' she queried as Theo shut the door, twisting the picklock to make it fast.

'Don't even think about it,' he said tersely. 'Help me wrap this thing up in my coat.'

They were crouched over it, padding the stem with the coat sleeves, their backs to the room, when the attack came. Filthy sackcloth descended in a smothering blanket, she heard Theo swearing and struck out with her nails, ripping against the cloth, then something hit her head, hard, and she went down into even deeper blackness.

Chapter Fifteen

'Nell! Nell, wake up.' Someone was calling her, which was most unfair when her head hurt so. Besides, she could not have overslept, it was still dark outside and the candles were lit.

Consciousness came back with a rush. She was sitting on something cold and hard and her hands were at full stretch over her head, which ached abominably. She was in a small stone chamber lit by guttering candles set side by side against the far wall and she wanted, rather badly, a drink, a privy and to ease the desperate ache in her arms.

'Nell!' It was Theo. Somehow she managed to turn her head and found he was chained beside her, his arms shackled as hers were, although as he was on his feet he was able to lower them so his elbows were bent.

'What happened?' she managed and saw raw relief on his face as she spoke.

'Someone hit us over the head—two people, it must have been.' So, it hadn't been her imagination or the ghosts of the past she had heard behind her after all. 'Are you all right?'

'My head hurts and I would kill for a drink, but otherwise I'll feel better if I can just stand up.' The relief when she scrambled to her feet, pushing up against the rough wall to help her shaky legs, was enormous. The chains sagged and she could clasp her hands together in front of her. 'Oh, that's better, my arms were coming out of their sockets. How are you?' Theo looked very white and there was blood on the shoulder of his shirt.

'I'll do,' Theo said, his mouth grim. 'At least they didn't want us dead.'

That was true. 'And we'll see who they are when they come back,' Elinor pointed out, nodding towards the candles. 'Two people—does that mean it is the Traceys after all?'

'Or Leon with a servant. Or Ana, with John, her groom, who has been noticeably absent from sight.'

'Even if we knew, it doesn't get us much further forwards, and it doesn't help us get out of here. What I don't understand is why they didn't just knock us out, take the Chalice and leave.' Elinor lifted her hands and peered at the heavy metal cuffs around her wrists. 'Where are your picklocks?'

'In my coat pocket.' And the coat was lying beside the candles.

'Oh.' Elinor reached out for him, finding that the chain ran freely through whatever it was secured to, high on the wall above. If she let one arm rise, she could straighten the other, almost as far as Theo. 'Can we hold hands for a little while? I'm feeling a bit shaky.' His hand clasping hers was warm, the fingers reassuringly strong and steady. 'Mama will want to know where we are.'

'That's true. And Hythe. He knows we are searching. I wish now I'd risked having him help me, but it would have been even harder to explain him if we were found than it was with you.' Theo's smile was obviously meant to be reassuring, but she was not at all sure he placed much confidence on his aunt thinking to search the dungeons, which was where they must be. 'It will take a while, though, for Aunt Louisa to start to worry and then to think of speaking to him. Plenty of time for you to tell me all the family news.'

It was a good attempt to keep her spirits up, although nothing was going to happen for a few hours, she was certain. Meanwhile, given the number of Ravenhursts, telling the news was a task that would take some time.

'And both Bel and Eva were expecting when we left England—the babies may even have been born by now,' Elinor was saying when Theo stiffened.

'Listen!'

Someone was coming. A key grated in the lock and the door swung open. '*Madame*, Julie—thank goodness!' Elinor slumped back against the wall in relief. 'You've found us. Someone hit us, dragged us in here…' Her voice tailed away as she saw them more clearly. Both looked grim, both were clad in old, dark clothes and neither made any move to approach them. 'Please, let us out of here.'

'You will be going nowhere, Mademoiselle Raven-hurst,' the countess said harshly. 'You have chosen to pry into my business, now you pay for that.'

'You took the Chalice from Theo?' Beside her he was silent, but she could feel the tension running through him as though he had touched her. If they came close enough…

'I did.' It was Julie. 'I had been following him ever

since Paris. He did not know me, even if he had seen me. And, of course, he did not expect me.'

'Then what happened to the late count?' It was hard to believe these two elegant Frenchwomen could be responsible for this, but there seemed no denying the evidence of her own eyes and ears.

'My late husband would have dragged us into notoriety and scandal again, releasing that dreadful, sinful, object on to the world. My son Leon is the first de Beaumartin for decades about whom one hears no sniggers, no repetition of the gossip. At last the past was buried, we could hold our heads up once more—and then Charles drags it out into the open again.'

'Scarcely, Madame,' Theo spoke at last. 'The Chalice was to go to a private collector.'

'Who would brag to his *select* friends, I have no doubt.' The countess took an angry pace closer, still a wary distance from their reach. 'Charles would not listen, would not hear my plans for a suitable marriage for Leon.'

'To Mademoiselle Julie, no doubt?' Theo waited until the younger woman nodded, her thin face intent and tense. 'No doubt he wanted a better match for his son?'

'She is like a daughter to me and she will make him a good wife—and one who will work to restore the family name. Charles would have him marry some society girl with no backbone, no commitment.'

'And your husband sold the Chalice to restore the family fortunes despite your objections and fear of scandal?' Elinor stared at the countess's implacable face. 'Did you kill him?'

'It was an accident,' Julie said passionately. 'We

were arguing in Paris, when I was trying to help her convince him it was wrong to sell the Chalice. He shouted that I was a nobody, that Leon should marry someone worthy, someone with a title and wealth to bring to the match. But I love Leon,' she said in a whisper, 'God help me, I love him.'

'So who killed the count?' Theo asked. Elinor was beyond words, staring at the two women in disbelief.

'It was an accident,' the countess said, her voice harsh. 'We struggled over the receipts, over the money. He tripped. When we saw he was dead, Julie followed you and took back the Chalice.'

'And where is it now?'

'Back in its hiding place, where it will stay for ever. Now I have found the inventory, I know nothing else is missing.'

'And you expect us to keep quiet about this?' Elinor demanded. 'Even if the count's death was an accident, you owe Lord X the money, you have assaulted us—'

'You will stay here,' the countess said, her voice eerily calm now. 'We will lock the door and we will not come back.'

'You would leave us here to die of hunger and thirst?' Elinor could hardly say the words.

'Let Elinor go,' Theo spoke over her. 'Let her go and she will promise to say nothing and I will give you access to all my money.'

'No! Leave you here? No!' She reached out for him, the chains tearing into her wrists as they stopped her, inches from him.

'I am not a cruel woman,' the countess said, placing a pitcher on the floor just within reach and stepping back. 'There is enough poison in there to kill you both, quickly.'

'Without blood on your hands?' Theo demanded.

'Exactly. I have no confidence I could kill you humanely by any other method.'

'You are a monster,' Elinor said with conviction. 'But *my* mother is not, and she will search for me and never stop.'

'I would do anything for my son's name.' The countess turned towards the door. 'And everyone, your mother included, will believe you two have eloped. In the morning all your clothes and possessions will have gone.'

The door closed behind her and the key rasped in the lock. Elinor turned and faced Theo, struggling to find calm somewhere in the sick turmoil of panic. 'Mama knows we do not want to marry, she will know something is wrong at once.'

'I agree. And together with Hythe they make a formidable team—but I do not intend staying here for however long it takes them to find us.'

'Good.' Elinor swallowed hard. 'Because I have to confess I feel just a touch…apprehensive.'

'When we do get out of here,' Theo said, smiling at her, his mouth a little crooked, 'remind me that you said that. Now then, let us be certain we cannot reach my coat and the picklocks.'

Fifteen minutes later, their wrists raw, they gave up every possible combination of stretches. The coat remained inches out of reach.

'Right.' Theo leaned back, peering up through the gloom at the point where their chains were suspended. 'I think these have been dropped over a hook, not run through a loop.'

'Which means if we can unhook them we can move

about the cell and get to the picklocks.' Elinor tried to throw up the chain, but it slumped back, jarring her sore wrists. 'That won't work, it is too heavy.'

Theo stood, thinking, then knelt down, one knee raised. 'Climb—if you can get high enough, you might be able to do it.'

She could get her feet on his knee all right and up to a crouch, her fingertips scrabbling at the wall for purchase. 'Now what?' He held out his clasped hands. Gingerly Elinor put one foot on to the linked fingers.

'Hold on.' Then he was beginning to stand, lifting her weight from a kneeling position with only the wall to lean on for balance. Elinor could see the veins standing out on his temples, hear the breath hiss from his teeth. But he was rising and she was higher, higher, until he was standing upright and she was swaying on her perch, her arms outstretched. 'Now, try and throw the chain over the hook.'

She tried, and failed, three times, constantly aware of the strain on his arms, of what would happen if she failed. The cell was cold, yet perspiration was trickling down her forehead and into her eyes. *Once more,* she told herself. *I'll do it this time.*

The chain snaked up, caught, hung poised for a moment, then fell, its weight pulling her with it to land sprawled on the stone floor. 'Nell. Nell, for heaven's sake, say something!'

'Ouch,' she ventured, sitting up and rubbing her knees. 'That hurt. Nothing is broken though.'

Theo wondered if he was going to faint. He never had before, but he supposed, leaning back against the wall, the periphery of his vision closing in and his ears full of buzzing, there must be a first time for every-thing.

He wasn't sure whether it was the pain—his arms felt as though he'd been racked—or the relief. Probably both.

'Theo? This is not the time to go to sleep,' Elinor said severely. He opened his eyes and found her standing right in front of him, her face white. 'Are you all right?' she managed when she saw his eyes focus.

'Yes. Get the picklocks.'

It took half an hour to fumble her shackles open and then, with her holding his in the best position, to free himself. At last the chains swung back against the wall and he was able to flex his arms. 'Are you still apprehen-sive?' he asked as she fell against his chest, wrapped her arms around his waist and pressed her face into his shoulder.

'No.' She looked up, her smile valiant, if a little tremulous. 'Why?'

'Because I thought it the bravest thing I ever heard,' he confessed, unsurprised to find his voice husky. 'To be chained in a cellar with a pot of poison to drink and to own yourself merely a little apprehensive.'

'I was lying,' she confessed, tipping back her head to look up at him. 'I was terrified. But I knew you'd get us out.'

'Let's get this door open first before we congratu-late ourselves.' The old lock was so large and crude he needed two picks to work it, but they were out into the passage in minutes. 'I'll lock it again.' He had to keep going, to think ahead and not back to what might have been. If Hythe and Lady James had been attacked, if they had not found the cell in time. If… Somehow he had to starve his imagination until they were safe away. 'We'll take the candles. I wonder if she would ever have opened the door again.'

Beside him Elinor shuddered. 'She must be mad. They both must be. You know, I've had a horrible thought. What if Leon marries Julie and they have a son—and then Leon does something to upset them? What do you think his life is worth once there's an heir those two can fully control?'

'Not much. I'll write to him once we get clear. He may need some convincing, though. Would you believe such a thing of *your* mother?'

He did not wait for her answer, striding to open the secret panel and take out the Chalice. This time he did not wrap it when the hiding place was secure again, merely grabbed it by the stem and put his other hand under Elinor's arm. 'Come on.'

'Where to?' she asked as they slipped out into the silence of the great hall.

'To the bedchambers.'

'But we can't take anything or they'll realise we are free.'

'We need to speak to your mother, let her know what is going on.'

Aunt Louisa was, all things considered, extremely calm about finding her daughter and her nephew in her bedchamber at four in the morning, both of them filthy, battered and clutching an artefact of such indecency she had to examine it twice with her quizzing glass before she was prepared to believe the evidence of her own eyes.

Alarming in nightcap and flannel robe, she listened to their story in silence. There was, Theo admitted, something to be said for the scholarly turn of mind.

'The woman is insane,' she pronounced when they had finished. 'So, what do you propose we do now? Call in the authorities?'

Theo had been thinking about that. A descent on the *mairie* with a demand to see the mayor and order the arrest of the most powerful woman for miles around seemed doomed to failure. It would take some time to convince Leon of his mother's appalling crimes and, even if convinced, he might act to cover them up, rather than to restrain her.

'There is no one we can trust,' he concluded and saw from her nod of approval that she fully agreed. 'I will take the Chalice and get it back to England.'

'And what about me?' Elinor demanded.

'I can drop you off with Madame Dubois; you can hide in my old room. Aunt Louisa will pretend to believe we have eloped and will set off in pursuit, collecting you from St Père on the way.'

Both women regarded him in silence. Finally Elinor said flatly, 'Very well. I do not like it, but I would be a burden to you on the way, I can see that.'

He expected his aunt to agree, but she looked at her daughter incredulously. 'I never thought to hear you so feeble, Elinor! I am not happy with you hiding with some woman I do not know, and I am not convinced of our safety if they should find us together. You will go with Theo.'

It was like someone handing him an unexpected gift. Days with Nell, just the two of them, the gypsy existence on the road they had joked about. The life those sketches had pictured so vividly. He looked at his aunt, the incredible suspicion forming that she was quite deliberately throwing them together. Surely she did not really want him to marry Elinor? Did she?

Elinor looked at him and, just for a second, he thought he saw his own desires mirrored there. Then she said, with no colour in her voice, 'If you feel it better, Mama.'

'We will go to Maubourg,' he said, the idea coming to him from nowhere. 'It is closer than Paris and the coast and you said Sebastian and Eva have gone back there for the baby to be born.'

'Very sensible,' Lady James approved. 'You can send that hell-begotten object to your patron in the diplomatic bag.'

'I think not,' Theo said, imagining some clerk in the Foreign Office unwrapping it and requiring medical attention. 'I will write to Lord X from there, though.'

'Maubourg?' Nell was frowning at him.

'Where better to be safe than a castle surrounded by guards? We will get down to the stables and wake Hythe. He must take the carriage and drive to Avallon to have Lord X's men set free. He will also provide a false trail, setting out to Paris. Goodness knows if those two will ever check on us, or move the stone panel again and find the Chalice gone, but if they do then my carriage is distinctive enough to give them something to chase. We can drop off on the road to Avallon and hire a chaise.'

He felt invigorated now, despite the lack of sleep, the blow to the head, the horror of believing he had brought Nell to her death. They were alive, relatively unscathed and he had days in her company ahead. Not that she seemed very happy about the prospect. *My poor love. She must be exhausted*, he thought, wishing he had the right to take her in his arms and carry her off to his bed. To sleep. Just to watch her sleep.

'Right. I imagine we must get a move on,' Lady James was saying briskly. 'I will find a spare toothbrush and soap and under-things from my wardrobe so it will appear nothing of Elinor's is missing. That is a weakness in their little plot, is it not? If *I* were eloping, I would certainly pack a bag!'

The thought of her mother doing such a thing at least produced a faint smile on Elinor's lips. Theo watched her with concern. Had he finally found the limit of her courage and endurance? Or was she appalled at the thought of spending days alone with him after his insane proposal up on the hill?

'No, they had thought of that, apparently. I'll see what I can find of mine that won't be noticeable,' he said, thankful for an excuse to leave Elinor alone with her mother for a few moments. She was probably desperate to cry on her shoulder.

He was back in the room only minutes later to find that, far from weeping in a maternal embrace, Elinor was briskly packing a small valise. 'They've been in my room, as they said they would,' he announced tersely. 'There's a valise gone, drawers pulled out—it looks as though I packed in a hurry. Yours—unless Jeanie left it in a mess—is in the same state.'

'They may be wicked,' Elinor remarked, 'but they are not stupid. Have you found anything you can bring?'

'Here.' He handed her a rolled shirt with his spare razor inside. 'If I take a valise now, they may spot it.

I'll buy more as we go. By some miracle they didn't find my money.' She took the things, pushed them into her bag and snapped it shut.

'Mama?'

'I find myself more diverted than I have in many a year,' Lady James remarked. 'Now, look after Theo— he appears to be managing very well, but one can never tell with men—and do not worry about my researches. I will pretend to set out for Paris, then double back once I am sure I am not being followed. I shall go down to Avignon—you may meet me there.'

'Of course, Mama. We can always complete the Burgundian work later,' Elinor agreed colourlessly.

'Come on, Nell.' He picked up the valise. 'We haven't much time before the servants will be up.'

'Yes, of course. Goodbye, Mama.' She kissed her mother and followed him out, into the unknown. *No,* he thought, sending a penetrating glance sideways at her face as they slipped through the trees down to the stables, *she hadn't reached the limits of her courage and endurance. She will keep going as long as I ask it of her.* The realisation left him strangely shaken—what would it be like to be loved by this woman?

Chapter Sixteen

Elinor sat in the jolting coach while Theo washed and dressed her raw wrists. He had dismissed her protests that his were worse and should take priority with a curt, 'Do as you are told', and for once she found she had no will to argue back. It was taking all her strength to stay awake and upright and she had to manage that, at least to tend to his wounds in her turn.

She should be feeling relieved that they were alive, that they had a plan and were heading for safety, but all she could feel was wave after wave of paralysing horror at what they had escaped. If Theo had been less resourceful, less strong, less…Theo, they would be in the dark by now, the candles gone, facing the prospect of dying together. Theo had sounded full of confidence, but they had both known what would have happened if Hythe and Mama had not found them in time.

Would she have told him then that she loved him? Probably not—it would only have added another burden to his shoulders for the sake of indulging herself.

She would have died never knowing what it was like to lie with a man, to show him with her body how much she loved him, to learn passion and tenderness from him. She would have died a virgin and Theo would have been lost to her for ever. Hazily she wondered if she had been given a second chance.

'Nell,' he said gently. 'You can lie down now.'

'No, I will bandage your wrists.' She forced her eyes open and reached for the basin with the stained water that was slopping around on the carriage seat.

'Nell—'

'No! Stop fussing. Just let me…' She dragged down a steadying breath and controlled the urge to babble of her terror. 'Just let me do this.' In the face of her outburst he was silent, holding out his hands for her to clean the dirty, raw scrapes and wrap the bandage around each wrist. 'There,' she said, tying the last knot. 'That's done.'

The carriage seemed to be swaying wildly, the lamps on their gimbals were fading, surely? And she was falling. 'Nell, my love,' said a voice gently and then everything faded and was gone.

Elinor woke to broad daylight, to even wilder swaying. 'Theo?' She was alone in a small carriage, wrapped up in a rug on the upholstered seat. Sitting up was an agony of bruises, stiff joints and, when she knocked her wrist, sharp pain. Doggedly she unwrapped herself from the rug, pushed her hair back from her face and made herself remember. It had not been a nightmare, then. But where was Theo?

The window let down on a strap. Elinor leaned out precariously and caught a glimpse of him up on the box, the reins of a pair in his hand. He looked relaxed, happy almost. 'Theo!'

He reined in and jumped down. 'You're awake—about time, Miss Ravenhurst, I thought you were going to sleep the clock round.'

'You said were going to hire a chaise—I thought you meant one with postillions. And where did you get those clothes?' He was dressed in a drab frieze coat and a rather battered hat.

'They're Hythe's. I thought it would attract less attention hiring just a chaise with no men. We couldn't wake you up—are you all right?'

'I'm fine. I think,' she added, trying a few experimental stretches. 'Are you?'

'Sore,' he admitted with a wry grimace. 'And I'll be glad to sleep tonight. But I'll live.'

'What time is it?' Elinor took the opportunity to study Theo as he dug his pocket watch out and checked it. He had said something as she had slipped into sleep, something that touched the edge of her consciousness, but which now she couldn't quite reach out and grasp. She wanted to hold him, hold on to him, needing comfort and wondering if he, too, felt the same hideous twist of fear when he remembered what might have happened. But you could not ask a man if he felt fear, and he would never admit it if he did.

When he looked up she saw there were dark smudges under the clear green eyes and the lines either side of his mouth were deeper. He looked older, harder and somehow different.

'It is half past two,' he said, pushing the watch back into the fob pocket. 'We'll stop at the next reasonable inn and get something to eat.'

'Where are we heading for?' Elinor asked.

'Arnay le Duc, but we may not make it tonight. I'm trying to take a direct route for Maubourg without using the most obvious main road.' He opened the carriage door, but Elinor shook her head. 'You want to come up on the box? I won't let you drive, you know.' The smile creased the corners of his eyes and she made herself smile back as he gave her his hand to help her climb up.

'Will they follow us?'

'The countess and Julie?' Theo untied the reins and gave the pair the office to move. 'Difficult. I doubt very much if they'll check on the cell—much too squeamish. What if they found us still alive? But they might check on the Chalice, worrying about whether it was safe to leave it there. Foolish to keep revisiting it, but people aren't always rational when they've something on their conscience. I prefer to be cautious for a day or two. I've given Hythe a letter for the count, and I have to hope he acts upon it, but one can never be certain.'

'What about Lord X's men? They'll be furious at being locked up.'

'Hythe is going to tell them to go back and tell his lordship we have the Chalice and will be getting it back to England. If they decide they don't trust me and come looking, it'll take a while to cast around before they pick up our trail.' He looked at her. 'Don't worry, Nell.'

'I'm not. I'm just making sure I understand where everything, and everybody, is,' she said, trying to focus on the practicalities and not on the fact that she was alone with Theo, not just for an hour or two, but for several days.

'Well, the Chalice is under the seat wrapped up in

a horse blanket and without a scratch on it, which is more than can be said for us.' There was an edge to his voice, which made her want to take his face between her palms and not let him go until he told her what was wrong. That was not possible as they drove, but she could try just asking.

'Theo, what is wrong?' He shot her an incredulous look, one eyebrow arching up. 'No, I don't mean the fact that we are careering about the countryside with a valuable erotic art work hidden in the carriage and have left Mama with two murderesses. There's something else.'

He had his eyes back on the road, his gaze focused on the road ahead and for a moment or two she thought he would not answer her. Elinor slipped one arm through his. 'Theo?'

She did not receive a very warm response. He neither pulled away, nor, as she hoped, squeezed her arm against his side. 'It occurs to me that I have not been taking very good care of you, Nell.'

'You saved my life,' she protested, incredulous.

'I put it at risk in the first place. And besides, if you weren't so determined and brave we would never have got out of there. I have dragged you into this mess, I made love to you and now, as you say, we are careering about the countryside in a thoroughly improper manner.'

Something hot, confused and miserable turned over in Elinor's chest. 'I have free will and a brain! You did not drag me anywhere, I went where I wanted. After that first kiss—if you can call it that—I wanted what we did at least as much as you did, and if I hadn't, I'd have told you so. I thought we were friends, Theo. I thought we were in this together. But, no, I am just a woman who was apparently dragged along at your coat tails, who was waiting passively to be kissed, or not, who—'

'Stop! Nell, I can't argue with you while I'm driving. You'll have to wait until we get to an inn if you want to scold me.'

'Scold you?' She dragged her arm free and clenched her fists in her lap. 'I don't want to scold you, you idiot man. I want you to treat me like an equal.' And that was the heart of it, she realised. She loved him, admired him, wanted him. But she did not want to be treated like someone he had to cosset and protect. She wanted to be with him, not safe in England. She wanted to share the dangers and the adventures. She wanted, she realised with the clarity born of hunger and exhaustion and desperation, to live his life with him.

'How, exactly?' he asked warily.

'Treat me like a man. One who is not as strong as you, of course. One who doesn't have a good right hook in a fight. But I'm as intelligent as you are,' she asserted. 'I can take responsibility for myself.'

Theo looked at the slim, dishevelled, determined figure on the box beside him. Treat her like a man? Oh, no, never that. But treat her like an equal? That was an intriguing thought. He thought he had been, but his feelings for her were so overwhelming that she was probably right. His instinct was to protect Nell, cherish her—and all he had achieved so far was a variety of sexual experiences that had doubtless been highly unsatisfactory from her point of view, a fight from which he had had to be rescued, a scandal and a near-death experience.

'All right, I promise,' he said, meeting her stormy gaze. 'I can't treat you like a man, but I can treat you like the independent, intelligent woman you are. From now on, if I do not respect your decisions, you may remind me of that pledge.'

'Good.' Her nod was decisive, yet there was something else that was troubling her, he could sense it. But he couldn't force her to confide. 'Look, an inn. Theo, I don't care how disreputable it is, I am *starving*.'

As it turned out, the Coq d'Or was modest but clean, and the girl who came out as they entered from the yard was pleased to offer them a choice of rabbit casserole or a cut off yesterday's leg of pork, to be followed by cheese.

They made short work of the rabbit and still had appetite to attack the cheese, washed down with a *pichet* of the local red wine. 'Where are we?' Elinor asked the girl.

'Eschamps, *madame*. Do you have far to go?'

'Autun,' Elinor said promptly. It was a good answer, he conceded mentally. Prompt, with no hint of mystery or concealment, and quite plausible, given the road they were on. Theo tipped his glass to her, to acknowledge the tactic, and she smiled back, turning his heart over in his chest.

He wanted her. He wanted *this*. This companionship, this meeting of minds. This enjoyment. That he also wanted her in his bed, stretched out under him while he took that slender, agile body to heights of delight, while he buried himself in her, while he showed her, again and again, how much he loved her, was something he had to deny to himself, had, at all costs to resist.

* * *

In the event the road was better than he expected and the horses stronger than he had hoped and they drew into Jouey, just north of Arnay le Duc, as the light was beginning to fade. And there, by the side of the road, was exactly the sort of inn he had been looking for. Large, respectable, with stabling and grooms and the strong possibility of bedchambers that would give them both the good night's sleep they needed.

What he had not foreseen was the enforced, almost domestic, intimacy of the private parlour. Nell was delightfully wifely about the whole thing, insisting on checking the beds to see they were aired, frowning over the choices of food presented, consulting him, then ordering, sending the maid for more candles— creating, very successfully, the impression they were an established married couple. And, again, he had not thought to discuss the need to play-act with her in advance.

But admiration at her ingenuity was no protection against the insidious yearnings that were stirring in his breast. What if every day could be like this, travelling around the continent, searching for things to buy and patrons to sell to? Having adventures and having, every evening, the contentment of being together, sharing the day. Sharing the night.

'What is it, Theo?' He looked up with a start to find Nell, elbows on the table, chin on cupped hand, regarding him with a twinkle in her eyes. A bath, a change of linen and another good meal had restored her, both in spirits and in looks. He could have wished she had fallen asleep the moment her feet were over the threshold. 'You were smiling,' she explained. 'Wistfully.'

'That sounds maudlin,' he said, trying to make a joke of it. 'Don't I often smile?'

'Not like that. Not as though you had just seen something you loved very much, something in a daydream.'

'Very maudlin,' he confirmed. 'Just thinking about something I can never have.'

'Of course. I'm sorry.' She looked embarrassed and he suddenly realised she thought he had been thinking about the words he had let slip on the summit of the hill above Beaumartin. No doubt she had assumed he was pining after some unobtainable love. What would she say if he told her he was dreaming about her?

'Look.' The crackle of unfolding paper had him snapping out of his self-absorption. 'I asked the waiter for a map. It's a bit dirty and creased, but it shows Maubourg. How much longer do you think it will take us?'

'Four days, three nights, unless we hit bad weather or problems on the road or the horses weaken. I'm not intending to force the pace.'

Nell's face lit up. 'Four days? Oh, good. Theo, I'm enjoying this so much now.'

'You are?'

'Of course. Mind you, we need to shop.' That smile, the one that went right to the base of his spine, lit up her face. 'I never thought I'd hear myself say it, but I really, really, want to shop for clothes now. I never enjoyed it before—it was a chore when everything had to be so practical and, anyway, I was convinced I looked plain in anything I bought. You have given me pleasure in dressing up.'

'It's a good thing I've got plenty of money, then,' Theo teased, warmed by the thought he had done something so simple that had given her pleasure. He indulged a fantasy of playing at husband and wife, of shopping together, buying her presents and little luxuries. He would wager that frivolous indulgences, small pieces of frippery nonsense, had never entered Elinor's life. Well, they would now. 'Arnay will be fine for the essentials, I am sure.'

And Lyon for the luxuries. He would keep that as a surprise, find a modiste who could deliver in two days. It would delay them a little, but Nell would arrive at Maubourg with a wardrobe befitting the cousin by marriage of the Grand Duchess, whether she liked it or not. And he firmly intended that she would like it very much.

'Excellent, I'll make a list, then.' To his amusement she produced notebook and pencil in a most domestic manner. 'Linen, a robe. A plain walking dress. A cloak, I think. Yes, that's all.' Theo hid an inward smile at the modest list. 'What do you need?'

'More linen. Shoes—I've spent too long in these boots. Toothpowder.'

Elinor stopped writing and looked up. 'Brushes? A nightshirt?'

'Yes, those too,' he conceded. 'You are being very housewifely. I thought you had no talent in that direction.'

'I am merely being practical,' she said severely. 'Someone has to worry about toothpowder.'

'No,' Theo said, straight-faced, suddenly feeling relaxed and warm and in the mood for teasing. 'No one should have to worry about toothpowder, and certainly not the intellectual Miss Ravenhurst, who has a mind above such matters.'

'Beast.' She threw the notebook at him, missing by a country mile. Theo stretched out one arm and caught it.

'Why can't women throw?' he enquired, with every intention of being provocative.

'Because we do not waste our time in childhood chasing balls,' she retorted. 'Give me my notebook back.'

'No. I shall read it. Perhaps it contains your diary and every secret you possess.'

'You, Theophilus Ravenhurst, are no gentleman.'

'So I have been told.' He began to flick through the pages, not at all sure what he expected to find. What he did not anticipate was a pencil sketch of his head and shoulders. He was looking away, utterly focused, eyes narrowed. He could not place it, then saw the suggestion of a slender arch in the background and realised she must have done it that morning in the church at St Père, while they were sketching.

'Give it back.' She sounded tense. 'That is private.'

'It is very good. What are you so worried about? I've got all my clothes on.'

'Oh! You—' She dived for the book as it hung provocatively from his fingers, managed to get a grip and then was pulled firmly on to his lap and locked there by his arm. 'Let me go, Theo, or I'll bite you.'

'You wouldn't—ow! You little hell cat.' She was off his lap and round the other side of the table, eyes sparkling, her laughter a positive incitement to any red-blooded male. Theo gave chase, dodging, feinting, always his fingertips a fraction of an inch behind her until they faced each other from opposite ends of the rectangular polished wooden table. Theo vaulted up, took one long step and slid on his knees to her end, arriving just in time to snatch her into his arms and crash off the table on to the settle beyond.

'You idiot!' she managed, whooping with laughter.

'I have always wanted to do that,' he confessed, hiccupping faintly himself. 'I read about it in some novel and decided it was exactly the sort of thing a hero should be able to do, like swinging from the chandelier with a cutlass in my teeth. Naturally, not being a hero, I have never found a use for it.'

'You are a hero,' Elinor said, no longer laughing. 'My hero.' She was very still in his arms, her eyes wide on his face, their colour darkened to a complex green, far more subtle than their usual hazel.

'Nell,' he began, all the caution knocked out of him. 'Nell, my—'

'Monsieur?' The door banged open. 'Are you all right? I heard a crash. *Oh, pardon monsieur.'* The waiter went out again, pulling the door shut behind him with exaggerated care.

'I must go to bed.' Elinor slid off his knee, her face averted, every line of her body stiff. 'I'm very tired.'

'Yes, of course.' He sounded equally constrained to his own ears. What had he almost blurted out? *Nell, my love? My darling?* 'Have you everything you need?'

'Thank you, I will be fine.' She was not fine. She had never been like this with him, but there was nothing to be said that would not make matters worse. Theo lit a candle and passed the chamberstick to her. 'Sleep well.'

As the door leading to the stairs to their two bedchambers clicked shut, Theo sat down on the settle and stared at the notebook that had fallen to the floor.

It lay open at the small sketch of him. His own profile was intent, focused. It was the face of a man completely unaware his life was about to be turned upside down. Whatever happened he must not touch her again, not like that, not in any way but the most everyday and fleeting, because he very much doubted if he could control himself if he did.

Chapter Seventeen

Theo sat for a long time after the footsteps on the boards above his head ceased. Sat while the candles guttered and sent wild shadows across the room. Finally he got to his feet and climbed the stairs stiffly, like a man in pain.

On the small landing that served only their two rooms, light was still visible under her door. He raised a hand to knock, to ask if she was all right, then opened his fist and laid the palm against the door, listening, trying to feel Nell's presence.

The door jerked open so suddenly he almost fell into the room. 'Theo?' She was dressed in her mother's nightgown, several sizes too large and trailing on the boards, a shawl wrapped tight around her shoulders.

'Sorry, I had something caught on my boot and I was freeing it.' He rested a hand on the doorpost and tried to look casual. 'Is anything wrong?'

'I can't sleep,' she said tersely. 'Every time I close my eyes I'm in that damnable dungeon. I am so *cross* with myself. We escaped, we won, we are all right, for goodness' sake. So why am I afraid of the shadows?'

'Because we could have died,' he said. 'And you are intelligent enough to know that and have enough imagination to realise what it would have been like.'

Elinor made a brave attempt at a smile. Theo's fingers tightened on the door frame. 'I'm frightened of having nightmares. Eva told me she used to suffer from them, but Sebastian made them go away, by being there. Theo, I'm not used to being frightened of things I can't do anything about. It is different if you can fight back, but now I'm terrified of sleeping, and I must sleep, sooner or later.'

'Leave your door open a crack, and I'll do the same to mine. Then if you cry out in your sleep I'll hear you and come and wake you,' he offered. He would fight dragons for her, but how could he fight the ones in her mind?

'Thank you,' she said, the smile rather more convincing this time. But she was still frightened, he could see it in the very way she squared her shoulders and her chin came up. This was the woman who had faced death by his side, who had tackled two ruffians for his sake and, now she was afraid, all he could offer was to leave his door open.

Over her shoulder he could see the big bed with its heap of blankets and puffy goose-feather quilt. The landlord had given her the big bed and him a smaller one, presumably calculating that the husband would cross the landing to visit his wife and not the other way around.

'Would it help if I slept with you?' Her pupils widened so her eyes went dark. '*Sleep*, Nell. That's a big bed with lots of covers. You get into the bed, I'll lie under the quilt. If you are aware of my breathing, know I'm here with you, you will not dream.'

He had no idea whether that was true or not, but if she began to show signs of distress at least he could wake her instantly. 'I'll just go and undress.' He went into his own room before she could say anything and before his own will weakened. It was going to be sheer hell lying next to her, unable to touch her, kiss her, love her. But he had told himself he would fight demons for her. This scaly monster would be his own desires.

Elinor stripped all but one blanket and the sheet off the bed, slid in and turned over, as close to the far edge as she could get. It was a warm night, but now she felt fevered. She had not expected this. She had expected Theo to give her a brisk, reassuring, lecture to the effect that there was nothing to be afraid of, to pull herself together and not be foolish. That was what Mama would have done. It was what she had been telling herself, with singularly little effect, come to that.

The thought of making love with him was beginning to haunt her, but he would never risk touching her like that again, she knew. She loved him so much, and yet she was never going to be able to show him—not without him guessing her feelings. Then he would pity her, perhaps feel he had to renew that offer of marriage, and she would have to refuse again.

He was quick. Her tumbling thoughts unresolved, she lay listening to the sound of bare feet passing over the boards, the click of the door shutting, then the rustle of him sorting through the pile of discarded bedding. The far side of the bed dipped, there was some scuffling and a flapping sound as he shook the cover over himself. Elinor closed her eyes tightly, aware that the candle had been extinguished.

'You do not have to cling to the edge you know.' He sounded amused. Elinor shuffled back towards the centre a little. 'That's better. I'm told I don't snore.'

Ana wouldn't tolerate snoring, I'm sure, Elinor told herself, then smiled, feeling a little better. 'I'll prod you in the ribs if you do,' she replied, trying to make this sound normal. She had feared she would never get to sleep alone; now she was convinced she would be lying awake all night out of sheer embarrassment. 'Goodnight, Theo.'

'Goodnight, Nell.' He turned over once, then seemed to settle immediately, his breathing evening out. She rolled over on to her back and turned her head on the pillow. Beside her in the gloom the big body seemed completely relaxed. There was nothing to be afraid of, nothing that Theo would not protect her from. With a sigh Elinor closed her eyes and willed herself to sleep.

She woke to find herself lying on her back, hot, pinned under the covers by a heavy weight and with hot breath fanning the back of her neck. *Theo*. Had she dreamed at all last night? She could not remember. All she could recall was feeling safe and dreadfully self-conscious. Now, in the dreamy after-sleep state she still felt safe, and not in the slightest bit uncomfortable.

Elinor blinked her eyes open and turned her head on the pillow. It was still early, she could tell from the quality of the light through the thin cotton curtain. It shone on the bed, turning Theo's hair the red-gold of autumn leaves and highlighting the dark stubble over his chin and cheeks. It would not take much for him to grow a beard, she thought fondly, wondering how it would feel if she touched it.

He was very soundly asleep, lying on his side facing her, his right arm thrown over her waist. She liked the feeling of it, the sense of being claimed and held, but she wanted to touch him. She wanted, she admitted, to kiss him. Was it possible without waking him?

Cautiously she began to turn within the curve of his arm, sensing new things as she became wider awake. She was more conscious of the scent of him: clean, hot male. One shoulder was visible above the blanket, protruding bare from his shirt. There were old bruises on it and fresh scrapes, bringing vividly to mind the way she had scrambled and clutched at him as she had struggled to free the chain in the dungeon.

Then she was over, almost nose to nose with him. His lashes were long, even darker than his beard. There was a small, sickle-shaped scar just below his right eyebrow. He did have freckles after all, she realised, they just didn't show as much as hers because his skin was lightly tanned. *My love.*

Could she? Dare she? Elinor leaned in, her lips close to his so that they were breathing the same air, so close she could feel the heat of his skin warming her. Only half an inch more. She puckered her lips and he moved, just enough to bring their mouths together.

Was he awake? His eyes were still shut. Elinor held her breath, her lips against his, then he shifted his weight over her and kissed her properly, an open-mouthed, utterly sexual caress. His tongue thrust and claimed and explored, demanding she respond, and she followed, unafraid of anything, but not matching what he wanted. Wide-eyed, she held her gaze on his face, but his eyes were still closed. His weight on her was troubling and exciting, both at once. She wanted to struggle simply to feel his strength holding her, but she kept still, sensing that he was not fully awake.

It probably meant he did not know who he was kissing. Perhaps he was deeply asleep and thought she was someone else. Was he dreaming of the woman he loved hopelessly, the reason he would not marry? Or Ana? It should have made a difference to how this felt, the rational part of her brain tried to say, but her body was taking not the slightest bit of notice.

Theo's hands came up to cup her face, to hold her still as he plundered her mouth. Pinned under him, she could feel his erection, thrillingly, terrifyingly large. Her own body was on fire now, melting, twisting, aching. Between her thighs she felt the moisture, understood hazily what it was preparing her for. All she knew was that she needed his hands on her, his body possessing her.

He was not fully conscious, she was sure of that now. Was this the second chance, the opportunity to experience a man's loving after her brush with death? If she was careful, did not speak, he might make love to her without even realising. *Without knowing it is me. No.*

No, that was not how she wanted to be loved by Theo and it was wrong. It would be using him, just as shockingly as if he had seduced her while she lay asleep and unknowing.

Elinor turned her head away from the seeking mouth and pushed at his shoulders, her hands meeting linen on one side, bare flesh on the other. He grumbled, low in his throat, like a big dog whose bone has been taken away, and she smiled despite herself.

'Theo, Theo, wake up.'

His eyes opened full on her face and she saw him go white, watched as the colour literally drained from under his skin as realisation struck him. 'Nell. Nell, what the hell have I done?' He threw himself away from her, hurling back the covers, and sat on the edge of the bed, shoulders bent, his back to her.

'Nothing,' she said prosaically. 'You just kissed me, that's all. It was very nice, but I thought I ought to wake you up because you obviously didn't know who I was—'

'That's flattering for you, isn't it?' he said, back still turned, voice bitter.

Lord, he is going to start blaming himself for this. I can hardly tell him nothing would have happened if I hadn't tried to kiss him myself. 'Theo, look, it is not as though we had made love last night, is it? I mean,' she persisted, despite the fact that the back of his neck was becoming decidedly pink and her tongue was getting in a tangle, 'if that had been the case, obviously I would have been insulted you didn't remember who you were in bed with. But you were only in bed with me because I was frightened and it worked, I had a wonderful night's sleep.'

'Good. No dreams?' He sounded slightly happier now. She wished he would turn round, then remembered what little he must be wearing and how his aroused body had felt against hers. Better to get out of the situation as smoothly as possible.

'No dreams. What happened a moment ago, that was just, um, a reflex, I expect. I really don't think of it as anything else.' She turned over and pulled the covers up around her ears. 'I'll be lazy for a little longer while you go back to your own room. Could you ring for water?'

'Right.' She waited until the door closed, then sat up, arms round her knees, chin resting on top. It was a comfortable thinking position and she needed, above all, to think. Her body felt alarmingly alive, achingly unfulfilled. It was obvious that making love was pleasurable, otherwise people would not do it. But there was more to it than she had realised. It was as though Theo had been taking her body on a journey, but they never got there and that left a deep yearning for completion. Making love was apprently not like having a delicious meal where, provided one was not starving, one could stop after one course, having enjoyed a satisfactory experience. One needed to eat all the courses, or whatever the sexual equivalent was.

Her plait was tangled in the neck of her overlarge nightgown and she pulled it out, nibbling the very tip in a manner that would have earned her a severe telling-off from her governess, who had cured her of that childish habit years ago. Obviously it was perfectly possible to go through life without experiencing physical love, it was just that it was becoming very clear to her that she did not want to.

A few weeks ago she could have gone through life, aware she was missing something, quite happily. But now she knew Theo, knew she loved him, she did not want that ignorance. She wanted to know what it was she would never have.

Men, it seemed, were quite happy to make love to women they didn't love. So were some women—Ana, for example—but she had gathered that it was a very different emotional experience for the two sexes. So Theo might not be exactly appalled if she asked him. He might not guess her real reasons if he thought he had simply physically aroused her. After all, he had kissed her in the old quarry to answer her curiosity…

'Just the once.'

'*Madame?*' The chambermaid stood in the doorway with a steaming jug of hot water. 'I did knock, *madame*, but *monsieur* said to take the water in.'

'Yes, thank you. Has *monsieur* ordered breakfast?' Elinor smiled at the assurance it was all in hand and went back to brooding.

But how to persuade him when he was fully awake and aware of what he was doing? And persuade him without him guessing why she wanted him. Would he accept that it was intellectual curiosity? Not that that was very flattering to him. She would just have to play it by ear when the opportunity arose.

Breakfast was substantial. Elinor could not decide whether Theo was simply hungry or finding an excuse not to speak to her. His single-minded demolition of steak allowed her to study her emotions with a mind somewhat cleared by two cups of coffee.

She loved Theo. She was not just in love with him, although she had not realised that these were two separate things until she experienced them both. He loved someone else, she was certain, someone perhaps from long ago. Certainly someone unobtainable. Despite that impetuous declaration on the hilltop, he obviously did not wish to marry *her.* Not when he was thinking clearly. He might want a companion, perhaps, but that was all.

So whatever she did, she must not allow him to feel trapped. Elinor poured two more cups of coffee and pushed one over to Theo, then began to butter a slice of bread before realising she already had a neat stack of three pieces sitting on the plate. Theo accepted two of them with a nod of thanks and addressed himself to his food again while she spread preserves on the remainder.

And becoming pregnant would certainly trap him. But there were ways to make love without that happening, she was certain. She had heard whispers. Bel had been Ashe's lover for some time before their marriage and Bel was not a reckless woman. At least, she had not been until she fell in love. Theo would know.

'What are you brooding about?' he asked so suddenly she dropped her bread. 'You look as though you have a knotty problem in translation to puzzle through.'

'Things I want.' It was a miracle that she had not blurted out, *you*, he had made her jump so.

'Oh, shopping.' Theo pushed back his plate. 'We'll stop in Arnay le Duc first thing, then push on to Mâcon for the night. Then it's a relatively easy drive down to Lyon and after that Grenoble, the last stop before Maubourg.' She nodded, reassured that she had three days to decide what to do, and how to do it. 'You know what you want, then? Are you going to put it on the list?'

'No. I'll remember without any trouble.' She looked up and smiled but Theo was already on his feet, ringing for the waiter.

Arnay behind them, their valises reassuringly full of essentials, Theo sent the horses down the long road to Mâcon at a steady pace while Elinor packed things away and tried to snatch sketches from the bouncing seat.

After lunch she climbed back up on the box again, ignoring the effect of wind and dust on her complexion and the hardness of the seat under her. 'Why only a pair? Must we be careful with money?'

'No. I thought we would be expected to take four, and in any case there is no great hurry. I could buy another pair, I suppose, and make up a team.' He flicked the whip down to discourage a small pack of village dogs that had come tumbling and barking out of a farm gate. 'I might do that after Lyon, the hills will be steeper.'

'Is it difficult driving a pair?' He was still only using one hand for the reins, his whip hand only coming across when he needed to loop a rein to take a corner. She frowned at his fingers, trying to work out what went where.

'More difficult than a single horse, as you'd expect. Why? Do you want to drive?' He turned his head to grin at her. 'It will make your shoulders stiff.'

'I'll try for a bit. They seem steady enough.'

'All right.' He moved over to the right. 'Come into the middle as much as possible—now open your hands.'

It took five minutes of fumbling, and considerable confusion for the pair, before she was settled sitting snug against Theo, the length of his hip and thigh pressed against hers, his left arm round the back of her, resting on the rail. 'I'll keep the whip and help you with the reins when we come to a bend.'

Somehow, as they bowled along, the Burgundian countryside unfolding green and gold on either side, the rows of vines stretching like the marks of a giant comb up every south-facing slope, his arm came up and round her shoulders and his right hand came over and guided hers more and more until they were driving together. There was no need to talk, no need to do anything but feel the companionship and the shared pleasure in what they were doing.

It was like that first walk along the river bank. Theo would nudge her and she would look round to see a vivid patch of flowers in front of a cottage, or children playing tag in and out of the puddles around a public wash house. She would murmur and he would look up as a buzzard swept overhead, mewing, or a white horse in a field galloped down to whinny at their pair as they passed.

'There's Mâcon ahead.' Theo took the reins back. 'I don't remember a day when I've spent more time doing virtually nothing and yet enjoyed myself so much.'

'No.' Moving back to her side of the box and smoothing down her skirts before they reached the streets, Elinor nodded in perfect comprehension. 'It was like a day from childhood, taking sights and experiences as they came with no worries, nothing to do but be.'

Beside her Theo chuckled. 'I like that: *Nothing to do but be.* You are taking years off me, Nell. Hold tight, here we are.'

As he swung the team through the gates of the inn, Elinor watched his face: focused, intent, strong. No, they might have taken a day out of childhood, but this was not a boy. This was a man.

Chapter Eighteen

Mâcon, and a night spent chastely in their own beds lay behind them, Lyon was just ahead in the late afternoon sunlight. Theo had kept the reins the whole way, saying he wanted to get to Lyon before evening and Elinor had secretly welcomed the chance to recover from yesterday's stiff shoulders and aching back.

She stretched as they climbed down into the courtyard of the Phaison Blanc. Theo was negotiating with the landlord for rooms and ordering hot water immediately. 'Come along, upstairs for a quick wash, then we are going out.' He was up to something, she could tell. Some excitement was bubbling underneath. Willing to indulge him, Elinor hurried to do as he asked, reappearing in the courtyard to find him hat in hand, hair ruthlessly combed.

'Where are we going?' Without thinking she tucked her hand under his elbow and allowed herself to be guided along the crowded footway.

'We will be in a Grand Ducal court soon.'

'Yes, I know.' That was not news.

'I intend we look the part.' Theo stopped in front of a discreet green-painted shop window displaying a length of figured silk, a pair of kid gloves and a fan. 'In we go.'

Ten minutes later Elinor found herself abandoned to the mercies of a team of interested semptresses under the direction of their employer, who had received detailed orders from Theo. Bewildered, Elinor saw large amounts of money change hands while she struggled to keep up with the rapid-fire exchange of French.

'Theo—what on earth—?' She managed before he was out of the door.

'I'll be back, just going to find a tailor.' Then she was staring at a closed door and hands were tugging her gently towards screens at the back of the shop.

'Madame, s'il-vous plaît.' Abandoned, and not at all sure she knew her way back, Elinor surrendered to having her outer clothes stripped off, to the accompaniment of much interested comment on her divided skirt, and being comprehensively measured, prodded and subjected to length after length of fabric being held up to her face.

It was like being gently assaulted by a flock of small, but very determined, birds. Just why measuring her for one gown, which she supposed was Theo's intention, should take so much fuss, she had no idea, but she was tired and her French vocabulary failed her.

Theo reappeared over an hour later when she was sitting with her feet on a petit-point footstool, sipping a tisane and leafing through copies of *La Correspon-*

dance des Dames. This was the sort of thing her friends Bel, Eva and Jessica did, not her.

'Having fun?' Somewhere along the way he had acquired a cane and a smart tall hat and his breeches and coat had been brushed and sponged.

'No! Well, yes, in a way. But, Theo, Eva and Sebastian won't mind us turning up with just a valise between us, not once we explain. And one of Eva's ladies will be sure to be my size and won't mind lending some things, I am sure.' She looked him up and down as he stood in front of her surrounded by the shop girls. 'You are looking very much the thing.'

'Wait until tomorrow. *Merci, madame, à bientôt.*' Theo held the door for her and ushered her out. 'Now then dinner, a bath and an early night.'

'Yes, but I'm not—'

'Not tired? We've a busy day tomorrow.'

'Theo!' Elinor dug in her heels in, stopping in the middle of the square. 'Talk to me! I thought we were going on to Grenoble tomorrow.'

'No, we are going to Grenoble *next*,' he said patiently, steering her firmly across the road. 'Tomorrow we shop. We need clothes and I want to indulge myself.'

'By dressing me up? Theo, how many gowns have you ordered?'

'One or two,' he said evasively. 'It is a very stylish court, I don't want either of us to feel out of place.'

Elinor set her lips tight together and walked back to the inn in silence. Theo had cajoled her into new clothes in St Père, and he had been proved right. She *had* looked a dowd and it was gratifying to look one's best and have a pretty gown or two. But they were not in London, she was not attending court for social reasons and she was baffled by why Theo should want to continue encouraging her to shop.

She held her peace until after dinner, maintaining a flow of cheerful conversation that Theo obviously found disconcerting. When the waiter cleared the board and brought in a bottle of brandy he half-rose to his feet, expecting her to retire.

'Oh, no, you don't.' Elinor settled down across the table where she could watch his face, pulled a glass towards her and splashed brandy in the bottom—she rather thought she might need its support. 'Now Theo, why, exactly, did you take me to that *modiste* this afternoon? And what shopping are we going to be occupying valuable travelling time with tomorrow?'

He did not answer her immediately, pouring himself a glass of brandy and pushing his chair back so he was sitting at right angles to her. Elinor waited patiently while he loosened his neckcloth, stretched out his legs and generally made himself comfortable. If he thought she was going to be put off by such obvious tactics, he had another think coming.

'I've risked your life, dragged you across France, made you thoroughly uncomfortable. I thought you deserved a treat. I thought I did, come to that. I thought I would enjoy buying you pretty things.' He turned from his contemplation of the brandy to look directly into her eyes. 'I wanted to take you to Maubourg and show you off.'

'As your creation? You wanted to buy me things as you would your mistress?' She thought she was angry, but the mixture of emotions churning round inside her were difficult to interpret.

'As I would any lady I was fond of, who had taste, who I thought might enjoy it,' he said, his eyes narrowing as he tried to assess her reaction.

'Oh.' Put like that, it was hard to be cross. 'I am not used to being brought presents of that sort.' And, of course, no lady could accept any article of apparel from a man as a gift, not so much as a pair of gloves. 'I should pay you back when we get back to England.'

'This is a present,' he said, his voice level. 'I would be gratified if you would accept tomorrow as a present.' There was emotion behind the calmness, feelings she did not understand. Unless her fear the other night had shaken him, made him feel he needed to make reparation for that terrifying time in the dungeons.

And if that was how he felt, could she throw it back in his face? She could hardly be much more compromised than she was already and it was not as though anyone need know how she had come by whatever it was Theo was determined to give her.

'Thinking again?' he enquired, not unkindly, as she sipped her brandy. She was not certain she liked it, but it warmed right down to her toes. 'I love your mind, Nell, but I wish you'd let your emotions out sometimes.'

'Yes. Yes, I would very much enjoy for you to take me shopping and buy me things, Theo, thank you.' *There, is that emotional enough for him? He loves my mind? But I don't want him to love my mind, I want him to love me! Just how startled would he be if I showed him my emotions, asked him to make love to me?*

'Right.' He grinned at her, suddenly looking happier than he had all day. 'Drink more brandy, it is obviously

good for you. I told them that I wanted the gowns ready
for a first fitting before noon. I will go to my tailors at
the same time. Then there are all the other things, the
frippery things—we can fit those in around the fittings.'

'Frippery things?'

'Do-dads. Bits of nonsense men aren't supposed to
talk about. Absolutely nothing sensible or practical,
Nell, I warn you.' She found she was smiling back,
carried away by his enjoyment of his plans for her.
'Now, bed and an early morning.'

Theo lounged, with a total lack of concern for propriety, on the chair in Elinor's bedchamber and
watched her unpacking their purchases on the bed.
Four gowns: morning, walking, half-dress and full
dress; a froth of Swiss lawn undergarments and night
things; gloves and stocking; fans, slippers and shoes;
two shawls, a pelisse and three hats.

'Oh, my goodness.' She sat down on the end of the
bed and looked at him, breathless, and apparently in
two minds whether to laugh or cry. 'Theo, I just don't
believe all this now I see it all together. It is so beautiful. Thank you. I have never been shopping like this
before.' She whisked off the bed and was kissing him,
her hands on his shoulders, before he could brace
himself.

Oh, God, the scent of her. It had been torture all day,
being with her, watching her enjoyment as he coaxed
and teased her into trying things on, choosing between
pairs of gloves and then buying them all for her
anyway, seeing an utterly frivolous, fun-loving, playful
Nell emerge into the sunlight.

She had accompanied him, shockingly, into bootmakers, had insisted on checking the quality of the neckcloths he bought, dabbed cologne on the back of her hand and then on his new handkerchiefs and teased him into buying a waistcoat all the colours of autumn, which she said would go with his hair.

'I'm glad you like them,' he said mildly, exercising considerable control of his breathing. 'I think I can hear the new luggage being brought up.'

'Shall I pack for you?'

'No. I can manage, thank you.' The thought of her bent over the valises, folding his shirts, acting like the wife he wished she was—that was one torture too far.

It was as well, he thought wryly over dinner, to be careful what one wished for. He had fantasised about a day spent with Nell, indulging his desire to buy her pretty things and now he was having to live with the consequences. She was happy and sparkling and light-hearted. Which was wonderful. She was also treating him like an indulgent brother, which was not.

She left him after dinner with a gesture towards the brandy bottle. 'That gave me a headache, I think I will leave you to it, Theo.' Something of the sparkle had gone out of her mood; she looked serious as she stood, the door handle in one hand, a copy of Petrarch's poetry she had insisted on buying in the other. How like Nell, he thought tenderly, off she goes to bed to read four-teenth-century Italian in the original.

'Theo.'

'Mmm?' He was not sure whether he did not like her best when she was serious, her brow furrowed over a book, or deep in thought. The laughter was never very far away and the look in those clear hazel eyes…

'Theo, wake up! Will you knock on my door when you come up? Say goodnight? I'll be reading.'

'If you want me to translate, I can't, my Italian is strictly the modern variety.'

'No.' Her smile was oddly tense. 'No, I won't ask you to translate.'

How long had she got to wait? Elinor wondered, washing with the tablet of fine-milled soap that she had picked up to smell in the perfumers and which had been immediately added to the pile of Theo's purchases. She could change her mind, right up to the point where he tapped on her door, expecting to say goodnight.

Her new nightgown slithered over her shoulders, a virginal pure white that should have prodded her conscience. She tied the ribbons loosely at the neck, for the first time in her life thinking about dressing to please a man. *No,* she corrected herself firmly, *seduce him.* It had a matching robe, hardly more practical or modest. She slipped it on, wondering if it was as translucent as it felt.

Theo had seemed to like her hair loose, she thought, remembering the way he had weighed it in his hands before plaiting it on the river bank. Freed from its ribbon, the braiding shaken out, it rippled over her shoulders and down her back, a shifting veil.

A more assured woman would have scent and know how to use it, would place a jewel strategically, might use lamp-black to lengthen her lashes, or the petals from those geraniums on the window sill to redden her lips or cheeks. But she had none of those arts, or those accessories. Either he wanted her or he did not. All she could do now was to wait and see whether her nerve held.

The book she had bought was hard to translate, forcing her to concentrate as she struggled with the meaning. But it was not a good choice for the love-lorn wrestling with conscience and desire, filled as it as with sonnets written by the poet to his unfulfilled love, Laura.

'Wherever I wander, love attends me still, Soft whispring to my soul, and I to him.' That was lovely, and, sadly, implied that love would never let you alone.

'Sighing?' She had not heard the tap on the door. Theo was standing just inside, regarding her with affectionate amusement. He had taken off his boots, which was perhaps why she had not heard him. 'That is heavy stuff for this time of night. Are you having trouble with the grammar?'

'No, it isn't as bad as I feared. Theo—' Now was the moment to make up her mind, take that second chance. 'Would you come in and close the door?' He raised his eyebrows, but did as she asked, putting his chamber stick down on the dresser and watching her in the candlelight.

'Are you afraid of sleeping again?'

'It isn't that.'

She put the book down with care and stood up. How difficult could it be? He only had to say *no*. Theo's eyes widened as he took in her loose hair, the fragile white lawn garments. As though his gaze was being dragged, it travelled down her body to her toes, bare under the lacy hem.

'I want you to stay with me tonight, Theo, and make love to me.' A frank demand, not one of the careful phrases she had rehearsed, but at least it was said, even if her stomach did seem to have shrunk to a tight knot of apprehension and she could feel the colour rising in her cheeks. He was standing there, watching her, his face a mask, yet she sensed anger, not any of the other emotions she would have expected—embarrassment, alarm, pity.

'You do not have to pay for what I bought you today,' he said finally, and the rage was there, clear and cold in his voice. It was the tone she would have imagined one man would have used to another in the moments before rapiers came sliding out of scabbards. And something else. Pain.

'Oh, no! Theo, I would never… I was going to ask before today, before I knew what you intended.' She was normally so calm and articulate and now the words were tangling in her mouth and she found that, confronted with pure emotion, she had no idea how to put right what she had done. This was Theo and she was losing him.

Elinor fought down the panic and took a deep breath. 'I realised the night before last, when you slept in my room, how much I wanted to…' Her resolution died away in the face of his implacably blank expression. She tried again.

'Theo, I know I'm not going to get married, I have always known it. I would never settle for anything other than a love match, and I know I'm not going to find one of those. But I find I don't want to live the whole of my life not knowing about—' She swallowed hard. 'Not knowing about physical passion. It is not something a single woman can seek out, not without terrible risks, not unless there is someone she can trust, as I trust you.'

The anger was leaving him, she could sense it,

although she was still surprised by how quickly it had flared up in him, the hurt she sensed. Was it simply touchy male honour? Surely not.

'As you say, there are risks,' he said steadily, his eyes watchful on her face. 'Your reputation, if word gets around that we have been travelling together, is ruined anyway. But with your mother's connivance and the Maubourg court as cover, there is no reason why it should ever get out. Unless you become pregnant—and if we make love, then that is a very real risk, and one I am not prepared to take.'

Because, if that is the consequence, you will be trapped? one part of her mind asked. *He is quite right, said her common sense. You would* both *be trapped.*

'It is possible to make love without that risk, is it not?'

'Ah.' Theo came fully into the room, leaning against the bedpost, a faint smile lifting the corner of his mouth. 'My very well-read and very innocent Elinor, you are quite correct. But there is one proviso—you have to trust the man who is making love to you not to get carried away in the heat of the moment.'

'And you do not trust yourself?' she queried, sceptical. 'What exactly were your intentions those times you kissed me, might I ask? Were they completely dishonourable? Were you confident things would go no further than a kiss? Or were you going to risk the consequences and rely on disappearing back into your wandering life afterwards?'

'I intended to give you pleasure,' Theo said slowly, his eyes locked with hers, 'and I intended to take pleasure myself from doing that. You would still have been a virgin at the end of it. And the intensity of it made me realise that I should not involve myself with virgins and I resolved, somehow, to keep my hands off you in future. Don't blush like that, Nell, you cannot initiate this sort of conversation and expect it to continue in euphemisms.'

'I see. I beg your pardon for having implied any lack of honour on your part.' The apology came from stiff lips, but something warmed the cold green eyes and she sensed him relax a little. The wise thing would be to say goodnight, to stop this now while she was still safe from the emotional consequences of what she wanted so much. But she no longer wished to be wise. Or safe.

'Could we not pretend we are still in that study?' she asked. 'Could we not finish what began there?' His lids lowered, hooding his eyes, hiding his thoughts from her. She wanted to shake him, make him realise how much she was suffering from the need he had ignited in her.

'Theo, I know men have ways of dealing with frustration.' His expression of mingled shock and amusement had her smiling back for the first time since this fraught encounter had begun. 'Well, I do read, as you say, and all kinds of journals, including medical ones, find their way into the study at home, and I am bright enough to read between the lines. But you have made me want something I do not understand. And I want to understand it and I don't want to ache like this any more.'

He was going to refuse her, she was certain. Theo walked to her side, his face serious. 'Nell.' His big hand curved under her chin and tipped her face up. 'I am not sure about revisiting the study. That floor was dreadfully hard and this one looks just as bad. Would you settle for the bed?'

Chapter Nineteen

'Yes, I will settle for the bed.' It was difficult to keep her tone light to match his. The bed suddenly seemed very large, Theo seemed very close and it did not seem as though she was wearing very much at all, not with the way he was looking at her now.

'Just tell me if you want to stop, Nell. This is all about you, about your pleasure.' He had shed his coat and was loosening his neckcloth while she stood there like Pandora, wondering what on earth she had just let out of the box.

'That is rather selfish,' she demurred, reaching up to take the ends of the long muslin strip from his hands.

'I didn't say I wouldn't enjoy it, too.' Theo bent his head to help her pull off the neckcloth, then added encouragingly as she hesitated, 'I would like it if you took off my shirt as well.'

It was all rather leisurely, in contrast to that explosion of passion in the study. Elinor began to unbutton his shirt, her fingers fumbling a little. But the tension this slowness engendered was very real, knotting in her stomach, aching down the inside of her thighs. Between her legs a pulse began to throb with intimate urgency. Then her fingertips brushed skin and Theo caught his breath and she forgot to analyse how she was feeling.

As she pushed the linen off his shoulders, he pulled at the shirt so it came out of his breeches and fell to the floor and then she was standing, her palms flat on the naked chest of a man. It felt...wonderful. He looked wonderful. She had thought she had known what to expect, but it was not the tactile smoothness of tanned skin over hard, defined, muscle or the strangely arousing tickle of crisp hair or the intriguing way his nipples hardened when she accidentally brushed against one.

Theo moved his hands to push her robe open and the muscles of his chest shifted, rippling under her hands and she smiled, caressing down to explore as the fine lawn fell to catch at her elbows.

'Are you sure you haven't done this before?' Theo asked as her fingertips slipped into the tight waistband of his breeches. 'You seem to know all the right places.'

'Quite sure!' Worried she would do something wrong if she went any further, Elinor snatched back her hands and the robe fell to the floor at her feet. Theo made a complicated noise, somewhere between a growl and a sigh and pulled her against him, his hands sliding down her back from her shoulders to cup her buttocks, lifting her against the wonderful evidence that she was doing something very right indeed.

Then he shifted his grip again and the next thing she knew her nightgown had gone and she was quite naked against him, feeling his heart hammering as his hands skimmed over her back and her buttocks, caressing with a gentleness she did not realise a man could possess. How she got on to the bed she could not say, but Theo was removing his breeches, drawers and stockings in one movement that a part of her brain which was still functioning recognised as honed by long practice.

He was even more beautiful naked than clothed, she realised, staring at him with unabashed interest, not even the startling jut of his erection deterring her. Then she saw his eyes and realising he was looking at her in just the same way. *I ought to be shy, I ought to be hiding under this sheet,* she thought, wondering at herself, but all she could do was bask in the warmth of his gaze.

'I knew I was right about what was under those dreadful gowns,' he murmured, lying down beside her and gathering her in close for a kiss. That felt safer— wonderful and exciting and inflammatory, but at least familiar, as his mouth worked over hers. But then he moved, slid down against her, and that wickedly knowing mouth was doing things to her breast and to her nipples and she arched up off the bed with a gasp as he nipped the tense buds between his teeth.

'Theo! Theo?' She caught at his head, her fingers threading into the glorious red mane, but he kept moving, his mouth hot and wet now on her belly. Under his tongue the flesh was sensitive, responsive and she tried to move, only his hands cupped her hips, steadying her. 'Where? *Theo!*' He was nuzzling into the dense red curls at the apex of her thighs and she knew she was wet and hot and aching and it was the most shocking thing she could imagine. And then it became even more shocking as his tongue tip found something, found *her*, and teased and stroked while his hands pushed her un-resisting legs apart and his fingers searched and probed and slid inside just as the complex knot of sensation deep in her belly unravelled itself into something that sent her spiralling into an explosion of feeling that was anguish and was delight and was everything.

'Theo.' That must be her voice, murmuring. Some-how she was in his arms again and the thud against her cheek was his heart.

'Nell?' He was stroking her, gentling his hands down over her hot skin, stilling her quivering. Now, at last, she realised that *making love* meant just that. He might not love her, but he had pleasured her with loving care, was holding her with tenderness.

'That was…beautiful.'

'Good,' he murmured into her hair. 'Are you tired?'

'I'm not sure,' Elinor answered honestly. 'Why?' In answer, his hands began to move with more firmness and he turned her in his arms until he could kiss her, while those clever, wicked fingers searched out that hidden part of her and began to touch and tease while she gasped against his mouth and realised that, no, she was not in the slightest bit tired.

But what about him? What about his pleasure? Ex-perimentally Elinor slid one hand down between their bodies to where his heat was most intense and curled her fingers around him. It stopped his mouth on hers and his moving fingers stilled. 'Yes,' he said, his voice husky. 'Like that. Move like that—ah, Nell!'

She was clumsy, unskilled, she knew, but he didn't seem to mind and to feel the powerful urgency of his body responding to her while he drove her to the brink, brought her back, over and over, was utterly delicious madness. Then that tightening knot broke, shattered again, just as he surged in her grasp, his groan mingling with her gasps and she collapsed, limp, into his arms as he fell back shuddering with the force of his release.

Theo woke to find himself in a hot sticky tangle of sheets, hair and soft feminine limbs. He lay looking up at the ceiling in the faint morning light and wondered if he had ever felt better. Beyond the moment, beyond this bed chamber door, was a reality he did not want to think about yet. Time enough to face it. Half on top of him, her face burrowed into his chest, Nell slept, her breath stirring the hair on his chest in an arousing tickle. He thought about waking her, then contented himself with stroking her hair.

He had roused her once in the night, loving the way she responded to every caress with delighted surprise. And then he had been the one to be surprised when he had woken from a deeply erotic dream to find her small hand caressing him into total arousal. Half-asleep as he had been, he had almost forgotten the overriding need to preserve her virginity, had caught himself just in time as he brought his weight down over her.

Had he satisfied both her and her curiosity? he wondered. Was she going to put away this awakening, this knowledge, and become once again the respectable bluestocking spinster? She was so vulnerable, trembling in his arms. Would it take so very much to convince her to marry him?

A hand slid down his belly, its fingers teasing into the coarse hair, then tiptoeing up the rapidly stiffening length of him. 'Good morning, Theo,' she said, turning up her face to smile at him.

'You, Nell, are a hussy. Don't you want your breakfast?'

'No.' She had learned not to handle him as though he was breakable. In fact, Theo thought, abandoning himself to her wicked exploration, she learned everything, very fast. And if he didn't do something, now this moment, it was all going to be over very fast, too.

'Nell, *slowly*. Oh, my God…'

Elinor curled up at the foot of the crumpled bed and ate toast, heedless of the crumbs. Theo, up at the pillow end, had wedged steak between two halves of a large roll and was demolishing it, wolf-like. It had been his idea, this decadent picnic breakfast when she had declared herself too indolent to get out of bed.

'We've got a longish drive ahead of us, we will eat in bed and then you must get up' he had said firmly, ringing the bell despite her protests. 'What? They think we are married, stop blushing.'

But she hadn't really been blushing, she rather thought she had lost the capacity to, all in one intense night of pleasure. Of course, there was that one thing still not experienced, Theo had not taken her, claimed her body, possessed her. But he had taught her, shatteringly, the pleasure that a man and a woman could give to each other. There was one more night before they reached Maubourg. Would he come to her bed again, or would he take her literally and make last night the one and only?

Theo had demolished his steak, and his third cup of coffee, and was watching her while she daydreamed.

'What is it?' she asked. He looked so right there in her bed, his chest bare, the sheet draped precariously, with unselfconscious provocation, over his hips.

'Nell, won't you think again about marrying me?'

No! So he had not listened to a word she had said last night. Now he was going to be noble and honourable and want her to marry him. No wonder he had been so reluctant, he had known he would feel this the next morning.

'No, Theo. Thank you, but no. I cannot marry without love, you see. I know it was wicked of me to want to experience this, but I did mean what I said last night—please do not make me feel bad by trying to do what you see as the honourable thing.'

'Honour be damned,' he retorted. 'Nell, I love you—'

'Yes, I know.' She had to reassure him, the words tumbled out. 'You couldn't be a more loving friend and cousin. And I love you, just the same way.' *Lies, I love you in every way there is.* 'But you told me you would never marry, and I realise that must be because you love someone else, hopelessly—no, don't interrupt—and I know it is sad because she doesn't love you, but two wrongs don't make a right. Given my feelings, it would be wrong for us to marry. Truly, I don't think I could *stand* it,' she added with as much conviction as she could muster.

'I see. Thank you for being so clear about it.' Theo put his plate down and threw back the sheet. Shy all of a sudden, Elinor looked away, keeping her eyes on the pile of hat and dress boxes while behind her she could hear Theo hunting through the strewn clothing for his breeches and shirt. 'I'll send the maid up with water and to help you to dress, shall I?'

'Yes, please.' How painfully polite they were being to each other. Last night, this morning, there was not an inch of each other's body they had not caressed, kissed, explored. Now they would be discussing the weather in a minute.

The road to Grenoble was long, Theo, reserved, and the horses, tired. The magic had gone out of the journey and Elinor knew she had only herself to blame for that. How could she have failed to anticipate the emotions that would be unleashed by intimacy of that kind? He had been so right, back at the chateau. She kept trying to understand desire intellectually and all the time it was far too complicated for that.

Theo suggested that she must be tired and might prefer to travel inside where she could sleep. Elinor translated this, without much difficulty, as meaning that he wanted to be alone and could very well do without her company.

She sat in the chaise surrounded by the pretty boxes full of Theo's joyful purchases and felt very much like weeping. Which was not helpful, she decided, waiting in an inn while Theo had a local livery stables change the fittings and harness another pair to the carriage. She had got into this mess by thinking too much; now an excess of sensibility was no way to get out of it.

The only thing to be done was to keep reminding herself that she was actually better off than she had been before Theo had come back into her life. She looked better, she felt more confident, she had had adventures and experiences and she had learned that risking letting herself feel led to both the expected disadvantages and to undreamed wonders.

If she could just manage to school her awakened body into accepting that it had experienced quite enough sensuality and was now satisfied, she was certain she would soon feel very much better.

The unexpected touch of Theo's hand on hers made her flinch. As she got to her feet, he stood well back to give her room, and, instead of explaining that he had simply startled her, she found there was nothing she could say. Perhaps, she thought with sadness as she climbed into the carriage, there never would be again.

That night Theo had professed himself tired from so much driving and had retired with the brandy after an hour of very stilted dinner conversation, leaving her to the dubious pleasures of Petrarch and the private parlour with a view of rain-soaked rooftops. Even the glorious August weather had deserted them, making the last ten miles a miserable drag along muddy roads.

Elinor shut her book with a snap, rang the bell for a glass of red wine, wrapped her shawl tight around her shoulders, put her feet up on the fender and gave her future some serious thought. It would not hold Theo, she knew that, but she was beginning to wonder whether it would bear any relation to her life with her mother so far either.

There was nothing she did for Mama that a competent secretary who could draw could not do. She had her own money—not that she ever touched it or questioned the decisions of her trustees. Well, that would have to change if she was going to stop simply existing and start living.

She could afford her own companion, could afford to travel. Elinor stretched out a hand for her notebook and began to scribble.

Half an hour later the wine was untouched at her side and she had filled a page with tightly packed notes headed, *How Much Money Do I Have?* and finishing, *ITALY!*

She read it through slowly, stretched out a hand for the glass and fought down the rising knot of apprehension. Yes, she could do it. One tear rolled down the side of her nose and she scrubbed it away with an impatient hand. She was going to be lonely, but she rather thought she had been lonely since she was a child. Now she was going to be lonely on her own terms and in that, surely, there must be some happiness. It was just a pity it had taken her heart being broken to make her realise it.

Theo came down to breakfast dressed in cream pantaloons, shining Hessians with gold tassels, brand new linen and a coat of immaculate dark blue superfine.

'You are never going to drive dressed like that, surely?' Elinor asked, putting down the coffee pot. She had put on her new carriage dress in heavy Lyon silk, taken a good deal of trouble over her hair, and had chosen a pair of exquisite kid gloves in honour of her first appearance at the Maubourg court.

The words had escaped before she had given any thought to the fact that things must still be somewhat constrained between them, but Theo shrugged amiably enough. 'I've hired a groom to drive. I did not think my arrival looking like the driver of the London-to-Brighton stage would add to our consequence. We might be relatives, but we've got to get in the front door first.' He accepted the coffee she passed him—strong, black, one sugar, just as he liked it—and added, 'You look very fine.'

'Thank you.' Elinor scrabbled around mentally for things to talk about, then realised they were going to have all day shut up in the carriage together and stilted conversation was not going to be enough. 'I don't suppose you have a travelling chess set on you?'

'No, but I can buy some cards from the waiter. Do you play whist? No? Let me teach you, then when we get to Maubourg Sebastian can teach you how to be a sharper.'

'Sebastian? Is he really? From his days as Jack Ryder, do you mean? I wish he would talk about his adventures as a King's Messenger, but he is desperately discreet.'

'Rather more than a King's Messenger,' Theo remarked, slicing ham thickly. 'And still is, from time to time, when the government needs him. Although don't, for goodness sake, repeat that.'

'And Eva knows?'

'Apparently she says that so long as it doesn't involve beautiful young women, he must do as he sees fit.'

'What would she say about the marquesa?' Elinor stole one of Theo's slices of ham, beginning to relax a little.

'Ana? Eva has more sense than to fret about Sebastian's past—after all, her first husband was one of the most notorious rakes in Europe. But I would not fancy any woman's chances of escaping with a whole skin if they decided to set their caps at Sebastian now.'

Elinor envied the Grand Duchess her strength and her certainty. If she could be like that, then an independent life would be easy to achieve. And then she remembered Eva's confidences about her nightmares, recalled seeing the way she looked at Sebastian when she thought she was unobserved—perhaps Eva was not so self-assured. Perhaps it was a matter of application and holding one's nerve after all. They would be in the castle of Maubourg tonight and she would talk to her cousin by marriage, ask her advice. Not about Theo, of course—she was certain that she could never speak about what had happened to a living soul—but about making a break from her past and becoming independent. Eva would understand.

Chapter Twenty

It was past seven in the evening when the rumble of the carriage wheels over cobbles woke Elinor. She had been dozing in the corner of the carriage for an hour, worn out by a day struggling with the rules of whist and Theo's ruthless acquisition of a vast, if imaginary, fortune from her. Her lost wealth was represented by the litter of vowels on the carriage floor.

'Wake up.' Theo reached out and shook her arm, gently. The first time he had voluntarily touched her, she realised, since he had left her bed. 'Put on your hat, we are almost there. Here.' He held out her pelisse and helped her into it For a moment his fingertips brushed along the nape of her neck, then he was sitting back in his corner, gazing out of the window, leaving her to button up the garment and twitch her skirts into order as though nothing was amiss and her breath had not hitched in her throat with the shock of his touch.

The light still lingered in the sloping square before the wide sweep of steps. At the top the massive double doors, studded with knots of medieval ironwork and with a dragon's-head knocker in the centre, frowned down at them. The shadows from the tall houses were long and Elinor shivered as she stepped down into shade, suddenly a prey to doubts. 'Is it going to be all right, just turning up like this?' she whispered, as Theo turned from giving the driver instructions and came to take her arm.

'Yes, of course. This is Eva and Sebastian, don't forget.' He walked across the cobbles, ignoring the curious stares of passers-by.

'Yes, but I don't know Eva at all well, not really,' she worried. There was an imposing pair of guards in full silver-and-blue uniforms with plumes in their helmets and pikes in their hands at the foot of the steps and another pair at the top. As Elinor and Theo approached, the pikes clashed together in an unmistakable signal to stop.

Theo kept going, arrived at the foot of the steps and addressed the right-hand guard in French. 'Mr and Miss Ravenhurst to see Her Serene Highness and Lord Sebastian Ravenhurst.'

One of the top pair of guards pulled a large metal knob, producing a sonorous clanging from inside. Elinor, her still-sleepy brain conjuring up scenes from Gothic novels, stifled a nervous giggle. A wicket gate opened, words were exchanged with someone unseen inside, then both doors were thrown wide, the guards saluted smartly and they were climbing the steps to be met by a tail-coated major domo with a long staff in his hands and a footman on either side.

'This is very formal,' Elinor hissed in Theo's ear. 'But they seem to accept who we are.'

'Mr Ravenhurst, welcome to Maubourg. Their

Serene Highnesses will be delighted at this unexpected pleasure. *Madame.*'

'Monsieur Heribaut, it is a pleasure to see you again.' So they knew him; she should have guessed. 'This is Miss Ravenhurst, Lord Sebastian's cousin. I regret, but there has been an incident that has forced us to seek the hospitality of the Grand Duke without notice. Elinor, this is Monsieur Heribaut, the Chamberlain of the castle.'

'If you would care to come in sir, *madame*, I will—'

'Papa, please let me hold him!' The Chamberlain swung round as a boy walked backwards into the great hall talking to the man who followed him. 'I won't drop him, I promise, Mama said—'

The man, tall, broad shouldered, elegant in black evening dress was, Elinor realised, her cousin Sebastian, holding a very small baby against his shoulder and patting it on the back. Her mouth dropped open—this was not at all how she would expect to see him. The boy stopped walking and began hopping up and down on the spot, allowing a small flock of what Elinor assumed were nursery maids to catch up and hover anxiously behind them. 'Papa…'

'Your Serene Highness, Lord Sebastian.' The Chamberlain managed to cut through the chatter of the women and the boy's wheedling voice without raising his own. 'Mr and Miss Ravenhurst.'

Elinor, who was always rather in awe of her magnificent cousin Sebastian, swallowed as he turned. Then he grinned and strode over, an incongruous figure with his exquisite clothes and the baby, which had begin to dribble, she noticed, clasped to his shoulder.

'Theo! My dear cousin. And…' he stopped and stared down at her '…Elinor?'

'Yes, that's Elinor,' Theo said cheerfully, holding out his hands and receiving the baby with an easy competence that almost struck her speechless. 'We're on the run and need sanctuary and a good strongroom. Is this the latest Ravenhurst, then?'

'This is Charles James Oliver Ryder Ravenhurst,' announced the Grand Duke, aged ten, ducking under his stepfather's elbow and thrusting out a hand. 'He's two weeks old and has no hair yet. Welcome to Maubourg Miss Ravenhurst. Sir.'

'Your Serene Highness.' Elinor took his hand and produced her best court curtsy.

'Freddie,' the Grand Duke said, grinning. 'We're sort of cousins, aren't we, if you're a Ravenhurst?'

'My goodness, Theo and Elinor.' The lightly accented, richly feminine voice cut through Theo simultaneously talking to the baby and Sebastian and Elinor trying to explain to Freddie how she was related to his stepfather. The Grand Duchess, in full evening dress, sailed down the hall, her hands held out to them. 'My dears, how lovely. Are you eloping?'

'We most certainly are not,' Elinor began hotly.

'We are trying to give the appearance of doing so,' Theo said. 'Eva, you grow more beautiful every time I see you and your new son is utterly charming.'

'He is, isn't he?' she said smugly. 'I do think it was clever of us. Now Freddie, you take Charles very carefully and carry him up to the nursery and have your dinner.'

'But, Mama, you said I could eat with you—'

'We need to have a business dinner, Freddie. Papa's business, hmm?'

'I see. Secret stuff,' Fréderic said with a grin. 'I'll see you tomorrow then, Cousin Elinor.'

Elinor was not quite sure how Eva did it, but in two crowded minutes the baby and its attendants had been despatched to the nursery, a message had gone down to the kitchens to delay dinner, the Chamberlain was organising rooms and Sebastian's valet had material-ised and was sponging dribble off his coat.

'Come along.' Eva tucked one hand under Elinor's arm. 'Come up to my rooms and have a wash and then we can eat while they take up your luggage.'

'I'm so sorry, arriving like this,' Elinor tried to apologise as they climbed the stairs.

'I am delighted. Now tell me, how did you come to look so lovely? You were such a little brown mouse whenever I saw you before. Except for the hair, of course.'

'It was Theo.'

'Oho!' Eva's chuckle was enough to make Elinor blush to her toes.

'No! I mean he nagged me into buying new clothes and doing my hair differently. And we've been having adventures recently, which seems to have improved my complexion. Or something,' she added doubtfully, not at all sure herself why these days she seemed to be glowing. Unless Jeanie was right and love did that to you.

'But you *are* going to marry him?' Eva swept into the room, startling a middle-aged woman who was folding clothes on the bed. 'Hortense, this is Miss Ravenhurst, Lord Sebastian's cousin. She will be staying and requires a maid. Now she needs hot water, if you please.' The dresser bobbed a curtsy and hurried out. 'Do you want to change? Don't feel you have to, it is only us tonight.'

'Thank you, if it is all right, I'll just wash my hands and face.' Elinor sat down with a thump on the dressing-table stool. 'Eva, I am not marrying Theo.'

'No? But you are compromised, are you not?' Eva picked up a comb. 'You have been travelling with him. Here, let me take your hat, your back hair is coming down.'

'Yes, but Mama knows about it and I do not have to. I mean, I am still—' Goodness, but this was embarrassing.

'A virgin? Not such a rake as he likes to make out then, our Theo. But you are blushing like a rose! Only just a virgin, perhaps? So, he is a very careful rake.' She was teasing, but gently, and her smile was warm.

'Eva! We'll tell you all about it at dinner. No, I do not mean *that*,' she added repressively as the Grand Duchess's smile became positively wicked. 'I would like to talk to you later, though, just the two of us,' she added, suddenly shy now the urgency of assuring Eva that she did not *have* to marry had ebbed away, but realising she did need a woman to confide in. 'And, please, do not tease Theo about me, he keeps having attacks of being all honourable and noble and saying we should get married and he obviously doesn't want to. Nor do I, naturally.'

'Naturally? How very odd of you,' Eva remarked through a mouthful of hairpins. 'I think he is very attractive. Not beautiful like Sebastian—no one else is *that* beautiful—but so masculine. No? And intelligent, which you need.'

Elinor was saved from answering by the arrival of the dresser with a maid in tow. 'Annette, *madame*—she will look after you while you are here.'

* * *

Walking down to dinner twenty minutes later, Elinor wondered uneasily whether Theo had been having an equally embarrassing talk with Sebastian. It was too much to hope that Theo's arrival with her, unchaperoned, would not provoke his cousin into some kind of enquiry, if only a teasing one. And the last thing she wanted was anyone reinforcing Theo's conviction that he must offer for her.

Thank goodness Eva had dropped the subject. She was talking about fashions, admiring Elinor's carriage dress and marvelling that she had managed to have it made in such a short time. 'Even for Lyon, that is good work. Obviously Theo has shopped there before.'

'I am sure he has,' Elinor responded brightly. 'It is equally obvious he has a great deal of experience shopping with ladies. Women,' she corrected herself after a moment's thought.

'If you will accept one word of advice from me…' Eva slowed and stopped as they approached the doors flanked by liveried footmen '…it would be to forget the women who came before a man meets you. They will have taught him many lessons, for which you may be grateful, but it is only the ones in his life after you have met him that need concern you.' Her eyes flickered up to the portrait of a rakishly handsome man in ornate uniform hanging at the head of the hallway. 'And not even then.'

'Did it not hurt?' Elinor asked, greatly daring, remembering the tales of Eva's first husband and his legendary *affaires*.

'There is hurt pride and there is love betrayed,' said Eva drily. 'They are not necessarily the same thing. When you marry a man like Louis Fréderic there are many compensations, but the price is learning not to give your heart. But we are not talking about Grand Dukes here, are we? Marry for love, Elinor, or not at all.'

'That,' she retorted with conviction, 'is my view entirely.'

The dining room was small, obviously the space used for eating *en famille*. Sebastian and Theo rose to their feet as the ladies entered, Sebastian nodding to the butler. 'Bring the wine to the table, then you may all leave us.'

Theo pulled out a chair for Elinor, then circled the table to sit opposite her. Before them dinner had been set out *à la française*, but in a much reduced form with the desserts on a sideboard. She had been fearing a formal court service, full of pitfalls for the unwary and with no opportunity to relax and talk. This was perfect. Or it would be once she had got over the butterflies in her stomach that Eva's frank remarks had produced.

With everyone served, Sebastian put down the carving knife and looked round the table. 'Now,' he said with a smile, 'you must sing for your suppers.'

Elinor let Theo talk, occasionally chipping in a comment, but mainly eating and watching the faces of the listeners. Sebastian, she decided, must be a superlative card player, possibly even have the skills of a sharper as Theo had suggested, for there was not a flicker of expression on his face when Ana's name was mentioned.

Eva was less guarded, although she betrayed her recognition only by a slight narrowing of her fine, dark eyes. Then she laughed, a gurgle of genuine amusement. 'So, you keep your mistresses in the family, you Ravenhursts?'

Sebastian, well used to his wife, merely smiled lazily. Theo retorted, 'She was never my mistress, that would be like trying to domesticate a wild cat. As I was explaining, having visited the chateau…'

'And you decided to visit us rather than make for the coast?' Sebastian leaned over and cut himself a corner of cheese as Theo reached the end of the tale. 'That seems a wise choice to me, if the countess had discovered your escape and decided to give chase.' They had demolished both courses and now the port decanter was circulating and Theo was cracking walnuts between long fingers.

'I wonder if they did realise you had escaped,' Eva pondered. 'By now your man will have delivered the letter you left with him to the count. He will have to decide what to do about his mother.'

'Unless he has resolved to keep it quiet and not risk scandal,' Elinor pointed out.

'He will have your mother to deal with in that case, with Hythe at her side. And I was frank with him—if he does not deal with her, I will tell the tale all over Paris.'

'So, the excitement is probably over,' Eva said with regret. 'Now, where is this Chalice? I want to see it.'

'No, you do not,' Elinor retorted with a shudder. 'It is a work of art and absolutely horrible, to look at and to touch.'

'In that case, it can stay where it is. We will find you some large outriders to guard it on its way back to England. How long can you stay with us?'

'Until Hythe arrives.' Theo swirled his port and looked into the ruby wine. 'He can escort Elinor to meet her mother in Avignon, I will go north for England.'

And that will be that, the end of my adventure.

'But you have been travelling alone with Elinor,' Sebastian pointed out. 'You cannot just waltz off and leave her.'

'Apparently I can,' Theo said, not lifting his eyes from the glass. 'Our cousin will not have me.'

'I don't have to marry you,' Elinor snapped, suddenly wanting nothing more than sleep and nothing less than a pair of men trying to tell her what to do. 'And I am not going to be pushed into a marriage of convention I don't want with an unwilling man just to satisfy everyone else's sense of honour, respectability and propriety. And don't look at me like that,' she added for Sebastian's benefit, 'you aren't head of the family, the Duke is, and he isn't about to appear from Scotland and order us to marry, is he?'

Eva cleared her throat. 'I think the ladies will retire now, gentlemen. I wish to go to the nursery and Elinor is sorely in need of her bed, I am sure.' She stopped by Sebastian's chair as she passed, pressing down on his shoulder to prevent him rising, and bent to kiss him on the mouth.

Elinor averted her eyes and met Theo's. 'Goodnight.' She lifted her chin and swept out in Eva's wake.

'I apologise if I was rude,' she said as Eva led the way to the guest chamber.

'Sebastian can look after himself,' Eva said. 'If there is no risk of you being with child, then it will be a simple matter to cover up those days you two spent together. Naturally, you will mention if asked that, with my invitation to visit, I sent one of my ladies to chaperon you. Now, here we are.'

Elinor doubted she would ever find her way back through the maze of passages and staircases, but as there were liveried retainers around every corner that was probably not too much of a problem. 'That little door leads to a circular stair up to the west battlements. There is a range of chambers up there opening out on to the battlement walkway that we give to single male guests. There is room for them to walk up and down smoking their cigarillos and telling *risqué* stories. Theo is the only occupant at the moment.'

Now why had she explained all that? Elinor wondered as she looked round at the cosy bedroom that had been fashioned from the unpromising beginning of a stone-vaulted chamber. Even in the winter it would be snug, with its thick carpets on the flagged floor and the Aubusson tapestries lining the walls.

'This is lovely, thank you.' She decided not to comment on Theo's whereabouts; it was probably her own over-sensitivity to any mention of him. Eva was merely making conversation. 'Eva, I would appreciate your help in finding myself a suitable companion. I have decided that I want to travel and I would rather face Mama with a *fait accompli*.'

'This is rather sudden, is it not?' Eva perched on the edge of the bed, looking less like a grand duchess and more like a young woman contemplating mischief. 'Is it because of Theo?'

It would be easy enough to lie. Elinor found she was tired of dissembling. 'Yes. That and the fact that I find I cannot contemplate going back to the way things were.'

'Very well, I will help you find a companion. There is a very pleasant and cultivated widow in her forties living in the town. She dines here occasionally—her husband was one of the court physicians. She may be a possibility. But why don't you do the obvious thing?'

'What is that?' Elinor plumped down beside Eva. Something obvious would be rather a pleasant change.

'Why, marry Theo, of course.'

'But he doesn't love me, that's what I meant at dinner.'

'He doesn't?'

'No, he says he will never marry. The way he told me, I am sure there is someone he loves, but whom he cannot have. He keeps proposing, of course—but I think that's a mixture of loneliness and guilt and this maddening male honour.' Eva looked decidedly puzzled. 'He is by himself so much, except for lovers, of course, and I don't think he has become attached to anyone other than this woman he cannot have. And we get on very well, most of the time, so I expect he thinks I would be pleasant company. And the guilt—well, he knows he has compromised me and we were rather, er…'

'Was he good?' Eva enquired, ignoring Elinor's gasp.

'Very. He made me feel wonderful. And special,' she admitted finally 'Not that I have any basis for comparison. Eva, men don't talk about—I mean, Theo and Sebastian?'

'Theo is far too much the gentleman, and Sebastian would never ask. Women are far less inhibited about these things.' Eva smiled her wicked smile. 'But who is this woman he is in love with, I wonder? Not the marquesa, surely?'

'Lord no. He threw her out of his bedchamber at Beaumartin. She's like a cat, she whisked her tail and stalked off to find another mouse to play with.'

'Pretending she wasn't at all put out? The lady has style, that is obvious. But Elinor, my dear, you love Theo, don't you?'

The quiet question caught her unawares, still smiling at the thought of Theo's rejection of Ana and the way she had reacted. 'Oh, yes,' she murmured, then caught herself. 'Far too much to marry him like this,' she added firmly.

'Oh, dear.' Eva put an arm around Elinor's shoulders and hugged. 'And you don't want to tell him and the idiot can't see it.'

'He isn't an idiot—'

'They all are when it comes to love,' Eva said with authority. 'Mind you, women are too. I proposed to Sebastian, and a complete mull I made of it. Then Bel put her oar in and that made it worse. Too much pride on both sides, of course, but we came to our senses in the end, thank goodness.'

'You are so happy. And Bel and Ashe, and Gareth and Jessica. Perhaps I am just infected by the Ravenhurst fashion for marriages and I'm pining for something I don't really want,' Elinor said, trying hard to sound light-hearted about it.

'You sleep on it.' Eva slid off the bed. 'Ring if you want anything, Annette will come. I must go and look in on the nursery. Theo's good with children, isn't he? Goodnight.'

Elinor sat looking at the closed door for some

minutes after Eva had taken herself off with that airy observation, seeing not the solid wood panels, but the image of Theo with the gurgling baby in his arms.

Chapter Twenty-One

To Theo's decidedly jaundiced eye Eva was up to something. His mood, he readily acknowledged, was considerably depressed by a crashing hangover. Sebastian had rung for a second bottle of port, declaring that they were both in need of an exclusively masculine evening and somehow that had emptied in short order, only to be replaced with brandy.

Quite why Sebastian, who appeared to be in the best of spirits, should need to indulge in what turned out to be a solid evening's drinking, Theo had no idea. In the end he knew himself to be so disguised that he took considerable care to hug the inner wall when he came out of the spiral stairs on to the battlements and Bachelors' Walk.

He was aware of the conversation turning to women and the problems they caused a man, and could remember wondering if Sebastian was trying to pump him about Nell. But he had quite as hard a head as his cousin, and probably almost as much experience keeping his mouth shut. So why, this morning, he had the uneasy feeling that he had given away more than he intended, he was not sure. A guilty conscience, probably.

His mood was not improved by the presence at the breakfast table of the castle's librarian, a slender young Englishman with blue eyes, blond hair, a classical profile and considerable address. Theo wanted to strangle him, if only to stop him discussing, with every appearance of interest, Gothic architecture in Italy with Nell.

'He is such an intelligent young man,' Eva murmured in Theo's ear. 'Lord Finchingfield mentioned him to us when we were last in England—Phillip is the third son, you know—and he is working wonders in the library. It had been dreadfully neglected. I was sure Elinor would find him entertaining, and I appear to have been correct.'

'Indeed?' Theo applied himself to his ham and eggs, trying not to glare at Mr Finchingfield, who was making Nell laugh now. Nell never laughed at breakfast. And why did she have to look so damnably lovely this morning?

'If you have finished, Elinor and Phillip, there was something I wanted to discuss in the library.' Eva gestured to the footman who sprang to pull back her chair and left with the others behind her, still laughing over some shared joke.

Nell had hardly spared him more than a polite *good morning* when he had come in and had then pertly enquired whether he would like her to ring for a powder for his head. When he had growled at her, he had seen her bite the inside of her cheek to keep from laughing at him. Did he look that bad? A glance in the mirror opposite confirmed that he did. His skin was pale under the tan, there were shadows under his eyes and he had made a hash of shaving that morning.

Sebastian, to be fair, did not look much better, but at least he had the decency to eat his breakfast in silence.

'My lord. There is a lady at the front door.' The Chamberlain looked as though he was not certain that *lady* was the apt word.

'She has presented her card?' Sebastian raised one eyebrow at Theo, who shrugged. Whoever it was, it was nothing to do with him.

'My lord.' The Chamberlain proffered a salver. Sebastian lifted the rectangle of pasteboard and studied it with a perfectly expressionless face.

'The Marquesa de Cordovilla. Now, which of us do you think she is visiting?'

'The lady enquired for Miss Ravenhurst, my lord. Apparently she has a message from her mother.'

'Miss Ravenhurst is in the library with her Serene Highness and is not to be disturbed. Show the marquesa in here, Heribaut. Interesting,' Sebastian remarked. 'I wonder if she really does have a message from Aunt Louisa or if it is simply a ruse to get entry.'

'To what end?' Theo felt the first stirrings of amusement he had felt all morning. 'I am looking forward to seeing the meeting between Ana and Eva.'

She was as dangerous as a snake and as difficult to handle as a flock of cats, but Theo found no difficulty in understanding why he had entangled himself with this woman. Her sheer nerve, let alone her looks, made her stand out like a diamond in a tray of paste stones.

And she was on her best behaviour. 'Lord Sebastian,

Mr Ravenhurst.' Her curtsy was immaculate, her carriage dress perfection and butter would not melt in her mouth. 'I do appreciate the honour of a reception. And I see I am interrupting your meal—my apologies.'

'Please, join us, Marquesa.' A water ice wouldn't have melted in Sebastian's mouth, let alone butter. Theo resumed his seat as she took hers, smiling at the footman who set a place before her.'

'Coffee only, I thank you.'

'You have come from Beaumartin? Our aunt is well?'

'Indeed, yes. Your letter put the cat amongst the pigeons with a vengeance, Mr Ravenhurst. But perhaps I had better wait until Miss Ravenhurst can join us?'

'Heribaut, please enquire if her Serene Highness and Miss Ravenhurst are free.'

It seemed none of them could find a topic for conversation. Ana consumed black, unsweetened coffee, Theo pushed back his chair so he could see the door and Sebastian steepled his long fingers and sat, apparently deep in thought.

Theo suspected Heribaut had informed Eva who the unexpected guest was, for she came through the door first, a warm smile on her lips and her hand extended. 'Marquesa, how delightful. I have heard so much about you, such a famed connoisseur and expert in art.'

'Your Serene Highness, you are too good. I merely love handsome—I mean beautiful—oh, my English!—things.' As she sat again, Eva cast her husband a glance and winked. Sebastian's eyes crinkled in an appreciative smile, then he was serious again as Elinor entered. 'Ah, Miss Ravenhurst, I come with a message from your mama.'

'So kind,' Elinor murmured, waiting until the staff had filed out and the door had closed. 'Our cousins know everything about events at the chateau before we left.'

'As you may imagine, there was a great to-do once your flight had been discovered. Lady James was most affecting, reproaching herself for having spoken to you so severely that you felt elopement was preferable to the rigours of a society wedding. And so we continued, some of us grieving, some vastly entertained,' And I know which you were, Elinor thought appreciatively, 'Until breakfast the next day, that is, when Theo's man arrived with a missive for Leon.'

Theo had always thought the expression a cliché, but now, as they all sat around the breakfast table, the tension could have been cut with a knife.

'Hythe went to stand behind Lady James's shoulder, which I thought odd, until I glimpsed the pistols in his belt. Leon read the letter, twice, I believe, each time becoming a little paler. Then he asked Lady James and Monsieur Castelnau to join him in his study. Well, we were agog—at least I was, and the Traceys seemed most interested—so no one went out and we were all making the most dull conversation in the salon when down comes Leon and asks his mother and Julie to join them.'

Ana broke off to take a sip of coffee, quite deliberately prolonging the suspense in Theo's opinion. 'So we sat a little longer, none of us quite liking to comment on what our hosts must be up to—and then the screaming began.'

'Naturally, good manners must have held you in your seats,' Eva commented. 'How frustrating.'

'But, no! How could we resist—off we all went, up the stairs, the noise getting worse by the second, and there, outside the family suites on the *premier étage*, was Leon, in the act of locking his mother's door and Julie, biting and screaming, in the more than capable grip of Hythe. She was bundled into her room and by this time all the servants were there—you may imagine the chaos. To cut the story short, a messenger was sent to the family doctor, the servants informed that the countess had been taken ill with some sort of brain fever and that Julie was hysterical with worry.'

'Did anyone accept that?' Theo enquired. Thank God, Leon had believed his letter. The count should be safe now, whatever happened to the two women.

'The servants did, why should they not? The poor woman, grieving over her husband until it all becomes too much to bear? And the two young girls guess nothing—Leon packed them both off home in the company of his elderly relative. And Julie was known to be devoted. But myself and the Traceys? No, of course not. So, Leon tells us the whole story—he did not have much choice, I think. We all went down to the dungeons and found the scene of your imprisonment— and there was the poison. My blood ran cold, believe me.' She gave a theatrical shudder, but Theo saw the darkness in her eyes. Yes, that horrid chamber had affected her, more than she was willing to betray.

'And the rest of the treasure?'

'He showed us that too, before locking it away and asking us all to swear on the bible that we would keep all this secret, except from you.'

'But what will happen to the countess and to Julie?'

Elinor asked. They were the first words she had spoken since she had sat down. Sebastian and Eva had murmured comments, but Nell had sat impassive throughout. He wondered if she was finding it hard to listen to.

'The family doctor has found that the countess is deranged by grief and she will be confined at the chateau—for ever, I suppose. Julie will be sent back to her mother with an annuity, which will cease if she ever tries to contact the family again, or leaves Brittany where her mother lives.'

'How neatly it is possible to dispose of murder and attempted murder,' Nell said softly.

'How kind of you to come out of your way to tell us this, Marquesa,' Eva remarked. 'You must, of course, stay the night.'

'Thank you.' If Ana was offended by being asked for only one night, she did not show it. 'And it was not out of my way at all, I am travelling to the coast to take ship for Italy. Lady James had already sent to Avignon to arrange her lodgings, so it would have been inconvenient for her to detour.'

Inconvenient, but natural, Theo thought, protective of Nell's feelings. At least if she had any concerns about her mother's safety, they were now put to rest. He watched her while the others asked more questions, sorted out just what had occurred to their own satisfaction. She sat still, her hands folded in her lap. For a while he was deceived into thinking she had reverted to the way she used to deal with her mother, passively allowing it all to wash over her. But then she lifted her head, listening to something Ana said about her plans in Italy, and he saw he was wrong.

She was not happy, but she was thinking, planning—
he could see it in her eyes. His Nell was making a
decision, and she was making it with no reference to
him. But then, why should she? he thought with a bitter
jab at his own feelings. He had made love to her when
he knew he ought not to have done and yet he had failed
to give her whatever it was she truly needed.

'Theo!' It was Sebastian, who appeared to have been
talking to him for some time.

'Sorry, I was miles away.'

'I was asking if you wanted to ride out with me, see
the agricultural experiments I've introduced.'

'Of course, although you do realise I wouldn't
know a turnip from a potato, don't you? Nell, why
don't you come too?'

She was at the door, exchanging a word with Eva
who was bearing their latest guest off to her bedchamber. 'No, thank you, Theo. Mr Finchingfield is expecting me in the library.'

'Bloody librarian,' Theo muttered as he found
himself alone with Sebastian in the breakfast room.

'You didn't take to him?' His cousin looked surprised. 'Very competent, good family and all that. I
wonder if Eva is matchmaking—he's a excellent
choice for Elinor, I'd have thought.' Apparently not
noticing Theo's snarl, he added, 'Let's see if Freddie
would like to come with us. I'd value your opinion on
the pony I've just bought him.'

A librarian? For Nell? A pattern-book pretty young
man with respectable bloodlines and a sound knowledge of the classics? She would be bored to tears. Safe,
no doubt, no dungeons or pistols or scandalous love-

making with Mr Finchingfield, that was for certain, but where would all that fun go, that courage?

'I'll get my hat and gloves.' He took the spiral stairs to his roof-high chamber at a run, two at a time, all the way up, arriving with his breath tight in his chest and a burn in his thigh muscles and still wanting nothing more than to ruin the line of the librarian's perfect nose for him.

A day spent in the panelled library was soothing, Elinor found. It was light and airy and well organised and she admired the young librarian's enthusiasm for his task.

'But there is still so much to do,' he said with a groan, waving a hand towards the back of the room where stacks of books, dusty and disorganised, still crowded the shelves. 'The late Grand Duke was not interested, except for sporting subjects and, um… certain rather indelicate volumes. But he bought widely, just as he did works of art. The only trouble was, he neglected to replace the librarian when the last one died twelve years ago. And as for the archives, I haven't even touched them. They are a full-time job.'

He opened a door into another chamber, with stone walls and vaulted ceiling. Bundles of documents, rolls of parchment, tin boxes and wooden chests were crammed inside with great ledgers balanced on every flat surface. 'Goodness, what a treasure trove.' Intrigued, Elinor lifted the nearest scroll off its shelf and peered at it. 'This is fascinating.'

'I am glad you think so.' It was Eva, her skirts lifted clear of the dusty floor. 'I did wonder whether you would like to spend a little time here as our archivist. It would allow you to consider your plans and to make a considered choice of companion for your travels.'

Mr Finchingfield effaced himself and tactfully went off to his desk while Eva waited for Elinor's response. 'Naturally, we would pay you the same salary as Phillip. And you only need stay as long as you wish—just make a start and help me find a permanent archivist is all I would ask.'

Taken aback, she considered it. 'It would make things easier with Mama. I am sure she would be less anxious if I came here rather than taking off by myself.' Actually she probably wouldn't be anxious at all. Irritated at having to find a new secretary, that was all. But it would stop Theo fussing. She might even see him from time to time if he knew where she was. 'Thank you, yes, I would like that very much.'

'Excellent. We must find you a desk. Phillip! You have a colleague.'

At dinner she found herself seated next to Mr Finchingfield with the castle's Anglican chaplain on her left. Perhaps to dilute the impact of Ana, Eva had invited a number of people, including the widowed Mrs Massingham, whom she had suggested as a possible companion for Elinor's travels.

It made it easier to avoid Theo. Why she wanted to, Elinor was not certain, but instinct told her that he would not be happy with her plans and that having an argument with him would be more upsetting than she could cope with just now.

When the gentlemen rejoined the ladies and Eva presided over the tea tray, Theo finally cut through the group around her. 'Elinor, I was hoping for a word with you.' Next to Phillip's slight elegance and the chaplain's comfortable roundness he looked big, masculine and decidedly commanding. He also looked thoroughly irritated, although she doubted anyone who didn't know him well would notice.

'Why don't you join us?' she asked, knowing that was not what he wanted. 'Mr Finchingfield was just explaining his new classification scheme for the library, which sounds most comprehensive, only I am not certain how it would work for theology. What do you think, Dr Herriot?'

'Indeed, comparative religion may be the stumbling block with your ideas,' the chaplain began.

Theo shot her a look that showed he knew exactly what she was up to, combined with something else she could not fathom. Surely he was not hurt by her evasion? He must know she would only refuse him again if that was his intention in speaking to her.

'Theology is not my subject, you must excuse me.' He turned and went back to join the rest of the group clustered around the wide, empty hearth.

But that look, that darkness behind the clear green eyes, haunted her. Was she imagining things, projecting her own unhappiness at the relationship between them on to him, manufacturing feelings for him he did not have? But he did not look happy—there was a tension about him even when he was joking with Sebastian or engaged in a barbed flirtation with Ana.

She watched, half her mind on him while she tried to keep up with Dr Herriot's arguments. There he was, the man she loved, funny, brave, attractive, heart-stoppingly sensual, and she was sending him away. It was the right thing, of course it was. Only it seemed to be making neither of them very happy.

When the clocks struck midnight—a somewhat prolonged matter in a castle the size of Maubourg, despite the best efforts of the official clock-winder—Elinor was still awake.

She had gone up at eleven, washed and changed into her nightgown, thanked her maid and settled down in an armchair with an extravagant number of candles and a sensation novel from the pile that Eva had sent up. It had been a long day; she was convinced she would soon want to climb into bed. But despite the best efforts of the valiant heroine, trapped in a tower by her wicked guardian for reasons that were not entirely clear, she could neither concentrate on the tale nor fall asleep.

Assuming that he and Sebastian had not had another late-night session, Theo was in his bedchamber somewhere above her head. Was he asleep already, or reading? Perhaps he was planning the journey back to England with the Chalice, or his next buying trip, somewhere in Europe. Or perhaps he was sitting like she was, a book disregarded on his knee, just thinking.

Had that strange darkness gone from his eyes? Had he realised that he did not need to worry about her?

What she wanted, she realised, more than anything, was to be close to him. Not to do or say anything—what was there left to do or say? Just to be close.

Elinor scrambled out of bed and opened the clothes press, searching for something she could wear that she could fasten herself. The shabby old gown she had explored the chateau in was the only thing, and it was warm. Despite the time of year, it would be cool up on the battlements.

Tossing a drab cloak around her shoulders and pushing her feet into slippers, Elinor peered out of her door. Down at the far end of the corridor stood one of the guards who patrolled the castle night and day, but his back was to her. Soft-footed, she crept to the doorway Eva had pointed out and was through it without a sound.

The stairs spiralled up, opening out on to a paved walkway, perhaps ten foot wide, with the battlements on one side and a wall, broken by doors and small windows, on the other. There was no sound except the hoot of a hunting owl drifting over the river far below and distantly, faint music from the town. And all was dark, but for the spill of light from under one door and from around the edge of the heavily curtained window.

Theo was still awake, then. Elinor leaned against the door, flattening her cheek and her palm on the warm old wood as though against his body. She knew she could not stay there all night, sleeping across his threshold like a medieval page, but she did not want to leave.

Interspersed with the regular gaps of the battlements were darker areas, which proved to be alcoves with stone slabs for seats, perhaps to allow sentries to rest or shelter in bad weather. Wrapping her cloak tight around her Elinor sat down in one, put her feet up and leaned back. It was surprisingly comfortable and it gave her a clear view of Theo's door. She would stay until he snuffed out his candles and then she would go back down to her own bed and try to sleep too.

* * *

How long she dozed there, warm in her corner with only a cold nose and toes to betray the deepening night, she had no idea. Nor was she sure what brought her completely awake. The light was still showing under Theo's door, but there was no sound from within his room.

Then she heard it again, the brush of leather on stone as the sole of someone's shoe met an uneven slab. The person halted. Elinor could sense, rather than hear, breathing and muffled her own in a fold of the cloak. She saw the person move across the spill of light from under the door, silk gown swishing faintly.

The door opened, throwing the woman into silhouette. Elinor craned to recognise who it was and saw, before she hid it in the folds of her skirt, the long blade in her right hand, sparking silver in the candlelight.

Chapter Twenty-Two

'Ana.' Theo had recognised the intruder, but he had not seen the knife. His voice, just reaching Elinor, held only resignation and faint amusement. 'What the devil…?'

She tore off her cloak and wriggled out of her niche, running without any attempt at concealment to the door, throwing her shoulder against it as Ana tried to close it from the inside.

The force of the push sent the other woman staggering off balance. Elinor swirled the heavy wool cloak in her hands and threw it, enveloping Ana in folds of cloth. 'She's got a knife,' she gasped, trying to hang on to the flailing figure.

Theo seized her by the shoulders and pushed her unceremoniously into the corner of the room. 'In that case, leave her to me.' He dragged off the cloak and Ana emerged, blinking and furious.

'You stupid little witch,' she hissed at Elinor. 'Sleep with him if you want. Do I care? I have had him, I do not want him back—so you take care not to attack me again or you will be sorry.' She advanced towards them, the long knife glinting in her hand as she prodded it towards Elinor to emphasise every word.

'Ana—' Theo was edging to one side, attempting to keep his body between Elinor and the furious Spanish woman. 'Put the knife down—we don't want anyone to get hurt, do we?'

'Don't we?' she enquired ominously, then tossed the weapon on to the bed where it lay, its hilt glittering with gemstones. 'Bah! You could not peel an apple with that thing.' She kicked the cloak to one side and stood, hands on hips, belligerently regarding Theo, and Elinor, who was trying to push past him.

'You English are mad. I come here to deliver that thing to you for the count. He says you deserve something from the treasure—and I have something for you, too, only I did not expect you to be up here.' She scowled at Elinor, who sat down with a thud on Theo's chair.

He picked up the dagger, turning it over in his hands, then studying the hilt closely. 'Just for show, see, the blade is dull.' He ran his thumb down it. 'It must have been brandished during their rituals. If the stones are genuine, it is worth a great deal of money.' Ana had sauntered over to the dresser and was pouring herself a glass of wine from the decanter that stood there. 'I suppose it was too much to hope you might have given it to me during the hours of daylight?'

'I did not want anyone to see.' She tossed back the wine. 'How do I know if you can trust your cousins?'

'Then thank you for bringing it. What did he send Elinor?'

'A platter, a small one, but good work. You can have it tomorrow.'

'I would not want anything from that place.' Elinor shuddered, thinking about the scenes those glittering objects must have been used in.

'Sell it, then.' Ana shrugged and put down the glass. 'The man is full of guilt for what has happened. That, and perhaps he wants to ensure you hold your tongues. The Chalice has vanished into its hiding place again— the count wants to pretend nothing has happened, that his lies about his mother's collapse are the truth.

'Now I go to my bed and leave you to your strange courtship.' She leaned close to Elinor as she passed. 'It is easier to make love, my respectable English miss, if you are both on the same side of the door.'

'What the hell did she mean by that?' Theo, hands on hips, glared at Elinor. He was still partly dressed, coat and neckcloth gone, his shirt open at the neck, his shoes discarded by the bed.

'Don't glower at me,' Elinor retorted. 'How should I know what she means?' She wanted to go to him and finish unbuttoning his shirt, push it back over his shoulders so she could savour the skin beneath, touch it with her lips and fingertips…

'Why were you following her?'

'I wasn't,' she denied, then realised just where that statement left her.

'You were here already?'

'I couldn't sleep, I needed some air. Eva had shown me the stairs to the battlements.' His expression was sceptical; she couldn't blame him. 'Look at me, for goodness' sake. Do I appear to have dressed up for a seduction? I was sitting outside in one of those niches, that's all.'

Theo took one long step and caught her hands in his. 'For how long? Your hands are cold.'

'I'm not certain, I must have nodded off.'

'Why couldn't you sleep?'

Why couldn't he? she wondered. There was no book beside the chair, no papers. He must have simply been sitting there. 'I was thinking about what I am going to do next.'

'You are going to Aunt Louisa in Avignon.' If he had added *good riddance*, his tone could not have been any colder, even while his hands warmed hers.

'No, I am not. I have been thinking. I want to travel. I have my own money, enough to be independent, very independent. I wonder at myself for never seeing it before. I shall find myself a congenial companion and see Italy, Greece, more of France. But while I am making up my mind who to travel with, I will be staying here. They need an archivist and I am suitably qualified.'

'Travel be damned.' Theo let go of her hands and took an angry pace away. 'Eva is matchmaking. She'll have you married off to that milksop librarian in a month, wait and see.'

'Phillip is not a milksop,' Elinor retorted. Even as she spoke she wondered if he was correct. Was Eva matchmaking? 'He is a pleasant and very intellectual young man. There is no need to sneer at him because he does not go racketing about the country, almost getting himself and everyone else killed in the process.'

'So you blame me for that after all, do you? I cannot recall inviting you to explore dungeons with me or rush up to my bedchamber brandishing a pistol you cannot use.'

'You were grateful at the time, damn you. And if I hadn't been with you in that dungeon, you might be dead now.' She was too angry with him for tears, although she could feel them hot and furious, stinging her eyes.

Theo looked to be in a towering, inexplicable, rage and suddenly she saw why. 'Theo—are you *jealous*?' He turned away, giving her his back, and reached for the decanter.

'Why the hell should I be jealous of that youth?'

'I do not know, that is what is puzzling me,' Elinor confessed, her own anger ebbing away as she stared at the uncommunicative set of his shoulders. 'If you are pouring wine, I will have a glass.'

He set it down with a snap and walked away from her. When he turned, she saw that strange darkness was in his eyes again and his voice was flat. 'I do not understand why, if you want to travel, you will not do it with me, but need to find a stranger. Why, if you need a man, you do not take me. Is he so much more intelligent, is that it? Am I not up to your lofty intellectual heights?'

He was making no sense at all. Elinor stared, then took a deep swallow of wine and sat down. 'I do not want Phillip Finchingfield. He is a nice young man, with the emphasis on *young*. Eva is not matchmaking, she is amusing herself.' She had to work this out as she went along, and her own emotions were so tangled they were not helping one whit.

'How can I travel with you without marrying you? And I have told you why I will not do that. I cannot marry a man who does not love me.'

Theo was staring at her from across the room. Then, very slowly, he sat down on the edge of the bed as though standing was no longer an option. 'You would marry me if I loved you?'

'Yes, of course.' Too late she saw where this had led her: virtually into a confession of her true feelings for him.

'But I told you I did. I told you I loved you that morning after we made love all night. But you hushed me, misunderstood me to mean that I loved you as a friend and made it very clear you did not love me.'

'You meant you *really* want to marry me?' This couldn't be true, surely? Something this wonderful simply could not be happening.

'I do. I want to marry you even if you don't love me. Elinor…' Somehow he was on his knees beside her chair, her hands in his. 'Nell, I love you and I want you and I will do everything in my power to make you happy. I know you like our lovemaking, that we have fun together. That's a start, isn't it—if I can convince you I love you, you will marry me?'

'I believe you.' And she did. That shadow had gone from his eyes—this was Theo looking deep into her soul, Theo, his pulse thudding hard against her fingers. 'And I love you.'

He sat back on his heels and closed his eyes. 'For two intelligent people, we very nearly got this completely wrong, didn't we?'

'It isn't a language I am used to,' she confessed, freeing one hand so she could reach forwards and touch his face. 'I have no understanding of the grammar, or the vocabulary. We must learn it together.' He turned his cheek into her palm and smiled, opening his eyes so his lashes tickled the sensitive skin.

'What, the language of emotions? I think something almost got lost in translation. Let me try in English. Nell, I love you. I don't know how long I loved you, because I've never been in love and I didn't realise why I felt like I did, but I realised when we were on that hilltop overlooking the chateau. When I said I would never marry, it was because I believed I could not have you, not because of any other woman. I want to marry you and live with you and have children with you.'

'And we will travel together?' It was very difficult to speak with her heart so full, but somehow she managed it, her hand stroking the strong lines of the face she had once thought was only passably handsome. 'I am not being left at home, children or no children.'

'Nell, I thought I couldn't have you, that I'd lost you—how could I contemplate ever leaving you behind? I will place the orders for our caravan of carriages at once—I was drawing it, too, so I have both sets.'

'So that is where my sketches went. Theo, I have been looking everywhere for those. I was the woman in all of the pictures, you see.'

'Oh, Nell.' He gathered her in against his heart and rocked her gently. His body felt hard and safe and yet so gentle. 'When can we get married?'

'I don't...' She managed to twist round so she could look up into his face. 'Will your family want a big wedding? Uncle Augustus will want to marry us, won't he? In the cathedral.' Her heart sank. It would all take months.

'That will take too much time, I want to get started on that family immediately.' Theo stood up, bringing her up with him. 'Sit on the bed, Nell, I can't think while I'm holding you.' He paced across the room, then flipped open a map and stared down at it. 'I've got to take that damn Chalice back to England. I'll leave tomorrow. You get Eva to send you down to Avignon with a maid and some outriders. Break the news to Aunt Louisa and interview the English vicar down there—there's sure to be an Anglican church. I'll come right back. In a month we'll be wed, no longer, I promise you.' He paused, frowning. 'You know, I can't help but wonder if she meant this to happen. She's been mighty careless about throwing us together.'

'Theo.'

'Yes, my love?' He looked up at her, his hands flat either side of the map.

'Am I dreaming?'

'Not unless I'm having the same dream, too. Nell, I've never had anyone to share emotions with. Ideas, yes, fun, yes. But not feelings, not the deep ones. And I don't think you have either. We nearly got this wrong because we tried to protect ourselves against being hurt, took what the other said literally, without listening to the truth underneath. I'm going to try very hard not to do that any more.'

'Mmm. I think we should say what we think and what we feel, honestly. Don't you?' He nodded. 'Good, I am glad you agree, because what I want most of all, now, is to go to bed with you and for you not to have to be careful, just to make me yours.'

Theo just looked at her, his eyes hooded, as though his own desires were banked down behind the heavy lids. 'Are you certain? You don't want to wait until our wedding night?'

'No, but if you do—'

Suddenly Theo grinned, the first broad smile she had seen for what seemed like days. 'Nell, we can sit here all night being carefully polite over this or I can do what I have been wanting to do ever since I knelt on that river bank, plaiting your hair.'

'Really? Oh, I knew I felt something, sensed something, even then.' He came and caught her in his arms and it felt right, here in their lonely eyrie, high on the battlements of the great castle.

'In my fantasies I didn't dream I'd be undoing this frightful garment,' Theo observed. 'There go the buttons, never mind, you won't be needing it again.' The old gown slid from his hands and he stopped talking, his mouth curving into an incredulous smile. 'Nell Ravenhurst, you bad girl—not a stitch on under your gown!'

It was impossible to feel shy in the face of his obvious delight. 'I was in a hurry, I wanted to be near you,' she murmured, reaching for his shirt. 'And now I want to be nearer still.'

She had thought she knew what to expect and the thrill of his caresses and the fire in his kisses was the same, yet deeper, more intense. But her heart was pounding and something inside her made her breath come fast as she clung to his shoulders while his mouth roamed over her hot skin.

'Are you frightened?' He looked up and she wondered what he had seen in her expression.

'Yes. A little,' she admitted. 'I know it will hurt, it isn't that, it is just…'

'Just such a big step? I know, my love, I'll be as slow as I can.'

'No,' Elinor protested, 'not slow. Theo, love me now.'

His weight as he came over her was wonderful,

powerful, yet he took such care to lift it from her. She ran her hands over his biceps, feeling the muscles taut as they took his weight on his elbows. Her legs parted to cradle him and she sighed at how perfectly they seemed to fit together, how open her body was to him as he moved against her, slowly nudging while her untutored body began to open for him, his eyes holding hers, a smile in them that promised so much, promised his love.

It did not seem possible that he really could fit, she thought hazily, trying to think of nothing but those eyes, that love, while her body struggled against itself to tense up and deny him. 'Theo, I don't think—'

'Exactly,' he murmured. 'For once in your life, don't think, Nell, just trust me, let me in.' He shifted his position slightly, his hand slipping between them to touch the aching core of her and she sobbed, arched to meet the sweetly familiar torment and he surged strongly into her, carrying away the sudden stab of pain with the intensity of it.

'I love you,' she managed to gasp before all she could do was to surrender to the rhythm he was setting, carrying her with him, making her cry out, over and over as he moved within her, filling her perfectly, perfectly at one with her.

'Now, Nell,' he gasped and she opened her eyes on to his intent face, on to the eyes that held her soul. 'Come with me, Nell.' And she was. The twisting, surging pleasure he had taught her was there, all wrapped up in something bigger, more intense, something that was the essence of the two of them, together.

'Theo!' She thought she screamed his name, heard his shout, and then there were colours and pleasure she could never have imagined and finally soft, sweet blackness and the feel of his arms holding her safe, bringing her back into harbour after the storm.

'I love you so much,' Theo murmured into her hair.

Unable to speak, she burrowed up against his chest until she could take his face in her hands and see the brightness of tears in his eyes and press her lips against the strong line of his jaw. 'Always,' she managed. 'Always.'

'*Madame.*' Eva's dresser came back from answering the tap on the door. '*Madame,* that was Annette. She says Mademoiselle Ravenhurst's bed has not been slept in.'

The Grand Duchess fastened one perfect diamond eardrop and turned her head to check her reflection in the mirror before answering. 'Well, thank heavens for that,' she said with a touch of complacency. 'Please ensure that Monsieur Ravenhurst is not disturbed before dinner time.'

Afterword

Neglected throughout the eighteenth-century, the basilica at Vezelay slipped into near dereliction during the Revolution. By the time Theo and Elinor visited it was very dilapidated, and in 1819 the principle bell tower was consumed by fire. In 1834 Prosper Mérimée, French Inspector of Historic Monuments, saw it and was appalled. But he could find no one willing to take on such a colossal work. Finally, an unknown architect, 26-year-old Eugène Viollet-le-Duc, accepted the commission and in less than twenty years rescued this wonderful building. In 1979 the church where St Bernard preached the First Crusade was declared a UNESCO World Heritage site.

The verse from Petrach is from Sonnet 28, *To Laura in Life,* translated in 1795 by an unknown poet.

Dear Reader,

In the course of their courtship Ashe Reynard informed Belinda Felsham (The Outrageous Lady Felsham) that she should stop matchmaking for her bluestocking cousin Elinor because what Elinor needed was an intellectual, someone who could match her intelligence.

The problem was, where could Elinor, firmly on the shelf, find such a man? One who would see past the drab gowns and meek studiousness to the warm, loving, adventurous woman inside? Especially when she was convinced she did not want a man at all.

And then there was Theo Ravenhurst, in disgrace and, so his mother kept insisting, off on the Grand Tour. Only I had my suspicions that Theo was not pursuing a blameless course around the cultural sights of Europe but was up to something altogether less conventional. What would happen if these two cousins met, I wondered?

I hope you enjoy finding out and, if you have read the first three Ravenhurst novels, meeting again Eva and Sebastian, young Freddie and the indomitable Lady James.

Coming next will be The Notorious Mr Hurst. Lady Maude Templeton, having escaped marriage to Ravenhurst cousin Gareth Morant (The Shocking Lord Standon) has already fallen for the entirely inappropriate attractions of theatre owner Eden Hurst. She knows what she wants, and is not used to being thwarted, but this time it looks as though everyone, from Society to the gentleman himself, is set on her not getting her heart's desire.